LACE CURTAIN

LACE CURTAIN

Daughters of Ireland

Jeanne Charters

OPEN ROAD

INTEGRATED MEDIA
NEW YORK

ISBN: 978-1-5040-8021-7

This edition published in 2023 by Open Road Integrated Media, Inc.
180 Maiden Lane
New York, NY 10038
www.openroadmedia.com

LACE CURTAIN

Chapter One

October 10, 1870

Boston, Massachusetts

Sister Sarah reminds me of a penguin as she stands erasing the blackboard; all black and white and round. She's two big jiggly balls stacked on top of each other with a smaller one on top. Every bit of her is covered in black veils. When she turns around, the white wimple goes right up to her chin and down to her eyes and pinches. I wonder if it hurts. The worst of it? I know that underneath that top round veil, she's bald as an egg.

When Monsignor asks which girls in our class want to be Sisters, I never raise my hand. Sometimes, that gets me in trouble. But of one thing I'm certain, I will *never* let anyone shave my black hair off. It took too long to grow it this long.

"Nellie Kelly, stop daydreaming!" Sister hollers.

"Yes, Sister," I answer, glad she can't read my thoughts.

My mother scolds me if I say bad things about Sister. She says I'm too smart to be a smart aleck, but is it all right to think it? After all, I can't help what I think.

No question about it, Sister in her long, black habit, bobbing from foot to foot at the board, is the image of a penguin. Not that I've ever seen a real penguin, just pictures of them. Oh, and those penguins didn't have rosary beads wrapped around their middle. Sister must have two or three of them around her. One would never reach.

I can't let her catch me staring at her again, so I gaze down at my paper, pretending to pray to The Father, Son, and the Holy Ghost. Actually, I finished my quiz fifteen minutes ago. So here I sit, watching the clock and pretending to check my paper again while the other girls hunch over their tests like crows over dead rats.

Religion *is* dead in a way, especially its language—Latin! There's so much about crucifixion and suffering and blood. The most boring part of being a Catholic is having to learn Catechism. Nothing but rules, rules, rules. Wish the Church would come up with some new ideas. I guess I'm a terrible girl, thinking these thoughts, but I do think them. Don't tell Sister Sarah or Mother, though.

Hiding my face with my hand, I sneak my eyes over to the window. The sun glaring through the wavy panes sure doesn't warm things up much. They must be trying to save money on coal again.

My stomach rumbles, wanting lunch.

Hurry up, time! Hurry up! Hurry up!

At last, Sister glances at the round wall clock and clucks. She reaches under her desk to bring up the big copper bell and clangs it three times.

I shake my pen into the inkwell and wipe it on the rag in my desk. That black ink is impossible if it gets under fingernails. My mother made me soak my hands in a nasty mix of vinegar and ammonia last time that happened. You should have seen my fingers. For a week, they looked like the peeling varnish on the pews at church.

"Everyone, put on your shawls. It's chilly out!" Sister declares. It's pretty chilly in here, too. I can almost see my breath.

Brigid, Kate, and Lizbeth, the three first graders in the front of the classroom, stand and file out. Lizbeth pulls her shawl around her shoulders, then looks back at me and smiles, her big blue eyes shy yet mischievous. I cross my eyes and stick out my tongue at her. She laughs.

Lizbeth's my favorite and she knows it. If I had a little sister, I'd want her to be just like Lizbeth. But I don't have a sister, or even a brother.

The four second graders start out next, and then the third, fourth, fifth, sixth, and seventh graders. The room empties so fast you'd think someone had set off the fire alarm. Finally, it's our turn. The eighth graders. After eight years in this one room, it's hard to believe I'll be leaving it come summer. In a way I'll miss St. Augustine's, but I do wish it was bigger. At Boys' Academy where all the rich Protestant boys go, every grade has its own classroom. Sean O'Halloran goes there, though I don't think he's rich. And Sean's as Catholic as I am.

"Just one minute, ladies," Sister pauses. "I've graded your arithmetic tests." She holds the papers up in the air and bustles back to us, turning sideways so as not to smack her wide hips on the desks. My stomach clenches a little. I need to keep my marks up so I can get into Girls High next year. Mother and Da are counting on me. But Arithmetic is hard, and I'm never sure how I did.

Sister's round face betrays no expression as she hands me my paper, but I spot the word '*EXCELLENT!*' scrawled at the top. My 100% is right under the A.M.D.G. we always print. Sister has explained it's Latin from St. Ignatius and means "For the greater honor and glory of God."

I catch a glimpse of the paper under mine. It's Fiona Doggett's and it's covered with red X-marks. *Oh, no.* Sister doesn't look up as she hands Fiona her paper. I shove my test into my book bag, hoping Fiona didn't see it. She'd be jealous, and a jealous Fiona is meaner than a cat hung on a clothesline in the rain. When Fiona's mad, her eyes narrow into slits of blazing red fire. She's scary. When Fiona's scary, all the store-bought dresses in the world can't turn her pretty, and she has most of them. Actually, Fiona's not very pretty even when she's happy.

Once out of the classroom, I race past the brown wood walls of the hallway and glance out the window to the St. Augustine Chapel graveyard. My schoolmates have grandparents buried there. My father's parents are, too, but my mother's mother died in Ireland and her father's ashes disappeared somewhere. He was murdered by some old mobster here in Boston before I was born. We visit my father's parents' graves every Sunday after church.

Outside, cold air blasts my face like a slap of ice. My eyes water instantly. Before the tears freeze on my cheeks, I brush them away. Good heavens, it's frigid. And this is only October! What will February bring? I pull my shawl tight around my shoulders.

I run for the swing Father Ruzzo hung on the oak tree. Jumping on it, I start pumping right away. As I swing out from under the tree, the sun, a warming fire, hits my face. As I pump harder, the air pulls my hair into my mouth, but I spit it out. My breath pours out in a foggy mist as I soar higher and higher. The rope starts doing that topsy-stomach stall that happens just before flying back down.

Sister's yelled at me about swinging so high, but I can't stop doing it. How am I ever going to be a trapeze performer if I can't get used to heights? I'm still not sure if I want to be a teacher or fly on a trapeze in the circus. I lay back on the swing and extend my arms and legs out to the side, balancing perfectly. My skirt flutters above my knees, showing the lace on my pantalettes, but I don't care. These girls have seen pantalettes before.

I'm flying! I'm flying! Higher and higher! I bet no one in this school has ever flown this high before. Opening my eyes, I see people on Dorchester Street way beyond the fence. I want to shout to them. "Look at me! Look at me! I'm flying!" Higher, higher, higher!

Suddenly, Sister Sarah roars out the door yelling, "Nellie, get off that swing! One of these days, you'll break your neck, I swan. And pull that skirt down."

Darn! Who told?

Sister shivers and rushes back inside, her chubby bottom wiggling, two battling piglets under the black skirt of her habit. It makes me giggle out loud.

She slams the door. I pump twice more and ready for the jump. It must be timed perfectly or I'll land face first in the dirt like that time in sixth grade. The scabs lasted a month. My mother scolded me even as she plastered my puss with some foul-smelling ointment she got from Uncle Neo. The girls called me Smelly Nellie.

But no such mistakes this time. When the swing hits its highest point, I soar. Arching, then rounding my back, I pull my arms back next to my ears, and point the heels of my boots down. Suspended in the air, I pretend I'm the trapeze lady I saw in a poster from the Dan Costello Circus. When I hit the dirt in a hard-heeled landing, I am only two feet from the wire fence.

A new record! Brilliant! What a day! First, the A+ in arithmetic and now a record landing. Life is perfect.

Right then, a cloud passes over the sun and my shoulders tremble with the chill.

Skipping to stay warm, I join the other girls at the wooden table. As I unwrap my cheese sandwich, I look up and realize Fiona, her eyes narrow, is staring at me, eyes blazing. I hadn't noticed her sitting there or would have sat on the grass.

Actually, Fiona always looks mad about something lately, except when that disgusting Orville Mattison's around. She told us girls Orville said her brown eyes were his sparkly diamonds in the sunlight. Ever since he said that, she flutters her eyes all over the place on sunny days, but not today, not with that cloud.

Fiona likes Orville, and that confounds me. Most boys stink of dirty socks and rotten underwear. And the stinkiest of them all is Orville Mattison. Really. It's true.

Last winter, when Fiona and I were still friends, we had a snowball fight with Orville and some kids. I flopped down on my back and started making an angel, but that pig, Orville, jumped on top of me and put his hands on my chest. I kneed him so hard he screamed as if I'd stabbed him. He climbed off me, in a hurry. He stunk that day, and still does.

I uncap my jug of water and take a swig.

"Did little Miss Kelly get a perfect paper again?" Fiona spits sarcastically.

"Not sure," I lie, taking a bite of my sandwich.

"Oh, right." She laughs, but it's not a happy laugh. It's a laugh squeezed through an angry throat, with not a bit of belly in it. "You might be the teacher's pet, Nellie, but you don't know everything. There's things we all know that you don't." Her raspy voice is as ugly as her tight-grinned face.

What does she mean by that? What things? I think for a second that I should just ignore her and walk away, but my curiosity gets the best of me. I bite. "Like what?"

The other girls grow quiet and seem to be holding their

breaths. My sandwich sticks in my throat. Fiona's secrets are never happy ones. I grab my jug of water again.

Fiona sits back, brushing a crumb of bread from her uniform. "Oh, just an itty-bitty secret everyone knows but you." She fluffs out her hair.

A crow caws as another cloud passes over the sun.

I swallow too fast and hiccough. "What secret?"

"Oh, nothing." She grins and whispers something to Annie O'Hara.

"Fiona, tell me right now or I'll tell Sister."

Her eyes bug out. "Oh, no!" Her mouth twists. "All right, if you insist. What you don't know is that your mother was the whore of the Pilgrim's Dandy—that coffin ship—when she came over from Ireland. Everybody else knows." The hiss of her words bounces off the brick walls of the school house, a devil's echo. She rises from the table and pats her skirt down over her bustled rump.

The playground freezes into a tintype. There's no sound until a second grader leaps off one end of the teeter totter, bouncing the other-end girl to her backside. The one who lands wails, "Sister Sarah!"

Her cry sounds as if it comes through a cotton fog, but I don't take my eyes off Fiona.

What did she say? My mother? The whore of a ship? That's crazy.

"Take it back," I snarl. "You're lying."

"Am not. My mother told me." She turns away as though this is the end of our conversation.

I grab her by the shoulder and whirl her back to face me. "Your mother's a liar, too."

"Nuh-uh," Fiona shakes her head, "my mother was on that ship, and she knows."

There's Banshee blood on my mother's side of the family and she's always warning me not to lose my temper lest I unleash a

Banshee inside me, but this time I can't help it. I ball up my fist and hit Fiona square in the snoot. She squeals like a pig stuck for roasting. Blood spurts from her nose and down the front of her blue silk uniform.

Suddenly, Sister Sarah is between us, pinching our arms with fingers strong as a blacksmith's vice. "Stop that, you two brawling street urchins. I won't have you fouling the air of St. Augustine's with a donnybrook."

"She started it," Fiona whines, tears streaming down her face as she tucks her curls back into their topknot and wipes the blood off her face with her shawl.

"I don't care who started it," Sister yells. "I'm the one who'll finish it." She grabs me by the ear. "Nellie Kelly, in my office." She jams a finger into Fiona's collar bone. "I'll deal with you later."

My heart hurts from Fiona's lie, and I blink back tears. She used to be my best friend. I loved sleeping at her mansion on Beacon Hill and eating crust-less sandwiches cut in perfect little triangles by her maid. Her closet was a fairyland, packed tight with beautiful dresses. I'd die for such dresses. It was wonderful being Fiona's friend. Since last year, though, she hates me.

"Sit, Miss Kelly." Sister points to the leather chair opposite her desk. I fidget into it, pulling at the tight buttons on the seat. Her office is warm, and I feel perspiration pop out on my forehead. My eyes fix on the crucifix on Sister's chest. She settles in, huffs, and crosses her arms. "Now, Miss Kelly. What's this all about?"

What can I say? If I tell the truth, I'll be punished for repeating a bad word, whore. If I lie, Jesus on Sister's crucifix might start bleeding right down the front of her habit as a sign of my sinfulness. I've heard that sometimes Jesus does things like that for punishment.

"I asked what this is all about," Sister repeats.

I can't sit here quiet all day. She might take out her ruler and pound my hands like Sister Annunciata did to Maeve O'Grady's last year after she caught Maeve smooching some kid from Boy's Academy. After that, they shipped the old nun back to Ireland.

"I'm sorry, Sister," I mumble.

"Sorry for what?"

"For fighting with Fiona."

"Look, Miss Kelly. You can stall 'til the cows come home, but you're not leaving this office 'til I know what the fight was about." Her brogue is thick now, a sure sign she's mad.

I suck in a deep breath and admit, "Fiona said something bad about my mother."

"About Mary Kelly?" She gasps, her eyes round as two blue marbles. "Who could say anything bad about Mary? She's a saint, she is, a saint."

I dig my nails into the wooden arms of the chair. People are always saying my mother is a saint. They should only see the way that saint rubs up against my da, nibbling on his ear. It's embarrassing. I slump down in the chair.

"What exactly did Fiona say?"

The 'saint' comment made me so mad I don't even care if I shock Sister now, so I say it. "That my mother was the whore of the ship she came over from Ireland on."

The chubby face flames above the white wimple. She sputters something in Irish I can't understand and catches her wire-rimmed glasses just before they fall off the tip of her nose. For a minute, I think she's going to climb over the desk and smack me one, but she stays squatted there, like a little black-and-white hen. "This is a matter for Monsignor Varley."

Panic floods over me worse than the Charles after a storm. *No! Monsignor'll go to my house. My mother and da'll think he's visiting because of me getting good grades or something. My mother will make black-currant scones like he's the President or Pope or something. And then Monsignor'll tell them I hit Fiona. My da'll be so mad. My mother might cry. Think, Nellie, think.*

Taking in a deep breath, I say, "Sister, can't we handle this another way?" I clasp my hands into a steeple.

She doesn't answer.

I say a quick prayer to St. Jude. He always works. "What if I ask my mother to come here for a meeting with *you*?"

She pushes her spectacles up again. One eyebrow rises, and the other flattens, then she smiles. I think my idea makes her feel special, perhaps nearly as important as Monsignor. If that thought wasn't so funny, I'd feel sorry for her. Nuns beg for money at the Beacon Hill mansions; monsignors are wined and dined in those same houses.

She finally speaks. "Very well, Nellie. Tell your mother to be here tomorrow after school, and you with her. We'll settle this between us."

Good. My mother will say Fiona lied, and that'll settle it. Then, Fiona'll be the one in trouble. I won't have to watch my da's face when Monsignor says bad things about me. "All right, Sister. I'll tell her."

"Now, tell Fiona Doggett to get herself in here. Tomorrow afternoon, you get to confession, girl."

Oh, no! I hate confession.

CHAPTER TWO

Walking home, I'm still mad. *How could Sister believe Fiona and not me?* I bang my umbrella on the iron fence posts along G Street; the umbrella my mother makes me bring every day, rain or shine. She says Boston isn't as rainy as Ireland, but you never know. I feel stupid carrying it. But I do fancy the loud sounds it makes. Clink, clank, clunk. I stomp my feet to the clanging and chant the words of a poem we just learned by a man called Edgar Allan Poe.

"Tintinnabulations of the bells, bells, bells. Tintinnabulations of the bells, bells, bells." Lost in the rhythm of my chant, I feel better and I nearly don't hear the shout.

"Hey, Nellie, quit the tintinnabulations and come for a ride."

It's Neo, and he couldn't have shown up at a better time. Neo's my best friend in the whole world; more like a brother really. His father is my Uncle Kam; not a real uncle, of course. Anyone would know that by looking at us since their skin is the color of chocolate.

Uncle Kam was on the same ship as my mother when she came over from Ireland. He was a slave boy then. Now, my mother says he's as rich as Croesus. I love saying Croesus. It looks like it should be pronounced *Crowsus,* but it's *Creesus,* who was some rich Turkish King who lived a million years ago. So if you're as rich as Croesus, you're *really* rich. Uncle Kam is; made his fortune selling some African tonic. He traveled as a medicine man all over the Eastern states when he was just sixteen.

I run toward Neo's wagon, but stop when caution nudges. Craning my neck in every direction, I make sure nobody's nearby. The war to free the slaves is long over, but people around here still get ugly about coloreds mixing with whites. Mother has said it's the same way with her and Uncle Kam. I wish people weren't so mean. Fiona calls colored people *niggers*. Remembering Fiona, I get mad again, grit my teeth, and run to Neo's wagon.

Actually, it's more a grand carriage than a wagon. It has seats for four people and a purple fringed canopy. I rub the horse's satin flank and kiss him on the nose. I love horses. My father takes me riding a lot.

I scan the neighborhood quickly and climb up beside Neo. Tucking the umbrella under my legs and pulling the maroon velvet lap robe up over my knees, I sit back so I'm partially hidden by the canopy.

"Neo, I'm in so much trouble."

He turns toward me. "Why?"

"Fiona Doggett said an awful thing about my mother, so I socked her. I think I broke her nose. I have to bring my mother to see Sister Sarah tomorrow."

Neo's mouth hangs open in a big O. "You socked her?"

"Yep." I grin proudly. I can't help it, remembering how shocked Fiona looked. But she was no more surprised than I was; didn't know I could do such a thing.

"That's wild, Nellie. Maybe your mother'll be proud you defended her?"

I look him in the eye and cock my eyebrow. No answer is

necessary. He knows my mother better than that. She expects me to be a perfect lady. Perfect ladies don't break noses. Besides, Mother always takes Sister's side over mine. I'll probably have to stay in my room for the next year.

A red maple leaf drifts down onto my lap. It looks so pretty against the maroon.

Tucking the lap robe tighter around my knees, I toss the leaf. Enjoying the look of it dancing in the air, I ask him, "Did your school just let out?"

"I skipped." Dazzling white teeth flash in his dark face as he brings the reins down on Bucky's back.

"You did?" Neo is so brave. I thought it was brave of me to sock Fiona, but this is even bolder. I'd never have the guts to skip.

"Herrmann the Great is at the Boston Theater over on Tremont Street. I snuck in to a rehearsal."

"My parents took me to that theater once, to see *Romeo and Juliet*. It was so long and boring my rump fell asleep."

Neo laughs.

"Who's Herrmann the Great?"

"The greatest magician in the world, Nellie, that's who. He and his brother came over from France to do a tour." He stares straight ahead. "I want to be what Herrmann is, a great magician."

I pivot my head to stare at him. *A magician? What is he thinking?* The teachers at his fancy prep call him a genius. Mother tells me Uncle Kam was the same; he could read the stars and know what direction a ship was going and when it would reach land. Neo's grandfather was a witch doctor in Africa, and when a slave ship took him to the sugar plantations in Louisiana, he cured malaria and saved Irish slaves there. None of the normal doctors could do that. "But your father wants you to be a doctor."

He snorts. "No one in Boston would go to a Negro doctor, Nellie."

I could protest, but why bother. Both of us know he's right.

"What matters is what *I* want to do." Neo pulls the wagon over to the side of the road. "Watch this." He takes a nickel from his pocket and flips it from hand to hand, throws it up in the air, puts it behind his back, then balances it on his nose before he pops it back into the same hand he started with. He holds both hands before me, palms down and closed. "Tap the hand holding the nickel."

I saw where he put it. So feeling right as rain, I lift my finger and tap his left hand. When he opens it, it's empty. "But that's where it was. I watched carefully."

He laughs. "Try the other hand."

When I tap the right hand, he slowly uncoils his fingers. It's empty, too.

"What did you do with it?" I take his hands in mine and check up his sleeves.

Laughing harder, he reaches behind my ear. "Here it is, Nellie." He holds up the nickel.

A small colored boy wearing ragged pants and a faded shirt stands beside the wagon. He looks about six years old. I hadn't noticed him before. "Mister, how'd you do that?" the little boy asks, his eyes dancing like ebony fireflies.

"It's magic," Neo waves his hand. "Wonderful magic, young man." He slips the nickel into the boy's hand.

When the boy looks up at Neo, his eyes are full of wonder. "Thank you, sir."

"What's your name?"

"It's James, sir."

"You're welcome, James. When you grow up, maybe you can make magic, too."

As James walks away, still staring at the coin in his hand, a screechy voice yells out. At first, I think it belongs to an old woman, but a quick look shows it's a boy. "Hey girl, what you doing riding with that nigger?"

Neo ties up the reins and turns, slowly. "What did you call me?" The world freezes to silence.

The boy's size doesn't match his high voice. He's as large as a man. Red hair sticks out from under his cap like porcupine quills. As he advances toward us, anger twists his bulldog face. He pulls the cap further down over grey eyes that glare with meanness; eyes of someone itching for a fight. "I wasn't talking to you, blackie. I asked the pretty girl what she's doing riding with a nigger. Cause that's what you are, a nigger riding in a fancy carriage."

Neo has studied boxing since he was six years old. Perhaps I should warn this oaf? Before I can do that, Neo glides smoothly to the cobblestones, moving as if he's made of liquid. I grab my umbrella from the carriage floor and jump down to the street, hoisting it over my head.

Neo lifts his fists in a classic boxing pose as the boy hurtles toward him, his arms flailing the air. Neo dances to the left, and the boy stumbles into space, nearly falling to the stones. When he swivels back toward us, his face is crimson.

"Are you sure you want to fight me?" Neo's voice is calm and quiet.

"You bet your black ass I want to fight you, nigger. You shouldn't be riding with a white girl, and you know it."

"We're friends," Neo explains.

"Niggers can't be friends with white girls," the boy squeals, sounding now like an Irish fishwife. He lunges again. This time, his arms wind-milling wildly, he runs headlong into a lamppost as Neo slides gracefully to the right. The boy sits simpering at the base of the post.

Neo turns to step up into the wagon when, without warning, three other boys emerge from an alley and circle the red-haired boy. Two of them rush Neo, surprising him. One jerks his knee up. Neo yelps in pain and falls to the street, clutching his belly. Now, the four bullies surround me. Fear and fury fight in my brain.

"My, this is a pretty one." The one with the porcupine hair wipes snot from his nose. "Maybe it's time she got a taste of me. That'll swear her off black meat for good."

I point my umbrella toward his belly and charge, but he wrenches it from my hands before I can connect. He grabs me, laughing. Two boys lift my feet and carry me toward the alley. I twist to see Neo rushing at them, still clutching himself. Then, he spreads his arms and springs onto their backs, a snarling pit bull. He fights fiercely, but they have him outnumbered.

Slammed onto my back in the alley, I whisper "The Memorare." "Remember, oh most gracious, Virgin Mary, that never was it known that anyone who fled to thy protection, implored thy help, or sought thy intercession was left unaided."

I open my eyes to see the brute with the porcupine hair kneeling on my shoulders. Saliva slides down his chin onto my uniform. He stinks of sweat and beer and cigarettes. I gag from the stench. Out of the corner of my eye, I see that Neo is also sprawled on his back, a muddy boot pushing into his stomach. He struggles mightily, but two boys beat him while porcupine hair holds me down with his knees. He begins to unbutton his pants.

Suddenly, a man's voice breaks through the roar of panic in my head. "Stop! I said stop, you little bastards."

Two hands grab the one kneeling on my shoulders and throw him to the curb. I hear bone slamming into stone and vomit spurts up into my mouth. I roll to my side and spit it out.

The porcupine boy yowls in pain and twitches on the cobble-stones, blood pouring from his mouth. His jaw hangs slack and shattered.

I pull up on my elbows as my eyes travel up the long, navy trousers to the stern face of my father.

CHAPTER THREE

My mother pulls me into her arms as if she'll never let go. "Did they hurt you? Did they?" She tips my face up and looks into my eyes. Her chin trembles and her eyes glisten with unshed tears. My mother never cries and seeing her this close to crying frightens me.

"No, Mother. I'm fine, but they beat Neo up pretty bad."

"Kam will know what to do with Neo. You're my concern." She touches my face gently. "Did that boy touch you in any way?"

"No, Mother. Da came along just in time."

"Thank God." She takes my hand and leads me to the table where we sit down opposite each other, my hand still cradled in hers.

Since she seems so relieved that I'm all right, this might be a good time to find out the truth about what Fiona said. *How will I do that without letting her know what I'm asking? I'll be sneaky, that's how. I'll change the subject.*

"Mother," I say, cupping her hand in mine tenderly. "You never talk about the ship that brought you over from Ireland. All I know about it is that it's where you met Uncle Kam. What was it like?"

She darts a quick look at my father. "What makes you ask

about that now?" She stands and gets her apron from the drawer. "This is not a good time for that discussion. We have different fish to fry this night." She ties the apron around her waist. "Are you certain that boy didn't touch you?" The tears spill out, and it hurts me to see them. She doesn't want to talk about the ship now. Perhaps tomorrow.

"I'm sure, Mother." My voice is calm and reassuring. "Nothing happened to me. I'm fine."

She stares into my eyes for a long moment, then says, "I'll bring dinner," and heads for the stove. From the way she stomps her feet, I can tell she's not through with me.

My da sits in his usual place, slipping me a sideways grin. "You're in for it, girl."

She slams the platter of stew down, fills my milk glass and mutters, "Daniel, say grace, please."

Why is she still upset? Nothing happened to me.

She doesn't waste any time after the Amen. "How many times have I told you to be careful, Nellie?" Her jaw is clamped so tight, her chin quivers.

"I *was* careful, Mother." I grit my teeth right back at her and fold my napkin onto my lap. It wasn't my fault what happened, but if I argue with her, my father will bellow at me louder than the three o'clock whistle at the iron factory.

He calmly eats his stew; his beer dark and foamy beside the bowl.

"Careful doesn't get you dragged into an alley in broad daylight. Do you have any idea what might have happened to you?"

In all honesty, I don't. I shake my head, wordless.

"I guess it's time we had the talk." She takes a cleansing breath.

As she leans closer, I catch the scent—chloride. She smells like Kathleen's Haven, the birthing center. I begin to breathe through my mouth. Do I need to confess to the priest that the smell of my mother makes me sick? I hope not. Father Ruzzo thinks she walks on water, like Jesus Himself. Well, I'll never smell like that when I'm a teacher or a trapeze artist.

We finish our dinner in silence. When she does look at me, she shakes her head again; reliving something awful. She tells me to brush my teeth and get to bed. I run to the yard to pump the water. Tears of frustration mingle with the water in the bucket. *It's so unfair. All I did was ride in Neo's carriage. What's wrong with that?*

Not one of my friends has to brush her teeth two times a day. When I complain, my mother tells me I'm lucky to have a toothbrush; that when she was a girl in Ireland, they used birch branches. Just imagine. Birch branches. She got her first toothbrush when her father traded a salmon to a British sailor for it. I rinse and spit.

Some of the Irish here don't have teeth. My family's teeth are perfect, and so are the O'Hallorans's. Kathleen O'Halloran was the first one to give my mother work. She and Tommy had two girls, Shannon and Molly, and my mother helped bring them up. When Kathleen was nearly fifty, she had another baby. My mother knew she was too old to deliver safely, but she did all she could to try and save the woman. In the end, though, all she could save was the baby. Baby Sean, named after Sean Boland, my mother's father. I don't think my mother ever really got over losing Kathleen O'Halloran in childbirth. That's why she named the clinic Kathleen's Haven. Her picture hangs in the front hall. She's a big, happy-looking woman with a rolling pin in her hand. It's a funny picture, but everyone who knew Kathleen loves it.

Sean doesn't look a bit like Kathleen nor Tommy. He's so handsome and they're rather plain. When Sean graduates, he'll go to Harvard next year. Everyone says he's brilliant . . . and spoiled rotten. At least that's what my parents say. They would not approve if they knew Sean is the one boy who makes my heart beat faster each time I see him.

Sean's sister, Shannon, is married and has five children already. His sister, Molly, works with my mother and is just about the smartest person I know. I think Molly knows I have a crush on her brother, and once she cautioned me, "Sean is mean, Nellie. Don't set your sights on him. He's a heartbreaker."

I laughed at her. "I think all boys have cooties, Molly. Sean, too. Don't you worry about me." In truth, though, he's the only boy I like in a special way. I adore Neo, of course, but he's like a brother. Sean is nothing like a brother.

I am thinking about all this as I put the lid back on the baking soda and put it away in the kitchen. Passing through, I give my parents a quick kiss on the cheek. My mother doesn't speak to me but doesn't pull her face away either.

Brushing my locks its usual hundred strokes. I part it in several sections and look at my scalp. Some girls in town have head lice, and the thought of those little white bugs roaming around my head is enough to make me itch all over.

In bed, I pull my old rag doll close to my heart but then toss her to the floor. I'm a big girl now. But she looks up at me so sadly that I pick her up and put her beside me on my pillow. I loved her so much when I was a child, but a girl shouldn't be playing with baby things when she's almost fourteen, now should she?

After lighting the kerosene lamp, I pick up *Little Women* off the table. The second volume arrived at the library yesterday. I loved the first book, I want to be just like Jo when I grow up, strong and smart.

Tonight, I can't get interested in the story, though. What happened today scared me more than I want to admit. What would've become of me if my father hadn't been walking by? What would they have done to me in that alley? I'm strong, but not strong enough. I shudder and turn off the lamp.

My eyes won't close. I still feel Porcupine boy's rough hands pushing me down. It was dark in the alley. Neo was helpless. What if Da hadn't shown up? But he did. But what if he hadn't?

The shudder turns into trembling all over, and I almost cry out for my mother. Stop it, Nellie. Only babies scream for their mothers. Rolling over, I bite my pillow, hug my doll, and begin to pray. *Hail Mary, full of grace . . .*

I close my eyes tight, but they fly open when I remember. *At breakfast tomorrow, I have to tell my mother Sister Sarah is expecting her after school. How will I explain that? Maybe I'll tell her I had an argument at school with Fiona but leave out the part about making her nose bleed. Yes, that's what I'll do. My mother will be upset. She knows Fiona's mother, Agnes. The Doggetts have given lots of money to Kathleen's Haven.*

Why did Fiona tell such an awful lie?

CHAPTER FOUR

After I fall asleep, I have wonderful dreams about teaching young girls. I see myself in a starched white blouse and navy-blue skirt standing at a blackboard. The children smile and raise their hands with each question I ask. One little girl looks just like Lizbeth.

I am in the middle of the dream when my mother's voice wakens me. "Nellie, come to breakfast." Climbing out of bed, I pull on the pink chenille robe over my white nightgown. This Christmas, I hope I'll get a new one. These sleeves are nearly up to my elbows. "Growing like a beanstalk," mother always comments after looking me up and down. "Soon, you'll be taller than I am."

I hope not. The boys from the Academy are attracted to short girls. When Sean O'Halloran is around, I try to slump myself shorter.

The wooden floor is so cold it reminds me of when I was four and ran out the front door barefoot into the snow. My da chased me and grabbed me up into his big warm arms and bundled me back into the house. Then, my mother carried me to the stove and rubbed my feet with a wool blanket. Even as she scolded me, she was laughing.

I scoot my feet into the flannel slippers my parents bought for my birthday. They feel good. The smell of pancakes drifts into my room, making my mouth water. I'm so hungry. It must be awful to be hungry all the time. Sister Sarah makes us pray for the poor, starving, pagan babies in Africa. That's where Neo's family came from and seems a million miles away.

When I get to the kitchen, my mother says, "Nellie, love, good morning."

Well, that's good. At least she's speaking to me.

Her smile is bright, but I cringe at her brogue. It sounds low class. My da's accent doesn't bother me as much as hers does. Nothing bothers me about my da. He's so handsome all my girl-friends envy me. Everyone thinks my mother's pretty, too, but that hair of hers is wild. No matter how many pins she puts in it, it always comes loose and falls down around her face. None of the other mothers have bright red hair.

"Here're your pancakes, Nellie." She slides a plate towards me. "The maple syrup came fresh from New York yesterday. Your Uncle Tommy got an extra bottle from the delivery wagon for us."

"He's not my real uncle," I mutter.

"Don't be a snot, Nellie. Tommy's the closest thing you'll ever know to an uncle, and he loves you like his own."

She's right, of course. I love Uncle Tommy. He's funny and sweet and Sean's father. *Why am I being such a brat?* Sometimes, I hate my contrary nature, but I can't seem to help it.

As I slather the syrup on my pancakes, my da comes into the kitchen. He wears a white shirt, black vest, a black frock coat, and grey trousers. He walks over to my mother and puts his arms around her. "Good morning, Mrs. Kelly." She laughs and hugs him around the neck.

I don't get it. He acts like he hasn't seen her for weeks even though they slept in the same bed last night.

He kisses her on the lips, then comes to me. "And you, too, Miss Kelly." I get my kiss on the cheek. He smells good. Last year, he started wearing cologne when he goes to his office. "Better hurry up, Nellie. You'll scarce have time to dress before I take you to school."

"Don't forget the penny in your shoe in case of an emergency," Mother reminds me for the umpteenth time.

I've had that same penny in my shoe since I was ten.

"And remember, no talking to strangers, Nellie." Then, in a hushed voice, "We will speak later about how babies are made."

I've heard stuff about that from girls at school, but I don't believe them. Maybe now I'll get the truth.

I run to the pump, brush my teeth, and go to my room.

In minutes, I'm dressed. I can't put off telling her any longer. Da's outside rigging the carriage. "Mother, Sister Sarah wants a meeting with you after school today."

She stops wiping the table. "Why?"

"Fiona Doggett and I had an argument yesterday at recess."

"An argument? About what?"

I fidget, trying to put off telling her more, until my da yells, "Nellie, come on. We'll both be late."

"About something nasty Fiona said about you."

I grab my lunch bag and race for the door. When I turn to wave goodbye to her, she's bent over the table.

That's odd.

On the way to school, women on the streets gawk at my father like love-struck school girls. I'm used to their staring by now, but I still sit up straighter, proud to be sitting beside him. He lights a cigarette, holds it between his fingers and squints when the smoke drifts up and over the brim of his Homburg. My mother begs him to stop, but I love it; the smell, the look, the way his eyes crinkle as he draws the smoke into his lungs.

He started smoking cigars during the War but changed to Bull Durham cigarettes a couple of years ago. My mother nags him that taking smoke down into his lungs might be unhealthy.

He scoffs at her. "How can it be unhealthy, Mary? Tobacco grows from the earth just like potatoes. Besides, lots of men smoke now. I even saw a woman with a cigarette down at the wharf."

I'd smoke, too, when I grow up, but my mother believes the only women in Boston who do that are shady ladies. I'm not sure what a shady lady does, but I don't think she's a trapeze artist or a teacher. But it would be fun to blow smoke rings the way Da does.

As I picture myself with hazy rings pouring out of my mouth, my father asks, "So, Nellie, could I interest you in a ride Saturday?"

Could he ever! "Yes, oh, yes, Da. What time? I want to practice my jumps and see if I can stand up on the horse." I'd done that a few years back in the alley behind my house. Until my mother caught me and yelled me off the horse.

"Around ten in the morning, I think. I talked to Tim and he has two horses for hire in the morning."

"Which horses?"

"Barney and Thelma."

"Can I have Barney, Da?" Barney's spirited and fast.

He chuckles. "I suppose so."

I decide to show him my arithmetic paper from yesterday to seal the deal.

He studies it and his face breaks into a big smile.

"Sister says I'm even smarter than Sean O'Halloran."

Da throws back his head and laughs loudly. "Don't let Tommy hear you say that, Miss. He doesn't believe any girl can best Sean at anything."

Thinking of Sean makes me smile. He's nearly as tall as my da and, though his hair is the color of sunlight, not midnight black like Da's, he's almost as handsome. I saw a razor nick on Sean's cheek last week and teased him, "Ah, the baby O'Halloran is shaving, is he?"

Sean stuck out his middle knuckle and punched me in that soft spot on my arm boys always hit. I still have the bruise, and sometimes I push down on it, remembering the pain when he hit me.

"Even Molly says I'm smarter than Sean." I put the paper away and tighten the buckle on my book strap. "And since he's her brother, she ought to know. Molly is just about the smartest person I've ever met."

"Your mother taught Molly everything she knows, Nellie. Molly's been her intern ever since she opened the clinic."

"Well, Molly'll be teaching Mother a thing or two one of these days. She knows of a woman named Dr. Clemence Lozier who's opened a medical school for women in New York City. There're only a few students now, but Molly hopes to attend it someday."

"Oh, she does, does she?"

"Once Molly's a doctor, I bet she'll live in a grand mansion the same as the Doggetts do. Oh, Da you should see that place. Last time I was there, Mrs. Doggett was dressed in a rose-colored silk dress with a huge hooped skirt. She looked like an illustration in *Godey's Lady Book*, like an angel."

"Gah, Agnes Dooley Doggett? An angel? Ah, Nellie, I could tell you tales about Agnes that would curl your toenails." I look at him expectantly, but he shakes his head. "No, that wouldn't be Christian, so I'll keep my own counsel. But Agnes was not always the fine lady she presents herself to be now-a-days."

"Da, tell me."

"No, that'll be my last word on the subject, Miss. Just know that particular grand lady isn't fit to blacken your mother's boots." He clamps his lips together in a way that says forget about prying further. Once my da makes up his mind, he doesn't change it. He's stubborn as a mule. So am I, I guess. Everybody tells me I look like him, too.

Sister Sarah stands in front of the school, herding girls inside. I wish I could go the Academy with the boys. It isn't fair that girls must make do with this one-room school house.

But that might change. People talk about a college opening for women soon. It's in Wellesley, and I hope to go there when I finish high school. Sister told me I'm the only girl in our class who could pass the entrance exams.

Just a few more years, and I'll be ready. Then, I'll be a teacher . . . after I'm through being a trapeze artist. Whichever one I am, I won't smell like chloride.

CHAPTER FIVE

When Sister rings the lunch bell, I grab the sack out from under my desk. Inside it, I'll find a cheese sandwich on brown bread and an apple, same as always. I wish my mother could come up with something more exciting once in a while, maybe ham or roast beef. But those are only for dinner in my house.

If I complain, I'll get the lecture about how my mother's mother and sister, Ellen, starved to death back in the old country. Blah—blah—blah. My real name is actually Ellen, but my da nicknamed me Nellie.

"Nellie Kelly," Da sings when he dances me around our living room. He's done that since I was a little girl standing on his feet. Now, I come nearly to his shoulder. It's fun being tall when I dance with him. When my mother looks at the two of us whirling around the living room, her face looks bright as a sunbeam.

I stand in line waiting to get out to the playground, Fiona Doggett sticks her ugly, swollen nose up in the air as she passes me. Last year, that would've hurt my feelings so bad; and to tell the truth, it still does. She was my friend then, but no more, and I don't know why.

When I get outside, there's Adelaide Mahoney waving me over to the teeter totter. Adelaide's been my best girlfriend since

Fiona turned snotty. When I tuck my lunch sack down the front of my dress, the apple juts out big and round in the center of my chest.

Adelaide laughs. "You look like you have two little bosoms and one big one in the middle. Actually, I wouldn't even call them bosoms, they're so small."

I look down at my uniform. "I don't care. Big ones would just get in my way."

"My bosoms started growing when I was eleven," she answers, "and they haven't stopped since."

She's right. She looks almost as big as the three women in the pictures at the burlesque house over on G Street. Neo and I snuck over to see the poster one day after school. The women on the poster had huge bosoms, which were half uncovered. And their hair! It was colors no normal person has ever grown on their head.

If my mother knew Neo and I did that, she'd switch me raw.

I'm curious about why boys are so obsessed with bosoms. One Sunday at church, I noticed Andrew Turner's eyes bulge out as he stared at Adelaide's chest. I think her bosoms are even more interesting to *him* than Fiona's sparkling eyes are to Orville Mattison.

"I'm getting off," Adelaide warns me just before she jumps off her end of the teeter totter. We sit down on the grass with our backs against the wooden fence, and I take my lunch sack out of my front.

Adelaide pulls her sandwich out of her lunchbox and starts eating. A thick coating of butter covers the white bread and there's ham inside. Her family's maid buys the bread at Quincy Market three times a week and then cuts Adelaide's sandwiches into little quarters with no crusts. Maids always do that. Mothers don't.

My bread is coarse and brown and a little stale. My mother's not a great baker.

As Adelaide bites into her sandwich, she sticks out her little finger. She says that's the ladylike way to eat, so I do the same, though I never feel as dainty as Adelaide.

"I have a secret," she announces.

Her voice sounds playful, the way it was when she told me about how babies are made. I didn't believe her then and I still don't. My father would never do that to my mother.

"What?" I stretch my legs out on the ground and try to cover my ankles with my skirt. Sister says ladies shouldn't show their ankles.

"Well, I don't know whether I should tell you or not."

I've learned the best way to loosen Adelaide's tongue is to act as though it I couldn't care less about her latest bit of gossip. So, I say, "Then don't."

She takes another bite from her sandwich; her pinky quivering with excitement. "But I think this is something you really should know."

"Adelaide, don't talk with your mouth full. You have butter running down your chin."

She grabs the white linen napkin from her lunch box and wipes her face, then settles back against the fence. She's dying to tell me her secret, whatever it is. Her arm is vibrating through her coat. I can feel it as it presses against mine.

"Very well, Nellie. Finish your sandwich, then I'll tell."

I try to take small bites and chew each one thoroughly. I don't want Adelaide to think she has the upper hand. I'm getting really curious.

After I swallow the last bite of my sandwich and drain the water from my jug, I put the apple away. I'll save it for after school. "All right, Adelaide. What is it?"

"Well, you know Andrew Turner?"

His face materializes before my eyes. Brown hair, brown eyes, pimples. "Of course, I know him. He lives on my street. We used to play tag together when we were little."

"He kissed me."

None of my friends has actually kissed a boy. I turn and look at her.

"Really?"

She's as proud as if she had just swum the length of the Charles River or walked all the way to New Hampshire. She puts her hand up next to my ear and whispers; her words rushing with excitement. When she's finished, she sits back against the fence once again, a smile triumphant on her face.

I can't believe what she just said. I've never heard of such a thing. "He did that?"

Her eyebrows rise in confirmation.

"Why?"

"It's called French kissing. I guess because they do it in France."

"Wasn't it disgusting?"

"Yes, it was at first; but then it began to feel good."

"And he tried to touch your bosoms?"

"Yes, but I stopped him. That's a sin."

"What about the other?"

"I don't think so. After all, France is a Catholic country, so it must be all right."

CHAPTER SIX

I slump into church. Sister let me out of class early with orders to go to confession. The glow of the candles and scent of incense nauseate me, although I usually like them. I hate confession. It's so close in the little wooden box and the kneeler hurts my knees even though I double my skirt up under them. Before I started doing that, the splintery kneeler snagged my stockings every time. The Catholic Church obviously believes you must suffer for your sins. That's why they made confessionals so uncomfortable. But Sister's orders are Sister's orders.

Each week, I usually make up sins to tell the priest; such as, I disobeyed my parents or had an impure thought, which is a lie. I've never had an impure thought in my life. But it's a sin, so it gives me something to say. Today is different. My heart beats wildly in my chest, and my knees are shaking. *Why am I so scared?*

The little wooden door slides open. "Bless me, Father, for I have sinned. It's been five days since my last confession." I say it in a rush before I run out of breath.

"Go on, my child." His voice sounds tired, and I can see his cheek braced on his fist through the nearly transparent veil that separates us.

My face burns and my stomach feels sick. Deepening my voice to disguise it, I inhale. *Dear God, don't let him recognize me.* "Yesterday, I had a fight with Fiona Doggett during recess."

A weary sigh. "And why did you do that?"

"Because she told a hateful lie about my mother."

Silence. For a long time. That's peculiar. Father Ruzzo usually has a comment for everything in or out of confession. My mother calls him gabby. Eventually, he asks, "What did Fiona say?"

I pause and then decide to just blurt it out. "She said my mother was the ship's whore when she came over from Ireland. I'm sorry, Father, for using that word, but that's what Fiona said." I wipe the perspiration off my forehead on my shawl. "So, I socked her in the nose."

He shakes his head. I can see it through the veil. "Do you know what your mother went through to get out of Ireland, Nellie?"

Well, if that doesn't fry the fish, I don't know what does. He knows it's me. I was silly to think otherwise. If I can make out his face, he can make out mine. "Yes, Father," I say in my natural tone. "She tells me all the time how lucky I am to live in America and have food to eat. My Uncle Kam, too. The two of them tell me and Neo over and over and over again about how bad things were." *What does this have to do with my sin?*

"Ah, young people, so smug." His sigh flutters the veil toward me.

My skin prickles. Now I have to listen to the same sad song from a priest? "That's my only sin, Father. Please give me my penance." I know my voice sounds cold, but I don't care. I'm frustrated with him, with my mother, with Sister Sarah, and most of all, with Fiona Doggett, for getting me into this pickle in the first place.

"For your penance, make a good act of contrition."

I begin, "Oh, my God, I am heartily sorry for having offended thee, and I detest—"

Before I can finish the prayer, he interjects, "And then, go home and tell your mother everything Fiona said."

What? I can't tell Mother that! She'd probably cry. I wouldn't blame her after hearing a lie like that. I don't want to make my mother cry. I stammer through gritted teeth, "But Father, my mother's coming to school in a few minutes for a meeting with Sister. Can't you just give me a few Our Fathers and Hail Marys? Or even a rosary?"

Quiet.

"At the meeting with Sister, you will tell your mother exactly what Fiona said and then listen with an open heart."

What a strange penance. Listen with an open heart? What does that mean? "But Father, I can't tell her Fiona called her that awful name."

"That's your penance. Do it if you want to receive communion on Sunday. Now, say three Our Fathers and three Hail Marys and get the devil out of here."

Without another word, he slides the little wooden door shut.

CHAPTER SEVEN

After confession, I arrive back at school to find my mother climbing down from our wagon. She sees me and smiles, but I don't smile back because I'm frightened this meeting with Sister will hurt her. And if Sister doesn't tell her what Fiona said about her, I'll have to do it when we get home.

Why am I trembling? For some reason, Father Ruzzo's penance is troubling me terribly. *How does a person keep her heart open anyway? And why would he tell me to do that? I've never heard of such a penance.*

As soon as she ties up the horse, I take her arm. "Hello, Mother. This way to Sister's office."

"For heaven's sake, I know how to get there, Nellie." She laughs and kisses me on the cheek. "I do wish you'd call me 'Mam' like a proper Irish girl."

"I'm not an Irish girl, Mother. I'm an American girl."

"So, something's wrong with keeping the good parts of our heritage, love? Lord knows there's enough we need to forget. Would it kill you?"

Yes, it *would* kill me is what I want to say, but don't. I don't *feel* Irish. I have no connection to Ireland. It's just a place far across the ocean whose people become maids and blacksmiths here in

America. The rich women check their Irish maid's dusting with white gloves, and the Brahmins look down their aquiline noses on the poor Irish men shining their shoes. No one will look down their skinny nose at Nellie Kelly, not if I can help it.

Mother and Sister exchange a quick hug. I start for the chair with the tufted buttons, but a glare from Sister moves me to the hard wooden one beside it. My mother takes the soft leather chair.

"How've you been, Sister?" my mother asks. "Lumbago any better?"

Sister shakes her head. "On cold days, I fairly want to scream, Mary."

My mother raises her eyebrow. "Using that liniment I gave you?"

"Oh, I keep forgetting it."

My mother points her index finger and wiggles it up and down.

"I know, I know. I'll use it, I promise. How goes things at Kathleen's Haven?"

My mother smiles. "Very well. The Okafor Foundation gave us another thousand dollars last month. That'll keep us going for quite some time."

"Praise God." Sister looks heavenward. "That place has saved the lives of so many women in our parish."

My mother lowers her head and smiles again, then directs her attention to the nun. "So, Sister, Nellie tells me she had an argument with Fiona Doggett yesterday?"

"More than an argument, Mary. Nellie punched Fiona in the nose. Might've broken it. I could scarcely stop the bleeding."

My mother jerks her head toward me; her mouth wide open. At first, she looks furious, but then a curtain of pain sweeps over her eyes. The anger I could take; the pain I cannot. I turn away.

She's is clearly disappointed in me. "Nellie?" she questions. Glancing back, I see her mouth silently trying to form the next words.

"Mary," Sister's voice soothes, "Fiona is not blameless in this incident."

"Perhaps not, but Nellie is my concern." She turns again to me. "What did she do to make you behave with violence?"

She waits for my answer, but my mouth is frozen against repeating Fiona's words. *Why am I so afraid to say them?*

"Nellie, what did Fiona do?" she repeats more firmly.

Tears convulse into sobs. My body jerks with the force of them. Mother kneels in front of me and takes me in her arms. She wipes my face with her linen hankie. Her comfort feels so good that I relax into her arms. "Hush, love. It's all right. Tell me."

I can't. I just can't. I look to Sister Sarah, my eyes imploring her to spare me this.

"Mary, maybe it's best I tell you." She leans forward and puts her elbows on the desk. Her chubby neck digs into the hard wimple.

My mother stands very straight and sits down again but doesn't let go of my hand.

"Fiona told Nellie that you did bad things on the ship that brought you from Ireland," Sister stammers.

My mother slumps in her chair, shaking. "Oh, no."

"I hate Fiona," I hiss.

My mother straightens and turns to me, taking my chin in her fingers. "Nellie, never let someone make you hate them. Hatred will eat you from the inside out. Believe me, I know."

"But it's right to hate someone who hurts you with a horrible lie." I turn to Sister Sarah. "Isn't it, Sister?"

Sister sputters for an answer, but my mother beats her to the words. "It's never right to hate, no matter what."

"But it is a lie, isn't it, Mother?" I hold my breath waiting for her answer.

She doesn't respond, her face is stony.

Why doesn't she answer me? "Tell me it's a lie, Mother. Please tell me it's a lie." I find myself teetering on the edge of the hard chair.

She stands. "We'll discuss this at home, Nellie. I'll answer all your questions at home."

Sister rises and comes around to her. "Mary, I'm so sorry about all this. If I could've stopped the girl, I would have, but it happened when I was inside."

"It's not your fault, Sister. Nellie will be in school tomorrow morning, I assure you. We'll be leaving now." Her back ramrod straight, we leave the classroom.

CHAPTER EIGHT

She pours me a glass of milk and lights the fire under the tea kettle. A plate of chocolate cookies appears on the table before me. My favorites. She must have baked them this morning before she went to work.

But my stomach is so tight I don't take a cookie. After she's explained things and proven Fiona the liar she is, then I'll eat one.

Sitting in this kitchen has never felt strained before. Though I'm tired of hearing the story of how the pretty linen tablecloth belonged to some woman on the ship with a daughter named Ceili, I'd almost welcome that story now. Mother walks to the whistling tea kettle without a word. The pendulum on the grandfather clock swings back and forth, back and forth. My father bought that clock for my mother for their tenth anniversary. She loves it and dusts it every Saturday. It ticks off minutes so slowly. When it chimes, I nearly jump out of my skin.

My mouth is dry, so I take a sip of milk. It doesn't help.

Why won't she just tell me Fiona's story is a lie and get this whole mess over with? I wipe my hands on my skirt. The pump outside is dripping. She must have not pulled the handle all the way up when she got the tea water. That's not like her.

My mother brings her tea to the table and takes off her apron.

Leaning towards me, she cradles my right hand into her two hands, and I'm glad I wiped mine dry. She'd have noticed in a heartbeat my wet, shaky palm. She is quiet for a long time, which scares me even more.

My head begins to ache from the silence of the room, so I start to chatter. "Father Ruzzo told me I must tell you the whole story and listen with an open heart, whatever that means." I shrug as if to toss off his words.

Her eyebrows spike into arches. "Father Ruzzo?"

"Sister Sarah made me go to confession."

She releases my hand and leans in to sip her tea. Her brow knits, and I see her jaw flexing and forming wrinkles on her white skin. She's always pale, but today her face looks chalky. "Go ahead, Nellie. Tell me everything."

My words pour from my mouth in a rush of nervousness. "Fiona told me an awful lie about you. It made me so mad I socked her. That's it."

"What did Fiona say?"

"It was just a lie."

"What did she say, Nellie?"

I slump back into my chair and cross my arms over my chest. *How do I say what I must say?* I take in a deep breath and blurt out, "Fiona called you the whore of the ship from Ireland. She said you did bad things with sailors. Had sex with them. I told her it was a lie and smacked her one."

My mother sits slumped over her tea. I want to touch her but can't move.

When she raises her eyes, they are blurry with tears, or maybe mine are. I'm not sure. There's no color in her face. Even her hair seems to be fading. I can't bear to see her like this. I get mad at her sometimes, but I don't want to see my mother hurt, so hurt she looks like a breathing corpse. I never want to see that.

Her fingers grasp my hand again. I feel the trembling from my hand and from hers.

"Nellie, you're shaking. Please remain calm."

How can I be calm with this stranger who used to be my mother sitting before me looking hurt? It's making my heart pound so loud I'm surprised she can't hear it. Why doesn't she deny this lie? Why isn't she marching me over to the Doggett's house to demand an apology from Fiona? I remember when our neighbor, Blanche, lied and said I'd stolen their newspaper. My mother nearly chewed her face off. She's always been like a Banshee when it comes to defending me. Why isn't she furious now? Why is she so quiet?

"There's something you don't know, Nellie . . ." She exhales forcefully. "Something I've tried to protect you from all these years." She looks so tired.

My brain whirls, trying to understand what she's saying. I was prepared for anger, even for a violent outburst, but not for this sad, quiet woman sitting across the kitchen table from me. Now, she's clutching my hand so hard it hurts, so I wrench mine away from her grasp.

She picks up her teacup but is trembling so it spills on her hand. She yelps in pain, then puts the burned finger in her mouth. She stares at me. Her mouth opens, closes, then opens again. "What Fiona told you is true."

CHAPTER NINE

I sit frozen, as cold as I've ever been in my life, although the wood stove is roaring and sun creeps through the curtains.

And then, and then . . . my mother tells me the story of the ship . . . for the first time.

She weeps as she expresses a tale of being sold to the sailors of the Pilgrims Dandy by an evil woman; that she thought she'd be a serving maid to the crew; that what happened to her was not of her own will but forced upon her, violating her repeatedly; that they beat her and tore her body so she thought she'd never heal. Raped unmercifully. Then her voice becomes shaky, breaking with each word, and she takes my hands in hers. "I thought . . . that's what . . . what could have happened to my . . . to my baby girl . . . in that alley . . . with those thugs."

I do not speak. I cannot speak.

She tells of three men: one with a bald head and an ugly tattoo, one with a wooden peg for a leg, and one with teeth so rotten his breath smelled like death. How she fought them, kicking and screaming, but was overpowered. How she was planning to throw herself over the rails to the sharks but was rescued by a young slave boy. "That boy was your Uncle Kam. They—" She clears her throat. "They visited their evil onto him as well." Tears flow with each word.

How could that be? Can a boy be raped? My eyes searching her face, I mutter, "How old were you?"

"Thirteen; a flat-chested naif, a full year from my first blood."

The same age I am now. Though I got my first blood last year, I still feel like a child. *What kind of monsters would do such things to a child?* Then I remember those boys in the alley and know that such evil does exist. I shudder, saying timidly, "Does Da know?"

"Of course, he knows." She sniffles and attempts to wipe her nose with the back of her hand, letting out a deep sigh.

"But he married you anyway?"

Her gasp shakes me to my very core.

"I didn't mean it the way it sounded," I say, reaching for her. "I'm sorry, Mam. I'm just so confused."

Her face is a mask of misery.

"I asked because you're always telling me that I must remain chaste—that no man will marry me if I don't. But he married you."

"He was on one of those ships, too, Nellie. He knows what they were like."

"But he could've had any girl in Boston. Didn't he want someone pure?"

Suddenly, my upper arm is caught in a steel grip. I am pulled to my feet and whirled around like a rag doll.

My father's face blazes with rage. "How dare you talk to your mother like that, girl!" He slaps me hard across the cheek. "Go to your room! Now!"

My mother jumps toward him, grabbing onto the lapels of his jacket. Her voice is low, a growl sharp as a winter wind. "Daniel, yesterday, that maggot, Fiona Doggett, told Nellie what happened to me on the ship. We're talking it out now. You'll not interfere."

She turns from his raging face and pulls me into her arms. "He didn't mean it, Darlin'. He didn't know."

But the rage is still there. I can see it and fairly feel the heat of it radiating from my father to me. His eyes blaze with hatred as my heart shatters into a thousand pieces. I stumble toward the kitchen door, sobbing and rubbing my throbbing cheek. He's *never* struck me; never gazed at me with anything but love and pride.

"Nellie!" he yells.

I whirl to face him. Maybe he'll say he's sorry; maybe he'll take me into his big, warm arms, but he does neither. His eyes remain cold. "Did Fiona tell you what her mother did? She who ran the biggest cathouse in Boston?"

"Be still, Daniel." My mother grabs his arm. "One evil won't help another."

I'm shocked to stillness. She's never spoken to him with disrespect.

"Nellie, come back here and sit down. We'll say a prayer and eat our dinner," she says. "I'll answer any questions you have about what happened." She holds out her hand for me.

I look at my father who motions toward the table. I say nary a word but sit down at my place. Father sits and Mother ladles three bowls of soup she'd prepared earlier that afternoon, then places them before us.

I put my spoon into the soup, pushing it forward as I've been taught to do. It's good, full of beef and vegetables and barley, but I don't really taste it. I drain my milk and then, through the numbness, my curiosity gets the best of me. "You say they did the same thing to Uncle Kam?"

She nods, her eyes cast down.

My father turns scarlet and pushes his chair back. "I'll leave that one to you, Mary. I'm going to the porch for a smoke."

Her eyes follow his departing back, then she rises to put tomorrow's bread, now risen, into the stove, and sits down. What she explains to me is even worse than the other; beyond belief, disgusting.

"They did *that* to Uncle Kam?" I start to shiver and cannot stop the flow of lamenting tears for both my mother and my dear, sweet uncle.

The next day at lunch, Fiona comes up to me in the school yard. Her nose is swollen and both her eyes are raccoon black.

Good! I did break it!

"Nellie," her posture's ram-rod straight, "Sister told my mother what I said, and I've been ordered to apologize to you. I'm sorry." It sounds forced and not the least bit sincere.

I turn on my heel and show her my back. I'll never forgive her. I itch to tell her what I know about *her* mother but won't. She'll find out in due time. At least, I hope so. Besides, I don't really know what a cathouse is, but the way my father said it, it must be really bad.

CHAPTER TEN

ONE MONTH LATER

I haven't spoken to Fiona since that day and don't intend to ever speak to her again. My mother essentially explained what a cathouse is. I can't believe Mrs. Doggett actually used to run one, and I thought she was so high class. My father always said you can't shine shit, but Mrs. Doggett certainly polished up pretty well, didn't she?

At least I now understand why my mother was so scared when those boys dragged me into the alley—no wonder, after what she went through. Truth be told, I'm pretty scared, too. Boston can be a dangerous town for a girl. Things are moving so fast around here.

Today is Thanksgiving! My family has been invited to the Okafors' house for dinner, an annual event for us. I'll get to see Neo, Uncle Kam, Aunt Imani, and, most of all, Martha, their housekeeper. Martha is my favorite person on earth.

We leave at four o'clock. Dinner is at six, but it's a long ride from South Boston to Joy Street. I sit bundled up in the back of our wagon and stare at the stiff backs of my parents. They still seem mad at each other most of the time. It might be because she nags him so much about smoking. But I also wonder if they worry about me socking Fiona and if I'm becoming like a banshee. All that's sure is that they're not like they used to be. *Have I caused this trouble between them? Am I to blame?*

Their posture is as cold and frigid as this November day. Neo says I shouldn't blame myself, but who else can I blame? I started this whole mess.

"Watch those pies, Nellie," my mother says over her shoulder. "Don't let them fall."

I brace the pies with both hands; one pumpkin and one mincemeat. Mincemeat is not my favorite, but my mother always adds lots of apples to it, so it's pretty good. I can't wait to see everyone, especially Martha who has been like a second mother to both me and Neo as far back as I can remember.

The sun is gone as our wagon clip clops up the cobbled streets and past the Boston Common. *Good! We're almost there.* A lamplighter in a tall black hat stretches a long pole up to light the gas lamps along the road. He waves and shouts, "Happy Thanksgiving!" as we pass him.

"And to you, sir!" my father tips his hat and shouts in return.

A slight mist rises from the yards as cold air glides over the city. A dog barks when we pass it, and dazzling chandeliers shine from each window of the mansions along Beacon Hill. Through the wavy glass of the windows, crystals dance like fairies in the gathering darkness of the night. I wonder what's happening behind those gleaming windows? Do some of them hide secrets like the Doggetts'? Obviously, things are not always what they appear to be.

We're close to Joy Street, also known as Nigger Hill, though my mother forbids my using that term, which is odd since that's what Neo calls it. Joy Street is situated on the back side of Beacon Hill. I suppose it's there because the Brahmins want their servants close.

The air is clear and frosty, and I puff out big clouds of white.

I laugh out loud. "Look, Mother, it looks like I'm smoking cigarettes, too."

She jumps on her chance. "Don't you *even think* about smoking cigarettes, Nellie Kelly. It's bad enough having him stinkin' up my house." She glances over at my father, and he gives the horse an extra lick with the reins.

At least I got her to talk.

I close my eyes and think about the evening ahead. Things are always special, even magical, at the Okafors. Their home is so grand. Not stuffy like Fiona's house, though it's every bit as big. But there's no coldness at the Okafors, no fake formality. Mother says Uncle Kam made his fortune as a medicine man selling some tonic from Africa. He doesn't travel any more, though; he sells it through something called mail order, and the orders keep coming in. Must be good stuff, I figure.

With everything so awful at home, I want to feel Martha hug me again. Martha has been the Okafor's housekeeper since before I was born. She came from Georgia and claims to have special powers for divining things. She thinks she and I were mother and daughter in a past life, and that's why we love each other so much in this one.

When I asked Father Ruzzo about past lives, he humphed and said we only get one on earth and the next one in heaven; that to believe anything else is a sin. But I do wonder sometimes. Why else would I love Martha so much?

At the top of Beacon Hill, I see the glow from the Okafor's mansion down below us. Neo's house glistens like a diamond shining in a black velvet case. Its turrets rise above its neighbors like a castle. And the lights, oh, the lights. Candles and oil lamps gleam from every window. Yes, it looks magical.

It's a wonder their neighbors don't hate the Okafors, considering the difference in their houses; but Mother says they all love the Okafors. Because whenever someone on Joy Street needs help, Kam or Imani is the first one at their door. They give whatever is needed—food, money, or comfort. So rather than jealousy, there's love. Mother says to remember the lesson in that. Maybe so, but I'm pretty sure I'd feel jealous if I lived in that ugly shack next door. It looks so sad and dark.

The wraparound porch at the Okafors is entwined with bittersweet vines. It's almost five-thirty and the moon is rising. Pumpkins carved and illuminated by candles blink from their scary faces on the railings of the porch. I swear, the house looks grateful it's Thanksgiving night and that we are coming to visit it.

I run up the twenty-eight steps to the porch, carefully balancing the pies. Neo and I counted them when I was six. We used to play here often when my mother was working. It's the best place in the world for hide and seek. When I climbed the big maple tree in the back, Neo didn't find me for nearly an hour.

"Nellie, hold your horses," my mother yells from the street. "Wait for your father and me before you ring that bell."

I dance from one foot to the other as the two of them climb up the stairs. My da's breathing heavily when he reaches the porch.

"All right, ring it."

I do.

The door swings wide in seconds, and Martha stands there, her ebony face beaming with pleasure. "Miss Nellie, just look at you. You taller than last time I saw you and prettier than any girl on Beacon Hill. Come to Martha."

After she takes the pies from my hands and puts them on a table, I melt into her arms. She is soft, a velvet pillow, not thin like my mother and Neo's. When I was smaller, I would sink my face into her warm belly or chest and stay there for as long as I could. She never let go in a hurry like most grownups did. Now I'm taller than she is, but her arms feel just as tight around my waist. I rest my chin on her head, inhaling the scent of turkey, sweet potatoes, and the musk that is Martha.

"You wanna cookie?" she asks.

"Martha, you spoil her rotten!" My mother laughs behind me.

"She deserves spoilin', Miss Mary. She be my favorite girl in thte whole wide world. Same as Neo's my favorite boy."

No one in her right mind would ever refuse one of Martha's cookies. "I'd love one, Martha."

She reaches into a basket on the hall table, handing one to me. I bite into the crunchy bliss of molasses and pecans.

"Could you spare one of those for me, Martha?" my father pleads.

"Sire 'nuf, Mister Daniel." She offers him the basket. "Now, take off dose coats and give 'em here. I'll hang 'em up for you and take these pies to the kitchen after I announce ya. Thank you kindly foe bringin' 'em."

My parents shrug out of their coats and hand them to Martha as my father crunches on his cookie. I do the same and pass her the white bunny muff Neo gave me for my last birthday. She rubs the soft fur against her face. "Oooh, I loves this thing." Then, she places it on the closet shelf and closes the door. "Come on, now." She leads us into the living room.

Uncle Kam and Aunt Imani sit in front of a fireplace that takes up a whole wall. They are sipping small glasses of wine. Candles blaze from every corner. When they see us, they stand and hurry to embrace us. They are as beautiful and sleek as panthers, moving gracefully through space.

"Nellie," Aunt Imani says, turning my face gently in her delicate fingers. "You're prettier every time I see you. Those blue eyes of yours will break many hearts."

Imani's bronze silk gown glistens in the light of the fire and candles. Her hair is swept up into curls at the back of her head and the effect exactly matches the bustle low on her back. Diamond ear bobs sway against her dark cheeks. She takes my breath away.

"Let me get a look at you, Nellie." I pivot towards Uncle Kam. "Yes, my wife is right. You are becoming a great beauty." When he turns to my father, I see a dusting of grey at his temples. He's the handsomest colored man I've ever seen. "Better keep an eye on this one, Daniel."

My father grunts and nods his head.

Mother hugs me. "She's a good girl."

The words warm my heart. *Yes, I am a good girl.*

Uncle Kam leads me to the sofa and sits down beside me. "What do you think you will become when you are grown, Miss Nellie Kelly?" For a second, I remember what my mother said the sailors did to him, but I push that thought away. There's no room for ugly thoughts on a night like this.

"A trapeze artist, Uncle Kam, or a teacher. A teacher of science, I think. No one has taught me any science, but I've read a lot of Mother's books, and it interests me."

"A science teacher!" he exclaims. "Wonderful. Where will you train?"

"I hope at the Wellesley Female Seminary. They're saying it may open later this year. Sister Sarah told me my grades should get me in when I graduate from Girls' High." I feel very puffed up at sharing this.

"I've heard of Wellesley. I understand that Governor Claflin plans to sign their charter soon."

"I've heard that, too," my father adds.

Mother seems surprised by his words. "You did?"

"Yep."

"Why didn't you mention it to me?"

"I didn't think it was important. Nellie's only thirteen, after all. By the time she's old enough for college, she might want to get married."

My mother shakes her head. "What happened to the man I married, the one who waited for me until I got the Haven up and running?" She sits down next to Imani. "Next thing, he'll be saying women shouldn't get the right to vote."

"I'd never say that, Mary, and you know it. I just don't think Nellie's as driven as you were."

That stings me to a response. "Da, I am driven. I *will* be a teacher."

"And who will you teach? Boys? Science isn't offered in girls' schools."

"But by then?" Aunt Imani asks.

My da shakes his head. "Who knows?" he walks to the blazing fireplace. "Mind if I smoke?"

"No, I don't mind," Imani says.

"*I* mind," Mother addresses Imani. "It can't be healthy to take smoke into your lungs."

Da shrugs and opens his brass cigarette carrier and extends it to Uncle Kam. "Join me?"

"No thanks, Daniel. They make me choke." He brings my father a glass of amber liquid. There is one ice cube in it. "It's Irish."

Da sips the drink and smiles. "Delicious." He lights his cigarette from an ember and draws in deeply. A red glow appears at its end. I don't care what Mother says, I think he looks marvelous smoking, like one of the elegant gentlemen I see at Quincy Market.

Uncle Kam addresses Da, "You know, Daniel, Mary just might be right about tobacco. Her intuition about things related to health is usually spot on."

My father lifts his eyebrow doubtful, "Do you really think so?"

"Possibly. People are getting sick in their lungs from something ever since the war, and it's not consumption. I wonder if there's a connection. Nobody smoked before the war." When Uncle Kam talks medical matters, people listen. He brings a wisdom that few medical doctors seem to have.

Da looks at the cigarette. "Maybe I should quit."

Uncle Kam shrugs. "Your choice."

The two of them stand by the fireplace sipping their drinks. My da throws the cigarette into the flames.

"That looked like a decision, Daniel."

"I think it was, Kam."

Martha bustles into the room carrying a tray filled with cheeses, meats, and olives. In her other hand, there's a plate of those delicious cookies. I grab one.

"Nellie," my mother calls out. "Take it easy on the cookies. Don't want to spoil your dinner."

"Where's Neo?" I ask Martha.

"Lord only knows. That boy's always off somewhere. He be back soon 'nough. He knows you're comin'."

Almost as if he heard his name, Neo calls through the door. "Hello, all! Happy Thanksgiving! Be right there. Just want to put these books in my room."

He's back in a heartbeat and sits next to me. After he's greeted my parents, he asks me, "Nellie, want to play checkers?"

"Sure, I do."

"Mother, is it all right if Nellie and I go to the library?"

"Certainly, son. We'll let you know when dinner's ready."

He grabs my hand and we run out of the room. The library is down a long hall behind the living room. The oriental carpet on the library floor is soft under my feet, and there's a rolling ladder to help us reach the higher shelves, the same one Neo and I used to roll around on when we were children, until Martha caught us.

We settle at a carved table with a checker board on it. The checkers are made of ebony wood and white elephant tusks. I pick up a white one and marvel at its weight.

"Nellie, I've a plan I want to talk to you about," Neo arranges the black checkers on his side of the board without looking at me.

I start to arrange my checkers. "What kind of plan?"

"Well, you know how our parents are always talking about the adventures they had when they were young?"

"Oh, yes." I roll my eyes and study the board to consider which piece to move first.

"I think we need to make our own adventure."

I move my checker and stare at him. He looks excited. Neo is so adventurous, not a scaredy cat like I am. I wish I could be more like him. "What do you think we should do?"

"You know how good I am at magic tricks? And how you're always pretending to be a trapeze artist?"

"Yes, Neo, but that's just for play."

He jumps me and takes my checker. "Not for me."

Darn, he always beats me. I shake my head, confounded by this conversation. "What are you talking about? What do you mean, 'not for you.'"

"We belong in the circus, Nellie. The circus. This summer, when the circus comes to New York, let's go there and join it. That's an adventure we'll never forget."

Chapter Eleven

"Dinner's served," Martha announces from the library door.

"Leave the board set up," Neo says. "We'll play again later."

As we walk toward the dining room, I whisper, "Are you insane? We can't run away. Our parents would go daft."

"We'll leave them notes and tell them not to worry; that we'll be back before summer's end. If we don't tell them where we are, they won't be able to track us down."

"But how would we get to New York?"

"I've got that figured out. I've been saving my allowance. Save yours, too."

"I don't get an allowance."

His eyes bug out a bit, but he recovers quickly. "No matter. I'll have enough for both of us."

Has Neo lost his mind? I wonder. His idea is impossible. I force myself to not laugh out loud, but I can still feel the grin cracking my face. How would I ever get away from my mother? And Uncle Kam and my father would have the police on us in a flash. But to tell the truth, in spite of the impossibility of such a thing, excitement bubbles inside me at the thought. *No*, I tell myself, *such a plan, whatever kind of plan it is, can't work, can it?* But I can't run away and join a circus; not just before I start Girls High School. It's crazy.

"Just think about it," Neo whispers. "You don't have to decide tonight. But Nellie," he stares into my eyes, "it's our chance for adventure; maybe even a bigger adventure than our parents had."

My mind is tumbling all over itself as we enter the dining room. *How could we sneak away without getting caught? And more confounding, how could I ever travel to New York with a colored boy? It would be a scandal for sure.*

At the entrance to the dining room, I stop, my eyes wide. The room looks like a picture in a story book. Candles light the linen-covered table and more tapers flicker on sconces encircling the room. A fire cracks and blazes in the fireplace. The table is set with china that has hand-painted flowers around the edge. The platter for the main course sits table center next to an ornate silver bread basket. Next to each plate is a matching salad dish and there are knives and forks of heavy silver beside them, too. I hope I'll know which fork goes with each course. At home, we eat everything on one plate, and it's a rustic earthenware, but these dishes shine with the patina of fine china.

"Nellie and Neo," Martha calls out, "y'all come in here an' help me bring things to the table."

We hurry to help her, loading up our hands with platters, bowls, and a gravy boat, all filled to the brim with the delicious food Martha has been preparing since dawn.

When we're finished with all the serving dishes and the table is complete, a huge, brown turkey sits in front of Uncle Kam. A bowl of mashed potatoes swimming in butter is in front of my father, and escalloped oysters sit next to cooling cranberries. And there's Martha's stuffing, the best stuffing I've ever tasted, smack in the middle of the feast. I know it's the best I've tasted because a little fell on the kitchen floor, and I scooped it up and into my mouth before anyone could see. Martha's sweet potatoes, drenched in butter, brown sugar, and cinnamon is next to the stuffing. The final bowl holds Brussels sprouts. Neo glances at them and then to me. An understanding passes between us. Neither of us will touch them.

The feast is completed with homemade yeast rolls so light they could float off the table and sweet butter fresh from the dairy.

We sit down, eyeing the food hungrily.

"Martha, we want you to join us for dinner," Aunt Imani states.

"Oh, no, ma'am. That wouldn' be proper."

The discussion happens each Thanksgiving, and every year, the outcome is the same. After much coaxing from everyone at the table, Martha sits down with us. She looks tired but satisfied with the feast she has presented.

"As I carve this beautiful bird, I want each of you to say what you're thankful for this year." Uncle Kam looks to his wife. "Imani, you start."

Aunt Imani thanks God for the love in her life. Her eyes sparkle like the diamonds in the earrings floating round her face as she looks at Kam and Neo.

"Mary," Aunt Imani says.

My mother lowers her eyes and when she raises them again, they are glistening with tears. "Thank you, God, for Daniel and Nellie, and for putting Kam on that ship with me. Without him, I'd have died." She quiets and turns to my father who starts to speak, but then she speaks up, "No, wait, I nearly forgot. Thank you, also, Kam, for keeping Kathleen's Haven afloat during the tough times." She lifts her wine glass in a toast. "Now, Daniel?"

"For friendship, love, and fine Irish whiskey, and for a wife who nags me so I can get it through my thick Irish skull that she just wants me healthy." He looks happy as he raises his glass, then kisses my mother's cheek. "Kam?"

Uncle Kam smiles. "I'm grateful that Hammacher Schlemmer invented mail order. Because of that, I can stay here in Boston with my family and still make money from my tonic. The Okafor name is now respected in America. Martha?"

She stammers, "Thank you, God, that my lumbago's stopped actin' up. Also, I'm grateful to have Miss Nellie and her parents at this table. My little girl's gettin' grown up and beautiful."

My face blazes hot, but I do love the attention.

As always, the children are last. Neo's grateful for learning magic tricks. I mention my bunny muff and its warmth with winter upon us.

My mother whispers to my father, "All I ask for is to see you stop the cigarettes, Daniel."

"I've quit," he declares before all.

She raises her eyebrows, grins, leans over, and kisses him on the cheek.

And I have yet one more thing to be thankful for.

CHAPTER TWELVE

APRIL 1971

Things at home seem almost normal now. My mother and father are nice to each other most of the time, unless he gets her Irish up—like when he tracked snow all over her freshly-waxed floors on Christmas. She screamed so loud I almost believed the old stories about banshee blood on her side.

This Christmas, Neo gave me bunny fur ear muffs to match my muff and I wore them every day. I needed those ear muffs. Winter was brutal in Boston this year.

But now, it's nearly summer. As I sit in my classroom, a big fat robin lights on the windowsill. He looks in at me, bobs his head up and down, and flies off to the budding apple tree outside the school fence. That bird seems to be saying, "Come on out, Nellie. It's getting warm." It's a silly thought, but it makes me smile.

"Miss Kelly!" Sister taps her desk. "Daydreaming out that window is not going to get you into Girls High, you know."

"Yes, Sister," I answer, returning my attention to the blackboard while the smile still devils my lips.

"Only two weeks until your final examinations, girls," Sister states, her eyebrows raised.

I look around at the other girls and, happy as I am, feel a pang of sadness. I probably won't see some of them again, at least not every day. For Bryn and Sheila, this year will end their education. No matter how hard they study, their future is sealed. They'll get jobs as maids or at the laundry. My heart hurts for them. They're sweet girls and certainly smarter than Fiona Doggett will ever be. But their families need extra money, so at fourteen, they'll put the books away and go to work. What a shame.

I'm lucky and know it. My mother has always planned on me going to high school. She keeps a tin on the kitchen counter, and every night, she puts a few coins into it, then cleans out my da's pants pockets for change and throws that in, too. She's done that for years. Each time the tin is filled up, she deposits the coins into a bank account for my school. When Da or I try to sneak a coin out, she yells like crazy.

Girls' High is not a big, fancy building or anything. I've walked by it often. But when I see girls walking home after school, their eyes are happy and they walk fast with their shoulders back and their chins lifted as though they're proud.

These are girls with dreams. I have dreams, too. Even more important, I have the grades to make those dreams come true.

Some of the pupils at Girls High live on Beacon Hill. I worry they might look down their noses at me because of where I live and the way I dress. When that worry comes, I remind myself that when I finish high school, Wellesley will be there. I'll be the first person in my family to go to high school. I'll probably even be the first girl in South Boston to go to college.

Sean O'Halloran is going to Harvard and plans to study law at Georgetown after he graduates. That's good, but he wasn't the first boy in South Boston to go college.

Fiona and Adelaide will go to a fancy finishing school in Philadelphia. Their grades certainly couldn't get them into Girls

High, but their fathers' money opens doors for them and always will. They could go on to college but won't. They'll learn drawing and sewing so they can marry rich men, then manage a staff of maids just like their mothers do.

I used to wish my da worked at one of the big law firms in town instead of on his own, defending our poor Irish neighbors. He doesn't make much money, but I'm pretty proud of him. He helps people who can't afford the big firms, and he always wins his cases. His reputation is so good that last year a patent law firm on Liberty Square tried to hire him. Patent lawyers make lots of money. There are so many new inventions now, and they're all rushing to get patents before someone else copies their idea.

A tailor named Ebenezer Butterick invented tissue paper patterns and now most every house in Boston has one right next to the sewing machine. He's making a fortune. And two years ago, an engineer named Christopher Sholes invented a machine that actually types words on paper. Our world is changing fast.

When Da refused the job with the firm on Liberty Square, I asked him why; and he said such work would bore him. I was mad then, but now I'm glad now. I know that with an education, I'll be able to make my own way, too.

In truth, I'm pretty proud of what my parents do. Perhaps when I'm a teacher, I'll teach poor children. Though I do hope I'll make enough money to afford some pretty clothes.

I'd probably make more working at a fancy boarding school somewhere, but I don't think my parents would approve. In truth, I'm not sure I'd approve either. My da always says you must do something that lets you respect yourself. Teaching thick-as-stumps rich girls like Fiona would never let me do that.

As examination day nears, I study every minute I'm home. My parents take care of my usual chores. My father washes the dishes so I won't have to, and even tiptoes around the kitchen so as not to disturb my homework. And he never smokes.

Some parents just want to see their daughters married or bringing in money to the house. Not mine. Yes, I'm lucky, and I thank God every day I was born to Daniel and Mary Kelly.

CHAPTER THIRTEEN

"Nellie, the postman just brought me a note from Sister Sarah. She wants a meeting with me." It's the week before examinations and my mother looks suspicious. "Do you know what this is about?" She cocks her left eyebrow and grins. "You didn't whack anyone else, did you?"

I shake my head. "No idea, Mother. And no, everybody's nose is intact."

She laughs and hugs me. "Perhaps she wants to give me some good news, like you've been selected to speak at commencement?"

"I don't think so. Sister hasn't said anything about a speech to me."

"Well, the note says you're to be with me. The meeting's for this afternoon."

I'm still puzzled when I go into the classroom, Fiona is circled by the other girls, all buzzing like insects. Until they see me and quiet down. Sister Sarah gestures me out into the hall.

"Nellie, did your mother tell you about our meeting this afternoon?"

"Yes, Sister, we'll be here."

Sister doesn't look happy; not like she's going to ask me to make a speech or anything.

After school, Mother meets me at the door to my classroom. She's washed her hair and dressed in her Sunday outfit, a green jacket and skirt that complements her red hair and small waist.

"You look pretty, Mother," I say, meaning it.

"Thank you, love. I figured I'd dress for the occasion. Who knows what Sister has to say."

Remembering the nun's hushed manner earlier today, I begin to worry a little. She surely didn't seem like someone with cheery news to tell us, but maybe my imagination is getting the best of me. That happens to me sometimes. When we get to Sister's office, she has brought in extra chairs. And there sitting on two of them are Fiona and her mother. *What on earth are they doing here?* A third chair is occupied by none other than Orville Mattison, Fiona's sort-of boyfriend. *What an odd trio they make, sitting there stone faced and stiff as boards. Truly, an ungodly trio.*

"Hello, Agnes." Mother's voice is cordial.

Mrs. Doggett tips her head slightly and shifts uncomfortably in her seat.

I sit down. The chair is hard and stiff-backed. I move around in it, trying to settle my bony backside into a comfortable place. I soon realize that's impossible, so I sit up straight as a rod and cross my ankles. Fiona is slumped into the tufted chair across from sister's desk. Oliver looks nervous as a squirming worm on the end of a hook.

Sister speaks. She seems as uncomfortable as I feel. "I've called you all here today to discuss a matter of grave importance. It involves a serious breach of St. Augustine policy." She leans forward and stares at my mother. "Mary, on Monday, Fiona told me something very disturbing."

I swivel my head toward Fiona. She stares straight ahead, as if she's been put into some kind of trance. When I catch her mother's eye, Mrs. Doggett looks away.

"Disturbing?" my mother asks.

"It involves a matter of morality," Sister answers.

I'm so shocked I blurt out, "Whose morality?"

"Yours, Nellie." Sister looks as if she's ready to cry.

Matters of morality involve breaking the sixth and ninth commandments. Breaking those commandments will spoil a girl's reputation faster than a runaway horse. Every girl in South Boston knows that from the time they're born.

"But I've done nothing immoral, Sister."

Sister removes her glasses and rubs her hand over her eyes as if she has a headache. When she looks up, her eyes are sad and tired.

My mother's hand covers mine. Turning to her, I see she looks frightened. I feel sick to my stomach to see her looking that way when I don't even know why. Then, she asks Fiona, "Fiona, what did you tell Sister about Nellie?"

"What everybody in eighth grade already knows," she stammers.

"Fiona, I asked what you said. Please honor me with a response."

Fiona inhales deeply. "That Nellie let Orville touch her."

"Is that true, Orville?" Mother asks, pinching her lips together.

He nods; his face red as a stormy sunset.

I jerk toward him and say, "Orville, that's a lie."

He squirms in his seat. Behind his back, I see him cross his fingers. "No, it's not. No, it's not. Remember that time in the snow?"

I can't believe my ears. I kneed him until he nearly cried when he touched my chest that time. I'm in the air before I know what I'm doing, going for his eyes. "Take it back, liar. Take it back."

Hands grab me around the waist and slam me back down onto the chair. Twisting around, I see the hands belong to my mother. "We'll not handle this with violence, Nellie." She turns toward Sister. "Where does Fiona say Orville touched Nellie?"

Sister's face blazes red above the wimple. "Uhhh, well, from what I understand it was . . ." She lowers her eyes and points to the place under her crucifix.

"On the breast?" Mother asks.

Sister closes her eyes once in acknowledgement.

"I think it's a disgrace that a student at St. Augustine's would behave in such a manner," Mrs. Doggett remarks.

My mother stands, glaring down at Mrs. Doggett. "Disgrace, Agnes? You dare speak of disgrace?"

Sister begins to sputter, some words formed, others simply utterances. "Oh, dear Lord, I didn't know what to do about this." She grabs her crucifix in her right hand. "So, I had to speak to Monsignor. If I hadn't told him, he would have shipped me back to Ireland. I know he would have."

"You spoke to Monsignor about this?" I whisper.

"Yes, Nellie. I had no choice."

"And what did Monsignor say?" my mother asks, leaning in closer.

Sister looks so sad I nearly pity her until she states, "That Nellie must be expelled from St. Augustine's. Immediately."

CHAPTER FOURTEEN

That evening, when Mother tells Da about the meeting, I can hear him yelling as I lie in my bedroom. My pillow is soddened from tears. Why would Orville say such a thing? Fiona likes Orville. Sometimes, she says she loves him. I have never been near the boy. Except for that time he tried something in the snow, and I hurt him for that.

Without a graduation certificate from St. Augustine's, I can forget about Girls High. That means my dream of going to Wellesley will never come true. My future is over, shattered by a vicious lie, and there's not one thing I can do about it. I'll have to become a maid and wait on people like Fiona for the rest of my life, or maybe work in the laundry until my hands are raw and rough from soap and scrubbing.

One thing is certain—I won't go back inside St. Augustine's church. If my church can abandon me over a filthy lie, I want no more to do with that church.

But there's one thing I can do and will. I will confront Miss Fiona Doggett.

I sneak out of the house the next morning and hide behind the big maple tree across from school, the school I can no longer attend. When I see the carriage drop Fiona off at the corner, I run and, before she can escape, grab her by the wrist and pull her behind a fence. I back her up against a tree. She squirms and starts to yell, but I hold her firm.

"Let me go, Nellie. You're crazy."

"Not crazy enough to make up lies about somebody. Why did you do that?"

"Orville says it's true."

"You know it's not. You were there that day when I kneed him. You heard him squeal. You know he's lying." I squeeze her upper arm. I hope I leave a bruise. I twist harder.

"Owwww."

"Tell me the truth." I keep twisting.

She looks around, her face contorted in pain. Finally, seeing no one to help her, she leans in toward me. "You're the one who knows everything, Miss Smarty Pants." Her face blazes with anger. "You're the one wanting to go to college, aren't you? Well, you don't deserve it."

"Why?" I am so honestly confounded I can scarcely speak.

"Because you're the teacher's pet, and Father Ruzzo's pet, and all the girls like you best."

"No, they don't."

"Sure they do, and Orville said you're beautiful. He said you're the prettiest girl in the school and will probably be the prettiest girl at Girls High. So, I smacked him."

I shake my head, trying to clear my brain. *Teachers pet? All the girls like me? Me pretty? No.*

"After I smacked him, he wanted to make up, tried to kiss me, tried to touch me on top, and I smacked him again."

"But why did he lie?"

She tries to pull away again. "None of your business."

"What do you mean none of my business? He's lying. Why?"

She puts her face right up into mine. Her grin is the nastiest thing I've ever seen. "Because I said if he told Sister you let him touch your bosoms, I'd really let him touch mine."

CHAPTER FIFTEEN

Walking home from St. Augustine's, I feel chilled to the bone even though spring is bursting its blossoms and the sun has melted all the snow into grey rivulets of water, which run into the cobblestones. I walk into my house and find my mother.

"Where were you?" she asks.

"Talking to Fiona."

"Oh?" She sits down at the table, waiting.

I sit down opposite her. "Mother, I swear that everything I'm about to tell you is true. Fiona admitted she was lying; that she made it all up; that she's jealous of me. She actually bribed Orville to lie in return for letting him feel *her* chest."

She shakes her head in disbelief and pins her curls up into a messy topknot. "Well, Nellie, that seems too farfetched to be made up. Fiona admitted that?"

I nod ten times. I know it was ten. I counted. Ten times is definite! Then, I cross my heart.

"All right then, we'll have to have another chat with Sister Sarah."

At 3:30, we walk to my father's office. He is at his desk studying a brief in his shirt sleeves. She tells him the whole story. "Daniel, come with us. We're going to fight the Catholic Church."

"Bring 'em on!" he shouts, putting on his frockcoat.

Sister Sarah is not in the classroom but bustles into it, stopping abruptly when she sees us. Her face is shocked, but she sits at her desk and gestures at us to sit down. The circles under her eyes look as though she hasn't slept for days.

The three of us sit at the little desks in the front. My da wriggles around until he can stretch his long legs out into the aisle. My mother puts her elbows on the desk top and crosses her arms.

When I look around the room, there's a memory in every corner. I think back eight years to when I started first grade here and sat up front. Through the years, I began to realize I was smart. That's when I started planning for my future. Now, because of one girl's lies, that future is doomed, unless we can make Sister understand enough to believe us and do something about it.

My mother tells Sister everything Fiona said, and the old nun surprises me half to death. She starts to cry. My mother jumps to her feet and runs around her desk, to rub Sister's shoulder. "Now, now, Sister. Don't cry. Just make things right."

"But I can't do that, Mary," the nun sobs, her double chin trembling on her wimple. "Fiona's father went to the Bishop. Monsignor is furious."

My father, always so calm and analytical, shocks me. He smacks his palm on the desk, stands up, and yells. "I don't care how mad that old fart is. He's got to be told the truth."

"Daniel, watch your mouth," Mother admonishes; her voice a warning.

Sister wails loudly and puts her forehead on the desk. "Mr. Kelly," she mumbles, her voice scarcely comprehensible through the sobs, "We told Monsignor we think the story is fabricated; that Nellie isn't that kind of girl. I told him and so did Father Ruzzo, but he won't budge."

My da seems unable to form words. He, who usually has an answer for every problem, sputters in frustration. That scares me more than anything. If my father can't figure out what to do, who can? "Tell him again, Sister. If Monsignor won't listen, I'll go to the Bishop."

Sister lifts her head from the desk. Her eyes are bloodshot and threaten to spill over again. She sighs deeply. "Father already tried that, Mr. Kelly. He traveled to Springfield and told Bishop O'Reilly he absolutely had to see him on a matter of great urgency. The Bishop kept him waiting for more than six hours."

"And?" Mother prods.

"And when Father Ruzzo told him he believed a great injustice had been done to Nellie, the Bishop said, 'It's out of my control.'"

"Why?" my father shouts.

The nun hesitates, swallows, then takes a drink of water from the glass on her desk. "I don't want to believe this, Mr. Kelly, but Father Ruzzo thinks it's because Mr. Doggett was a major contributor in setting up the Diocese in Springfield earlier this year. Financial contributor, I mean."

My father sits down. It nearly kills me to see him look so defeated. He begins to talk to himself, as if we weren't in the room. "I'll sue the Diocese; that's what I'll do. I'll eat the head off that feckin' maggot O'Reilly. That's what I'll do."

"You'll sue the Catholic Church, Daniel?" My mother's voice is tired and soft.

"Sure as shit I will, Mary. Just watch me."

When he says that, I know I must stop him. How I don't know, but my father must not sue the Diocese. It would destroy his law practice, everything he's worked so hard to build. Whatever it takes, I'll do it.

* * *

The next day, I go to the laundry and apply for work. The owner tells me he has no tubs available. Yesterday, Adelaide promised she'll keep her ears open for anyone looking for a new maid on Beacon Hill. Just hearing her say that makes my stomach sick.

My parents talk in the kitchen when they think I'm asleep. I sneak and listen. Mother pleads there has to be another way. His way won't work. But my da is as stubborn as she is, and their argument grows heated.

What can I do? Expelled. When I think about it, I shake my head to scare the thought away, but it doesn't work. Sleep won't come because I'm sick in my soul. All my plans, all my parents' scrimping and saving for my future, and it's all dashed by a lie. I stare into the dark, but no solution comes to me. My future is ruined. I mustn't allow my father's career to be ruined as well.

He used to joke. "Money talks in the Church, and there's no sense pretending differently. It screams its power all the way across the Atlantic to Rome."

Fiona's father is one of the richest men in Boston.

My mother told Uncle Kam and Imani what happened, and he's trying to reverse the Bishop's decision. But I have no faith Bishop O'Reilly will listen . . . to a black man.

I must see Neo. If ever I needed my friend, it's now.

CHAPTER SIXTEEN

On Saturday morning, there's a note on the kitchen table from my mother. A woman is in labor at the Haven and I'm to stay in the house until she gets home. My father is at his office preparing the brief we interrupted yesterday.

That's perfect. I'm free, and Neo won't be in school. I'll scour all his usual haunts until I find him.

I start at the library. He's often there on Saturday. It's a long walk, and a disappointing one. His wagon isn't outside. I head for the docks. Sometimes, he goes down there with friends to see the ships unload cargo. He likes to smell all the exotic spices that come in from India and Indonesia and some other places I've never even heard of.

I walk the length of the dock looking for him. Sailors scramble up and down gangplanks carrying bags on their backs. At one large vessel, I look up, shielding my eyes from the sun, and see a young boy swinging from the rigging on a mainsail. My heart soars at the sight. How I'd love to do that. But flying high cannot happen for me now. The childish part of my life is finished. I curse Fiona under my breath.

I watch the boy for nearly half an hour until, without warning, an arm snakes round my waist and pulls me close. The arm belongs to a massive sailor, surrounded by laughing chums. A black cigar hangs soggy in his mouth.

"Well, look at this pretty young thing." The cigar stinks. I push him away and turn to leave.

His buddies mock him. "Poor Angus. The maggot can't even stand up against a girl."

He looks around at them, juts out his chin, and advances after me. "Oh, a tough one, she is; strong as a lad."

I swivel and point my umbrella toward his eyes. "Keep your distance, Angus. My da is Daniel Kelly, and if he finds out you put your big hams on me, you'll be in the county jail before you can finish that cigar."

At first, I didn't know whether it's the umbrella or if he recognized my father's name, but he backs away, puts up his hands, and laughs to his chums a bit nervously. "Whoa, Miss Kelly. Don't be telling your father nothing. I meant you no harm, just joshing around, you know?"

"Next time, think twice before you *josh* with a strange girl." I put my umbrella on my shoulder like a Springfield rifle, turn my back, and walk away. That felt good, strong and powerful.

My next stop is at the magic shop near the docks that opened earlier this year. Neo's wagon sits out front. I should have known that's where he'd be. Hurrying inside, I spy him. He's surrounded by a crowd of people, clerks and customers alike. He stands on a crate, his back to me.

When he angles to the side, I see that he's holding up a piece of plain white paper. He begins folding and refolding it until it's down to the size of a Penny Red postage stamp. Then he waves and circles it high in the air, so that everyone can inspect it.

He spots me and winks.

He waves a wand over the tiny piece of white paper and begins to unfold it, moving faster and faster with each movement. I stare at his speeding hands. Without warning, the paper begins to change color to a light, then darker green. I blink my eyes, trying to clear the illusion. *That's impossible. The paper was white. How can it turn greener and greener before my eyes?*

When it's completely unfolded, he waves it triumphantly in the air, transformed into a ten-dollar bill.

"How did you do that?" a boy about ten years old asks; his eyes wide and excited.

"It's called magic, my boy," Neo answers, laughing. "Pure magic."

CHAPTER SEVENTEEN

"How *did* you do that, Neo?" I ask when we're in his wagon.

"Can't tell you, Nellie. A magician never shares his secrets." He brings the whip down lightly on the horse's back and puts on a big top hat.

"Where'd you get that hat?"

"Swiped it from my father's closet," he answers. "He has so many of these, he'll never miss one. How do you like it?" He taps the brim.

"Nice, Neo. Makes you look quite grown up."

He grins, smug in his newfound maturity. "How'd you know where I'd be?"

I laugh. "Magic, Neo. Pure magic."

He laughs back. "*Touché.*"

Neo has studied French, Spanish, and German and is proficient in all of them. It's a bit showy when he throws in a foreign word, but it's impressive, too.

"Why were you looking for me?"

I tell him of Fiona's treachery, my parents' reactions, and my disgust with the Catholic Bishop who probably sold me out for a donation from Mr. Doggett. I actually speak the words that have plagued me since this whole mess began. "Sometimes, I really wonder if I'm meant to be a Catholic."

He turns to me, incredulous. "Really, Nellie?"

I straighten my back. "And truly."

"Yes, well, sometimes I wonder if I'm really meant to be any religion," Neo answers. "But for now, we're stuck with one of them. The question is, what do you intend to do about it? Being expelled, I mean."

Without warning, I burst into tears. I've tried so hard not to cry because when the tears start, I fear they'll never stop.

Neo leans away, startled; stares at me for just a moment, then orders, "Stop that!"

I cringe at the harsh authority of his voice. He's never spoken to me like that.

One thing about tears, though, once you start them, it's really hard to stop. At least it is for me. I try, but the tears keep rolling down my face. "Uh, uh, uh," I mumble, helplessly.

"I mean it, Nellie. Stop it. It makes you look weak."

"I *am* weak."

"No, you're not. You're the toughest girl I know."

Now there's a surprise. I've never thought of myself as particularly strong, let alone tough. But his words, or his tone, or something about him startles me so much that I snivel once more, wipe my nose, and stop crying.

"That's better. Now, let's figure this out. What's the worst thing about getting expelled?"

"That I'm an embarrassment to my parents."

"They'll get over it."

Neo's right, of course. Eventually, they will get over it. I take a deep breath. "That I won't be able to go to Girls' High. That I'll never get into Wellesley now. That my life is ruined." I nearly start up with the tears again, but he interrupts.

"You're being dramatic! Stop it!"

I gasp. "No, I'm not."

"Yes, you are. Your life is not ruined. There are ways you can get into Wellesley when the time comes. We just need to figure them out. Think."

He pulls the carriage to the curb and we get out at the Boston Common. He points at a bench. I sit down and he takes the other end. I know he doesn't want anyone to think he's too close to me or there'll be trouble. Even with three feet between us, passersby give us the evil eye. I know what they're thinking and, though I hate that I can't be close to my best friend, that's how it is.

"All right," Neo begins, "you will get into Wellesley. With your brains and your parents' reputations, they'll welcome you. But you do have to get a high school certificate first."

"Yes."

"So, let's go see Father Ruzzo."

I slump. "That avenue is closed."

"We have to start somewhere. Maybe we can reopen it."

CHAPTER EIGHTEEN

We go to the church, Neo and me in one pew and Father Ruzzo in front of us. He swivels around to face us. "First, let me say I am appalled at the Bishop's and Monsignor's actions, Nellie. Nobody really believes Fiona's accusations."

"So, what can you do about it?" Neo asks, a bit boldly, I think.

Father Ruzzo shakes his mostly bald head. "Nothing, I'm afraid. I don't have that kind of power." He looks miserable, so miserable I wish I could reach out and touch his face and tell him it's all right.

But Neo's body stiffens beside mine. "Very well." He stands and looks down at me, eyes filled with anger, turns, and, without a word of goodbye, strides up the aisle to the door. His footsteps sound definite, determined. The door squeaks open, letting in a moment of sunlight, then shuts with a muffled slam. It's very quiet. Father Ruzzo looks up at the crucifix hanging over the altar, then down to his clenched hands.

I fluster for a moment, "I'm sorry, Father. I didn't mean to put you in this position."

He doesn't answer, just lowers his head and shakes it side to side. "It's wrong, Nellie. I'm so very sorry. I promise I'll keep trying to make this right. I'll never give up. You have my word."

"Thank you, Father. Goodbye then." He's already said he's powerless. What can he do that he hasn't already tried? I walk out of my church.

Neo waits in the carriage. He gestures for me to climb in and pulls it away from the curb. We ride in silence. The nerves in my neck tighten painfully. His jaw is clamped and I wonder what he's thinking? Finally, he reins in the horse when we reach a deserted section of South Boston. "You were right. Our hands are tied and the church won't help you." He turns to face me, his eyes sparkling. "But this might actually be a blessing in disguise."

A blessing? Is he crazy?

"So, let's consider what opportunity this mess opens up to us."

"Opportunity?" I ask, genuinely confused.

He tips the top hat, leans back, and smiles. "The opportunity for us to have *our* adventure; to join the circus."

After a moment, it all comes back to me; his talk at Thanksgiving. Much as it appealed to me as a lark, I had not taken his words seriously. Nor could I take them seriously now. "I can't do that."

"Then what will you do? Get a job as a laundress or maid? Or perhaps someone will take pity on you and bring you in as governess? You can teach a couple of spoiled brats, I suppose. Of course, it won't be like teaching in a real school, but you can make do."

At his sarcastic tone, my Irish temper flares. "What do you mean, 'make do?' We're talking about my life. For as long as I can remember, I've wanted to be a real teacher, in a real school. This is so unfair."

I start to blubber. He ignores me. "Why can't you at least understand how hard this is for me? Why can't you be my friend?"

He starts loud and gets louder. "I am your friend but think. This is our chance for an adventure. For us to prove to our parents we're as tough and grown up as they were at our ages. Aren't you tired of hearing stories about how bad they had it as young people? Once I go back to prep school and you're at Girls High, we'll never get this chance again."

"How can I go to Girls High without a certificate from St. Augustine's?"

He rubs his forehead and tilts back the top hat, then adjusts it back in place; a sign he has reached some conclusion. But what is it?

He swivels to face me. "I guarantee you, even as we're sitting here, my father is talking to your mother and dad about making that happen. He can do anything. You know that."

Neo's right. Uncle Kam *can* do anything. Look how he beat the banks and the Brahmins to help my mother open Kathleen's Haven. And he has even more money now than he did back then, maybe even more money than the Doggett's.

I feel a tiny ray of hope. At first, it's just a warming around my heart, but soon it passes up to my head and all the way down to my toes. "Maybe you're right. If I'm gone for a while, my father will be distracted from suing the church, which would save his law practice." I work this all through my brain for a while, and when I'm done, I turn to Neo. "Maybe we *should* have our adventure this summer?" My heart begins to race.

"Take the question mark off that sentence, Nellie. We will have it. We leave in two weeks."

In spite of all the questions, all the doubts, all the fears that cloud my brain, my heart pounds hard. I feel it in my throat. Maybe if I'm out of Boston, this whole mess with Fiona will simmer down, maybe even get resolved. Spend some summer time with a circus? I'm a strong girl. If I can't be a performer, I can rig trapezes and tight ropes. I love being high in the air. I'm not scared of that or much else . . . except hurting my parents and worrying them senseless when they find me missing. But I'll leave a note, assure them I'll be all right; that I'm with Neo and we'll look out for each other. Just like she and Uncle Kam did all those years ago. I'll leave a very good note. Maybe I'll call her mam in the note. She'll like that. I'll make sure they know we'll be back before fall, before school starts again. It'll be the best note I can write. I'll start composing it tonight.

Neo's smart. I'm smart, too. He's sixteen, about the same age Uncle Kam was when he met my mother. And I'm almost fourteen, my mother's age when she got on the ship out of Ireland. If they could have a great adventure, so can we. A circus!

CHAPTER NINETEEN

During the next two weeks, I change my mind a thousand times. *This is crazy. No it's not. Are Neo and I insane? No, it's our one chance to prove our independence. The girls at St. Augustine will call me a tramp, but they'll be really jealous. Especially Fiona! Ha! Oh, but my mother will die from worry.*

No, my note is really, really reassuring. In it, I tell her I'll be with Neo who will protect me just like Uncle Kam protected her on the ship.

But, what about my da? She'll handle him. She always does. It'll be good for them to have some time alone. And it won't be that long.

On July 7, 1870, well before dawn, I creep barefoot toward the front door, scared but excited. My father's snores roll at me from their room and my mother's light sleep breathing follows each sound he makes. A board creaks under my foot; her breathing stops. I freeze in the middle of the living room and hold my breath. Soon, her gentle exhalations resume as I hear her roll to her side. The bed squeaks and she sighs softly.

Good. She's still asleep.

I exhale slowly and walk toward the door, making my steps long and my landings soft. I had unlocked the door earlier, anticipating this moment. My hand goes to the brass knob and slowly, so slowly, I begin to turn it. *Good, not a sound.* I oiled it yesterday. That was Neo's idea.

I begin to push the door forward. The hinges don't squeak. I oiled them, too. When it's all the way open, I step gingerly out to the front porch, careful to ease out my satchel so it doesn't touch anything. I walk to the steps and put the satchel down, then creep back and slowly pull the door shut. The only sound is the startled bark of a dog, angry at being awakened before the sun is up.

I'm out. And my mother and father stayed asleep.

As promised, Neo's carriage is parked in front of the Donahue's house in the next block. I grab my satchel and run silently down the cobblestones. As I climb up beside him, he puts his forefinger to his lips. I pull on my boots.

We ride away, at first very slowly, then several blocks from my house, faster. He whispers, "Any problems?"

"Not a one. Our plan went like clockwork."

"Did you leave them the note?"

"Of course. I told them I was with you and not to worry; that we'd be back before summer's end; that we wanted one adventure before you had to buckle down at school and I found work. I promised my mother I'd be very careful and not talk to strangers or anything."

He tips a pretend hat in acknowledgement. He isn't wearing the top hat. It might attract attention.

It is still dark when we reach the train station. The train's there; its engine belching out smoke.

"Stay here and be quiet," Kam tells me. "I'll buy two tickets."

I do, and in a few minutes, he climbs back up and we pull away.

"We'll park the carriage at Mendel's. No one'll be there yet."

He whips the horse lightly and we head toward the apothecary. Old Mr. Mendel passed away two years ago. The business is now run by his son, Abel, with Uncle Kam's help. Mother told me that Uncle Kam is the real owner of the apothecary now and pays Mr. Mendel's son an exorbitant salary to run the store.

Neo tethers the horse, leaves a pail of water and a block of hay beside him, and gives him a carrot. He'll be fine until Abel opens the store.

Now we run, satchels in tow. It feels good, after all the quiet and stealth, to just run full-out down the dark streets back to the train station. Boston is so beautiful at night, illuminated only by the faint glow of gas lamps and stars. I imagine I am a phantom gliding swiftly across the cobblestones while all the rest of the world is asleep.

The trees in front of the brownstones are in full bloom. A weeping willow drapes her branches gracefully and brushes my face as if to say, "God speed, Nellie. Come back."

Neo is faster than I am, but not by much. As we run, he whispers, "Nellie, you sit in the front car of the train. I'll go to the back. It will cast suspicion if we're seen together. Our parents will have the police after us as soon as they see our notes."

He holds out his hand for me—two tickets and a dollar bill. I grip them tightly. One ticket is for the train and the other for the steamboat that will take us from Fall River to New York City.

Breathless, we stop near the train station.

"You go first." He adjusts his clothing and wipes his brow. "When we get to Fall River, take the dollar and get some lunch. Meet me at six this evening at the pier. Look for *The Bristol* steamboat. You can't miss it."

I climb up the iron steps of the train and take a seat in the first car after the locomotive. It's not crowded; no one looks up to see me. Most of the people are sleeping.

Now that I am situated, I put the tickets and money in my pull-string purse. Searching through my satchel, I take out the book my mother gave me yesterday, *Twenty Thousand Leagues Under the Sea*. It's quite an adventurous tale that everybody who's anybody in Boston is talking about it. Maybe someday I'll write a book about the adventures I have this summer.

Though I'm still scared about my parents and what they'll do when they find my note, my excitement builds. Neo is right. We do have the right to an adventure of our own; one that'll make our parents realize we're as grown up as they were on that awful coffin ship.

It's our turn.

CHAPTER TWENTY

Lulled by the soothing sound of train wheels on tracks, I'm in a dead sleep, the book open on my lap, when the conductor yells, "Fall River, Massachusetts, next stop."

Grabbing my purse off the seat beside me, I pull the drawstrings and yank out the gold pocket watch Neo lent me for our journey. He has two—one Swiss, one English. Mine is the English one.

When I click it open, I see that it's nearly three o'clock. No wonder I'm hungry. I'll have time to get food in my belly and meet Neo at the pier at six. I've never been to Fall River. My da says it's even more industrial than Boston.

Inside the train station, I see that the big grandfather clock has exactly the same time registered as my pocket watch. *Good.*

As I turn to walk out onto the street, I see Neo standing at another exit. After we make eye contact, he turns away and leaves.

Once outside, I'm stunned at the crowds of people who propel me along the sidewalk. It's so different than Boston, where you often encounter smiling ladies and gentlemen dressed in the highest fashion of the season. These people walk eyes down, the men's heads covered by workmen's caps and the women with scarves tied over their hair. Their clothes look as if they haven't seen a washing in months, and their faces are not much cleaner. Grime covers everything. Even the stones under my feet feel sticky with dirt. Smoke stacks belch tall plumes of gray and white smoke. Signs read Beattie Granite Quarry and Sagamore Mills.

It's terribly warm and so humid the clothes stick to my skin. A few red, white, and blue streamers remain on lamp posts and hang as limp reminders of the recent holiday. The doors to the factories stand open. Curious, I stick my head inside one of them. Women pull what looks like grey cotton from huge bales on the floor, wrapping its strands around spindles. Men crank the spindles until they spin in circles round and round. The air is thick with dingy fiber flying from the whirling spindles. Some of the workers have handkerchiefs covering their noses and mouths. Others cough and spit all over the floor. Within seconds, I can't breathe and return to the street.

I gulp in air, though in truth, even the air outside is dense with dust and fiber. The red and white July 4th streamers are grimy and grey.

How can people live like this?

On a corner, a sign points to the pier. *Maybe it'll be cleaner down by the water.* I follow the sign and walk three blocks.

The ships at this harbor are larger than the ones in Boston. Though I don't recognize the flags on them, the looks of their crews tell me they come from India, China, even Egypt. Dock hands carry bulging bales down the gangplanks and pile them into wagons. I smell tea and exotic spices coming from the bales. On one bale, an ivory tusk sticks through the burlap.

The buildings near the water are different. In the main part of the city, the factories were grey granite. On the waterfront, red brick structures line the streets. Even through the stench of dead fish, I welcome the smells of salt air after the dense, filthy air up in the town.

My stomach rumbles, and I stop in my tracks looking around for a grocery sign. Suddenly, a delicious smell drifts toward me and I follow it to a man standing outside a tavern. His hair is white and his blotchy face is a mass of wrinkles. His fisherman's cap is pulled down to shield his eyes from the sun.

"Fish and chips," he yells out. "Fresh from the fryer." He holds up a sack. The grease is already seeping through the paper. His accent is English, but crude, not at all like the English gentry on Beacon Hill back home.

When he spots me, he shouts, "Fish and chips for the pretty girl. Come on over here, Ducks. Twenty cents'll buy enough to fill up two of your skinny frames."

My mother's kitchen is a meat and potatoes place. She isn't partial to fish because she hates its bones, so we seldom have it at home. I figure for my first real adventure, I need to have a new kind of meal. I walk up to the man and hand him my dollar.

"No change, girlie?"

I shake my head. "This is all I have."

He grumbles some, then digs into his pockets until he plops eighty cents into my extended palm. "Here." He hands me the greasy sack and a small paper cone of brown-colored liquid. "This is malt vinegar. It goes on the fish."

"Have you anything to drink?"

He pulls a bottle from under his cart. "You're in luck, girlie. This just came in from England today. It's called Schweppe's ginger ale. It's been sitting on ice all afternoon inside the tavern."

More adventure. "I'll take one. How much?"

"Ah, a bit pricey, but it's worth it, girlie. Forty cents."

I think he's picked me out as the unworldly girl I am. That seems a huge price, but nothing is too dear for the first meal of my adventure. I lift my chin, "I'll take it." I hand over the forty cents.

He hands me a glass filled to the brim with a yellowish colored liquid. Bubbles float from the bottom to the top. When I lean down to smell it, it tickles my nose, and I giggle. The man gives me some brown paper. "You'll need this to wipe off your face and hands after that fish, dearie."

I walk to a bench near the docks, sit down, and open the bag. I put the glass of ginger ale beside me and balance the vinegar-filled cone between my knees. Then, I pull out a piece of fish. It's very crisp and greasy and smells good. Wondering if I'll like it, I take a bite. Not one bone.

Dipping the fish, I chew and crunch the fish and love the vinegary flavor. The chips are crispy potatoes cut in wedges and cooked brown outside and soft white inside. I've never tasted better potatoes in my life, though my mother would tan my hide if she heard me say that. I gulp the ginger ale and a rush of fizz up my nose makes my eyes water. It's good.

When I've finished, I throw out the trash and take the glass back to the fish-and-chips man. He looks startled. "That was fast! Pretty *and* hungry, huh? Did you like it?"

"Best thing I've ever tasted."

Chapter Twenty-One

At six o'clock, I walk into the ferry station. Right in front of me is a big wall calendar with a pretty girl in a red, white, and blue bonnet smiling. It's July 6, 1870. I can't believe I left Boston only this morning.

Neo sits on a bench in the back of the big room. We lock eyes. I pull open the strings of my purse and remove the steamboat ticket from it, holding it up so Neo can see. Then, tugging the strings again, I go out to the pier and look for the *Bristol*.

The ship is much bigger than I expected, and the smoke stacks are already building up heads of steam for the journey to New York City. Two decks of white-painted wood tower above the main deck. It looks like a wedding cake. The big paddle wheel at its side has a sign *BRISTOL* running above it. Sailors carry bales marked tobacco and cotton up the gangplank while passengers scurry past them. Families with children tote luggage and mingle with men in waistcoats carrying leather briefcases.

When I hand the porter my ticket, he says, "You're in a bunk adjacent to the Grand Salon, Miss. You're lucky; it's a lower bunk."

That's not luck. That's Neo's planning.

"The lavatory is down the hall from your bunk," the porter continues. "People will probably be queued up for it right now. The dining room's on the second deck. Dinner service will begin as soon as we sail."

As I make my way toward the Grand Salon, every few steps is a canary in an ornate metal cage. Their singing makes for a beautiful chorus. I stop and stare into one of the cages.

A woman behind me says, "There are 250 canaries on this ship, girl. Mr. James Fisk, the owner, has named each one of them. See, there's a name on that plaque at the front." The name *Mary* is inscribed on the bronze. For a moment, my eyes blur, thinking how worried my mother probably is at this very moment. But then, I remind myself I'm entitled to this adventure. I'll be perfectly safe with Neo.

In search of my bunk, I saunter through The Grand Salon. It surpasses my wildest dreams of luxury. Ceiling-to-floor fluted pillars and walls brocaded with gold enclose decorative niches every few feet. Each niche has a marble statue of some Greek god. Crystal chandeliers hang from ceilings gleaming with gilt. Purple velvet settees line the long salon, and shiny black floors are covered with oriental rugs thicker than the ones in Neo's home. I wonder how much each of those carpets cost; probably more than our little house in Boston.

Leaving the Salon, I find my bunk and toss in my satchel. All I packed, along with my book, is an extra pair of pantalettes and one clean blouse.

"On deck, everyone!" a sailor yells.

Amid a flurry of passengers, I hurry to the main deck and position myself at the rail. Impeccably uniformed sailors stand at attention as a distinguished gentleman with white hair climbs up onto a platform. He wears a lavish navy-blue uniform with gold buttons and braid across the shoulders.

"That's the Admiral," a woman next to me whispers.

"Ladies and gentlemen, I am James Fisk, owner of *Bristol*. I hope you find her to your liking and that your trip to New York is a pleasant one. Bon Voyage to all." He picks up a megaphone and yells into it. "Set sail!" With that, he jumps nimbly off the platform as the ship, with a small lurch, pulls out into the bay, heading South.

We're on our way. I've never been on a real ship before, and for a moment, my legs feel wavy and weak. But soon, I am striding the deck like a seasoned traveler.

The adventure begins.

The dining room is on the main deck. Passengers file into it and sit at white linen-covered tables set with china plates and ornate silverware. The carpet in this room is lush and cushiony. I'd love to take off my shoes, but that would be scandalous.

More chandeliers hang from the gilt-covered ceiling, and canaries chirp and sing throughout the room. I remember the forty cents still in my purse. *I'll grab a sweet here later.*

Back downstairs, a line stands outside the lavatory. I want to see what's in there, so I take my place at the back of the line behind a stout, elderly lady who smiles at me.

At home, we still use chamber pots and the outhouse, but I've read of fine homes that actually have water closets inside. When I get to the front of the line and open the door, a porcelain toilet, a throne of sorts with a chain hanging from its side, sits there. I sit down, make a small tinkle, and wipe with the papers so I can pull that chain. When I do, the flushing noise is loud, then everything swirls and disappears.

I adjust my clothes and go to a small sink on the back wall. I turn a spigot and water rushes out of the nozzle. *What a wonder!*

Feeling a bit hungry, I dry my hands and leave the lavatory to walk back up the stairs and into the dining room. I am startled by a loud argument at the opposite end of the room. Passengers shift uncomfortably in their chairs. Standing on tip toe, I spot Neo standing before a man wearing a tuxedo. I guess the man's a waiter. Neo's nostrils are flaring as he gestures with both hands toward the man, then throws up his hands and storms out of the dining room. When he sees me, he averts his eyes, but not before I see his anger.

"What happened?" I ask the waiter.

"We had a complaint about that young man being seated here," he answers, shaking his head. "Some colored folks think they can mingle wherever they want since the slaves got freed. Well, not here they can't. We have standards. Would you like a seat, Miss?"

Although I had planned on spending my last forty cents on a treat and glass of milk, I shake my head and leave. If Neo can't be served here, I won't spend a penny of his money in this place.

Sadly, I climb back down the stairs, pull open the curtain and slide into my bunk. Soon, the sound of the paddle wheel and the rolling of the boat in the water sends me drifting to sleep.

I dream of flying.

CHAPTER TWENTY-TWO

JULY 7

A shrill whistle awakens me. I jump and hit my head on the upper bunk.

"Damn it, stupid. Watch your head. You woke me up," a female voice complains vehemently from above.

"Sorry," I answer timidly.

Pushing up on my elbows, I peer through the tiny porthole. Yes, it's really true and not a dream. I slept away from home last night, on a boat that's carrying me away from Boston and to the largest city in America.

Craning my neck and looking to the left, I see tall buildings off in the distance; and I'm instantly alert and excited. This must be New York City! I pull aside my curtain and try to brush the wrinkles from my skirt.

Outside my berth, a line of people stand there, waiting at the lavatory. Oh no, now, I really do need the facility. Fidgeting from foot to foot, I reach into my pocket and make sure my toothbrush and baking soda are tucked there. After a few minutes, only two people are left in front of me. One is a skinny, elderly woman, the other a girl slightly older than I am. *Which one of them will take longer*, I wonder, as I continue to fidget. The old woman is out in a jiffy, but it turns out the young girl is in there for what seems an eternity.

I'm next, and when the girl finally emerges, I glare at her, run in, and close the door. After I relieve myself, I use the Gayetty paper, pull the chain, wash my hands and face, then finish with a quick tooth brushing.

I can hear my mother's voice. *Brush up and down, front and back, and then sideways, Nellie. Get in the crevices.* It's good to remember how her voice sounded. A wave of longing washes over me. I didn't expect to miss her. I knew I would feel guilty about her worrying, but not to miss her. Oh well, this adventure is worth a little homesickness. I run a brush through my hair, pull it back and tie it with my ribbon, and pinch my cheeks.

Grabbing my satchel from the bunk, I make my way to the upper deck. Neo leans against the rail, his hand shielding his eyes from the morning sun. Standing next to him, but pretending to ignore him, I whisper, "Where did you sleep?"

"In Steerage, of course."

I don't tell him about my nice bed. "Are you starving? I am."

A quick glance at him answers my question. "Get food," he murmurs, slipping a dollar bill into my hand.

I order glasses of milk, sweet rolls, and apples. I ask the waiter to put them on a tray to take outside.

"Wouldn't you like to sit down and order, Miss?" he asks.

"No, thank you. I'd rather eat on deck."

He prepares the tray, then holds out his hand. "That'll be fifty cents."

I pay him. Let's see now, with the forty cents left over from yesterday and another fifty, I still have nearly a dollar. The clinking coins make a reassuring sound as I pull the drawstrings shut.

Neo sees me and indicates a smoke stack. I go behind it and, in seconds, he's beside me, grabbing an apple from the sack. "I could hardly sleep I was so hungry," he murmurs, chewing noisily.

I set down the tray and take a huge swallow of milk before I start on the sweet roll. I'll save the apple for last. My mother thinks an apple cleans the teeth from other sweets. In spite of myself, here I am obeying her lectures.

The whistle blares, and the ship begins to slow down. The pier is in sight, so I run to return the tray of dishes to the dining room and to make sure I left nothing in my bunk. Back on deck, I join the line of passengers and walk down the gangplank. My legs nearly buckle under me when I hit the deck.

I turn to the right as Neo and I had discussed and wait for him at the corner of a busy street. So many carriages, each appearing to race the others to get somewhere, it's a wonder they don't crash together in their frenzy.

"Where's the circus?" I ask Neo who stands behind me.

"On Flatbush Avenue. We'll find it."

As we begin to walk, I scan the people we pass. There are lots of colored people here, as well as people with slanted eyes, speaking languages I don't comprehend. It will be easier to blend in here than it ever would be in Boston.

Circus posters blaze from store windows. One shows a lion, its mouth open, eyes and teeth lethal, looking ready to devour anyone who comes too close. Another has a picture of two clowns with scary faces and painted-on smiles. Something about those clowns makes my skin crawl. One poster has drawings of midgets and giants and a woman so fat she seems ready to explode out of her skin.

I stop and stare at the largest of the posters: THE FLYING FLAUBERTS. On it, two handsome men hang by their knees on trapezes. They are suspended high above the ground with no net under them. Their arms are extended toward a beautiful blonde girl who floats between them as if suspended by a pillar of air. A a dazzling smile wreathes her perfect face. She clearly has no fear of flying free and unsupported in space. I want to meet this girl. Neo stops and stares at her, too.

At a corner called Flatbush Avenue, I glance at him and nod. I turn onto Flatbush and begin walking down it. Neo follows. In a vacant lot at the end of the street is an enormous canvas tent. It looks taller than the buildings around us. On the right side of the tent are cages of lions and tigers, striped horses and monkeys, all growling, whinnying, and screeching their heads off. The smells of the animals mingle with the heated scent of sawdust, which is more exciting to me than the whiff of a French perfume I once smelled at Mendel's Apothecary.

At the left side of the big tent is a smaller, narrower tent with strange pictures in front of it. There's a man with two heads, a huge woman with tattoos covering her body, and a tiny man looking up at a giant. At the center of all this is a big sign: ODDITIES. Under the sign, up on a platform, stands a real man dressed in black jodhpurs, a red jacket with brass buttons and golden braid on his lapels, wearing a top hat. He yells and gestures wildly.

"Step right up, ladies and gentlemen, to enjoy the strangest, most horrific, exciting sights on earth. Don Costillo's Oddities! No freak show at any other circus rivals the assemblage of human anomalies you'll see behind this tent flap!" He narrows his eyes in a scary way. "Or are they human? Come in and find out! Only five dimes!"

Fifty cents? Is he crazy? Who can afford that? As I turn away, there's Neo standing about ten feet back. His mouth is open, and his eyes are wide. Watching him closely, I see his Adam's apple jump in his throat. He actually looks afraid. I swallow hard.

CHAPTER TWENTY-THREE

Neo pushes me toward the man in jodhpurs. I swallow the lump in my throat. We had agreed that I should speak to people first because I'm white and a girl and will probably get a better reception. I inhale a big breath and stride forward. By the time I get to the man, he's stopped his yelling and has stepped down, his back to me. He's getting something from behind the tent flap. He raises a brown bottle and swigs from it.

I can hear my mother's voice. "He's an alkie." And he probably is, but I need to talk to him and hope he'll help us find work.

"Sir," I say just loud enough to get his attention.

He jumps and swings around to face me. His round face is covered with red blotches. He caps his bottle and returns it to the back of the tent flap. He smiles. "Well, hello, Miss Pretty. And who are you?"

My brain searches for an answer. Neo and I hadn't discussed what our names would be, but they must be made up and quickly. "Uhhhm, I'm Felicity the Flyer. I want to be a trapeze artist."

I turn around and gesture for Neo to come closer. "And this is Omar of Africa. He's a magician."

Neo tips his hat solemnly.

"We've got plenty of magicians," the man asserts.

I feel Neo slump beside me.

"And who are you, sir?" I ask in a voice Sister Sarah would call bold as brass.

"Phineas, the barker." He tips his hat, bows deeply, and nearly falls over.

Neo jumps forward and steadies the man. "Mr. Phineas, sir, I'm also a mind reader." His accent is thick, a combination of British and French, I think. I'm proud of him. He's a great bluffer.

"A mind reader?"

"Oh yes, sir!" I exclaim. "Omar's amazing. I'll bet he knows exactly what you're thinking right now." I turn to Neo with a questioning grin.

Neo's eyes widen some, but he recovers quickly. "You're wondering how it is that I speak such good English, aren't you?"

The man looks at me. "If he's from Africa, how can he talk English at all?"

"Oh sir, he's a genius, you see," I say. "It took him only two weeks to learn the language when he arrived in America."

Neo's seriousness nearly makes me giggle.

"How'd you get out of Africa?"

"I built a raft that carried me out the Gambia River basin into the Atlantic Ocean. That took me to Rome. I worked outside the Coliseum as a mind reader and finally got onto an ocean vessel that landed in Boston where I joined a small circus."

I raise my eyebrows at Neo. Good story.

"And where'd you two meet?"

"In Omaha." Neo almost convinces me, though I know better. "We got tired of playing small towns and decided to hit the big time. So, here we are."

Omaha, is it? I look at Neo in admiration. He's getting to be as good a fibber as I am, though I never knew I was good at it till this very day. White lies. I'll remember them, though, for confession.

"How old are you two?" the man asks, looking us up and down.

"I'm sixteen," I blurt out. Another lie. I mentally make an Act of Contrition.

"And I'm eighteen," Neo chimes in.

"Well, Miss Felicity, we already have a flyer. See the picture of that pretty blonde there? Her name is Angelique. She comes from France."

In spite of myself, I feel a bit relieved. I'm fearless on the swing at school but am not confident about how I'd do on a real trapeze. "I'm also an excellent equestrian, sir." This is not a lie. My da had me on a horse's back when I was three and taught me to jump fences at eight. There's not a horse in Boston I can't ride. "I can stand on a horse's back while it's in full cantor." This is stretching the truth some. I did stand on a horse's back once in an alley behind the house, but the horse wasn't moving, and my mother caught me and screamed me off it.

Neo glances over at me, his eyebrows arched. I lift my chin. *I can do it if I have to.*

Phineas reaches behind the tent flap and swigs from the brown bottle again. When he swivels back to us, he swerves unsteadily and his nose is red as a radish. "Tell you what," he slurs. "We'll have a chat with the Ringmaster. He makes all the decisions around here when it comes to the big tent."

Does Phineas have a touch of resentment in his words? I think so, but another swig on the bottle seems to soothe him. "Maybe the Ringmaster'll take you on as an apprentice," he says to me. "A pretty girl in tights standing on a horse could be a fetching sight for the yokels," he swivels to Neo, "and I could probably use an African mind reader here among the freaks."

"Could I slip in a few magic tricks, too?" Neo asks hopefully, waving a handkerchief in front of Phineas's face, turning it into a cravat, which he deftly ties around the man's scrawny neck.

Phineas grins, tightens the cravat and tucks it under his jacket. "Not bad. Maybe. Get yourselves back here at four this afternoon, after the matinee. You'll meet the Ringmaster."

"We'll be here," I say quickly. I don't want him to change his mind. I don't own tights and know my mother would kill me for wearing them in public. But this is a circus! What else would I wear? I'm so excited I forget to separate from Neo as we walk back down Flatbush Avenue . . . until a big man wearing a brown homburg hat spews, "Off the curb, nigger. You can't walk alongside a white girl."

Neo bristles but jumps into the street; the muscles in his neck contracting.

We check the time and see it's nearly two. That gives us two hours to get something to eat and plan our strategy for meeting with the Ringmaster. Jingling the change in my pocket, I say, "I'll run in that restaurant up ahead and get some food. I have money left over."

"I'll be waiting." He points to a park across the street.

In the restaurant, I elbow my way up to the counter. "Could I get two sandwiches, please?"

The woman behind the counter has red hair like my mother's, but it's brassy red and straight as a stick. "I suppose you can," she answers with a sneer. "This is a restaurant after all."

She acts mad at me about something, but I decide to ignore her rudeness. "Two hams on rye bread, please. Mustard on one, mayonnaise on the other." I start to turn away, then remember and turn back. "Oh, and do you have any ginger ale?"

"How'd you hear about that already?" the woman asks, squinting her eyes at me. "It only came in yesterday."

"I had some in Fall River. I figured it must be in New York by now." My, I am feeling sophisticated.

She turns away, uncaps a big jug, and pours two glasses of the sparkling golden beverage. Then, she plops a piece of ice into each one. Thirsty, I take a sip, loving the tickle of the bubbles up my nose. *Wait'll Neo tastes this!*

After a few minutes, she brings two sandwiches to the counter. I pay the bill and say, "My friend and I are going to eat in the park across the street. I'll bring the saucers and glasses back when we're finished."

"No skin off my nose if you don't," she answers. "But I'll guarantee you my boss will be after your ass if he don't get them back. He's the toughest guy in Jersey."

"I will, I promise. But isn't this Manhattan?"

"Nah, that's two miles that way." She points across the water.

Neo sits on a bench; his left foot twitching in excitement. "Sit at the end of this bench, Nellie. Act like we're not together. We don't need trouble."

I do as he says, placing his sandwich and glass of ginger ale on the ground in front of him.

He takes a sip and wrinkles up his nose. "What's this?"

"It's called ginger ale. I had some yesterday in Fall River. Like it?"

He raises the glass to his lips and takes a big swig. He sneezes loudly. "That's really bubbly!" He crinkles his nose, laughing. "Yeah, it's tasty."

As we eat, we discuss what we'll say when we meet the Ringmaster. When our plan is in place, Neo wipes his mouth on his sleeve, crumples up the sandwich paper and drains the glass. "I'll tell you one thing, Nellie. I'm going to meet that Angelique, the blonde flyer. She's beautiful. She may well be my first love."

His first love? Is he crazy? Has Neo forgotten he's colored?

Suddenly, a huge black crow lights on a street sign near us. His beady eyes stare at me, and my breath stops in my chest. I don't know why.

CHAPTER TWENTY-FOUR

At four o'clock, we are again in front of the Oddities tent. Phineas opens a flap and shows us in. Looking at his pocket watch, he says, "Good, you're right on time. Wait here. I'll be back."

In minutes, he's back with a very tall man whose slick brown hair gleams with pomade. He is the skinniest man I've ever seen. This must be the Ringmaster. His eyes are blue and cold, and his handlebar mustache curls down nearly to his chin. His tight black suit, white shirt, and tall black hat make him look eight feet tall. He smokes a long cigar, and when he takes it from his mouth, the end is soggy with spittle. He grins a yellow grin, and the sight of those teeth, pointed as a wolf's, makes the hair stand out on my arms.

"Meet the Ringmaster." Phineas waves his hand palm open, with flare. "Sal, this is Felicity and Omar. She's a fancy bareback rider, and he's a mind reader. I think I can use him in my Oddities show. I told Felicity maybe you'd take her on as an apprentice."

The yellow grin fades as his blue eyes squint at me. "How old are you?"

"Sixteen, sir." I gulp.

He begins to slowly circle me. His eyes are boring into my back so that I can almost feel them penetrate my skin. "How are your legs?"

Though startled, I lift my chin, turn, and stare back at him. "Good. They get me where I want to go." I try to make my voice sound tough.

"Show 'em."

My mother will kill me, is my first thought. My second is *if I want to work here, I'll have to wear skimpy costumes like I see on the posters.* So, my second thought wins out. I lift my skirt.

"Petticoat, too." He sucks air between his teeth and rolls a piece of straw from one side of his mouth to the other.

Blushing, I raise my petticoat almost to my knees.

"Roll up them pantalettes, too."

Gritting my teeth, I follow his orders. Neo turns his head.

"Good legs," the Ringmaster murmurs to Phineas who agrees appreciatively.

"Okay, Missy, drop the skirt. You'll do . . ." he saunters off, "if you can handle the horse," he tosses over his shoulder.

He returns in minutes, leading a monstrously tall, white horse with no saddle on its back. "Show me," he commands.

"What kind of horse is he? I've never seen one so big." My stomach is fluttering.

"A Percheron."

"What's his name?" I ask, scanning every square inch of the animal.

"Bianco."

This horse's shoulders are level with my eyes. "I'll need a boost to get on him." I try to keep my voice steady.

Sal motions me over.

I put my hand on the horse's nose and pull down so that I can look into his eyes. They stare, unblinking and uncaring. I run my hand along his withers and down his front leg. "Hello, Bianco," I say, staring up into the flat, black eyes. "You and I are going to be friends." *Please God, let this be true.*

Neo puts his hand under my left foot and lifts. I swing my right leg over the horse's back and grab onto the mane. At first, Bianco rears, startled by this unfamiliar burden, but he gentles quickly and I grip his sides with my thighs. The ground looks a million miles down. Lightly, I touch his flanks with my ankles, and the massive animal begins to move. *Good. He's well trained.* I walk, then trot him around the sawdust-covered ground in a circle.

"All right," the Ringmaster yells, "show me a trick!"

"Coming right up!" A frantic glance at Neo reveals his terror, but his dark eyes also will me to succeed.

And succeed I must if I am to stay here. I kick Bianco's flanks harder, and the horse moves into a gentle canter. He's becoming comfortable with me. Now, *I* must perform.

I kneel on the broad back, holding onto his mane with both hands. We continue around and around in the pattern I've established. Still kneeling, I let go of the mane and extend my arms out. Neo claps, but the Ringmaster never changes his expression. Focusing my eyes, I think hard. *How should I do this? One foot at a time? Or a quick spring to standing?* I decide the latter.

Praying to the Blessed Mother, I jump up, gauging where the horse will be when my feet land. It seems I'm in the air for minutes, but I know that is not possible. Finally, my soles fall solid onto Bianco's undulating back. I keep my knees bent slightly, and then come to full standing and try not to look down at the ground. I'm at least twenty feet in the air.

As the massive animal moves, I adjust my body to his rhythm, bending and straightening my knees in accordance with his gait. After a time, it feels like a dance, a divine dance between girl and horse. When we move as if we are one being, I raise my arms and point my hands to the side in victory. My smile surely stretches to my ears. We continue to circle.

The Ringmaster shouts, "Enough!"

It's over! I did it! I look at Neo and see pride beaming from his face. "Watch this!" I leap into the air and land in a perfect straddle on Bianco's back, bracing my thighs as I land so as not to hurt my lady parts. I bend over and kiss the great horse on the neck. "Thank you, Bianco. Good boy." I pull him to a stop and leap to the ground, pirouetting as I land.

"Okay," the Ringmaster says, "you'll be an apprentice rider in the parade when we get to Manhattan Island tomorrow. You'll start at fifty cents a week, plus grub, and you'll sleep in the girls' car on the train. I'll introduce you to Bridey, the bearded lady. She'll show you around."

As we walk toward the big tent, Neo whispers. "How did you do that?"

"Magic, my boy, pure magic."

CHAPTER TWENTY-FIVE

We left home only two days ago, but it feels like a lifetime.

"The evening show starts at 6:30," Phineas informs us, lifting the flap on the big tent. Its bleachers are empty now, except for a few people scattered around eating. He leads us across the sawdust and nimbly jumps into the big wooden ring. I follow him, walking on the ring, my arms extended. I glance back. Neo/Omar is staring around the tent with shining eyes. Looking up, I see two trapezes. The sight of them thrills me and sets my heart beating faster.

On a low bleacher at the far side of the tent, a woman with long, black hair sits with her back to us. She faces a bald man next to her. His face is filled with pure adoration. As we draw closer, I realize the man's shirt sleeves hang empty at his sides. No arms. He smiles at the woman, as his right leg bends toward a plate of fried chicken between them. With two toes, he picks up a drumstick as easily as I would with my fingers at our kitchen table. His foot brings the drumstick to his mouth and takes a big bite. *How can he do that?*

"Bridey and Wilbur," Phineas stands with his hands on his hips, "I want you to meet some new additions."

The woman turns to face us. I jump, startled. She has a full, black beard that hangs to the top of her abundant bosom. As she catches the astonishment on my face, her dark blue eyes smile. She's seen this reaction before. Well, of course, she has, unless that beard is fake. I steal a side look at Neo/Omar and am surprised that he appears to hardly notice it. He steps forward and bows to the woman.

"The girl is Felicity," Phineas says. "She's our apprentice bareback rider. The dark one is Omar from Africa. He reads minds. Kids, meet Bridey, our bearded lady, and her husband, Wilbur, the armless wonder."

Bridey's smile grows wider, though it mostly shows in her eyes. Her mouth is obscured by a bushy moustache. Wilbur looks up at us with a grin so warm I smile back. He now grasps a fork in the toes of his left foot and casually puts a piece of potato into his mouth, wipes his face with a napkin held in his right foot, then jumps up to his feet.

"Welcome," he says sincerely, bowing slightly.

What a marvelous man! He doesn't appear to be one bit sorry for himself. I wonder if I could ever be so resourceful if I lost my arms and hands?

"Oooh, *álainn*," Bridey whispers, taking my hands in both of hers.

I reply, "*A bhuí le.*"

She claps her hands delightedly.

"What's that all about?" Phineas asks.

"She said I'm beautiful in Irish," I tell him. "I thanked her."

"You speak Gaelic?" Neo whispers.

"Just a little."

Wilbur, surprisingly tall and skeletal thin, grins down at me. He stretches his right foot out toward Bridey who takes it and pulls herself to standing, whereupon she wraps me in her arms. "Ah, little colleen," she croons into my cheek. Her beard tickles my face, but I don't mind at all.

"Bridey's from a place called The Dingle Peninsula," Wilbur explains. "She spoke only the Irish language till she came here two years ago. Her brogue's still a little thick, but she's working on it."

"Bridey, my mother's from Cork and my father from Mayo."

"Oh, I knew the map of Ireland was on your face, sweetheart."

I smile and accept a kiss on the cheek; a very fuzzy kiss.

"Can you write?" she asks me, her eyes wide.

My head bobs up and down.

"*Taibhseach*!" she squeals. "Will you teach me?"

"Perhaps," I say; sad that I won't be here long enough. "I do want to be a teacher someday, or at least I did."

She claps her hands again and grabs me into an even bigger hug.

"I want you two to show them the ropes," Phineas tells them. "Take 'em under your wings. Wilbur, in your case, guess it'll be your feet. Show them the mess area and where they'll sleep." He turns to me. "Bridey and Wilbur are married, respectable like. When we leave here tomorrow, you'll sleep in the female car on the train, Felicity, and Omar'll be with the roustabouts. But first, we have to get over the Hudson River. Tonight, the girls bunk on this side of the big tent," he points to the right, "and the boys, on that side," then left. "Mats are rolled up over there." He points to a place behind me. "Now, I'll get back to work while you two get acquainted with the other oddities."

"Excuse me, please," Neo/Omar gets his attention. "You say Felicity will earn fifty cents a week. What about me?"

"You'll get whatever you can scrounge from the stooges after you read their minds." As he walks away, he throws over his shoulder. "You better be as good as you say you are."

Neo looks at me, panic in his eyes. "Nellie, I can't read minds," he whispers.

Wilbur, standing nearby, says. "I heard that."

"You did?" Neo says, his voice quivering with fear.

"Yeah, I was born without arms, but God compensated me with strong legs and the best ears in the world. I really *can* hear a pin drop."

Neo hangs his head, then looks Wilbur straight in the eyes. "I'm afraid I'll fail at reading minds. I'm actually a magician. Please don't tell Phineas."

Wilbur smiles gently. "Ah, don't worry about that, boy. People change their minds every second. Just take a good look at 'em, see if they're looking happy or sad, and take a guess. You'll probably be right some of the time. Oh, and don't call her Nellie. Her name is Felicity, right?" He winks.

"Right," Omar answers. "Thank you, Wilbur."

CHAPTER TWENTY-SIX

Bridey holds my hand as we approach a massive woman eating a huge sandwich. It's at least four inches thick. Wilbur has taken Neo/Omar off in a different direction.

"Marge," with Bridey's accent it sounds more like Mahrsh, "this is Felicity, the new girl. She rides horses."

Marge looks up at me from her place on the floor and stretches her mouth to a giant "O" to take another bite. A monkey screaming from a nearby cage distracts me for a moment, but then I focus my attention back on Marge. She is the largest human being I've ever seen. I'd always been told fat people are jolly, but Marge doesn't look one bit happy. As a matter of fact, she looks angry. I wish I had a napkin to wipe her chin, which is covered in mayonnaise. She rubs her forearm across it. "Where'd you come from, kid?"

I sputter a few words, trying to recall what lie Neo told Sal about where we met, but I can't remember. That's the problem with lies. If you forget what the lie was, you might get caught, then people stop trusting you. Anyway, that's what my mother always says.

The thought of my mother hits me right in the chest with a stab of grief. Right now, she's probably crazy with fear wondering where I am. Or so mad at me she doesn't care if I ever come back. *We won't be gone that long,* I tell myself. *We'll go back before school starts for Neo.* Remembering that I don't have a school to go back to, I want to cry, but don't.

If I have to spend the rest of my life scrubbing floors on Beacon Hill, so be it. At least, I'll have had one great adventure the summer of my almost-fourteenth year. *I'm Felicity, Queen of the Air, no, Queen of Bareback Riding. Well, Queen of something anyway.*

Instantly, I recall Neo's story. "I met Omar at a circus in the Midwest we were both working at. Maybe Indiana. I can't remember. He was a magician then. All our shows were one night, and we traveled a lot between Indiana and Nebraska." I was getting really good at this lying stuff. "The towns become a blur after a while."

"Tell me about it," Marge complains. "I've been doing this crap since I was ten. I don't know where I was last week." Suddenly, she lets out a belly laugh. Her massive stomach rolls on itself like dough being kneaded. "Or maybe my memory's bad because I like my beer a little too much, huh, Bridey?"

I notice a large pitcher on the blanket she's sitting on. She picks it up and pours herself a giant mug. I smell beer. Before I can blink, she's downed the beer, tipping her chin up and her head back. She finishes with a loud burp. "Scuse." She looks me up and down. "So what's your talent, cutie pie?"

Now, I'm cutie pie. Mercy, her mood changes quickly. "I really wanted to be a flyer on the trapeze, but Sal says you already have one. So now I'm a bareback rider."

"Oh, yes, Miss Angelique. All the men think she's the cat's meow. But they should only have to share a room with her. What a bitch!"

I blush at the word. Since I started to talk, my mother has threatened me with a mouth full of soap for swearing.

"She's not a bitch," Bridey quickly takes up for the absent girl, "just young. I like her."

"Oh, Bridey," Marge huffs, hauling her mountain of flesh up to standing. She plants her legs wide apart and pats her belly in satisfaction. "You like everyone. It's absolutely disgusting." She burps again.

But nothing about Bridey is disgusting to me. Her arm around my waist is solid and warm. She makes me feel at home. I look into her soft, blue eyes. I must ask the one question that's deviled me since I first saw her. "Do you mind if I ask if that beard is real?"

Marge laughs. "I wondered about that myself when I first met her."

"Pull it," Bridey answers.

I give it a gentle tug. "Oh my, it certainly is real, isn't it? Do you like having it?"

She tilts her head as if she's never been asked that question before. "*Like* it?"

She scratches her beard and smoothes down her moustache. "I didn't like it when I was young. Everyone in my village laughed at me. My mother tried to shave my face every day, and my father wouldn't let me come to church with them. I needed to get away from people who didn't love me. So, when the circus came to Killarney, I joined it. I was sixteen. Wilbur was in that circus." She smiles. "Wilbur adores my beard. Rubs his face in it and sings love songs to me sometimes." Her eyes glow with memory and I notice for the first time that her eyes are beautiful, with eyebrows that arch perfectly and lashes so long they nearly meet her brows. "So yes, I like my beard now," she coos softly.

Marge combs through Bridey's beard with her fingers and gives her a playful pat on the cheek. "Yep, you lucked out with that husband of yours. He's a prince, and I oughta know. I've married three of them, and not one of them was worth a plugged nickel. All of them said they loved my bein' in show business. But once I married them, each one tried to put me on a diet." She throws up her hands. "Don't they know that without this," she puts her arms around herself and squeezes, "they'd starve? Not one of those three could earn a dime." She shakes her head in disgust.

Bridey hugs Marge and turns to me, "Come, we'll meet the others."

After saying goodbye to Marge, the two of us stroll, our hands entwined, through the circus midway. The sawdust feels fresh and soft under my feet, and I become so accustomed to the odor of horse manure that I hardly smell it. I do watch my step, though. No one seems to be picking up after the animals.

"Charlie!" Bridey calls out. "Give me two bags!"

The man she yells at stands behind a cart loaded with peanuts. He scoops some up and puts them into two paper bags. Bridey tries to give him some coins, but he holds up his hand and shakes his head. "Tell Wilbur hello for me."

She hands me one bag and I start cracking open the shells.

"Just dump those shells in the sawdust," she waves palm out. "Everybody does."

As we amble along munching on peanuts, Bridey pulls me over to a tiny man. He can't be over two foot tall. When he sees my stare, he breaks into a tap dance. He ends it with a great flourish of tapping that leaves his right leg extended toward me, then bends at the waist. "Ta-da! I'm Tiny, the smallest man in the world."

I extend my hand. "Hello, Tiny."

"Thank you, Miss. . . ?"

"Felicity," Bridey answers for me. "She's our new bareback rider."

"Well now, Miss Felicity, you're as pretty as a picture if I do say so myself. If I were a little younger, I'd stand on a ladder for a kiss from you."

"What about Opal?" Bridey asks, patting his shoulder playfully.

"Ah, Opal, my true love. Felicity knows I was just kidding, don't you?" He looks at me expectantly. I consider teasing him just for mischief, but he looks really concerned.

"Sure, I do."

"Good. Opal is my only real love and always will be, though loving her does have its challenges."

"Challenges?" My eyes open wide.

"Opal is attached to her twin sister, Pearl," Bridey answers.

"That's nice," I murmur. "I'd love to have a sister."

"No, I mean *attached*. They're Siamese twins."

"Oh." I'd seen pictures of such twins in a book at the library. How awful that must be!

"Here they come now." Bridey tips her head toward the incoming light.

At first, the two women appear to have their arms around each other. But a closer look reveals they are joined at the hip. I wonder how it would feel to be joined for life to another person. One of the women looks miserable, but the other beams with pleasure. The one with the smile leans down and kisses Tiny on top of his head. The other has no choice but to join her twin in the bend, and she grunts in displeasure.

Tiny kisses the smiling twin on the hand and turns her to meet me. "Opal, this is our new bareback rider. Felicity, meet Opal, the love of my life."

"Nice to meet you, Opal."

"Hello, Felicity." She points to the woman attached to her hip. "This is my sister, Pearl."

Surly, Pearl hisses, "Hello."

At that moment, a giant animal whose movement shakes the ground walks across the runway. The animal is being led by a young boy with a rope.

"What is that?" I ask, breathless with wonder.

"An elephant, our ticket to the big time," Bridey answers. "He's new here, too. Give him a peanut."

I start to shell it, but Bridey advises, "No need. He'll take care of that."

With that, I hold out a peanut. The elephant rubs a massive trunk against my hand and scoops the peanut up and drops it into his mouth. His skin is as soft as the softest suede. Fiona's father brought her a pair of suede gloves back from France last year, when we were still friends, but Fiona *never* met an elephant up close. "Should I give him another?"

Bridey winks at me, so I do just that. I love this elephant. It's the gentlest animal I've ever seen. And so big! He lumbers off, following the boy.

"It's wonderful meeting all of you," I say, turning back. "All good wishes for happiness to you and Opal, Tiny."

He looks up into Opal's adoring eyes. "Thank you, Felicity. I want you and Bridey to be the first to know something. At the end of this season, I will make Opal my wife."

Opal smiles and kisses him on the head.

"Congratulations," I say, my heart warm with joy for them.

Pearl shudders.

Chapter Twenty-Seven

Bridey, never letting loose of my hand, strolls me around the circus midway for an hour. When she's satisfied we've seen everything of importance, she shows me where we'll sleep tonight. "Pick out your mat and pillow, Felicity, and leave a coin on it. No one will take it."

I choose a blue mat and a soft pillow and hold it up for her approval. She nods. I lay them out on the sawdust and put a penny on the pillow.

Bridey has more advice. "You might want to move that when you see where others bunk down. Don't sleep next to Marge. She snores terrible. Also, stay away from the twins. Pearl is so jealous she pulls Opal's hair and makes her cry. Opal is one loud crier."

"Why's Pearl jealous?"

"Opal has a man. Tiny is short, but male."

"Hmmm." I must ask the question deviling me. "How in the world can Opal marry Tiny? I mean, wouldn't he have to marry both of them?"

Bridey shrugs and rakes her fingers through her beard. "They've talked about it and have come to some kind of agreement. It'd be good if Pearl had a husband, too, but who'd want to marry her? She's so mean." She suddenly grabs my arm. "I smell food. Come, let's get some before they run out."

We follow our noses to the grub tent. About fifty people are already seated at long tables inside. A delicious aroma comes from whatever is being cooked. A man in a tall purple turban dishes out big spoonfuls of the aromatic food onto plates.

"What is that?" I ask curiously.

"Some kind of curry," Bridey explains. "The cook is Turkish. Last week, it was an Italian. We pick up different cooks in each town. My favorite was the noodles in red sauce the Italian cooked last week. *Ach tá stobhach na hÉireann an chuid is fearr.*"

I recognize the Gaelic. *But Irish food is still the best*, I translate to myself.

But from the scents rising from my dish, I'm not sure I agree. Cabbage never smelled this good.

We sit down, and my first taste of curry sparks a new and exciting response from my taste buds. Irish cooking is plain. This is rich, thick, and spicy. I wish my parents could taste this food, especially Da.

At the table next to us, Neo sits with Wilbur who picks up a piece of meat on his fork with his foot as if it's the most natural thing in the world. Across from Neo is a man who, even sitting, towers over everyone in the tent.

"Who's that with Omar and Wilbur?" I ask Bridey.

"That's Jasper, the tallest man on earth. He loves to paint. His pictures are beautiful. Sometimes, they sell them on the midway."

Jasper's face is gentle and smiling. *Neo is probably dazzling him with one of his jokes. Oops, I mean Omar. I must remember.*

Wilbur stands on one leg, picks up a pot of tea with the opposite foot, and expertly pours cups for all his table companions. "Your Wilbur's quite accomplished, Bridey."

"Accomplished?" She cocks her head. "That's a new word to me. What's it mean?"

"It means he can do so many things in spite of his handicap."

"Handicap?" Her brow knits.

"Well, yes, having no arms. That's a handicap."

"Wilbur has no handicap." Her voice sounds a bit flat.

Perhaps I offended her. I am contrite. "I'm sorry, Bridey. You're right. He is perfect. And so are you. You're both lucky."

Her expression brightens. "Yes, luck of the Irish, I guess, or the power of prayer. I prayed for a kind man like Wilbur when I was a girl in Ireland. Who knew I'd find him in the circus?"

After a long sleep, I rise refreshed the next day. This day, Neo and I learn all about our new home: where the costumes are, where the boat is docked that'll take us across the river to the train when we leave New York, and all about the troupe we will be living with. They are mostly sweet people, welcoming and kind. It would be awful if they weren't, considering how intimately they live to each other. It strikes me that this circus is a true family, as loving and protective of each other as my parents are of me.

When Wilbur and Bridey introduce us to beautiful Angelique, the trapeze artist, I am disturbed at the way she and Neo look at each other. Their eyes lock and seem unable to turn away. He cups her hand in both of his.

"*Enchanté.*" He finally bows low to kiss her hand.

Angelique blushes and laughs softly. "*Merci,*" she answers, not removing her hand from his.

They stand staring into each other's eyes until I nudge in and say, "Hello, Angelique, I'm Felicity."

She drops Neo's hand and turns to shake mine. "*Bon jour,* Felicity." Then, she angles back and gazes up at Neo from under impossibly long lashes.

Perhaps Angelique is color blind. Maybe the French are like that. She sees only a dark, handsome young man who's clearly besotted with her. No American white girl would look at him like that. It would cause a scandal.

In America, there's still anger against free blacks, even in the North. I've read tales of kidnappings and murders in Boston. Uncle Kam was almost killed by a lynch mob when he and Mother were young. Things haven't changed much.

The memory of my mother's face as she told me that story stabs me in the heart. Homesickness overtakes me, and all Neo's reassurances haven't dispelled my guilt. I nearly scream out, *I want to go home!*

But then I see Bianco tied off near the tent, and I remember. This summer is my time for adventure. Afterwards, I'll probably have nothing to look forward to in Boston except the drudgery of life as someone's maid—maybe even the Doggett's. Fiona would love to see me dusting her dresser as she goes off to her posh boarding school. I couldn't stand that. No, I will never work for the Doggett's.

That night, I take the penny off my pillow and lie down on the straw mat. Staring at the ceiling, I come to a decision. I will ride Bianco flawlessly. I will have my adventure. Then, I'll accept the lowly life in store for me. At least, I'll have memories.

CHAPTER TWENTY-EIGHT

In the morning, I find Bridey bent over a large trunk in the costume room. All I can see of her is her round bottom. Her hands emerge out of the trunk, each of them grasping handfuls of net, color, and glitter. She pulls herself up, holding out two costumes, one white and one yellow. She places the yellow one up in front of me and squints. She grunts and throws it back into the trunk. Now, she holds up the other one. It is a poof of snow-white net with spangled stars. Bridey's eyes are nearly as bright as the spangles. "Yes!" she exclaims. "Put it on. These tights and ballet shoes, too. You'll wear them all when you ride in tomorrow's parade."

As I go into a dressing room, her voice trails after me. "That costume belonged to Angelique, but she grew out of it last year. One day, she was a little girl. Next day, boom!" I glance out and see her hands making circles over her chest. "She grows bosoms. Happens to girls sometimes."

I hope she's right.

I take off my dress and pull on the white tights and ballet shoes, then I slip the costume over my head. It's tight, but perfect. The top has tiny straps holding up a low-cut bodice. My mother would have a stroke that it's so bare. Looking down, I'm grateful for my small chest. If I were as big as Fiona or Adelaide, I'd spill right out the top of it.

The legs on the costume are cut high like a trapeze artist's. Thank heavens for the tights, which grant some modesty. As I turn in front of the full-length mirror, the costume catches sunlight through the top of the tent and sends out sparkles to its walls.

When I walk out in the costume, tights, and shoes, Bridey sighs. "If I ever have a daughter, I'd want her to look just like you. Sit." She runs outside the tent and returns with a handful of white daisies.

"Sit," she orders again, pointing to a small stool in front of mirror. Bridey brushes my hair straight down to my waist and then pulls it up and twists it into curls on top my head. After she's secured it with hairpins, she weaves the daisies into the topknot and pulls a few strands down around my face.

Her fingers are deft and certain. "I used to do Angelique's hair when she was younger. Now, they hire a professional hair dresser. She says she likes my styling better."

When she's finished, she stands back and inspects her handi-work. "Perfect!" she declares and hands me a mirror. In a way, I wish my mother could see me. She'd not approve of this costume, but I do look pretty.

"Where's Angelique's mother?"

Bridey's face clouds. "Her mother passed when Angelique was three. Now, it's just her, her father, and brother."

Poor Angelique. Mad as I used to get at Mother for nagging me, I miss that concern now. *What must she and Da be thinking? This very minute?* I shake my head to clear the guilt.

"Why the head shake?" Bridey's concerned.

"Nothing."

"Time for bed." Bridey turns her back as I strip off the

glittering costume, then hands me my dress. I slip it over my head and remove the ballet shoes and tights and hand the whole costume to her. She wraps a shawl around my shoulders and leads me barefoot back to the sleeping tent. The sawdust caresses and warms my feet.

I begin to get excited. I'll not sleep this night, thinking about riding in my first circus parade. I have practiced every spare moment with Bianco. No one else gets to ride him. Now I can do a handstand and splits on his back. I doubt I could do that with any other horse, but Bianco has learned to trust me. When we move together, he feels like an extension of my own body.

Bridey kneels down beside my mat and puts her hand on my head. "Sleep well, child. Ask your guardian angel to protect you." She kisses my forehead. "We'll touch up your hair again come morning."

As I close my eyes, I whisper the prayer my mother taught me. "Angel of God, my guardian dear, to whom God's love commits me here, ever this day be at my side to light, to guard, to rule, to guide."

The next thing I know, a bright sun creeps through the flap of the tent and hits my eyes. I did sleep after all and wake feeling wonderful. It's parade day. And though nobody knows but me, it's August tenth, my fourteenth birthday. I've been away five days.

Don't worry, Mother. I'm having the time of my life.

CHAPTER TWENTY-NINE

Phineas informs us that someone named Boss Tweed has personally cleared the route for the parade around the city and back to the big tent. I don't know who Boss Tweed is, but everyone acts mighty impressed with him.

The troupe vibrates with excitement as we assemble. We will march right into the heart of Manhattan. Phineas has given us a lineup. I'm in position number fourteen, on my fourteenth birthday, a good sign. A roustabout helps me on to Bianco's back.

Angelique will be the final act at parade's end at position twenty. She passes me smiling. "*Bonne chance*, Felicity!" Her beauty takes my breath away.

She walks daintily to the back of the assemblage on such high silver heels I fear she will twist her ankle on a cobblestone. When she arrives at the golden litter that will transport her, Neo helps her onto it. He and three other boys hoist her high into the air. She sits up there, smiling and waving, a princess to the people at her feet.

When she looks back down at Neo, her gaze frightens me. This morning, I found them sitting close together under a big elm tree. He was tracing the lines of her palm with his finger.

Can't they see how dark his finger looks against her skin? Don't they care what people will think?

Suddenly, Bianco's flanks quiver in nervousness. Perhaps he's sensed my anxiety. I pat his nose and nuzzle his ear and give him a nibble of carrot. Up ahead, the circus band begins to play, its big horns blasting through the mid-morning traffic.

The Ringmaster takes his position at the front of the band and raises his baton. We freeze to attention. He lifts his baton over his head, then slams it down. The horns strike a startling note. He pivots to the front and starts to march. The band follows him down Riverside Drive, trumpets blaring "The Battle Hymn of the Republic."

Marge has refused to walk. She's in a horse-drawn carriage right behind the band with a banner proclaiming her "The Fattest Woman on Earth." The horses begin a labored plodding forward. Like magic, her surly mouth turns up into a beaming smile. She waves and laughs, all the time dropping chocolates into her mouth.

"That's the only way the Ringmaster can get her in the parade, lots of chocolate," Bridey had told me.

Jasper the Giant, and Baba, an African midget, are paired in the march. Baba dances and turns cartwheels as Jasper strides with stiff arms and legs. He looks even taller next to the tiny Baba.

Cyril, the one they call "The Missing Link," roars from a lion cage at the people assembling on the sidewalk. His close-set eyes glare out from under matted hair through the bars, setting kids to screeching. I laugh to myself because Cyril is the gentlest person in the entire troupe and speaks with the voice of a soprano. But he does a great, fierce act, and children shrink back against their parents' legs. It's too bad they can't know him as the sweet soul he is.

Torch the Flame Thrower, swipes a blazing stick into and out of his mouth while Opal and Pearl follow behind him, their arms around each other. They look as though they actually like each other.

I wait patiently until it's my turn, then say, "Go, Bianco!" as I gently nudge him with my feet. That's all it takes for the giant horse to prance into a gentle canter. His reins are white and studded with spangles that match my costume. He arches his massive neck and snorts proudly. I think he knows it's his time to show off. I kneel on him, and then jump high into the air and land in a perfect split in the middle of his bare back. He doesn't break his stride for a second. I roll myself up and lie on my back, then spring to my feet again. After that, I kneel down, placing my hands squarely on his back, and lift into the air. The people on the sidewalk cheer. I nod to their applause, thrilled by their excitement.

"Good boy," I whisper into his ear, and then flip back down so that I'm riding with both legs on one side of his huge body. Bianco never lowers his head and never takes one misstep.

I continue my acrobatics all the way back to the tent on 14th Street. When the Ringmaster enters the tent, strutting with his baton, the band blasting away behind him, a loud roar goes up from the crowd. It sounds like there are a million people in there. When I get inside, I don't see an empty seat.

The screaming of the crowd excites me. I can't wait to show them what I can do. I pirouette on the horse's back, a ballerina dancing to the beat of the music, then leap into the air, higher and higher. I land solidly and the crowd roars its approval. Just as I begin another leap, a firecracker explodes behind me. My body is high in the air as Bianco startles, breaking into a gallop. From that height, I fall, missing his back by inches. I slam into the sawdust. Everything turns black.

CHAPTER THIRTY

The first face I see upon waking is Bridey's, sleeping on a chair next to my bed. Her face is streaked with tears and lined with worry. I moan and her eyes fly open.

"Felicity, you're awake?"

Though I dare not speak lest it make the pain in my head worse, I blink.

"Thank Jesus!" she exclaims and runs out of the compartment. In minutes, she's back accompanied by Neo and Angelique. Their faces blur before my eyes, but I recognize them.

"Nellie," Neo says, then immediately corrected himself. "I mean Felicity." He turns to Angelique. "Her sister's name was Nellie. I get them confused." He leans down and whispers in my ear. "Felicity, do you know me?"

I blink again.

"Am I Omar?" he asks.

I'd forgotten we were playing this game with our names and grin, except even a smile hurts, so I stop.

Angelique takes my hand. "Do you remember what happened, Felicity?"

Why won't they stop asking questions?

"Leave her be," Bridey says, her voice scolding. "She just woke up. Let her rest."

I close my eyes again and hear them saying my name, Bridey praises Jesus for answering her prayers.

A hand touches my forehead. It is calloused and rough. Phineas. "Now don't you worry about nothing, Felicity. You took a nasty fall off Bianco when he bolted. The doctor says you're going to be okay. Just keep your eyes closed."

Bianco? Ah yes, I remember. I obey Phineas. I have no choice.

I hear Neo say to Angelique, "Is it all right if she stays in your bed?"

Her voice whispers softly, "Yes, if you promise that someday I will be in yours."

Bridey tells me later that during the two days I slept, I often cried out "Mam." I remember none of that. The last thing I recall is hitting that sawdust.

It's strange that I cried for my mother. I figured I was tougher than that. Perhaps her rules had provided a safety net that I didn't appreciate. Now, as I lie in Angelique's soft bed, watching through the train's window as towns whiz by, tears flood my eyes as I remember her face.

Angelique has given me her private compartment for my recovery. That is good of her, though I do wonder if she might have an underlying motive. Her father and brother share the next compartment and might notice if she sneaks out to see Neo.

I'm probably being unkind, but whenever anyone from the troupe visits my bedside, they whisper gossip about the two of them. "They're together all the time." "They can't keep their hands off each other." "Who do they think they're kidding?"

I want to scream, "Stop your chatter! My head hurts!" but I say nothing.

Each time I awaken, my headache is so blinding I cannot

open my eyes to the sun. The sounds of the train pounding on the tracks causes my brain to throb. After a time, the pain eases and, though I'm sore and bruised nearly everywhere on my body, the circus doctor doesn't think there's any permanent damage, I do have a concussion. Blessed sleep returns.

CHAPTER THIRTY-ONE

On the fourth day, the train grinds itself to a noisy, steamy halt. Neo helps me to my feet and cajoles me to stay up. "Come now. We're going outside for some air. We have a show today."

As we climb down the metal steps to the cobbled walk of a strange town, he says, "You must get back on Bianco." His voice is harsh. "You slept for two days and have laid there for two more. It's time."

"I fell only four days ago. Quit nagging me." I peer about, eyes squinting, head pounding. A station sign says Plattsburgh, New York. It barely registers in my brain. I have no idea where that is.

"Nellie, if you don't fight your fear, there's a decent chance you'll never get over it."

"Be quiet, Neo."

I turn my back on him and cross my arms over my chest, angry. He's not the one who was thrown and knocked unconscious. He's not the one who still has bruises in places no decent girl can show. Besides, I'm not so sure Neo knows what the word "decent" means any more. He and Angelique make no effort to hide what is happening between them. Everyone gossips about the scandal of a black boy courting the beautiful French flyer.

"Get over it." He forces me to turn back and look him.

The roustabouts unload the screeching animals off the train and into their cages. People mill around us, bumping me. I feel violated with each shove and jar.

"I don't want to get over it. I want to go home." I don't realize my voice is so loud until I see Tiny stop, looking concerned.

Neo takes my arm roughly and pulls me away from the crowd. "That's crazy, Nellie," he whispers. "We've only been gone one week. School doesn't start for another month."

"What school?" My voice is quieter, but bitter as bile. "You may have a posh school to return to, but I have nothing. I want to go home. I miss my parents." As I say the words, I realize how true they are.

"Think about it, please. You don't mean that."

"I do mean it. You only want to stay because of your affair with your blonde girlfriend." *There, it's said. What I've wanted to say to him for days.*

A man carrying a straw mat jostles my shoulder. "Move it, Missy. You're in the way."

Neo walks behind a stand selling maps. When he faces me again, the look in his dark eyes is anguished. *I've never seen him like this. Why is he so miserable?*

He bursts out, "It's not an affair, Nellie. We're in love. I want to marry her someday."

My mouth flies open. Doesn't he know this is impossible? People stare if Neo and I even walk down the street together. Their faces scowl with hatred as they raise their hands to cover whispers.

When he moves back near the train, he looks so desperately sad that I put my arm around his shoulder and hug him, not worrying about the crowd milling around us.

"After another white girl, nigger?" a passing tent rigger says, pushing Neo's shoulder. "I saw you mooning over that trapeze artist yesterday."

Neo whirls to face the man, his fists raised. The man is elderly, probably in his sixties. His leathery face is creased by a thousand wrinkles. His sparse hair is white. He brandishes a tent rope on his left hand. "You lay a hand on me, nigger, and you'll swing before dark. I promise you that," he snarls.

Neo lowers his fists and strides away, his head hanging. I spin back and face the old man. "You, sir, are an evil man. You don't know what you're talking about."

He shrugs away.

I run after Neo. "Pay no attention to him. He's a fool."

Neo turns to me, and I am shocked that tears, hastily wiped away, still dampen his cheeks. He shakes his head. "It's impossible, Angelique and me."

I quicken my pace, wanting to stay with him, desperate to make him feel better. I decide on a plan. "Neo, you're right. I do need to get back on Bianco. I'll be more careful next time."

His hands still shake, but he forces a small grin. "You mean you're actually going to listen to me about something? Stubborn Nellie Kelly is willing to concede?"

"I am."

Just then, a roustabout leads Bianco down to the platform.

"Then, let's go to the stable." Neo grabs my hand. "Now."

He signals a wagon headed to the fairgrounds. We load our trunks onto the back and climb in.

He's called my bluff, and there's no way out.

Twenty minutes later, my knees tremble as I stand beside the giant white horse, caressing his flank.

"Change your mind?"

"Did you fake the tears to make me do this?"

A smile flits across his mouth. "I'm good, Nellie, very good, but even I'm not that good a magician. No, the tears were there, but now it's time to focus on you. When we go home, you'll be proud if you get back on that horse."

Gritting my teeth, I take in a deep breath. "All right. Bianco, here I come."

I spring to the bare back from a nearby stool and grip with my knees. Neo puts the bit in Bianco's mouth and fastens the bridle, then hands me the reins. "I'm proud of you, Nellie."

One soft kick to the flanks and we're off. Bianco, my magical animal, moves under me. Once again, I feel one with him, moving in rhythm as though our bodies and souls are joined in a dance.

"Good boy," I murmur, nudging him again with my foot. He increases his speed to a canter. "Here we go, Bianco." Breathless with excitement and, yes, fear, I kneel on his broad back, then jump to my feet. Bianco parades me around the midway like a grand prize he's showing off to everyone. Jasper and Tiny cheer our passing, and I wave to them joyfully. I'm a bareback rider in the circus, I'm good at it, and I've never felt more powerful. One fall didn't kill me.

When we've gone the length of the ring, I jump into a mid-air split and come back down perfectly on Bianco's back. "Good boy," I croon. "Let's go back. You get a carrot."

CHAPTER THIRTY-TWO

Bridey is quivering with elation when she takes me in her arms. "You rode, Nellie!"

I grin, realizing word does travel fast in the circus.

My heart warms and my confidence soars as many in the troupe congratulate me—even Pierre Flaubert, Angelique's father and the star of the circus. "Good job, child." His voice is so heavily accented I can hardly understand him, but there is no mistaking his kind smile and the way his eyes crinkle at the corners the way my da's does. "Ready for the parade?" He pats my back.

"Yes, sir!"

He touches my cheek softly. "*Tu es gentille.*"

At the site of the event, families mill around wanting to see us. Children with large eyes and gaping mouths watch roustabouts roll cages with monkeys and horses off the wagons and into cages.

The crowd cheers as the great tent is pulled up. I elbow my way through the people, excited to get dressed for the parade, happy as a child on Christmas morning.

At last, I'm ready.

Bianco stands waiting for me, bobbing his great head eagerly. "Let's go, my friend," I rub his snout and climb up "It's time."

Bridey didn't want to pull my hair up in pins lest it gives me a headache, so today, my black hair is loose and flying behind me, so in contrast with Bianco's stark whiteness. The great horse carries me through the downtown streets of Plattsburgh, New York, as though I am the most delicate thing on earth. He steps around any uneven cobblestones that might break his gait. It's as if he remembers my fall. I swear I think he does.

Plattsburgh's pretty, downtown shops have their doors wide open to welcome customers. This town is much smaller than New York or Boston, and it feels sriendly. Maybe someday when I'm grown up, I'll live in a town like this.

The parade starts on Main Street and will end at the fairgrounds where the tent is pitched and waiting.

As we travel through the town, I move effortlessly to standing and then execute a hand stand on Bianco's steady back. When we reach the fairgrounds, I jump off for just a second. "Here, buddy, good job." I give him a carrot, then spring again up onto his back.

This time, our promenade around the inside of the big tent is flawless. My confidence and footing never waver. At the finale of the ride, I do a split leap and land on my feet in the sawdust, bow to applause then lead Bianco back to the stable. His massive head seems higher than usual. He's as proud as I am. As I brush him down, I tell him, "Good boy! Good boy!" over and over again.

Once he's cooled off, I leave the stable. Looking for Neo, I head for the food tent. On the way, I am stopped every few steps to receive congratulations from roustabouts and performers. What good people they are.

Scanning the crowd in the food tent, I don't see him. He must be still working.

He is outside the Oddities tent, holding the hand of a plump, middle-aged woman. Her hair is poorly hennaed and she wears a frilly bonnet trimmed in paper daisies and white lace. Neo's eyes are closed.

As I move closer, I hear him say, "I believe you are thinking about someone dear to you who has passed on."

The woman sniffles hard and her eyes mist over. She removes her wire-rimmed glasses and wipes her eyes on the sleeve of her rose-colored dress.

Neo continues, "Is the someone you lost a man?"

The tears erupt into sobs. Her double chin quivers in grief. "Yes, it was my husband. He died last year of the typhus."

Neo gently raises her face to look into his eyes. A white hand-kerchief magically appears in his fingers. He dabs the tears away. "Only his body is gone from you, ma'am. His spirit remains. I see him hovering there, right over your shoulder."

The woman jerks to look.

"No, no. You can't see him, my dear lady. It's not your time for that. But you will see him again someday. He wants me to tell you that."

"I will?"

"Yes, and he says to remind you that he loved you, still loves you, will always love you."

The woman's face shines with joy and relief even as she blows her nose in Neo's handkerchief. "Oh, thank you, young man. That makes me feel so much better." She extends the soiled handkerchief back to Neo.

He shakes his head, refusing to take it from her. "Don't thank me. Thank him." He gestures to the air above her shoulder.

"Yes, yes . . ." She looks up. "Thank you, Ebenezer. I love you, too." She swivels her head back to Neo. "Now I can live my life as he would have wanted me to live it. I just needed to know I'd see him again." She turns and leaves the tent.

"Neo, that was beautiful," I say quietly as I come closer. "How'd you do it?"

He chuckles. "A little magic, a little razzle dazzle, and a lot of imagination."

"You mean you didn't really see anything?"

"Of course not, Nellie. What do you think I am, a mind reader?"

I stammer in confusion. "But you were so convincing. I thought you really saw that man over her shoulder."

"I'm a magician, remember?" He brushes sawdust off his trousers. "So, how'd the ride go?"

I remember my reason for wanting to find him. "It was incredible, Neo. Bianco was perfect. Everyone is so excited."

Neo pats her shoulder. "I told you so. You can't give in to fear."

"Come on, Neo. Let's have lunch to celebrate, and I'll tell you all about it."

He slows his pace. "Can't, Nellie, not today. Tomorrow, though, definitely tomorrow."

"Where are you going in such a hurry?"

"I have an appointment. An important appointment."

Appointment indeed! And I bet I know exactly who that appointment is with.

CHAPTER THIRTY-THREE

I follow Neo, stepping lightly and at a distance. Once, he turns as though he hears me, but I jump behind a pile of rope.

Good, he didn't spot me.

He walks across the runway and past the entrance gate. "Hi, Neo!" the ticket taker calls out. "Be sure you're back before the next show."

Neo waves and is quickly on his way again. When we're outside the circus grounds, it's more difficult to conceal myself. The ground is flat and treeless, so I stay further back, always looking for a place to hide in a hurry. The area he's walking into now is thick with trees. That'll make it easier to hide.

Reaching a clearing, he tilts his head back and whistles. I recognize the melody. It's called "Only Love Can Tell." The fiddler from the circus band played it for me once. Neo stands very still, studying the branches around him, tilting his head so as not to miss a sound.

The branches part on the far side of the clearing. Neo turns toward the sound. Angelique rushes out of the forest and into Neo's arms. "*Mon amour,*" she says. "I've missed you."

Neo kisses her and my heart nearly stops. Strangely, I'm jealous, wishing I could experience such love. Neo is so tender as he pulls his lips from hers and looks down into her face. He takes her chin in his fingers and slides his hand up into her long, blonde hair. He kisses her again, longer. Angelique moans as if she is going to weep. I'm frozen to the earth.

Can this be ignored? Should I pretend I didn't see it and go on about my business?

Probably, but I can't. This love could get Neo killed.

Angelique looks so white, wrapped there in his dark arms. Trembling, I step forward, out of the coverage of the trees.

"Neo, Angelique, stop."

Angelique screams and backs away; her eyes wide.

Neo speaks first. "Nellie, are you crazy? How dare you follow me?"

Angelique whimpers by his side, covering her face with her hands.

"I mean it, Neo. You two are playing with fire. Surely you know that. What if you get caught? Think of Angelique."

His face crumples. "That's all I do think about. I don't care about myself, but she mustn't be hurt." He starts to walk toward me.

Angelique throws her arms around his neck. "You can't leave me, Neo. You mustn't. I love you so much." Her sobs melt my heart and, obviously, his, because he grabs her back into his arms and strokes her hair.

"Shhh, love, shhh," he whispers. "I'll never leave you. You know that."

I want to scream, "I'll tell. I'll tell your parents," but I can't force my mouth to say the words. That would be a child's taunt, and this is not a childish matter. They're both sixteen years old. Lots of people that age get married, but those are usually people with few prospects. Not like Neo. Not like Angelique. He's brilliant and accomplished. And she's so beautiful, she could be an actress. She could be famous like the girl who played Juliet at the Globe. That girl was not nearly as pretty as Angelique.

So, I stand there a foolish child, gawking, until the tears start coursing down my cheeks. Neo sees me crying. He and Angelique come to me encircling me with their arms.

"Hush, Nellie. Don't cry. It'll be all right," he consoles.

"How can it ever be all right?" I question him in a muffled scream. A dreaded thought comes to me, and I realize it's not the first time I have had that thought. "What if you get her in the family way?"

Neo shakes his head. "That won't happen. We'll remain chaste until we're married. That's a promise we made to each other and now to you."

"Married? There's not a church in Boston that'll marry you, Neo. You know that."

"Yes, I do know that." He chuckles bitterly. "I can just see my parents' church if I showed up there with Angelique and a marriage license. Racism goes both ways. But I have a plan."

"What plan?"

He pauses as if he's not sure he wants to share more. "Have you heard of Frederick Douglass?"

"Of course, I've heard of him. Who hasn't? Seen his picture in the newspaper, too. He's always speaking for equal treatment for the coloreds."

"Do you know where he found equal treatment?"

I shake my head.

"In Ireland. Your country. In Ireland, Frederick Douglass was treated as an equal. He even wrote a book about it. Angelique and I will find a church in Ireland to marry us."

"But you're not even Catholic, Neo. All the churches over there are Catholic."

"Not in Dublin, I've checked."

CHAPTER THIRTY-FOUR

This has been a whirlwind week. We've performed in towns all the way down the Hudson River—Glens Falls, beautiful Lake George, and Saratoga. This morning, we took the parade through the streets of Albany, a city whose brownstones remind me of Boston. This is the state capital of New York and most of the streets have the Dutch names of its early settlers.

The crowds on those streets are elegantly dressed and more subdued than in other towns we've visited. We pass the State Capitol building and stop in front of the Albany City Hall where Mayor George Thacher is introduced. He welcomes us to his town in a long, windy speech. It's hot, and I wish he'd finish. I don't want Bianco to get overheated.

We finally enter into the big tent, which is set up in Thacher park on the outskirts of downtown. This park was named for Mayor George Thacher's uncle, John Boyd Thacher, a former mayor himself.

I give Bianco a bucket of water, and he drinks thirstily. The clowns cavort with the children in the audience. Maurice, the French clown, lets a little boy play with his big red nose and then squeezes a rubber bulb under his costume, which sets off a noisy bleat. The crowd screams in laughter.

The big bass drum pounds a frantic beat. Roustabouts run around the ring and dim the kerosene lamps circling it. The Ringmaster takes his place in the center of the ring. His black suit and top hat make him look impossibly tall and skinny. He holds a bullhorn to his lips, and his deep voice bounces off every canvas wall of the tent. "Ladies and gentlemen, boys and girls, now we come to the *piece de resistance* of The Don Costillo Circus, the greatest circus on earth, the Flying Flauberts, featuring Miss Angelique Flaubert, the soaring angel of the heavens who comes to New York direct from Paris."

The torches circling the ring flare red, blue, and yellow as Angelique arrives at center ring. She reclines on a purple velvet litter carried by her father, Pierre, her brother, Jean, one roustabout, and Neo. All four men are dressed alike, in black costumes that reveal every muscle of their chiseled bodies.

Her sky-blue costume is cut high over matching tights. Her hair is a vision of spun gold dotted with stars and is pulled into a high, loose chignon. Golden tendrils circle her perfect face.

The four men lower the litter to the ground, and she delicately jumps to the sawdust, then flits from one to the next, bestowing upon each man a fleeting kiss to his cheek. She lingers longest at Neo. The crowd hushes, surprised at her display of affection to a Negro.

She dances daintily around the ring until she's ready to climb the rigging to the flyer's perch. Jean ascends hand over hand to the catcher's swing. The two of them swing back and forth, back and forth, closer and closer to each other with each pass. Jean drops from sitting to a position hanging from his knees. Angelique stands on her trapeze, accelerating its movement. As they swing higher and higher, it appears they will collide mid-air. Each near miss results in a hushed gasp from the crowd. For moments, it appears that all the audience packing the big tent stops breathing, eyes glued to the two bodies swinging above them.

Suddenly, at the top of her ascent, Angelique jumps from her trapeze, does a high backward somersault in space, then extends her body straight downward. The audience seems to stop breathing. Then, at the last possible second before Angelique will smack into the sawdust, Jean grasps her ankles and swings her higher.

The crowd doesn't notice her father, Pierre, on the perch until he snatches the trapeze she jumped from and swings it toward the two in the center. When it returns to Pierre, he pushes it back harder toward Angelique.

Jean releases Angelique from his grasp, sending her soaring nearly to the top of the canvas tent and again, she dives toward the floor. At the last second, the trapeze her father swung catches her under the knees, and she swings again upside down across the center of the ring, throwing kisses at the roaring crowd.

Angelique does a spectacular double somersault in the air and lands lightly on the perch next to her father who stands there, muscular arms casually crossed over his chest. The audience, berserk with excitement, screams her name. "Angelique! Angelique! Angelique! Angel of the sky!"

The Ringmaster screams through his bull horn. "And now, the great Pierre Flaubert will demonstrate the trick that has made the Flying Flauberts the greatest trapeze act in the world." He points toward the top of the tent. "Do you see that ring hanging from the center up there?"

Every face in the tent cranes upward to spot the shining metal ring attached to the peak of the tent. It gleams in a spotlight. The Ringmaster's voice booms through the horn. "Pierre Flaubert will now execute his world-famous swing to ring trick; the death-defying stunt that has stunned audiences across Europe and America."

Pierre brightens the lamps on his perch upward. He waves to the crowd, his silver hair a shining halo. Pierre's physique in his skin-tight black costume is stunning. He is lean, taut, and exquisitely muscled. Except for his hair, he could be a man half his age.

Angelique stands beside her father and pins a St. Christopher medal to his shirt. Though the crowd can barely see the pin, they roar in approval. The gesture has been well publicized since we arrived in New York. Jean stands on the opposite perch, holding a trapeze in his hands.

Pierre begins to swing, his pumping body carrying him higher and higher. When he's close to the ring, he flies from the trapeze and misses it. No one notices the trapeze swung to him by Angelique until it catches him under the knees. The crowd, thinking he fell, erupts in screaming.

Pierre stands and waves to the audience. Now, though, comes the serious part. He drops from standing to catch the trapeze in his hands. He swings higher and higher; higher than before. The crowd is nearly silent except for a baby crying somewhere in the top of the bleachers. That wail, though no one outside the troupe knows this, is produced by a thirty-year-old midget who makes an extra dollar for crying on cue. It is a perfect contretemps to the hushed breathlessness in the tent.

One powerful kerosene lamp is lighted and directed through a funnel toward the ring attached to the center pole of the tent. All other lights are extinguished. As eyes adjust to this one focus, Pierre swings toward the ring. After five swings back and forth, at exact center, he propels himself up. Gasps become audible in the big tent as his hands approach the ring.

He grasps it in the fingers of his left hand. He extends his right hand out to the crowd in triumph, a grin creasing his face. The crowd roars approval and Pierre bows to the audience, still grasping the ring.

But this time is different. We are startled by a sound we've never heard before. It's the sound of metal scraping against canvas. Pierre looks upward. What he sees flexes his body into an ungodly angle. "No!" he screams.

The ring is pulling loose from its mooring. Pierre yells something in French and gestures wildly for a trapeze. Angelique, seeing what's happening, swings one toward the center. As he falls, ring still in his hand, he desperately tries to propel himself toward the swinging trapeze. He misses it by an inch.

"*Merde!*" he screams as he falls toward the ground. Time freezes into disbelief. Mothers shield children's eyes. The form in black plummets toward the ground like a rag doll, slamming into the sawdust with a heavy thud; a sickening symphony of cracking bones.

People leap screaming from the bleachers trying to escape the horror. The Ringmaster strives to control them but can't. Ankles turn and children fall, crying in pain, to the floor. One woman, heavy with a baby screams that her water has broken.

In the chaos, no one notices as Jean drops to the ground from a high trapeze and runs to his father. Angelique seems frozen on her perch, eyes wide with horror, her hands covering her mouth.

When Jean reaches Pierre, his moan fills the tent to its peak. It is the sound of pure anguish.

CHAPTER THIRTY-FIVE

In shocked silence, the audience files out of the tent. Heads shake in disbelief. They thought this was another trapeze trick; that Pierre would stand and laugh at the great joke he had played; that he was alive and would fly again.

But slowly, reality dawns. "Why isn't he moving?" "This is a trick, isn't it? Isn't it?" In minutes, the crowd realizes that the horror is real. The great Pierre Flaubert is dead.

I push through the throng of people searching for Neo and Angelique. Tears blur my vision. "Have you seen them?" I ask. Each person shakes his or her head. I don't know where to turn.

As I stagger into the women's quarters, Bridey sees me. "Ah, thank God, girl. I couldn't find you in the crowd. Are you all right?"

Crying harder, I say, "Yes, but, oh, Bridey, it was awful. And I can't find Omar and Angelique. I must find them!" My voice is high, near hysteria.

She grabs hold of me tightly. "Felicity, try to be calm. The Ringmaster says they're holed up in the train with her brother, trying to figure out what to do."

A male voice calls out, "Are you decent in there?" It is Phineas.

"Yes, come ahead," Bridey answers.

Phineas looks as devastated as Bridey and I feel.

"What're we going to do, Phineas?" Bridey asks, her voice cracking.

"We'll close down the circus for the rest of this week. Then, we'll see." He shakes his head. "Why did that ring pull loose?"

Neo's voice calls from outside the door, "May I come in?"

I fling the door open and grab him into my arms as I would a child. His back is quaking; his eyes red and raw from crying. "Where's Angelique?" I ask.

"In her compartment with Jean. They must leave the circus. They can't go back to France because of the war. Napoleon the third hates Pierre. Apparently, they served in the army together years ago and Pierre called him a fool." He sinks down miserably to the sawdust of the floor. "They're talking of going to Montreal. They have an aunt there."

"When will they leave?" I ask, massaging his shoulders.

"As soon as they can arrange the burial," he replies, then whispers. "I planned to speak to Pierre tonight and ask for Angelique's hand. Now, now . . ." He lowers his head into his hands and chokes back tears.

The week drags by in a blur of grief. Pierre was respected by every member of this troupe. His burial is quiet and desperately sad. He was a consummate performer and a gentleman. Every person had been touched by his kindness.

Angelique and Jean decide they will definitely go to Montreal where Pierre's sister lives. She's the only relative they have left.

On Sunday, Neo and I take Angelique and Jean to the train station. We are a somber foursome.

The trip will be long and difficult. Neo researched trains to Montreal, and they are few and far between. The best he could do was find a train to Northern Vermont that sometimes has a transfer to Montreal.

Before the two of them board, Neo whispers to Angelique. "Write to me. I will be faithful, my love. When I graduate, I'll come for you. I'll take you to Ireland and we'll be married there. Wait for me."

CHAPTER THIRTY-SIX

When the circus finally reopens in Troy, New York, a town across the river from Albany, a pall of grief hangs over the entire troupe. Yet, Phineas keeps telling us the show must go on.

I'll put on the spangly costume and jump on Bianco's back as though everything is exactly as it's supposed to be, but it's not. Pierre is dead. Angelique and Jean are gone to Canada. Neo is so sad he scares me. He won't even talk to me. When I try, he looks at me with red-streaked eyes and remains mute.

Bridey tries to console me with her warm arms, but her grief is as deep as mine. Wilbur fears she's going to cry herself to death.

I put on my costume and ask her to do my hair. She loves doing that, and I want to distract her from her sadness. She does an especially beautiful job today, and I tell her so. As I gaze in the mirror, I am surprised at my reflection. I look older. Can turning fourteen have made a difference? My bosom is beginning to swell a bit, and I see sharp angles in my face that used to be round and childish. For the first time, I see the girl my da bragged about back in Boston; his pretty Nellie Kelly.

I do my tricks on Bianco flawlessly. The Ringmaster leads the crowd in oohs and aahs each time I land a difficult leap. The audience would never suspect my heart is breaking.

As I finish my last stunt, I jump to the sawdust, pirouette for the crowd and take a deep bow. As I crouch there, listening to the applause, two black boots slam into the sawdust in front of me. The boots of a man.

I remain kneeling, strangely afraid to confront whomever stands there. In slow motion, I lift my eyes up to his face. His hair is short and blonde. He has a hint of a beard now and his eyes are very blue and angry; the visage of a young warrior.

"Sean?" I gasp. It is Sean O'Halloran. My heart stops.

He grabs me roughly by the arm and pulls me to standing, glaring down into my eyes, an angry Viking on a quest.

"What are you doing here?" I ask, confused and flustered.

"I think the question should be, what the hell are you doing here, Nellie?"

Sputtering and incoherent I follow the pull of his hand as he drags me out of the circus ring. The audience hushes, confused. Phineas wrings his hands and Bridey's mouth hangs open in disbelief. I wrench my arm away from Sean and bow again to the crowd. "Thank you! Thank you!" I yell. "Everything's all right. This is an old friend."

But Sean is far from friendly. Red-faced and snarling, he orders, "Follow me! Now!"

The Ringmaster announces the next act through his megaphone and I, not wanting to bring more attention to this embarrassing scene, follow Sean out to the back of the tent. "How did you find me?" I whisper.

He stops and faces me. "Half of Boston is looking for you, Nellie. Your parents are crazy with worry. Your father talked to Sister Sarah and found out you were always talking about trapezes and circuses. Right now, there are people canvassing every circus in the East. Molly, Shannon, my father, your mother and father, Mr. and Mrs. Okafor, and lots of other people Mr.

Okafor hired. You're lucky I'm the one who found you and not your mother."

Neo runs around the corner of the tent but stops in a hurry when he sees Sean, who stands over him, glaring in rage. "Are you crazy? You're sixteen years old. You should know better. She's a thirteen-year-old child."

"Fourteen!" I yell. "And, I'm not a child. I've done something you'd never have the guts to try. I joined the circus. I'm grown up."

"A grown-up wouldn't pull such a stunt, you silly fool. Grown-ups are responsible. You should be thinking about school, not joining a circus."

"That's why I ran away! I have no chance for school. Fiona Doggett cooked that goose for me with her lies. You must know that. Everybody in Boston knows."

Sean shakes his head. "Since you've been gone, your parents have visited the new Principal of Girls High. Father Ruzzo smuggled out your grades from St. Augustine's. The principal has agreed to meet with you, but you're the one who'll have to convince her that you're suitable to attend her school. Better hope she never learns you've pulled this crazy stunt."

CHAPTER THIRTY-SEVEN

As I stand there trying to comprehend what Sean is saying, Neo approaches him. He extends his hand. Sean smashes Neo's hand away from him. "Are you crazy? Taking her off to join the circus?"

Neo casts his eyes downward, embarrassed in front of those observing the scene. A handful of performers and roustabouts circles us.

Suddenly, Sean lunges at Neo, his fist raised as if to strike him. I jump on Sean's back, kicking his ribs with my heels as I would a horse. He shrugs me off him, and when he turns to me, his eyes are flaming.

The rage in those eyes frightens me. Someone could get hurt here. I've never seen Sean so enraged, and I must calm him down. "Sean," I say quietly. "I am not a kid. I'm fourteen years old; older than my mother was when she sailed from Ireland. Neo protected me like a brother."

"He's not your brother!" he yells. "He's a nigger!"

Quiet falls over all of us. No one in this group ever used such an ugly word in front of us. Bridey steps next to me and circles my shoulders with her arm. Wilbur stands beside Neo.

"Young man," Wilbur reprimands, "we don't use such language

here. This boy is our friend and he has suffered a terrible loss. Please apologize."

Sean's laugh is mean. "I'm here to take both of these *friends* of yours back to Boston. His father is paying me a pretty penny for doing just that. Now get out of my way." He shoves past Wilbur, nearly knocking him off his feet.

Bridey puts her arm around my shoulders and whispers in my ear. "Be careful of him, Nellie. He's a bad one."

Bad one? All I've ever heard from the O'Hallorans are raves about Sean. He's the smartest. He's the handsomest. They've all worshipped him since the day he was taken from Kathleen's dead body. My mother says they spoiled him rotten.

"Come on, Nellie," he insists, roughly grabbing my hand. "You, too, Blackie."

I try to embrace Bridey, weeping into her shoulder, but Sean pulls me roughly away from her "Oh, Bridey, will I ever see you again?" I hold onto her for dear life.

"Hush, *Mo Cuisle*. If God wills us to meet again, we will. Just take care of yourself. She kisses me softly on the cheek and whispers, "Try not to be alone with that one." She looks at Sean. Her words of caution startle me. I've never thought of Sean as dangerous.

But he seems so as he wrenches me from her arms. "I'll leave the costume in the trunk."

Her hands are shaking as she waves me on.

We do not speak again.

I take off my costume with Sean standing guard outside the tent. I hold it up and turn it around, sparkling in the light. It is so pretty. I loved wearing it and will miss it. I hug it once and toss it into the trunk. Another girl will wear it now.

When I've changed, Sean pulls his wagon up to our tent, and Neo and I silently load our few belongings into it. I take with me only what I brought into this adventure—one small satchel and a drawstring purse. I climb up beside Sean. Neo sits miserably behind us. It is a quiet ride, except for the steady clopping of the horse's hooves.

As we ride, I steal glances at Sean's face. He's handsome all right, but his angry mouth looks set in granite. He's heavy on the whip and I flinch for the poor horse. That is something my father would despise. I hate it as well. A chill ripples my shoulders and I wish I had a shawl. *Where did that come from?* It's August and quite warm, but the chill remains and intensifies each time I look at him.

I remain silent until we ride into Rensselaer, New York. "Did you tell my parents you found me?"

His grim mouth tightens even more as he brings the whip down smartly on the horse's back. "Of course. I sent them a telegram while you packed. Yours, too, Neo."

"Did you hear anything back from them?" I ask.

"Just 'Thank God.'"

"How are my folks?" Neo asks.

"Your father is worried sick, but healthy otherwise. Haven't seen your mother."

I look back at Neo. He slumps down into his shoulders.

"And mine?" I ask.

"They're all right, but your dad is working himself to death."

"He is?" Alarm takes my voice higher.

He turns to face me, relaxing the whip in his hands. "Yes, he thinks he drove you away over some fight you had."

I lower my head.

"He spends all his time at work on pro bono cases. He's not making any money, but he doesn't want to be home. People say it reminds him that you're not there."

My father used to love being home. *Oh, Da, I'm so sorry.*

"I've got to hurry this horse along now. I want to make it to the train tonight." He whips the horse heavily, and once again, I cringe for the poor animal.

We ride along more quickly, but in silence. We are all deep in our own thoughts.

I should never have run off with Neo. If I'd stayed in Boston, Da wouldn't be spending all his time at his office. It's my fault. I know it is. I'll never do anything bad again.

We settle in on the train and I try to sleep; but each time I close my eyes, I see my father's worried face. The iron wheels on the train track seem to repeat, *You're to blame. You're to blame. You're to blame.*

The next afternoon, the train pulls up to the Boston terminal, and through the steam on the window I see them. My mother and father with Uncle Kam and Aunt Imani. They all look older than before; just a few weeks ago. *How can that be?* But there's no doubt that my father looks thinner, and my mother's red hair, pulled into a topknot, seems dull.

As we pull closer, I see that her topknot is streaked with silver. *Why did I never notice that before?* The train grinds to a stop. Sean climbs down the steps first, and then offers his hand to help me down. Neo follows. I'm so scared I don't want to get off, but I must.

My mother rushes to me as soon as my boot hits the platform. She is crying as she catches me into her arms and holds on as though she'll never let go. Even though my father's haggard face tells me how worried he's been, he smiles. He doesn't look mad any longer.

Aunt Imani is sobbing, but Uncle Kam simply says, "Neo, we're going to have a talk when we get home."

Neo is resolutely miserably.

We had been so convinced that running away to join the circus was something we owed ourselves. We thought we were entitled to our great adventure, yet coming back to these sad people feels awful.

My mother wipes the tears from her eyes. "Nellie, what you and Neo did was terrible."

Terrible? "I'm sorry, Mother. We wanted to have an adventure like you and Uncle Kam had."

My mother looks at Uncle Kam and shakes her head.

Uncle Kam speaks sternly. "That *adventure* as you call it was forced on us, not of our choosing. We both nearly died on that hell ship. What you and Neo did was foolhardy and cruel."

Cruel? We never intended cruelty. We just wanted our adventure. And we did have it, for a while.

CHAPTER THIRTY-EIGHT

Uncle Kam takes us home in his carriage. My mother refuses to let go of my hand for a second. She sits straight as a board, but when I steal a glance at her, there are worry lines I never noticed before . . . and so much gray in her hair. Her jaw is clenched tight and she grinds her teeth together.

My father hardly speaks.

"Mary, do you want us to come in?" Aunt Imani asks. "Or would you want to come to our house?"

"No, dear. Nellie needs to have a nice home-cooked dinner She looks thin."

I look thin? No, she's the thin one. She and Da.

Neo and I exchange a miserable goodbye. He forces a quick smile and waves as the carriage pulls off into the gathering dusk.

My legs are heavy as we walk up the five stairs to our front porch. They felt light as air that morning I met Neo for our adventure. No more. A few weeks can change things so much.

"Nellie, I want you to help me with dinner."

I follow her into the kitchen and pick up an apron. As I tie it on, I make a vow to myself. I hurt my parents, especially my father. Now that I'm home, I must make him happy again. I close my eyes and pray. *Dear God. I promise never to disobey again.*

As I pick up the knife to peel the potatoes, Da's voice calls out, "Nellie, come into the parlor for a bit," My mother tilts her head to his voice and smiles, so I put the potato and knife down on the table.

When I go into the living room again, Da pats the space next to him on the davenport. As I sit down, he puts his arm around me. It feels so good I want it to last forever. "Mary," he calls out "is there any stout in the house?"

She laughs for the first time since I got home. "Yes, love, there is."

"I'll get it." I jump to my feet and go into the kitchen to pour him a glass. My mother grins at me. "He gave up spirits while you were gone. He even started praying."

"He did?"

"Believe it or not. That's all the man did, work and pray. You sit with your father and tell him all about your time away. I'll peel the potatoes."

"Do you mind?"

"Nah, love. He needs you more than I do right now. Keep him company." I take off the apron and join him on the couch, handing him the beer as I sit down. As he sips his drink, I tell him about riding Bianco and my tricks, and about Phineas, Wilbur, and Bridey. "Da, she was from Ireland, Killarney, and she had the biggest, blackest beard you ever did see."

"She did, did she?" The sound of his laughter warms my soul. I snuggle closer to him.

"Oh yes, and she was so kind. She was like a mother to me."

I feel him stiffen. "Nellie, no one can ever replace your mother. You know that now, don't you?"

"Yes, yes, of course I do, Da. I'm so sorry I made you mad that time I said something mean to her." Laying my head on his shoulder, his bones cut into my ear through his shirt. "How much weight have you lost?"

"I don't know. It seemed to fall off all of a sudden."

"Was it when I left?"

"I just don't know, Nellie."

But I know.

Chapter Thirty-Nine

After we say Grace, dinner is a quiet affair, in spite of my mother's gaiety. She has made a horseradish sauce for the beef and mashed potatoes. She tells me she got the recipe from *Godey's Lady Book*, then chatters about how Uncle Kam has arranged for me to meet with the Principal of Girls High and how she herself got my grades from Sister Sarah after Father Ruzzo ordered the nun to give them up. She had to promise Sister she would never tell Monsignor how she got them.

"That dear little nun is so scared of being sent back to the old country, she doesn't know what to do." She laughs at that, though I don't really see much funny about it.

My father eats his food with relish.

My mother comments, "Daniel, you haven't eaten that much in weeks."

With that, he helps himself to more mashed potatoes.

We continue eating until my father speaks. "Nellie, you have an appointment on Tuesday with the Principal. She wants to meet with you alone."

My stomach clenches. *Did Uncle Kam make a donation to the school to get me this appointment? And if he did, that doesn't mean they'll let me in, not after what I've done. But then again, people do lots of things for money.*

"What's she like?" I ask. "The Principal, I mean."

"Her name is Miss Spencer, and she's new in Boston, from London. No one knows much about her." Mother pushes her food about, preparing another fork full.

I glance at her to see if she found the word "London" distasteful. Neither of my parents favor British people. It's all about the way the English treated the Irish. I guess Britain still controls Ireland, but Ireland is fighting now for home rule.

"Is she old? Miss Spencer?"

"I've heard she's about my age." Mother takes another bite and looks for my reaction.

She's old. "What did she say about my running away?"

"We've only spoken by letter. I mentioned the circus, but she didn't comment on it."

She didn't comment? How can that be? Most Boston head mistresses would find such behavior scandalous. I bet she'll be afraid to take a chance on such a reckless girl. "What do you think I should wear?"

"Something simple, I think . . ." She pauses in thought. "Your white blouse and navy skirt would be grand."

As if I have many choices. Besides my school uniform, I have only two skirts and two blouses. I certainly can't wear my uniform. That would just remind this Miss Spencer that I'd been expelled. I wish it were colder, then I could carry my bunny muff.

The doorbell rings, startling me. "Please answer it, Nellie," mother orders.

"Uncle Kam!?" I was startled to see him. *What could have brought him all the way back here?* "I'll get my mother."

"I want to talk to you," he answers sternly. He walks to the kitchen and states, "Mary, Daniel, I just want a word with Nellie."

"All right, Kam," she answers, a question clouding the simple words. She'll ask him later what this is about. I'm certain of that.

We sit down facing each other.

"Are you mad at me?" I ask him.

He pauses. "More disappointed than mad, Nellie. And much more disappointed in Neo than I am in you. He's older. He should have known better."

I sniff hard, trying to hold back the tears. "Oh, Uncle Kam, we're both so sorry. We just wanted an adventure."

His dark eyes flare with anger. "Stop saying that. Your mother and I did not choose the adventure we had. It was forced on us."

With the way he looks and speaks, the dam breaks and the tears flow. "Uncle Kam, please forgive Neo. He's been very badly hurt."

He becomes still and stiff.

"That's why I want to talk to you. Neo won't tell me anything. What do you mean, hurt?"

Should I tell him? I have no choice; not with those eyes boring into me like that.

"Did he mention Angelique?" When I see the confusion on his face, I think I should have held my tongue.

"He mentioned no one. Who's Angelique?"

"She's a French aerialist in the circus. She's sixteen, same as Neo."

It takes a moment for the words to sink in. "And what is she to Neo?"

I'm tired of secrets, and he needs to know this. "She and Neo are in love and want to marry someday. But . . . but . . ."

"But what, Nellie? But what?"

"But her father fell from the trapeze and died, so Angelique went to Canada with her brother. She has an aunt there."

He stares into my eyes even more deeply. "Is Angelique colored?" He puts his hands on my shoulders.

I hesitate just a moment too long. His hands begin to grip harder. "Nellie?"

By now, I am crying hard. Tears flow down my face and my nose is running.

He gives me a handkerchief.

I compose myself first. "No, Uncle Kam, she's a beautiful, blonde white girl."

He closes his eyes and shakes his head. "Oh, no."

His face crumples and I want to explain; to make his concern go away. "Neo says someday they'll go to Ireland and get married; that the Irish accept colored people better than Americans."

He releases my shoulders, still shaking his head. "Well, hopefully, another girl will come along while they're apart, a girl of his own race. He's only sixteen after all."

"Yes, that could happen." I pretend to agree with him, but I don't believe my own words. If Uncle Kam had seen the way Neo and Angelique look at each other, he wouldn't think so either.

CHAPTER FORTY

I dress carefully the following Tuesday morning. This is the day of the appointment with Miss Spencer. As I pull on my lisle stockings and black boots, my hands shake. I'm more nervous than I want to admit, even to myself.

Brushing out my hair, my mind flings things back and forth, a flurry of croquet balls bouncing off the mallet. *What if I don't get in? And what if I do get in? Will I be able to pass the courses? And if I do pass them, will I really be able to go to Wellesley College? What makes me think I'm so special? I know one thing for sure, I don't want to be in a circus ever again, or fly from a trapeze. I want to be a teacher. But what if I'm a terrible teacher? What then?* I say a silent prayer, *Dear God, I promise I'll be a good teacher.*

With my hair is finished, tied up in a navy ribbon that matches my skirt, I pinch my cheeks and dab a little Vaseline on my lips. It'll dry before my mother notices it. She doesn't approve, even though it has no color. I started putting Vaseline on my mouth when I was in the circus. Actually, all us girls put it on our teeth so our lips wouldn't stick to them as we smiled at the audience.

My da is already sitting at the table in the kitchen. I kiss him on the cheek.

"Ah, Nellie Kelly, don't you look grown up? Pretty as a sunset on Galway Bay."

"Thanks, Da."

"But you'd best rub some of that grease off your lips. Your mother will not approve."

I'd forgotten that he'd feel it with the kiss. "Yes, sir." I pretend to rub my mouth with my napkin. "Da, will you take me to my appointment?"

"Yes. I'd planned on that. We have an hour before we have to leave."

It strikes me that my father is still the best-looking man in Boston. Lots of people think Robert E. Lee, that General from the South, is the handsomest man of our time. But I saw a picture of Lee in the *Boston Globe* when he died earlier this year, and he doesn't compare to my father. Besides, Lee had white hair.

Mother bustles into the kitchen. She's always in a rush, it seems. "A messenger just came with this note." She holds it up in the air. "Berthe McGonigle is in labor, and her time is on her. She needs me." She paces the kitchen floor as nervous as a cat in a room full of rockers. "How can I take Nellie to her appointment?"

My father stands. "Mary, love, I want to take her."

"Well, that's good, isn't it? Are you feeling good?"

"Yes, right as rain."

"All right, but don't overdo it."

"Quit your worrying, woman. You're enough to turn my hair grey."

"I see a few specks of silver there right now." She grins mischievously as she runs her fingers through his thick hair.

"And I see a couple of snowy strands in that red mop on your head as well, Mrs. Kelly." He pats her bustle.

I turn away, happy to see they're not ready to eat each other's heads off any more.

She pulls on her cloak, gesturing. "Nellie, come here."

She sits on the sofa, and so do I. "Do you know what you're going to say to Miss Spencer?"

"Yes, Mother. I'm going to tell her how important it is for me to go to Girls High; that I love children and want to be a teacher and help other girls."

She pats my thigh, "That'll do," she says, then stands determinedly.

"Of course, I don't know what her questions will be. What if she asks why I ran away and joined the circus?"

She sits back down and takes both my hands in hers, staring deeply into my eyes. "Nellie, it's always best to just tell the truth. If this Miss Spencer is as smart as I've heard she is, she may understand better than you think." She kisses my cheek and prepares to leave. "I must hurry. Poor Berthe is probably frightened out of her wits. It's her first, you know."

Oh yes. I can only imagine how terrified poor Mrs. McGonigle must be. Once, I helped my mother deliver a baby at Kathleen's Haven, and once was more than enough. The whole thing scared me to death. So much yelling and blood everywhere. Poor woman had no idea what she'd go through to push that baby out of her. And then, it ended up looking just like a baboon.

My mother had said, "Oh, he's beautiful."

I saw her with new eyes that day. She could fib better than me.

She pulls on her gloves. "Must go, Nellie. Good, good luck."

"Thank you, Mother."

How much luck will I need at this meeting? What's she going to ask me? Will she like me? If she doesn't, I'll be a disappointment to my parents and to Uncle Kam and Aunt Imani.

Dear God, please send me every bit of luck you can muster. Amen.

CHAPTER FORTY-ONE

As we pull up to the stately brick building off Newton Street, a flock of butterflies battle for space in my chest. Girls High. Dedicated earlier this year. This new school is on the same site as another one built before I was born. Before that, there was no high school education available for women anywhere in Boston.

It never seems right that boys have had opportunities in this town forever, like Sean and Neo. Both went to fancy prep schools and now Sean's at Harvard and Neo's off to Howard. But things might be changing. Mother talks about Suffragettes, a newspaper called *The Revolution,* and equal rights for women. Around here? Well, I don't know.

We arrive at the school and father pats my leg. "Good luck, Nellie."

"You can't come in with me?" My heart stalls a beat.

"Nope. Miss Spencer was very specific. She wants to see you alone."

I kiss him on the cheek. Though it's hollower than I remember, his color looks good. Thank God. I can't afford to worry about him.

I square my shoulders and walk up the stone steps to the front door of Girls High.

Inside, I look around for a sign indicating the Principal's Office. I don't see it. Walking up the big stairway to the second floor, my knees tremble. I grab onto the railing.

The building feels cold, though it's still balmy outside. Then I see her office. Miss Corinne Spencer, Principal. Taking a big breath, I brace my knees against the shaking.

I knock.

From inside, a voice rings out, "Come in, please." It is tinged with an accent. *Irish? No, my mother said she came from England.*

I open the door.

She sits primly behind a large mahogany desk. A tiny woman, about the same age as my mother; not pretty, but not homely either, with bright eyes that look intelligent and interested.

"Miss Spencer?"

"Yes, and you must be Miss Kelly."

"Yes, ma'am."

"Please be seated."

I sit very straight and cross my ankles the way ladies should. She never takes her eyes off me. That makes me jittery again, but I clasp my hands in my lap to stop them from trembling and try a small smile.

"So, you want to attend Girls High this fall?" Now the accent is stronger and is clearly British. In spite of my parents' loathing of the sound, I find it attractive.

"Oh, yes, Miss Spencer, more than I can say. It's what I've wanted for so very long."

"I also heard you scared your parents out of their wits recently by running away to the circus."

I lower my eyes. "Yes, ma'am." I knew she'd bring it up, but I don't know what will please her and what will make her think I'm callous. I decide on honesty. It's all I can manage.

"Yes, ma'am. And I'm sorry they were so scared. I left them a note and I thought that would reassure them. Plus, I was with a family friend whom they trust."

"A young man, I understand?"

"Yes, Neo. He's the son of my Uncle Kam. We've grown up like brother and sister."

"And he's a colored boy?"

Again, I lower my eyes. "Yes, ma'am." *Is she a racist? If she is, she can keep her school.*

"Didn't you realize what people would think?"

I look her in the eye. "Yes. But you see, I don't see Neo as different than me." I feel myself getting mad about this questioning but calm myself down. *Is she as bad as some Americans? I hope I'm wrong.*

"Do you think I'm judging you based on Neo's race, Nellie?"

Again, honesty is the best policy. I take a deep breath. "Yes, ma'am, I kind of do think that."

She grins, and her face becomes beautiful. "To tell you the truth, your disobedience in this instance makes me want to know you better."

What? "But, but, I thought everybody in Boston would think I was awful for doing what I did."

The grin widens. "I'm sure many in Boston do feel that way. It was a terribly bold thing for a girl your age to do."

I lower my face, hoping I look demure. "Yes, ma'am."

"Nellie?"

I lift my eyes to her gaze. "Yes, ma'am?"

"I'm of the persuasion that bold is not necessarily bad in young women."

"You are?"

"Yes. Have you ever heard of the *Ladies of Langham Place*?"

I strain my brain but come up with nothing. "I don't think so."

"They're a London-based group of women trying to achieve reform in the treatment of women."

"Reform?"

"Yes, particularly in the area of voting."

"Oh, like the Suffragettes?"

Again, the smile. "Precisely. Years ago, I attended The Seneca Falls Convention in America. I met a woman there named Susan Anthony. Do you know her name?"

"Yes, ma'am, I do. My mother says if she wasn't so busy, she'd work with Susan B. Anthony. She's read all about her in *The Revolution*. She's mad because after the War, coloreds were allowed to vote, but women aren't."

She smiles broadly. "Ah, I see then where you get your gumption, from your mother."

Really? I've never thought of my mother as having gumption, but I guess she does. She came over from Ireland alone and by the time she was seventeen she had opened Kathleen's Haven. When I think of some of my friends' mothers, it seems all they do is buy new clothes and go to the hairdresser. I guess my mother does have gumption.

All of a sudden, Miss Spencer becomes very serious. "Well, I received your test scores from a Sister Sarah via a man named Father Ruzzo."

I am so nervous.

"Your grades are excellent, particularly in Mathematics."

Mathematics? Oh, Arithmetic. "Thank you, ma'am."

"I believe you're the kind of girl we need to have at Girls High. A young woman with gumption—with guts." She titters a bit at that. It did sound funny with that high-class English accent.

"Are you saying I'm accepted?"

"Why, yes indeed, Miss Kelly. That's exactly what I'm saying."

CHAPTER FORTY-TWO

My father waits outside in the wagon. When he spots me coming down that long staircase, he turns the page on his newspaper and folds it. I climb up beside him and decide to try a little joke.

"Well?" he asks.

I turn my lips down and try to look sad, but then I notice his hands are trembling. He is as nervous as I was earlier, and it would be cruel to keep him in suspense. Besides, I don't want to contain my excitement another minute. "I'm in, Da. I start in September! Oh, that's next month!"

"Then why the long face when I first saw you?"

I giggle. "Just trying to trick you."

He grins and pulls me in for a hug. His shoulders relax under my fingers. "Sometimes I could murder you, girl. You with your tricks." The horse stops nodding his head and pulls the wagon away from the curb, following the gentle tug of Da's hands on the reins.

"I thought you'd get in, Nellie." He keeps his right arm around me, controlling the reins with his left hand. The pressure of his hand on my shoulder makes me feel safe. "You deserve it. And by the way, you can thank your mother and Uncle Kam for keeping up the pressure. And, Father Ruzzo really went to bat for you." He chuckles. "He took on the whole Catholic Church hierarchy and they didn't even see it happening. If they ever figure out all he pulled, I'm afraid they'll defrock him."

When we get home and tell my mother, she dances an Irish jig right in the middle of our living room. Da grabs her in for a kiss and a whirl, and I clap my hands for them. My heart swells, seeing them so happy.

She had put a large corned beef in the stove this morning before leaving for work in case we would have something to celebrate this night. And do we ever!

Come evening time, we have a party, a rare occasion in this house. Uncle Kam, Aunt Imani, and Neo come over, along with Uncle Tommy, his crabby-faced wife, and Molly and Sean O'Halloran. And Martha, of course. Wonderful Martha.

Flowers fresh from the garden fill every vase we own, and my mother's new lace curtains flutter from the living room windows. Her tablecloth, saved from the ship, and restored to immaculate, mended condition, covers the kitchen table. It's topped with plates, glasses, utensils, bottles of whiskey and wine, and a pitcher of fresh-squeezed lemonade. An ice chest holds bottles of dark Guinness beer. The house smells delicious and rich with the scents of meat, vegetables, and baking breads and desserts.

It doesn't take long for the grownups' cheeks to turn pink from their drinks, and smiles wreathe every face in the room.

"You join your friends, Nellie." Mother scoots me out of the kitchen. "Molly and I will bring the food to the table and the guests can help themselves."

I grab the plate of Martha's magical cookies and take them into the living room, helping myself to one before I sit it on a side table.

Sean is the first to congratulate me. "Excellent, Nellie. You made it into Girls High."

"I sure did."

Molly grabs me in her arms. "I knew you'd get in. You're one of the brightest girls in this town."

"But not as bright as I am, right, Molly?" Sean squares his shoulders and stands to his full height. Looking up at him, I feel dainty and proud to be just standing beside him.

"That is to be determined, sir," she answers cuffing him gently on his cheek. "Don't you be getting all cocky on us now that you're in first unit at Harvard. It's easier for boys."

"What are you studying?" I ask, looking up at him and marveling again at how very handsome he is, and how tall. He's as tall as my da.

"Pre-law, with an eye to becoming the first Irish Mayor of Boston."

"But that's crazy. I mean, only the Brahmins ever get elected Mayor in this town, don't they?" I've heard that in this very room since I was a child.

"Not crazy at all, Nellie. The Irish population has grown so much we're nearly in the majority. We just need to be organized."

My father, overhearing, clamps his hand on Sean's shoulder. "Good for you, boy. Once upon a time, I thought I'd be the first, but the time wasn't right. I hope it's right for you."

Neo stands back from the others, his eyes guarded and downcast. I haven't seen him since we got back from the circus, and I've missed him. I walk over to him. "Neo, aren't you happy for me? You don't look it."

"You know I am, Nellie, but far from surprised. I knew that between your mother and my father, they'd figure this out. And Father Ruzzo helped a lot, too. You're smart. You deserve an education."

I hug him. "Thanks. You're a real friend." And he is. But he still looks unhappy. "Are you all right? You seem down in the dumps."

He drops his head forward and when he brings it back up, his eyes glisten. "I don't want to spoil your party, Nellie. It's just that I miss Angelique."

"Have you heard from her?"

"Not yet. I know I will in time. She'll write as soon as she has a permanent address."

"You must have patience."

He grins. "Yes, patience; not what I'm best at."

"I know, Neo. Can I help?"

"Just let me talk about her once in a while, Nellie. I can't even mention her in the presence of my parents. You're the only one here who knew her; who saw how much we care for each other."

I take both his hands and stare into his eyes. "Yes, Neo. Anytime you need to talk, find me. I'll always listen."

"Come on, you two, this is a celebration. Join it." Uncle Tommy's voice startles us. Then, he bursts into a slightly off-key rendition of "The Rose of Tralee." My mother and da join in, she in a clear soprano and he an octave lower.

I lead Neo over to the others. As we approach Sean, his face is set in a stony look of disapproval. He turns his back on us as we draw close to him.

Shocked by his behavior, I take his arm and try to tease him into a smile. He shrugs my hand away, stalks off, and fills his plate again.

As the song ends, my father raises a glass of stout. "To Nellie. The future belongs to you now, girl."

Molly and Neo lift glasses of lemonade and say, "To Nellie." Neo's smile lifts my spirits.

"Thank you, all." I am touched by the joy reflected in every face surrounding me—every face but Sean's.

But then, with no warning, Sean strides over to me, puts his arm around my waist and squeezes. I am embarrassed at this in front of my parents, but when I look up into his eyes, an electric current passes through me. I've never felt this before, and it frightens me. To escape those eyes, I jump away from him and smack his arm playfully. "You're fresh."

Still laughing, I search for my mother. Now, she's not smiling. I go to her and tilt my head, a question in my eyes. She kisses my cheek and murmurs. "Oh, love, many temptations may come your way. Mind them closely."

Her words confuse me, but she says no more, so I turn back to the crowd of raised glasses and, forcing a smile, thank them all again. Then, I take a big swig of lemonade. I need to cool down some.

CHAPTER FORTY-THREE

SEPTEMBER 4

I awaken to the excitement of starting high school this morning, and, though sunlight streams through my curtains, the air coming through the window feels cooler, like fall. A note on the kitchen table tells me my mother has left for work and wishes me good luck.

I hurry to dress and eat, then dance from foot to foot waiting for my father to come out to the wagon to take me to school.

We are quiet on our ride, lost in our own thoughts; at least I am, not sure whether to be happy or frightened.

Da kisses me goodbye and pulls away as I turn to go to the steps; seventeen of them made of solid stone. My book bag grows heavier with each step. In the bag are five big books: General Science, Geography, History, Arithmetic, and Home Economics.

Mother believes Home Economics will come in handy someday. I suppose I *should* learn to cook and sew. She's done it for me all these years. I'll have a different teacher for each subject, and *none* of them are nuns. Mrs. Krumholtz teaches Home Economics. She's the only Mrs. among them, which doesn't surprise me.

No more uniforms. Boy, am I glad of that. Mine from St Augustine was worn threadbare. Today, I'm wearing a new blue skirt and white blouse. My mother washed, starched, and ironed the blouse last night, and now it scratches my neck. I loosen the top button. Since I only have one other skirt and blouse, Mother offered to take me shopping this weekend at the Mercantile.

Girls are all around me; some bump me as they pass. They're all shapes and sizes, but each of them has one thing in common, a look of sheer terror. I thought I was the only one scared. On the top step, something slams into my arm, nearly knocking my book bag from my grip. I catch it just before it tumbles back down to the street and hug it to my chest.

Looking to see what hit me, I find a girl, frowning with remorse. "I'm so sorry. I wasn't looking where I was going. I am deathly afraid of being late. Please forgive me." Her hair is black as coal and very curly. Her eyes are black, too, with sweeping, long eyelashes. A tear is caught on her bottom lash, and it glimmers like a translucent pearl. She's wearing a black skirt, blue blouse, and a black shawl over her shoulders. She's small but round, and her skin is tawny and golden.

She plants her book bag on the top step and holds out her right hand firmly. "Rosie Marino."

Her hand is clammy with nervous perspiration, too.

"My name's Nellie Kelly. Good to meet you, Rosie Marino. Are you Italian?" The only other Italian I've ever met is Father Ruzzo, and he doesn't look at all like this girl. His skin is much fairer and what hair he has left is blonde, silvered by grey.

She looks angry at my question. "What if I am?"

Embarrassed, I stammer. "I didn't mean that in a mean way. I just don't see many Italians in South Boston and I wondered."

Her eyes stop flashing. "Actually, my parents were born in Sicily. They don't speak good English. Well, my dad does pretty good now, but my mother is hopeless. I was born right here in Boston."

"So was I!" I exclaim, excited. "My parents were both born in Ireland. They have brogues, but they speak English. That must be hard for your parents; not speaking English, I mean."

"Well, where we live in North Boston, most of the people speak Italian, so it's not much of a problem, except that I have to spend an extra hour on the streetcar before and after school."

This girl is nice, so different from my friends at St. Augustine's who are mostly fair-skinned and blue-eyed like me. She has a quick grin, and her eyes dance with mischief. I bet she'll be fun. As we approach the big wooden front door, I say, "What's Rosie stand for? My real name is Ellen Kelly, but my nickname is Nellie. Is Rosie a nickname?"

"Yes, indeed, Miss Nellie. My real name is Rosalia. That's what they all call me at home. My mother hates Rosie. She also hates all things American. Mostly, she hates my father's job, which brought them over from Sicily. He imports stuff. But she's stuck with America and us, too." She laughs loudly. "I'm Rosie to you, and don't you forget it or else."

"Or else what?"

She stops, staring up at me. "Or I won't be your new best friend, that's what."

I wonder what her father imports but don't really care. I have a new best friend. That's what counts.

"What's your first class?" she asks.

"Geography."

"Me, too." She squeals and points. "Look, it's right over there. Sit next to me."

I do, but the two of us get yelled at for giggling in class. Chagrined, we stop laughing. As soon as we walk out the door, we're at it again.

Giggling comes naturally with Rosie.

CHAPTER FORTY-FOUR

MAY, 1873

THREE YEARS LATER

"We're invited for dinner on Saturday at the Marino's house," I announce to my mother, Tuesday after school. "Rosie's mother wants to celebrate how well we've both done at Girls High."

And we have. Rosie and I are competing neck and neck for Top Student. I can't believe how quickly this time has flown by.

Soon, we'll be off for summer vacation. Since I'm sixteen now, I'll try to get work. Perhaps Uncle Tommy will hire me at O'Halloran's Pub. That's where my mother started out.

"Well, that's good," she says. "All I hear from you is Rosie this and Rosie that. I've been wanting to meet the girl for the longest time."

"So, we can go?"

"Of course, we'll go. Why would you think not?"

"Just that it's all the way in North Boston. It'll take an hour to get there. I have no idea what they'll cook, but I bet it won't be mashed potatoes."

"That's what's exciting about it, Nellie. From what I've read,

Italian food is delicious. I've never tasted it. Neither has your father."

"Will he be able to go? He's been so busy lately."

"We'll see. Ask Rosie to tell her family to plan for the three of us but ask their understanding if Da can't make it."

With that, she puts on her cloak and hat. "I need to get to the Haven. There's a full moon tonight and you know what that means, I'll spend the night."

"Lots of babies?"

"Absolutely. There's something about the pull of the full moon that brings babies. I have no idea what it is, but I always make sure Molly is there during Full Moon week to assist with birthing. It never fails."

"Has Molly mentioned Sean lately? How's he doing at Harvard?" I know the answer to this question but just want to talk about him. I haven't seen him for such a long time—and haven't really talked to him since that night at the party.

"Grand, I think." She pulls on a glove. "After next year, he'll go to Georgetown Law School. Kathleen would be so proud of that boy. Smart as a whip, he is, but . . ." She grimaces.

"But what?"

She shakes her head. "I don't know. I just get a bad feeling from Sean sometimes. Sure he's bright and, God knows, handsome, but sometimes I think he's more arrogant than grateful for his blessings."

"You talking about Sean?" Father cracks open the front door. "Don't let Tommy hear you say anything bad about that lad."

She laughs and opens her arms to him. "Don't you worry, love. When it comes to Sean O'Halloran, all Tommy hears from this mouth is praise." She stands on tip toe to kiss him. "How're you doing, love?"

"Good." He kisses her again.

"I'll be home in the morning. Molly will spend the night at The Haven with me. Full moon, you know."

"Okay, love, we'll be fine."

She turns to me. "Nellie, the roast is in the pan in the ice box. Get the stove good and hot and put it in around 3:30."

"I'll do that, Mother."

"Good girl." She closes the door behind her.

Come Saturday, the three of us are bundled up in our wagon for the trip to the Marinos. My da canceled an appointment to go with us and is looking forward to his first taste of Italian food. The May afternoon is soft, with warm breezes promising summer is near.

"What're Rosie's parents' names again?" Da asks.

"Matteo and Maria," I answer. "There's also a little brother called Matteuso."

"Hope they like Irish," he said, holding up the bottle of Tullamore Dew he'd bought special for the occasion.

Mother laughs. "Everyone likes Irish, love. 'Tis the nectar of the Gods."

CHAPTER FORTY-FIVE

When we pull the wagon up in front of a large white house on D Street. I am surprised at how fancy it is. It has two stories, a wrap-around porch, and beautiful lace curtains in every window. My mother scrimped and saved for years to get curtains like that. The house is not as grand as Neo's, but it is certainly respectable and much larger than ours.

Rosie opens the door and hugs me. "Nellie, so glad to see you." I introduce her to my parents, and she greets them with handshakes. Joining her, a trim, dark-haired man wearing a black frock coat and grey trousers extends his hand "This is my father, Matteo Marino." Over his white shirt, he wears a silk ascot in a red print pattern. His hair is slicked back and shiny, and his moustache swirls down into a perfectly manicured goatee. He presents quite a picture of sophistication.

"Welcome to my home," Mr. Marino says in a deep, heavily accented voice and extends his right hand.

"Mr. Marino," my father answers, taking the hand. "Daniel Kelly."

"Please call me Matteo. Come in. Come in."

My mother introduces herself and I do a slight curtsy before him. He grabs my hand. "No need to bow to me. I'm not the

Pope." He tips my chin with his finger and looks into my eyes. "*Bella, bella.*"

A lady joins him and helps us off with our cloaks. She is short and shaped exactly like a pear. Her shoulders and torso are narrow, but below her waist, she balloons out into a round ball. She is smiling and keeps bowing her head at us.

My mother extends her hand. "You must be Maria Marino. I'm Mary Kelly."

The woman looks up at my mother with beautiful dark eyes, Rosie's eyes. She repeats "Maria Marino, *si*," and pats her chest. It is then we all realize then that she really doesn't speak English.

A little boy hides behind his mother.

"That's Matteuso," Rosie tells us, "my little brother. He's a pest."

"Matteuso!" my mother exclaims. "What a beautiful name! How old are you, Matteuso?"

"Six," he answers shyly.

"You're tall for your age, aren't you?" Mother asks, warming up to him.

The little boy stands straighter, throwing his shoulders back. His grin reaches from one ear to the other. He's a beautiful child and looks like Rosie, but his features are finer, more delicate.

"Come into the parlor." Mr. Marino gestures. "Let me get you some wine."

My father steps forward. "Actually, I brought you some of this. It's Irish whiskey."

"Whiskey?" Mr. Marino smiles. "From Ireland?"

My father grins.

"Well, we will have to try it, won't we? Should I put anything in it?"

"Nah, neat is fine."

"I think I'd like the wine," my mother says. I'm surprised at that. She rarely drinks alcohol. She says she had to deal with so many Irish drunks while working at O'Halloran's.

Mr. Marino speaks to his wife in Italian, and she takes the bottle of whiskey from his hands and goes into what I assume is the kitchen. When she returns, she carries a tray with three glasses of whiskey and one glass of deep red wine.

Maria Marino serves her husband and my parents and puts a glass on a table next to the couch for herself. She returns to the kitchen and emerges quickly with three glasses of sarsaparilla for me, Rosie, and Matteuso. Then, she sits down and picks up her glass.

"*Cin Cin*," Mr. Marino says, clicking his glass against my father's.

"*Sláinte*," my father answers.

Rosie nudges my knee with hers; her dark eyes dancing with pleasure. She and I exchange pinkie squeezes, our hands hidden under our long skirts.

All remains cordial until Mrs. Marino takes a sip of that whiskey. She coughs and spits most of it down the front of her dress. Her eyes turn radish red and, when she can speak, she sputters, "*Merda*."

"Mama!" Rosie is obviously shocked. She turns to me. "Mama never swears, and that's a very bad word."

"What's it mean?" I ask.

"Shit," she whispers, then catches my eye as we both burst into laughter.

Mrs. Marino jumps to her feet as adroitly as her size allows and runs into the kitchen. My mother follows her.

My father admonishes, "Nellie, stop laughing," which just makes me giggle harder. Rosie, too.

Mr. Marino throws up his hands, "Well, Daniel, we may as well laugh, too." He slaps my father on the back and they click glasses again, then down the amber liquid.

From that moment on, any tension that existed in that room dissolves into easy conversation. When they re-join us, Mrs. Marino and my mother communicate through signs and smiles in a language that seems female and warm. My mother pays lots of attention to Rosie's little brother. He snuggles up close beside her on the couch.

When it's time for dinner, my mother, Rosie and I go into the kitchen to help serve it. Pans of chicken emerge from the wood stove. If food can smell divine, this food does. There's a bowl of odd-looking skinny noodles covered with a red sauce and cheese over that, another bowl of bright green lettuce, and, of course, bread.

Oh, Lord, the bread! It's drenched in butter and has a flavor I've never tasted before.

"Garlic," Rosie tells me.

Before we eat the feast, Mr. Marino says a prayer over the food. Thank heavens it's a short prayer; my mouth is drooling.

When he's finished, my mother adds, "Dear God, I have no idea what all has gone into this food, but from the smell of it, we're grateful. My prayer is that this is what is served in Heaven. Amen."

"*Mangia*," Mrs. Marino laughs, sipping her wine.

CHAPTER FORTY-SIX

After our meal, the two men go out to the back porch for glasses of some dark brown liquid. Mr. Marino offers my father a cigar, but Da declines. "No thanks. I quit tobacco."

We can see them and overhear their conversation from the kitchen, and my mother smiles at me when she hears his words.

Da sniffs the drink and grimaces slightly. "What is this? It's . . . interesting."

"*Grappa*," Mr. Marino replies.

Rosie and I have cleared the table, and Mrs. Marino is washing dishes. The three of us dry them while Rosie translates the conversation for her mother and mine. Since they're mostly talking about recipes, I soon grow bored with their halting conversation and start to eavesdrop on the men outside.

Mr. Marino holds a long, black cigar in one hand and the glass of *grappa* in the other. My father takes a sip and frowns.

Mr. Marino catches the expression and raises his eyebrows.

Father sputters, "An acquired taste, I'd wager. What's it made from?"

"Oh, the skins and seeds of the grapes mostly. In Sicily, we love it."

Da takes another sip. "Ah, that's better. Just takes some getting used to."

Mr. Marino smiles and leans forward, his elbows on his knees. "I understand you're a counselor."

"An attorney actually."

Mr. Marino shrugs. "Yes, that's what I meant. The language makes it difficult."

"It must be hard to learn a new language as an adult. The Irish had it hard in the beginning, and many still do, but most of us spoke English; at least some form of it."

"*Si*. I mean, yes."

My father seems to be enjoying the *grappa* more now. Soon, Mr. Marino is refilling his glass. "Are you well compensated for your work, Daniel?"

My father leans against the back of the chair. "I do all right. Mary puts every penny she earns back into the birthing center. She operates the place on a shoestring. We're not rich, but we get by. My friends tell me I take too many pro bono cases."

Mr. Marino's brow wrinkles. "Pro bono?"

"Yes, people too poor to afford a lawyer. Many of them Irish. I hate to turn them down when they ask. They are my people after all."

Mr. Marino acknowledges and takes a drag of his cigar. "I may have an opportunity for you."

Later, on the ride home, my father is cheerful. "Fascinating night, didn't you think, Mary? And that food! *Delicioso*."

She laughs at his stab at Italian. "Yes, Maria wrote down three of those recipes for me. The chicken in wine and the red sauce. Oh, and the garlic bread. That's what it's called, garlic bread. Actually, Maria told Rosie in Italian and Rosie wrote them. I'll try them sometime. The chicken was delicious."

"Wine, huh? That's his business. Marino's, I mean. He imports wines from Sicily. Also, something called olive oil. He has lots of contacts over there and they need a lawyer in Boston to handle contracts and negotiations. He thinks an Irish lawyer is just the ticket. The salary he mentioned was sizable."

"Really? Well, isn't that a corker? Are you interested?"

"Maybe. I need to think about that a bit. I just hope I don't have to drink that *grappa* all the time. It tastes like paint thinner."

She laughs again. "Well, your paint must be plenty thin by now."

He puts his arm around her and she rests her head on his shoulder. I'm surprised at how happy it makes me to see them loving again.

I wonder if I'll ever feel that way with a boy. I mean, a man. Most of the boys I know are pretty stupid, except for Neo, of course. But he doesn't count; he's my best friend and a Negro. Angelique didn't seem bothered by his color, but I don't think I have as much courage as she does. I hope that doesn't mean I'm prejudiced.

Neo hopes to visit her in Montreal when she has a permanent address. She and Jean drift from cousin to cousin for lodging now.

Neo and Angelique write each other faithfully every week, but it takes weeks for letters to reach them.

Lots of the girls at school have boyfriends who they talk about all the time. Some plan to get married after graduation next year. Is there something wrong with me that I don't have a boyfriend? Mother doesn't believe I should think of marriage or even keeping company until I have my education completed.

Most times, I agree with her.

But then I remember Sean O'Halloran, and my heart still races. When he put his arm around me at the party that time, I felt something, an electricity, from my head down to my knees. He really is exciting.

I've never admitted this to anyone, not even Rosie, but twice now I've had dreams about Sean, and when I woke up, my hand was between my legs. Each time, in my dreams, I awakened after having something like a convulsion, shaking all over, but it felt really good. I was wet down there. At first, I thought perhaps I had my monthly, but it wasn't blood. It was something else. And it's not like I had an accident and wet the bed or anything.

Each time it happened, it scared me half to death. But it was a different fear than I've experienced before. I felt guilty and almost as though I needed to go to confession. But how could I explain such a thing to Father Ruzzo? So, am I in a state of mortal sin or not?

I wish I could talk to my mother about this, but I can't. I'd be mortified.

What is happening to me?

CHAPTER FORTY-SEVEN

Two weeks later, Neo appears unexpectedly at my front door. He's on summer vacation from Howard. My mother is at the clinic and Da is meeting with Mr. Marino.

I pour him a glass of lemonade and we sit down on the front porch swing. I hope none of our neighbors see us together. Although most of them have seen the Okafors before, they've never seen me sitting alone with Neo.

Maybe *I am* prejudiced, but I think it's because I know some of our neighbors are. They say words like nigger and call Italians dagos and wops. That's why I've never invited Rosie here after school. I wouldn't want to take a chance on her hearing such things.

As we sit together sipping our drinks, I realize Neo is shaking. His shoulder next to me on the swing is vibrating. He's excited about something. Curiosity gets the best of me. "What is it, Neo?"

"I got a letter."

"Yes?" I needn't ask who it's from.

He pulls a folded envelope from his pocket and takes out the letter. "She writes she's finally settled in Montreal at 15 Rue St. Jacques. She and her brother are working as models in some designer's shop."

Maybe I shouldn't be surprised but am. After all, Angelique and Jean are both tall and beautiful, but I've never heard of shop models in Boston.

"And she wants me to come there. She wants to marry me," he concludes, putting the letter back into the envelope and returning it to his pocket.

My stomach tightens, wondering how people in Montreal feel about white girls marrying colored boys.

It is then I put words to my fears. "Neo, does she say how coloreds are treated in Canada?"

He takes a large swig from his glass. "She thinks it's better than in America. I've told her about the prejudice I've experienced here in Boston. Maybe it's worse in America because of the War. There was little African slave trade in Canada. Most of their slaves were native Indians.

"I've signed up to study French during my last year at Howard. That's what they speak in Montreal. By the time I graduate, I'll be fluent. I've told her I still think we'd be better off in Ireland."

"You graduate next year."

"Yes, and that's when I'll go to either Montreal or Ireland. Angelique has agreed to wait until then."

My heart sinks a bit, but I tell myself I just don't want to lose my best friend.

And lose him, I will. Montreal is in another country. Ireland seems like another world. Both are so far away.

He continues excitedly. "Angelique, Jean, and I plan to eventually join a Polite Vaudeville show. Angelique and her brother will do an acrobatic act, and I'll be a magician."

"Polite Vaudeville?"

"Yes, that's what such shows are called. There are a few of them starting up soon in Canada, and America, too. We can bring them to Ireland as well."

"So, you'll finally get your dream to do magic?"

His eyes dance with joy. "Yes, I've been practicing a lot of new tricks and hope that someday Angelique will join my act. I read about a magician who actually saws pretty girls in half."

"Saws them in half? How can they do that without killing them?"

"Magic, my girl. Pure magic." Again, that flashing smile. "I know how it's done."

I grin. "Of course, you do. But Neo, aren't you worried your father will think you've wasted your education?"

"Actually no. I told him about my plans, and he's willing to help us get started. I think he wishes I'd go on to medical school, but that's not the career I want."

"You're lucky he feels that way."

"I know that. Let's face it, my father has done very well following *his* dreams, and he respects my wanting to follow mine."

I close my eyes for a second and ponder. *What are my dreams? To become a teacher, of course. But lately, dreams of Sean plague me almost every night.*

It's been nearly a year since I've seen him, even casually; and I do wonder if he might have found someone he loves like Neo loves Angelique. That would break my heart.

I must find out if Neo knows anything about Sean. Trying to act as though his answer doesn't matter in the slightest, I ask, "So, do you ever see Sean O'Halloran around town?"

"No. I saw him once on a train to Washington. He's traveling there for interviews at Georgetown Law. He's been accepted and will go there next year. Sean lives a different life than I do."

"Oh."

Neo knows me too well to be fooled into thinking my question was casual. He turns and looks at me. "Are you interested in Sean, Nellie?" His eyes are piercing in their concern. They don't look happy.

What should I answer? I decide on the truth. After all, Neo is my best friend. "Yes, I do think of him sometimes. He's very attractive and seems to be planning a fine future."

Neo touches my shoulder and I jump at the contact. "He appears to be quite the catch, I suppose. But Nellie, be careful."

His words chill my heart. "What do you mean?"

He digs his toe into the porch and stops the swing as he seems to ponder his answer to my question. Finally, he speaks. "Well, one time we rode the same train back from Washington. I was riding in a different car, of course, but overheard his conversation in the diner. Some of the things Sean said don't sound as if he has a high opinion of women."

"Like what?"

Neo squirms as if he's uncomfortable. "Oh, the names he calls them."

"What names?"

"I don't want to repeat them to you, Nellie, but they're parts of the female anatomy. Derogatory names. Demeaning and coarse." He takes a breath before continuing. "Sean O'Halloran is not a gentleman. I wouldn't have him as a friend."

His words confound and concern me. I want to make them go away and try for a light-hearted response. "Ah Neo, he's just joking around. Don't you think?" He pauses then turns to me. "No, and I'm telling you the truth. Watch out for him."

CHAPTER FORTY-EIGHT

"Tonight, we eat Eye-talian," my mother announces.

It's nearly dinner time. I just got home, having stayed after school to help Miss Spencer with the next day's lessons. She's really taken me under her wing and thinks that maybe after I'm through at Wellesley, I can come back as a teacher at Girls High.

My father sits at the kitchen table, a bottle of stout in front of him. "Smells good, Mary."

He's right. A strong scent fills our entire home. One I've never smelled before in this place of beef, potatoes, and egg noodles.

"What're you making, Mother?"

"I decided to take a day away from the clinic and practice my cooking skills. I used Maria's recipes, and Mr. Marino dropped off a bottle of that cooking wine and a big clump of garlic at your da's office." She stirs a bubbling pot of red sauce on top of the stove. "Oh, he also brought a bottle of some sweet vinegar and the red wine they served at dinner.

"I made the noodles different, too. You use eggs as usual, but Mrs. Marino said to use semolina flour. I had to buy it at an Italian store in Quincy. And, I've been cooking that tomato sauce all day." She falls into a kitchen chair. "I'm tired."

"From the smell of it, it'll be worth it, Mary." Da is hungry and starts to dip a piece of bread in the pot.

She jumps up and takes the bread from his hand. "Don't! You'll spoil your appetite. We'll eat in one hour."

He laughs and pulls her in for a kiss.

She backs away, putting her hand over her mouth. "I don't think you should get close to me. I chopped all that garlic and it has a terrible stink. Now, so do I. I hope it tastes better than it smells."

I pick up her hand and take a sniff. She's right. For once, something is stronger than the chloride.

"Darlin', could you get me a wee glass of that wine? I need a rest."

I pour her a glass and ask, "Can I taste it?"

She looks at my father and neither of them seems to know what to say. "Here, have a sip, love." She extends the glass toward me. "You're almost seventeen. It's time you know how alcohol tastes."

I sip the wine and start to choke. "How can people drink that? It's awful."

My father laughs. "You think that's bad? Wait'll you taste that *grappa* Marino serves. It'll peel the paint off your gizzard."

I sputter, "I want to finish my homework."

"Go ahead, sweetheart." She pats my back. "I want to ask your father about his meeting with Mr. Marino."

I hurry and leave my door open. I want to hear what he has to say, too.

"So, Daniel?" Mother is most curious.

"Well, intriguing, it is, Mary. The money is very good, and that would be a good thing what with Nellie going off to college next year."

"I hear a 'but' in your tone, Daniel Kelly."

He wipes his forehead with a handkerchief and sits back

against his chair. "I'm just thinking about it, Mary. I could still take on pro bono cases if they're warranted. I wouldn't be working full time for Marino. This is a big decision."

"You can always say no, Daniel."

"But that might be as foolish as old Donohue's jackass. I like Marino well enough, and the work's just contracts and negotiations. I can do that stuff in my sleep. But something about the whole thing makes me uncomfortable."

"Sleep on it, love. You needn't make a decision right now, do you?"

"No, though he'd prefer to have an answer by next week."

She gets up to stir the tomato sauce, which is nearly bubbling over on the stove. "Don't want this to burn. I've been boiling and peeling tomatoes all day to get it ready and then chopping that stinkin' garlic till I can hardly breathe. It better be good."

And it is very, very good; though not as good as Mrs. Marino's. But I'd never tell my mother that.

CHAPTER FORTY-NINE

"Guess who I met at Quincy Market last night?" Rosie teases at lunch the next day. Her dark eyes flash in excitement. She wears a red scarf around her neck and looks quite exotic in her blouse and skirt with her black curls and gorgeous dark eyes.

"Who?"

"A certain male friend of yours whom I think you fancy very much."

"Neo?" Rosie had met Neo once when we ran into him at the Boston Common. But why the teasing game about him?

"Nope."

I wait in silent frustration. If she sees I'm curious, she'll drag this out as long as she can. She's leaning in and breathing fast, a sure sign she's dying to tell me. I pretend to stifle a yawn.

She blurts it out, "Sean O'Halloran, that's who."

I rest my back against the chair and sip my milk, feigning indifference. "That's nice."

"Oh, my Lord, Nellie. He's so handsome."

I shrug casually, determined to appear nonchalant even though my heart is racing. "So?"

"So, he told me he wants to invite you to a football celebration party at Harvard in three weeks."

"What's football? I've heard about it but don't know much about it."

"It's kind of a combination of rugby and soccer, I think. From what I hear, it's all the rage in colleges now."

"Oh, does Sean play it?"

"I don't think so, but Harvard's had a football team for two years now, and they'll play Yale next month for the first time. It's a huge competition, Nellie."

"Why's the party at Harvard?"

"Because nobody can get to Connecticut to cheer the team. You can take a train from Boston to Albany or from New York City to New Haven, but there's no train from Boston to New Haven. So, Sean's Club is hosting a party the night before the team leaves for the game."

"How will the team get there?"

Her eyebrows rise in consternation. "I don't know. For God's sake, Nellie. I'm telling you Sean is inviting you to a party at Harvard. Aren't you excited?"

I don't respond right away. I'm trying to figure how I'll ever get my mother to let me go.

"Nellie, it's a party at Harvard!" she exclaims. "I told Sean your mother might let you go if I went with you."

Would she? Maybe. I know she wouldn't let me go alone.

"He says his roommate would be happy to escort me. Oh Nellie, wouldn't that be the most marvelous thing in the world? A college party?"

"So, we'd both go?"

She squeals and claps her hands.

I can't believe it. *Sean wants to take me to a party? He must like me, too. If I tell my mother it's just a friends-of-the-family invitation, maybe she'd consider it. After all, she birthed Sean. And I've gotten straight A's ever since I got to high school. Miss*

Spencer says I'm a shoo-in for Wellesley, maybe even a scholar-ship. And after all, I'm seventeen years old. Some of my friends from St. Augustine are already married. Fiona married Orville last week. Word is she's expecting, but my mother tells me not to gossip. And after all, Harvard's practically next door to Boston.

I turn to Rosie. "Let me think on this, Rosie. If I can figure out a strategy, the two of us may be taking a little trip to Cambridge."

Chapter Fifty

My mother sits down at the kitchen table. The stew simmers on the wood stove, and the fresh-baked bread warms on the back of it. "You look tired, Mother. It's been a long day, hasn't it?"

"You could say that."

I pour her a glass of the Italian wine. "Here, perhaps this will refresh you."

She looks at the glass, then raises her eyes to me. She knows me well; suspects I have something my sleeve. Her thirst wins out. She takes a sip. "Ahhhh."

After I finish setting the table, I sit opposite her, prepared for what I know will be a tough argument. I'd rehearsed the night before in bed.

"Where's Da?" I ask.

"He has a meeting with Patrick Collins at the Irish Fellowship. He'll eat there."

That means he'll be late.

That's good. Perhaps I can convince one of them more easily than both of them together. Although, I think my father will be the softer of the two.

I had showed my mother my report card earlier. My lowest grade was a ninety-seven and that was in Home Economics. Maybe that, along with the wine, might soften her up some.

In an offhand way, I casually broach the subject of my going to Cambridge. I act as though it's not an issue for concern at all. She hears me out with more patience than I'd expected. But then she rears back in her chair, her eyes wide with disbelief. "Are you daft, Miss?"

I take in a deep breath and cross my hands on the table. "No, Mother, I'm not daft. Sean is an old family friend. You know I'd be safe with him."

"Nothing about this sounds safe to me, girl." She pulls herself to her feet and starts to dish out two bowls of stew. "Or proper. You are too young to go off alone on a train to Harvard."

"But I didn't tell you the whole plan, Mother. I won't be alone. I forgot to mention Rosie will go with me. Sean is introducing her to his roommate for the party. We'll be perfectly fine."

She hesitates. Does that mean she's considering it? But then she puts the steaming bowl in front of me and says, "No, Nellie. You're too young." Her tone sounds final as she sits down and picks up her spoon.

Her words indicate the case is closed, and I almost give up on what looks to be a hopeless plea. But I can't let this go so easily. Maybe I can try another tact. "Mother," I say in the most calm, reasonable voice I can muster, "I'm in my last term at Girls High. If I get into Wellesley next year, I'll have to ride the train every day." "And you will get into Wellesley. Everyone says so."

"Maybe, but that's not the point." I take her right hand gently. "It's time to let me grow up."

Her eyes flare. "Grow up? You mean like you thought you were when you ran away to the circus? You almost turned my hair grey with worry, you did." She takes her hand out of mine and points her finger at me. "Don't you ever pull such a thing again."

"I won't. I promise." I grab her hand again into both of mine and squeeze, looking deep into her eyes. "All I want is to go to a college party with an old family friend. A friend you brought into this world; whose named for your father. I'll be in college myself next year."

She pulls her hand away again and crosses her arms over her chest. "It wouldn't be proper."

"But it would, Mother. Rosie's going with me. You were younger than I am when you danced with Da at that St. Patrick's Day Dance. You had just turned sixteen, remember?"

"Of course, I remember, but I was with Kathleen."

"And I'll be with Rosie."

"Rosie's your age. Kathleen was older. And besides, girl, you'd have to stay overnight. You wouldn't be able to get back home the same night, now would you? Where do you think you'd be staying?"

My mind races for an answer. I hadn't figured that out yet. That was dumb. "I could stay in a rooming house with Rosie," I stammer, knowing she won't be satisfied.

Her lips turn down in a scowl.

Think, Nellie, think. You're losing this argument. Suddenly, I flash on a brilliant idea. "Or if it would make you feel better, a convent! We could stay at a convent on the Harvard campus."

"Is there such a thing?" She tilts her head to the side, daring me to give the wrong answer.

I hem and haw for just a second. "I'm not sure, but there must be one somewhere around there. A few Catholics go to Harvard after all. We'll ask Sister Sarah. She'll know."

She still looks skeptical, but she might be weakening, slightly. "I need to talk to your father about this, Nellie.

"Of course, Mother."

I'll tell Rosie to start convincing her father tomorrow. If she can get Mr. Marino to say yes, Da may follow his lead.

Chapter Fifty-One

My da didn't get home last night till quite late. I heard him open the door just as I was falling asleep. He called out softly, "Hello, love. I'm home." That was the last I heard before I was lost in a dream about Sean. It was a wonderful dream. In it, Sean gave me my first kiss. When I awakened, I still felt his lips on mine.

This morning, as Da joins me at the breakfast table, I blow on my porridge, trying to cool it down some. Since it's Saturday, I'm not in my usual rush.

"Tell your daughter what Patrick Collins wants of you?" Mother asks.

"Aw, Mary, the same thing as last time."

"And what is that, Da?"

"He wants me to get into politics."

"But Da, that's exciting. Think of all the ways you could help our neighbors."

He grunts and shakes his head. "Not as a member of this ward's Common Council. All they do is have meetings. They never get anything done. The Mayor is the one who makes all the decisions."

"Have you thought about running for Mayor?"

He chuckles. "Oh, yes. Mary, remember when I was going to be the first Irish Mayor of Boston?"

She smiles and takes a sip of her tea. "And I was going to save all the young women in Boston from unsafe pregnancies?"

"Well, you have saved a good share of them, love. Just don't let the church find out about the advice you're giving them."

I lower my head in embarrassment. I don't like such talk from him, though I don't quite understand what she's been advising.

She grins and gets to her feet. "Daniel, more coffee?"

He raises his empty cup.

"But you have saved mothers and babies, Mother." I am proud of her. "Everyone says so." People always speak of the good she's done in stamping out something called childbed fever. I shudder at the stories I've heard of how devastating that illness was. Things are better for women in Boston since Mother opened Kathleen's Haven.

Da turns to me. "As to why I won't run for Mayor, right now Boston has a thirty percent Irish population. That seems large, but not in comparison with the Protestant Republicans. I figure we're about five years out from getting an Irish Mayor in this town, and I don't want to waste my time sitting in useless Common Council meetings until then."

"So, you disappointed dear Mr. Collins yet again?" Mother asks.

"Afraid so. I hated doing that. He's so fiery and committed to his cause. Think that comes from his days with the Fenians."

I'd heard of the Fenians but knew little about them. "Who are the Fenians?" I ask.

"A grand bunch of fighting boys from the old country. Tough lads. They got a lot done."

"But not Ireland's independence." Mother interrupts him, a hint of sadness in her voice.

"Not yet, Mary, not yet. That will come."

Before Da leaves, I must speak to him about that party. "Da, I want to talk to you about something."

He raises his eyebrows. "What thing? Is it what your mother mentioned?"

Oh, she did talk to him. "Maybe. You see, Sean O'Halloran has invited me to a party at Harvard." I race my words so I can get them all out and, hopefully, convince him before she interferes. "Rosie and I would go together. Sean's arranging for his roommate to escort her. The party is for the football team who will leave the next day for a game in New Haven. We'd stay in a convent."

"Ah yes, I've heard about that game. This is the first time they're playing Yale, right?"

I light up enthusiastically. "Yes! Just think, Da, I'll be a part of history."

"Slow down, Miss. History is a bit of a blarney stretch. What did your mother say?"

It annoys me he asks that question. I'm sure he knows the answer. She turns from the stove, coffee pot hoisted like a sword. "She's too young."

I jump back in the fray. I must control this conversation or I'll never get to that party. "I'm seventeen years old. One year older than you two were when you danced at that Irish dance a hundred years ago."

He looks at her and grins. "A hundred years, huh?"

"And I'll be going with Sean, an old family friend. Think how bad Uncle Tommy would feel if he knew you didn't trust his son."

"Trust has nothing to do with this, Nellie," he counters.

"Of course, it does, Da."

This isn't going as well as I'd hoped. Tears well up in my eyes. Maybe if I let him see them it'll make a difference. I take his hand. "Please. Rosie and I will be together. Think about it, won't you?"

He pauses, casts a glance at my mother's back, saying demurely, "I'll think about it."

My mother walks from the stove. "Daniel?"

"I said I'd think about it, Mary, and I will."

My heart soars. I'm on my way to Harvard.

CHAPTER FIFTY-TWO

Except I'm not. After I went to my room, their talk got so loud, I put the pillow over my head. My father thought it might be a great adventure for me and Rosie, but my mother would not budge. And in the end, as usual, my mother won the argument. She should have been the attorney.

This morning, I pouted through church, furious at her for denying me this chance to be with Sean. I'll never forgive her.

On Monday morning, Rosie waits on the steps of school. She dances from foot to foot in excitement. She's nearly quivering. "What did they say? My father said I can go with you."

Miserably, I shake my head.

"Can't you convince them?" she asks, her voice whiny. "Make them change their minds?"

"You don't know my mother. Once her mind is made up, nothing changes it. She could swallow a stick of dynamite and not budge. She'd just sit there shaking her head." As I explain, my anger grows. It's so unfair.

"But I want to go," Rosie pleads, her eyes welling.

"And so do I. More than you can imagine. I'll keep trying, but I don't think I can convince her. She's ridiculous." *And ruining my life*, I think to myself. "Sorry, Rosie. Afraid no Harvard for us this time." In dejection, I slump up the stairs and into school. I have never been so sad, nor so angry with my mother.

The week passes in a blur of examinations. On Tuesday, *The Boston Globe* headlines the front page with huge letters proclaiming that on November 13, 1875, Harvard defeated Yale in their first match on the football field.

Later that day, I ask Rosie if she's seen the paper. "Not really." That surprises me because the whole town is buzzing about the game.

I really don't get all the excitement. After all, it's just a game. It's not like Harvard discovered a cure for consumption or something. When I try to talk to Rosie about the foolishness of the hoopla, she pretends she's not interested. I don't understand her. She seems to be avoiding me and runs off every time I try to get her into a conversation. She always has to study or get home and help her mother. Did I do something wrong? Is she mad at me? I'm confounded. But maybe it's just my imagination. I brush away my concerns. I'm too busy studying for tests to worry about Rosie now.

The following Saturday, Boston celebrates the victory over Yale with a huge parade. I ask Rosie to meet me and some other friends at the festivities, and she says she can't. Her father is out of town and she can't get a ride to downtown Boston. Her answer is confusing because it seems the whole city is planning to attend the parade, and I'm certain some of her neighbors would give her a ride.

What is wrong with her?

That Saturday morning, the music and excitement are so infectious that my friends and I clap and march in place as we wave American flags and cheer wildly. My eyes fill with patriotic tears when the Minute Men from Amherst march by solemnly playing their fifes and drums.

The crowd erupts in frenzied cheers when the Harvard football team strolls proudly next to the Red Stockings baseball team. The football captain carries a huge banner of a shield with red, white, and black streamers attached to it. The baseball players are resplendent in black and white uniforms and caps with knickers tucked into bright red stockings. They just won their fourth consecutive national title, and Boston has become a city burning with sports fever.

I whirl to catch a glimpse of the next band in line and my hand strikes the hard chest of a young man.

"Sean O'Halloran!" I exclaim. "You're home from school?"

"Sure am," he answers with a grin. "Wanted to see my girl."

He came home to see me, I think, blushing. *He's calling me his girl.* As I stand there, jubilant and flattered, Rosie rushes up to Sean. When she sees me, she sputters, "Uh, Nellie, uh, I've been meaning to tell you about this."

What is she talking about? "Tell me what?"

Her face reflects a picture of consternation and repressed joy. "Ummm, you know how your mother wouldn't let you go to Harvard last week?"

"Yes, of course I do."

"Well, see, since I already had permission from my parents, I figured why not go to the party?"

"You went without me?" *I can't believe this!*

She tries to look sad but is clearly so excited to see Sean that she can't contain her grin. She's all bouncing black curls and dark eyes sparkling in the sunlight.

I pivot back to Sean. "Did you fix her up with your roommate?"

He hesitates less than a second. "No. Since you couldn't come, I took her myself."

I whirl back to Rosie, expecting her to say Sean is lying. My mouth opens, but I cannot speak. Looking deep into her eyes—this girl who is my best friend on this earth—truth dawns. That's why she's avoided me this week. She didn't want to tell me.

Of course, that's it. When I look at Rosie now, I see betrayal . . . and absolute happiness. I shake my head, trying to dispel this awful truth. She's not my friend at all, which hurts even more than Sean's cavalier grin.

I was hurt in eighth grade by Fiona's lies about me, but this is worse. Fiona was never that close. Rosie and I shared everything. She told me about her first kiss and helped me clean up and find rags when my monthly stained the back of my skirt in tenth grade. She knew my every fear and desire. She knew I had not yet experienced a first kiss and that I very much wanted to. We helped each other study for tests and gossiped about other girls. She was my best friend.

How could a friend do such a thing as this?

I stumble away from them, aimlessly batting my way through the jubilant crowd.

My heart feels hard as the stones under my feet. Snow starts to fall, and my eyes blur. Blindly, I stumble into a young boy who screams, "Watch out, lady!"

Suddenly, I hear a shout in a deep, male voice. "Nellie!"

For a second, I imagine it's Sean wanting to explain. Maybe he wants to tell me it's all a big joke. My heart fills with hope as I look back.

What I see twists my heart into a cold knot. Rosie takes Sean's arm and, smiling up into his eyes, walks away through the throngs of celebrants.

Where are they going? To all the world, they are another happy young couple off on a weekend adventure. No one sees the evil, the betrayal, but me.

But I see it, and my tears stop as bitterness freezes my soul.

"Nellie!" the shout comes again. Desperate and confused, I see through the crowd the purple fringe of Neo's carriage. He waves and smiles. "Nellie!" he calls out again. I stumble toward him.

He's waving a letter up in the air. "I got a letter from Angelique. She accepted my proposal. I want you to help me buy a ring."

I stagger up into the carriage beside him. He is so thrilled he doesn't notice my wet cheeks as he continues to tell me of his plans.

"It will happen next summer after I graduate from Howard. We'll meet in Ireland. She's investigating passage on liners already. I'll do the same. We must talk to your mother. She can tell us where we might go from the Dublin Harbor for the wedding. It won't be big or fancy, but, Nellie, I want you there. My father will pay for your family's passage. He's already said he would."

"Uncle Kam knows about this?" I stammer, sniffling.

He trembles with excitement. "Yes, and he's given his blessing. He says our love has lasted through this long separation, so it must be true. He'll come to Ireland, too. I'm not sure about my mother. She's been ailing some."

I know this. My mother is worried about Imani.

With that, Neo pulls the carriage to the curb and turns to face me. When he sees my face, his eyes narrow in concern. He knows me so well. "Nellie, what is it?"

I burst into tears and speak of betrayal—of Rosie, of Sean—and that my heart is broken.

He takes me by the shoulders, right in broad-daylight Boston. "Good, Nellie. Better now than later."

How can he say that? My heart is broken, and he's saying that's good? What if Angelique did that to him? Would he still think it's good?

"I didn't tell you what I really think of Sean O'Halloran because I knew you were crazy about him."

"I still am."

He takes in a deep breath. "Fellows from Gettysburg say he's a snake, Nellie. Even his pals call him scum. He has no respect for women. I hear them joke about him on the train, I've actually prayed you would get over that louse, and you know I never pray."

He takes my hands into his and in a voice so sincere it breaks my heart, Neo says, "Nellie, you can do better."

CHAPTER FIFTY-THREE

JUNE, 1875

It's been six months since that awful day. When the acceptance letter arrived from Wellesley the following week, my parents whooped for joy. I was proud, too, but still felt devastated about Sean and Rosie. In truth, that hasn't changed.

Neo said I can do better, but right now, I don't think so. There aren't many men like Sean O'Halloran. He's smart and ambitious, tall, handsome, and funny; and he has a twinkle in his eyes that makes my knees go weak. Maybe Neo's wrong about him. He might just need a good girl to straighten him out. Maybe I'm that girl. I hope so with every fiber of my being.

Still.

Other boys have started paying attention to me. Boys from the Academy who never glanced my way before. Tommy Higginbotham asked me if he could speak to my parents about our keeping company. I was flattered but made an excuse. He's a nice boy, and very good looking, but he's just that, a boy. Not a man, not like Sean.

When I stroll the streets of Boston now, even grown men turn their heads as I pass them. I don't know if that ever happened before, but if it did, I didn't see it. Though I'm pleased at their attention, I never look back at them.

Last week, my mother mentioned Rosie. "How is she? Are you two still close?"

I made an excuse. I didn't tell her Rosie went off to Harvard that weekend and that now she and Sean are together. Though in my bitterest moments, I'd surely tell her that it's she who caused this. That if she'd let me go to Harvard that weekend, none of this would have happened. There's no point in telling her that.

When she pushes for information, I just say, "Oh, I'm so busy studying I don't have much time for Rosie anymore."

She shakes her head about that. "Good friends deserve attention, Nellie."

Yes, good friends do. But good friends don't steal the man you love.

At school, I work harder than ever. Rosie Marino will *not* top me in grades. She who was my dearest friend. She with whom I shared my deepest secrets. She who betrayed me, knowing it would break my heart. She'll not best me again—ever.

When I see her in class now, I pretend she's dead. But she doesn't look dead. She's glowing, and looking buxom.

Her breasts look larger than before. They strain against the buttons on her lacy blouse as if they want to pop free. Her face is fuller, too, and pretty in an exotic way I hadn't noticed before. Her skin is tawny and golden, and sometimes I think she wears lip rouge. She is so much a woman now, not a girl.

I hate her. Mother would say that's a sin; so would my priest. I've heard all my life at church that "the greatest of these is love," and that hatred is sinful. But I don't care.

Today, Miss Spencer told me I'm to make a speech at graduation since I have the highest grades in the class. Rosie is second highest. In spite of being tired and sad, that makes me happy. At least she comes in second in some things.

I work hard on my speech, mainly because I'm sure Sean will be there. I want him to recognize what he's lost. I wash my hair the night before and roll it up in rags so that the next morning, it will fall in soft waves over my new white graduation dress.

The Marinos will be at graduation, of course, and I hope they don't expect us to celebrate with them. If so, I will feign illness. I will not be in Rosie's company—never again.

The day of graduation is picture perfect, beautiful and warm. Cherry blossoms are beginning to appear on trees around school and their scent perfumes the air. This kind of day used to lift my heart with every breath I took. Not now. I thought I'd be nervous today and am surprised that I'm not. In fact, I feel numb.

I begin my speech, "Young ladies, we have before us a whole world of opportunity. We are the first graduating class of Girls High, a school that did not exist for our mothers and grandmothers.

"Some of us will go on to college and some will now go to work. Whatever you choose, be proud of what you've accomplished here."

I speak of the privilege of attending Girls High and of the opportunities our education will afford us. When I finish my talk, I smile at the applause and scan the crowd for Sean. He's staring at Rosie, a lopsided smile playing over his lips.

Tears come to my eyes. As I sit down, I look up to the heavens and swallow them down. I don't want to spoil this day for my parents. I remember so well their joy when the acceptance letter arrived from Wellesley. They were proud. My mother wept and my da grabbed me and danced me around the living room. I was his little girl again.

They brag to everyone who will listen about "the first high school graduate in our family."

I look out into the crowd and see the Okafors and a beaming Martha next to Neo. All our family friends stare at me with such love and admiration. Why can't I feel that for myself? There's Uncle Tommy and Molly with Sean. Now he's looking at me, not Rosie, and the intensity of his stare brings flutters to my stomach. *The rock of ice that is my heart melts a little. No, Nellie, that can't happen. He has hurt me too much, and I must steel my will against him. But he looks so handsome.*

After Georgetown Law, he probably will eventually enter Boston politics. With his looks and a law degree, voters won't be able to resist him. He may well be the first Irish-Catholic Mayor.

What about Rosie then? She could be first lady someday. A first lady who's nothing better than Sicilian trash. A first lady whose parents can scarcely speak English. Even as I think these wretched thoughts, I scold myself for their hatefulness. *What has happened to me?* I thought I was a good person, but now I'm not so sure.

CHAPTER FIFTY-FOUR

APRIL 30, 1876, SATURDAY EVENING

Dishes washed and dried, Da and I sit reading the Globe on the front porch as my mother knits a baby blanket. Soon, it will be dark. Suddenly, the sky to the East of us flares with a jagged shard of lightning. A deafening boom of thunder follows in seconds.

"I smell the rain coming." Da stands, takes a deep breath and leans against the railing. He gazes into the gathering gloom of the sky.

My mother, beside me on the swing, nods in agreement.

"Can you really smell rain, Da?"

"You bet I can. In Ireland, you learn to do that mighty quick. Rain comes and goes there so fast even a jackrabbit can't outrun it. The smell of rain warns you to pull out a Mackintosh if you have one. My da had one, so if he wasn't out on the boat, I'd filch it every chance I got." He laughs at the memory.

"What was he like, Da? Grandpa?"

He sits on the railing and cradles his head back against his hands as he continues to study the sky. "Grand man, your Grandpa Kelly. Big as a boulder, and strong." He turns to me and runs his fingers through my hair. "You got that Irish mop from him, as did I."

He's told me stories of his father and mother a hundred times or more, but I do love hearing them. I wonder if they'd have loved me. Da says they would. It's sad to think I'll never meet them.

My mother never talks about her parents. I think it hurts her to remember the way her mam passed and that her da was murdered by an Irish mobster here in Boston. Whenever she starts to speak of them, her eyes go dark, then she shakes her head and changes the subject.

Since I started college, I spend three hours every Monday through Friday on the Boston and Worcester train to get to and from school. I kind of like it. The clackety clack of the wheels soothes me, and by the time I get home at night, my homework is usually finished.

Weekends are special times of pampering by my mother and grilling about studies by my da. He's so excited with everything I'm learning. I do love Wellesley, and my teachers say I will someday be a fine teacher. The thought of educating young minds excites me.

It's funny now when I think how I used to want to make a life in the circus. It's good Neo and I experienced that. Now I know better. Spangly tights and trapezes hold no fascination for me. Though I do miss some of the people, especially Bridey with her beautiful dark eyes and soft hair. She warned me about Sean, and I wonder how she knew he'd hurt me. She met him once.

I haven't seen him or Rosie for months now.

As darkness gathers, a chill settles over me. I pull my shawl tighter around my shoulders and stand to pull a new leaf from the big maple tree in the front yard. Right now, in General

Science, we're studying the vascular system, and I marvel at how the veins in the leaf resemble the veins in my wrist.

As I sit down on the swing again, a carriage pulls up in front of the house. Mother looks at Da with raised eyebrows. His shrug shows that he's as bewildered as she is. We aren't expecting visitors.

A strange dark man drives the two horses, and when the carriage stops, my mouth opens in shock as Mrs. Marino alights from it. She turns to the driver of the rig and says something in Italian. He sits back and tips his hat over his eyes.

"Maria!" my mother exclaims. She sounds surprised, but her voice is warm and friendly. She goes down the steps and embraces the woman. Mrs. Marino's eyes are deeply shadowed and red. She looks as though she hasn't slept in a week. My mother takes her into her arms. "You're trembling. Come in to the kitchen for a cup of tea."

They go through the front door as my father and I stare at each other in surprise. Mrs. Marino out alone on a Saturday evening?

"What's she doing here?" I ask.

"Beats me," he says, then saunters out to speak to the carriage driver. "Hello mate, can I get you a brew? Come on up here on the porch lest you get drenched when the rain comes."

The man clearly does not understand English, but after a pantomime of gestures, he climbs down from the carriage and settles himself on the step beside me. We all smile at each other awkwardly, and I turn back to talk to my father who sits on the swing. "Is everything all right? You working for Mr. Marino, I mean."

He scoots over some on the swing. "It's fine. The contracts are pretty standard stuff, and the extra money surely does come in handy."

He gestures me up onto the swing beside him. When I settle there, he puts his arm around my shoulders. "School still going well, Nell?" He's taken to calling me Nell since I'm at Wellesley, and he still brags to anyone who'll listen that his little girl will be the first college graduate in the Kelly family. "If only my mam was here to see you. She'd be so proud."

"I wish she were, Da. School's great. I love Wellesley."

"It's all girls, right?"

"Of course."

"Miss the lads?"

What an odd question. He knows Wellesley's an all-female school. "Not really. I've never gone to a school with boys, you know. You can't miss what you've never known."

"That's true." He's silent for a moment and then asks another strange question. "Did you know Tim Donahue's girl is getting married soon. They posted the banns last Sunday."

"Yes." Marcy Donahue was one year ahead of me at St. Augustine's.

"Think you'll want to get married someday? I figure you can take your pick of just about any lad in this town."

Oh, now I see where he was going with his strange questions. I turn to face him, a grin teasing my mouth. "Probably someday, Da, but not any time soon."

He needn't know that the one boy I've ever cared about is now Rosie Marino's boyfriend. My friends at Girls High buzzed about the two of them all summer after graduation. It was all I could do to not scream at them to stop talking. They say Rosie is still living at home and not going to college so she can be here when Sean gets breaks from law school. I'm surprised at that. Rosie was determined to get into Wellesley just one year ago.

Da and I sit together and swing for a few minutes. Having

his arm around me warms my heart and my chilled body at the same time. His closeness feels good. I'm lucky to have him for a father. He's healthier now; strong and solid. A hope flashes through my mind. Perhaps someday, I'll sit on a porch with Sean's arm around my shoulders. That thought stabs me in the heart. Sean has made his choice, and it's not me.

As the evening darkens, I say, "What on earth is Mrs. Marino talking to Mother about? They don't even speak the same language."

"Well, the times we've had dinner with the Marinos, those two always figure out a way to communicate. It's a woman thing, I guess."

We pass the next half hour in comfortable quiet, both of us swinging and thinking our own thoughts.

Footsteps approach the porch from inside, and I stand. "Going for a walk around the block, Da."

He looks surprised but advises, "Take my Mackintosh with you."

As I stroll the familiar neighborhoods of South Boston, a soft rain dampens the stones beneath my feet. It feels good. I hear Ireland is like this a lot, misty and cool. I think I'd enjoy that.

Musing about my life in Boston and its many turns, I remember that come June, we'll be traveling to Ireland for Neo's and Angelique's wedding. It's doubtful Neo's mother will be able to come. She is now thin and weak, and no doctor seems able to help her. My mother says, "women's troubles." What does that mean?

I'm anxious to see Ireland for the first time. Mother and Da say it's beautiful. That if it weren't for the famine, they'd still be there. In a way, though, I'm glad they did leave Ireland. I probably wouldn't exist if they had stayed there. After all, they lived in different counties and might never have met.

I walk for nearly an hour and when I return home, the carriage is gone. My parents are in deep conversation at the kitchen table. Shaking the rain from my father's raincoat and hanging it up, I join them and ask, "What did Mrs. Marino want?"

Mother hesitates, which means she hasn't decided yet if she can answer the question. She looks at my da, her eyebrows raised. After a time, he gives his go-ahead. His face is sad.

"Nellie . . ." she says hesitantly, "what I'm going to tell you may hurt you, but you must hear it."

CHAPTER FIFTY-FIVE

As my father leaves us, he pats me on the shoulder.

"Sit down." Mother points to a chair.

Her tone is so serious. I take a deep breath into my chest. "All right." I sit.

She is twisting her apron between her hands, worrying the gingham until it looks ready to shred.

Why is she doing that? Why is she so nervous?

"Nellie," she begins, "this may be painful."

"All right," I say again, feeling nerves I didn't know were there tighten in my chest. Why does she look so serious, so distressed? Is there some problem with Da I don't know about? Perhaps something went wrong with a contract or something. "Just tell me, Mother, whatever it is."

She inhales a deep breath. "Well, love, it seems Sean O'Halloran, has created quite a mess."

Hearing his name brings a rush of blood to my head, and my face flames. "What kind of mess?" My hands begin to tremble. I clench them in my lap before she sees them.

"Did you know he's been seeing Rosie?"

"Yes, I knew, ever since you wouldn't let me go to Harvard for that football party. Rosie went in my stead." In some perverse corner of my soul, I hope she realizes now how she ruined my life.

She bows her head. "I didn't know that. Why didn't you tell me?" She looks sad and confused.

Why didn't I? Probably because I didn't want to talk about something that hurt so much. "Oh, I don't know." Suddenly, I am gripped by terror. "They're not getting married, are they?"

She seems surprised by the tone of my voice but hesitatingly continues. "Would that they were. But no, Nellie, they're not getting married."

My relief at her words stills my quivering hands. I wish I didn't care so much, but I do. "That's good."

"Not really," she answers. "That's why Maria came here today. She's desperately looking for help."

"What kind of help? Why from you?"

"She hasn't many friends in Boston and considers me one. Plus, she knows I run a birthing center."

"What does that have to do with Sean and Rosie?"

She shakes her head and bites her lower lip, clearly struggling for words.

Her words sink in. The birthing center part. "Mother, what does that have to do with Sean?" I repeat, my voice urgent.

When she looks up at me, her eyes fill with love and concern. "It seems Mr. O'Halloran has gotten Rosie in the family way."

Rosie's having Sean's baby? An image of them making love brings goosebumps to my arms. I shake my head to dispel the picture.

"But he refuses to marry her."

A wave of relief washes over me, a welcoming, cleansing salve. It's awful that I feel that now, but the relief remains. Probably, I should be ashamed of myself. Rosie was my best friend.

But she asked for it, didn't she? She shouldn't have gone behind my back with Sean. She knew I cared for him. In some peculiar way, I feel retribution for the pain last summer watching the two of them ogling each other at graduation. She's getting exactly what she deserves. But what about him?

Any boy will take a free handout if it's offered. I've known that since I was twelve. It was drilled into my head by my mother and the church and even by Da. "Don't let the boy taste the milk before he buys it, girl." Didn't Mr. Marino ever say that to Rosie? Somehow, I'm sure he did.

Rosie let Sean have the milk with no strings attached. She deserves everything she gets.

Cool as a cucumber, I ask, "So, what are the Marinos planning to do?"

"We're not sure yet, but I told Maria I'd help her."

CHAPTER FIFTY-SIX

The house buzzes for the next ten days with talks about Rosie. I go back to school, but Da tells me Mrs. Marino returns here four times during those days, each time looking more frightened and worried. I'm glad to not be around to witness the melodrama. Rosie's having Sean's baby. That's quite enough for me to ponder.

On Saturday, two weeks after her first visit, Mrs. Marino and my mother emerge from their kitchen conversation. Their expressions tell me something has been resolved.

As the carriage carrying Mrs. Marino pulls off from the front of our house, I follow my mother back into the kitchen. "Are things settled?"

"I think so." With that, she ties up her apron and pretends the matter is closed.

"How?" I persist.

She turns to me, her face unreadable. "I've met with Father Ruzzo and Sister Sarah, and they're helping us."

"In what way?"

"The Mercy nuns in Dublin take in girls in trouble. God love those nuns." She looks skyward.

"And?" Waiting for her answer makes me nervous. Her calmness is maddening. Does she think I can read her mind?

She turns to me, hands on hips, her mouth set in a determined line, "And we'll take Rosie with us to Ireland next month. Kam's agreed to help. Your father can't go. He has meetings scheduled with associates of Mr. Marino's in from Italy during that time. He can't get out of them. Rosie will have his passage. She'll share quarters with you. Martha is going in Imani's stead. I'll stay with her."

What did she just say? Rosie and I will share quarters? Not on my life we won't. "Mother, you expect me to room with Rosie? That's not going to happen. Why are we responsible for her? Why can't she go back to Sicily for God's sake?" I nearly scream.

She turns from the stove. The look in her eyes tells me the matter is settled, whether I like it or not. "Because someone must help the Marinos, Nellie. And never again let me hear you take the Lord's name in vain. Rosie can't go back to Sicily. She'd be a disgrace to her family there and here. In Ireland, no one knows her. The nuns will take good care of her until after the birth, and then make sure the baby has a good home. All in all, this is the best solution."

The best solution? I don't think so. I'll have to share my trip with the girl who betrayed me. I'd so looked forward to seeing Neo and Angelique married. And to seeing Ireland for the first time. *Why does no one think of my feelings?*

I am sullen for the rest of the weekend until my da can't take it anymore. "What's with the puss, girl? Put a smile on that face or put a veil over it."

So, I try.

We have two weeks until we sail. By then, my first year at Wellesley will be over. But I'm troubled by something and must get some questions answered. I must see Sean.

* * *

I know he's home from law school. Friends have seen him back in Boston during the past week. On Monday, pretending illness, I skip class and put on my prettiest dress, the blue one with the small hoop and ruffled sleeves. The one Mother bought me for Neo's wedding. Neither of my parents are at home or I'd never have gotten away with wearing it before then.

Carrying my pleated blue parasol, I walk to O'Halloran's Pub. I've never gone there alone before, but it's a short distance and familiar as my own neighborhood. On my way, two sailors whistle to get my attention. Should I be flattered or angry? It's never happened before. But they smile sweetly, so I decide to be flattered and smile back at them.

I arrive at three o'clock—a time I know I'll find the old pub quiet and empty—after the hectic lunch crowd and before the workmen arrive for their after-work pints.

As I open the front door, Uncle Tommy's voice booms out at me, "Nellie, what a pleasure to see you. The prettiest girl in Boston, I swan." He rushes up and grabs me in his burly bear arms for a hug.

"Uncle Tommy, how are you? Is Molly around?"

I know she's left for medical school in New York City, but figure it's a good ruse to explain my presence.

"Nah, she's off to school already. Didn't you know?"

Pretending ignorance, I shake my head.

"Molly's back at school, and Shannon is so busy with her three she can hardly visit her old da. The only bairn I've still got here is Sean." A stir on the stairs draws his attention. "And here's the lad now."

Sean lopes down the steps from upstairs. When he spots me, his smile is dazzling. "Nellie, look at you. A real beauty." He takes my hands and twirls me around to get a better look.

"Thank you, sir," I say, lowering my eyelashes. Being near

him again makes my heart pound. "Want to fix me a cup of tea?"

"Sure," He heads into the kitchen to prepare it, then taps a Guinness for himself.

When we settle in at a small table in the back, I tell him I'll sail for Ireland soon for Neo's wedding.

"Oh, he's really going to marry the Frenchie, huh?"

The way he says "Frenchie" bothers me, but I bury the feeling. I often don't understand Sean's vernacular, and I'm sure it's harmless. "Yes, on June 14th."

"Is she in the family way?"

I am shocked at the ease of his question. "No. They haven't seen each other since she went to Montreal, but they've both been faithful all these years. I think they're truly in love."

He grins and takes a long swig of the dark brew.

I decide it's time to speak my real reason for this visit. "Sean, did you know Rosie is coming to Ireland with me and my mother?"

"I heard a rumor."

"Not a rumor. It's the only way she can protect her family's good name. Have you seen her lately?"

He takes another swig of his beer. "Shit, that's good." He smiles and puts his hand to my face. "Be careful, Nellie. That tea's hot. Don't want you to burn that pretty mouth of yours."

"I'll be careful. Have you, Sean? Seen her lately, I mean."

"Nope. The last time I saw Rosie, she came up with a cocka-mamie story that she's expecting and I'm the father." He laughs out loud.

"Are you?"

"Who knows? I don't know how many boyos she's been with. She was certainly easy enough with me." He shakes his head. "She actually thought I'd marry her."

His words bother me. I don't believe Rosie's been with anyone else. She would have told me. "That's reasonable, Sean. You probably are her baby's father. Shouldn't you marry her?" I hold my breath.

He stares at me as if I'd said the stupidest thing in the world. "Are you kidding? I'm not marrying a guinea hen."

I am so startled by his words I jump in my chair. *Guinea hen?* "But Sean, you fancied her enough to get her in the family way. Don't you care?"

He leans his head back against his crossed hands. "Honestly, no I don't. She knew what she was getting into. She should have protected herself. I can't marry a dago, not if I want to be the first Catholic Mayor in this town. I'll need a fine Irish wife." He leans forward and looks into my eyes. "A wife such as you, Nellie."

I should despise him for his uncaring attitude. I should smack him in the face, and I know it. But honestly, all I feel is relief . . . and the possibility I still might end up as Sean O'Halloran's wife someday. *God help me.*

CHAPTER FIFTY-SEVEN

Today, we sail, and I've still told no one about my conversation with Sean. As my da pulls our wagon up to *The Gaelic Princess*, my mother talks about the difference from when she sailed from Ireland. "We'll all have cabins; no steerage this time."

I run up the gangplank, eager to explore the majestic ship docked before me.

Mother joins me on the deck while Da ties up the horse. "They say we should get to Dublin in three to four weeks. A miracle, that's what steam is. Our voyage back then took months because the wind stilled. I would never have lasted without Kam." She shakes her head. "At this age, a voyage like that would finish me."

She is forty-one years old and Uncle Kam is three years older. When they met on the ship in 1849, she was only thirteen and he sixteen. Her mouth draws tight. "It was a *coffin ship,* for God's sake. The bloody owners didn't care if it sank or we all died. They'd collect the insurance."

My father strolls up the gangplank and hears her. "Now Mary, don't think on the past. Those days of hell are over."

She grabs his arm and stares up into his face. "Ah, Daniel, I so wish you were coming. I shall miss you dreadfully."

"Someday, my love, I'll take you to Ireland for the honeymoon I couldn't give you when we married." He kisses her. "That's a promise. For now, let's look around this lovely scow."

It is hardly a scow. *The Gaelic Princess* is magnificent; a massive ship painted white and emerald green. Two large smokestacks belch out steam. She has two decks with wooden walks around each of them. I'll love strolling this ship.

In spite of my dread of spending so much time with Rosie, my excitement has built. Neo is getting married, and I'll be in Ireland. Nothing can spoil that, even sharing a room with the girl who stole my true love.

Peering out over the rail, I see the Marinos pull up down below. Mr. Marino is driving the horse, and his wife and Rosie are perched behind him. He helps them both down, and I am surprised at how swollen Rosie's body already is. No one's seen her for at least two months. From what I've heard, her family has been hiding her in their house.

When she glances up and sees me, she grins and then lowers her eyes. She's embarrassed. Well, she should be. Somehow, though, knowing that Sean has no intention of ever meeting this baby hits me straight in the heart. In spite of myself, I pity her.

Would I have been as foolish as Rosie had I gone to that party with him? I'm not certain I wouldn't have. Sean can charm the birds out of the trees when he wants to. Yes, charming describes him. Prince Charming.

And he still may be my Prince Charming someday. Who knows?

My mother heads down the gangplank and hugs Mrs. Marino. Mr. Marino kisses her on the cheek saying, "Thank you, Mary, thank you!" over and over again. My da joins her and shakes Mr. Marino's hand.

"All right, all of you," my father calls out, "let's get all the trunks unloaded and onto this ship." He lifts mine and my mother's down from our wagon and passes them off to a waiting deck hand. Then, he helps Mr. Marino tug Rosie's trunk off the back of their carriage.

The porter tells us, "I'll deliver these to your cabins." Mr. Marino slips some money into his hand.

As the young man begins to haul the luggage up the gang-plank on a pull cart, Rosie stands near me. She whispers, "Nellie, I know you're still mad at me. I am sorry."

For a second, I'd like to turn my back, but then the memory of Sean calling her a guinea hen jumps to my brain. "Look, Rosie, we'll never be best friends again, but let's make this trip as good as it can be."

She is visibly grateful.

Just then, the Okafors' carriage pulls up. Neo, his face beaming with excitement, climbs down. Uncle Kam jumps nimbly down beside him and extends his hand up to Aunt Imani. I haven't seen her since last Thanksgiving and her appearance startles me. She's haggard, and her skin has a dusty pallor, which she's tried to conceal with rouge. The two bright circles on her cheeks only make her look more tired and worn. Martha perches beside her, worry lines etched on her dark face.

"What's happened to her, Mother?" I whisper.

"I'm not sure, Nellie, but it's awful. I fear it's the wasting disease."

I've heard of this before; always in hushed tones behind gloved hands. They don't have a name for this illness, but it seems to kill everyone who has it; some very quickly, others more slowly. Poor Aunt Imani, she looks nothing like the vibrant, beautiful woman I remember.

Soon, though, I am wrapped in Martha's arms and enveloped by her musky scent and soft skin.

"Martha, we would prefer you share Nellie's cabin," Mother says.

I stare at her in open astonishment. Catching my obvious shock, she takes me aside. "Nellie, I know how you feel about Rosie, and I don't blame you. Martha's been another mother to you for years. Will you be happier sharing her quarters?"

I don't answer her question; I just take her in my arms and squeeze.

"So, that's settled. Martha will stay in Nellie's cabin and, Rosie, you will stay with me."

"Oh, Miss Mary. That don't seem proper," Martha starts, shaking her head.

My mother laughs. "Well, it's Nellie, Kam, or Neo. Take your choice."

If Martha can turn pink, I swear she does.

My father takes Mother into his arms and pulls me to them for a long embrace. "Gonna miss my girls."

"Daniel, sweetheart, why don't you change your mind. It's not too late. Kam will arrange it if you wish."

"Wish I could, love, but I have a court date set and promised to meet with those associates of Marino's. I have some questions to ask them. Some of their contracts don't seem legitimate."

"How so?"

"I'm probably just being a stickler, Mary. Maybe it's the legalese getting mixed up in the Italian dialect, but I need to know what's going on." He turns away and, with tears threatening his eyes, runs down the gangplank to our buggy.

CHAPTER FIFTY-EIGHT

My mother stands at the rail waving until he's out of sight. Then, she turns to me., "Let's find our cabins," brushing at her eyes. They've never been parted before.

Our cabins are on the top deck of the ship; and when my mother sees hers, she squeals with joy. "Look, a window!"

"It's called a porthole, Mary," Uncle Kam laughs.

My room is small with two beds on opposite walls. Covering the beds are blue spreads with bright colored fish and sails embroidered all over them. A tiny porthole looks out over the water and a kerosene lamp stands on the single dresser. I'm happy to see there's a bathroom attached. Two sets of white towels hang over a rack there.

As Martha and I unpack our things, she turns to me, "Miss Nellie, you mind roomin' with old Martha? Does it humble you to have a colored woman stayin' with you?"

I take her hands into mine and sit down beside her on a bed. "Martha, I cannot think of anyone I'd rather share this voyage with. I've loved you for years. I'm honored to have you here with me."

Her smile shows her relief. "Good, Miss. When Mister Okafor told me I be takin' Neo's mother's place, I couldn't 'magine how

I'd feel sailin' on a fancy ship and eating in an all-white dining room. He told me not to worry about it. I hadn't thought about how I'd have to share quarters with someone. Now that it's you, I'll be just fine. I'm just so sorry Miss Imani can't be at her son's wedding." She shakes her head.

"My mother is terribly worried about her, Martha. Do you know what's wrong?"

"No, Miss. She be doctorin' all de time tryin' to figure it out. Goes to one doctor after the next. In the meantime, I try to get her to eat more, but she won't do it. Says she's just not hungry." Her eyes brim with tears. "She looks like a skeleton."

An hour later, Martha and I walk out onto the deck to meet the others for dinner. I hold her arm to steady her against the rolling waves.

When we find our group, Neo links his arms through ours. If his smile was any wider, he'd crack his jaw. He's practically dancing with excitement. He's on his way to Angelique and, in a few weeks, he'll marry her. My heart warms. It's good to see my friend happy again. That's not been the case during the years since he left Angelique back in Albany.

Their love has weathered such a long separation. Clearly, it is true. I guess you know it when that's the case. I can't tell Neo, though, that I believe my true love is Sean O'Halloran. Neo's been very clear about what he thinks of Sean.

Martha and I join my mother at the rail.

"I so wish Daniel could have come with us," she wistfully wishes aloud. "I hope he'll see Ireland again, and that I'll be with him." Another example of true, lasting love. I want to experience that someday.

We lean against the rail watching Boston fade into the evening mist. The people scurrying over the wharf area appear to be tiny ants off in the distance.

Suddenly, Mother claps her hands. "Well, this isn't getting us fed, and I'm famished. Let's go eat."

The dining room is one deck down. Slowly, we walk down the steps bracing ourselves against the swaying of the ship. Martha and I both giggle at our careful steps and the way I hang onto the handrail. She treads behind me, one hand on my shoulder.

A crowd is assembled outside the dining room. We wait our turn and I am struck by its opulence. It's much larger than the one on the *Bristol* steamship Neo and I took from Fall River to New York so long ago, and even more elegant with high ceilings and silver chandeliers. The tables are covered in immaculate white linen, and each one is set with china Uncle Kam says was hand painted in Italy. As I pass an empty table, I momentarily lift a silver fork and am surprised by its weight.

Then remembering the *Bristol*, my heart constricts. What if they won't allow coloreds into this fancy dining hall? It happened before with Neo.

Uncle Kam eases my fears, though, as he approaches the *maître d* who welcomes him with open arms. Maybe with enough money, skin color doesn't matter. Many heads turn, though, as we pass their tables, some with disapproval. Uncle Kam and Neo glide confidently past them in their black frock coats and striped trousers. Martha lifts her chin and pretends to ignore the stares as if they're not worth her time or attention.

And they're not. My pride in Martha soars. It takes courage to ignore someone who hates you for the color of your skin, and no other reason.

I touch Martha on the shoulder. As she turns and smiles at me, I realize these people looking down their noses don't compare to the elegance of the Okafors or the sweetness of their maid.

Walking behind Uncle Kam, Rosie takes great pains to cover her stomach with her arms. The outline of her corset visibly bulges under the thin blue silk of her bodice.

Her dress has the empire waist that has had a resurgence in Boston fashion, but the slight protrusion below the waistband ruins its effect. Her head is down, and the sparkle that was always in her eyes is gone.

As we take our places, Rosie's bosom swells up and over the low neckline of her dress. Rather than seductive, she simply looks chubby. Her skin is pasty and her dour expression makes me forget she used to be so pretty. Even her curls don't bounce any more.

Pity rises for this girl who was my dearest friend, then I remind myself of what Sean said. She knew exactly what she was getting into. Of course, she did. Rosie's smart. Perhaps she thought she could trap him into marriage.

"Order whatever you wish," Uncle Kam says from the head of the table. "Don't worry about the price. It's all taken care of."

I study the menu and decide to try something I've never tasted. Lobster. When it arrives at the table on a gigantic plate, red and menacing, I am confounded. The shell is so hard. How am I supposed to eat this thing? It looks prehistoric and dangerous.

Neo picks up the nutcracker from my plate and cracks the shell of the monster. Then, he takes a tiny fork and pulls out a piece of white meat and feeds it to me. It is delicious. "Be careful, Nellie, don't let it squirt all over your pretty dress," he warns.

My mother asks for a taste of the lobster, and I put a morsel on her plate. "Oh, my!" She rolls her eyes in ecstasy. "I don't want to get too used to this. It's a mite expensive for a midwife's budget, I'm sure."

We finish up the delicious meal with something called *crème brûlée*, which is the most wonderful dessert I've ever tasted.

"I believe this used to be called English cream." My mother spoons a bite into her mouth. "Isn't it lovely? I can't believe the bloody English invented such a delightful confection."

Kam and Neo laugh, recognizing my mother's ongoing antagonism toward the British. She still prays for Irish independence from Great Britain. I don't really know why that's so important, but Mother thinks the British are at the root of every evil that drove her out of her country.

I am becoming more and more excited for this trip. Not just to see Ireland but also to watch Neo and Angelique reunite. I can't believe they're actually getting married. I mean, they only spent a few weeks together. But whatever they feel has stood against the four years and the thousands of miles separating them.

I'll bet Angelique will be the most beautiful bride in the world.

CHAPTER FIFTY-NINE

Two weeks have passed since we sailed out of Boston Harbor. I'm used to the constant lurching and swaying of the ship now, and my footing is steady as I stroll her decks. At night, the rocking lulls me into a deep, fast sleep. It's familiar and hearkens to something I can't believe I remember, my mother soothing me to sleep in the old rocker that still sits on our front porch. I felt so safe, so loved. And still do.

Rosie has not been so lucky on the ship. Every morning, she hangs over the rail vomiting the contents of her stomach. My mother tells me that's quite normal for a girl in "her condition."

Today, before lunch, she asked if she could talk to me about Sean. Though I'm at immediate attention hearing his name, a mix of excitement and pain tightens my heart. And, my anger returns, seething and painful. If she considers I'll be a sympathetic friend, she'd best think again.

We settle in two lounges on the lower deck. The upper deck shields our eyes from the sun, and the strollers-by can't hear us as they pass. The sound of waves is a great muffler.

Cracker crumbs sprinkle the front of her blouse. Though she starves herself at dinner to stop gaining weight, my mother told her crackers are good for settling an expectant woman's stomach.

"The thing is, Nellie," she looks all dreamy-eyed, "I really do care for him. He was the first and only man I ever loved. I would never have done what we did if I weren't crazy about him."

Oh yes, I can understand that. Sean is a man designed to drive a girl crazy. God knows he's done that to me. "What do you expect to happen now?"

She lies back on the chaise lounge. At my question, she rolls to her side and looks at me with dark, sad eyes. "He doesn't want to get married, but I hope he'll change his mind." Her eyes fill with tears. "After all, this is his baby, too."

I don't tell her what Sean said to me; that he called her a "guinea hen" and that she doesn't fit into his political plans. Although some evil part of me wants to hurt her as much as she hurt me, I can't bring myself to tell her those things. Instead, I say, "Sean is a typical hard-headed Irishman and they don't often change their minds about anything."

In spite of my anger, I do feel compassion for the fix she's gotten herself into. What's this girl, this smart, funny girl going to do with the rest of her life? Without college, without suitors? Who's going to want her now that she's *damaged?*

Her next question makes me sit up with a start. "Do you think we can ever be friends again, Nellie?"

I stand quickly and turn away. If I don't get away quickly, I fear I'll cry. "I don't think so, Rosie. You hurt me too much." As I walk off, she dabs at her eyes with her handkerchief.

Martha often rests in the afternoon in our cabin. That's when I explore the ship. One day, I stroll to the top deck and hang out over the rail. The wind whips my face and pulls my hair straight back and the flap of the sails sets a rhythm that thrills me. Sometimes, looking at the sails, I yearn to climb to the top of the masts. That would probably be as exciting as flying on a trapeze. But I better not do that. A girl who may one day be the First Lady of Boston must maintain her decorum.

Looking out over the vast ocean, I wonder what lies ahead for me. I'll finish college, of course, and become a teacher. But then what? If I get married, I'll probably not be able to teach any more. Most husbands don't want wives who work. My da is the exception. He told me, "I didn't marry a dishrag, and I don't want one. I married your mother because I love her quite a lot, but also because she has things in her life that continue to make her interesting. Keep that in mind, Nellie, when you pick a husband someday."

What would Sean O'Halloran think of having a teacher for a wife? Not much, I'd wager. I think he'd expect a woman to tend to him and their children. And, of course, look beautiful at political parties. How would I feel about that? Would that life make me unhappy, no matter how much I loved him?

Watching Rosie on this voyage, I'm really not sure I want to have babies. I said that once to my mother, and she answered, "You may change your mind when you're a bit older, Nellie. But if you don't, stick to your guns. Don't let a man boss you around."

But if Sean was doing the bossing, would I obey?

After one more week on the ship, I begin to feel restless. "When will we get there, Uncle Kam?"

"I figure we'll disembark in about six days, Nellie. Count your lucky stars. The voyage your mother and I took from Ireland was much longer than this one. The ship didn't have steam. When the winds died down, we drifted for weeks."

One more week? I can stand that.

CHAPTER SIXTY

Tonight, as I lay in bed listening to the waves caressing the ship, Martha breaks through my drowsy half sleep.

"Miss Nellie, you happy?"

I roll to my side and prop my head up on my hand. "That's an odd question. I suppose so. Why do you ask?"

She harrumphs and sits up. "It seems to old Martha you ain't as happy as you oughta be. I recall my girl being such a joyous child. I don't see that light in your eyes no more."

Should I tell her?

Martha has always been a second mother to me. Some strange bond binds us. I can't tell my mother how much Sean and Rosie have hurt me. She'd hover too much. But I need advice on how to handle my feelings. Sometimes, I think I'm jealous because Neo is going to marry his true love, while I'm being reminded every day on this ship that the man I love has gotten another girl in the family way.

I can trust Martha. If I ask her not to tell anyone what I say, she won't breathe a word.

The ship hits a huge wave at that moment, and I am nearly rocked to the floor. "Mercy!" I screech.

"Lordy, that was a big one," Martha murmurs.

As we settle back into our beds, I decide. I will confide in Martha.

"Martha, have you noticed that Rosie is, um, getting heavier?"

"Pshaw, that girl ain't just heavier. That girl's got a bun in her oven, sure as shootin'. Anybody can tell that. But what's that got to do with you bein' happy?"

"Well, see, Rosie and I used to be best friends."

"Uh-huh."

"But that's changed."

"Clear's day. You two hardly speak."

"The reason is Rosie stole a boy she knew I cared about."

"That girl hornswoggled your sweetie away from you? Well, if that don't beat all."

"Surely does."

"And is he the rascal who got her in this condition, Bae?"

"Yes."

"Well, he ain't no good. No good a'tall then. Cheatin' on a girl like you? That young buck is just plain crazy. You need to forget him."

I pause for a moment. "But you see, I still love him."

Silence. More silence.

"Martha, you asleep?"

She rises from her bed, lights a candle, and opens her dresser drawer. "Nah, but what you sayin' makes me jittery. I needs a little chaw to calm my nerves."

"You do chaw?"

"Yessum. For over forty years now." She chews and smacks her lips on the smelly chaw. After a time, she is ready to talk some more. "This be the same one brought you and Neo home from the circus?"

"Yes."

"My stars, girl. I knowed that one was no good the moment

I met him. He got that strut; that old cock-a-de-walk swagger. Old Martha loved a few like that in 'er time."

"You did?" I am shocked. I'd never thought of Martha having any life outside of the Okafor house.

"Uh-huh, even had a child by one a them. It died, though. A little girl. She even had blue eyes. Her daddy was the son of the plantation owner. Some folks say new babies ugly, but not her. She was pretty as a picture, just like you. She only lived six months. No matter how I tried, she just wouldn' thrive. But oh, Lordy, how I loved that child. Never loved nothin' as much as that since . . . 'cept you."

Except me? Is that why we've always had such a close bond? Because I remind her of her dead child? Whatever it is, I'm grateful. I love Martha, too. And trust her.

"Oh, he was good lookin' an' so strong he could pick me up like I was no heavier than a feather. His blue eyes was kind, an' his hands so gentle he made me feel things I never felt before or since. Yessum, he was special."

After that night, I confide in Martha often as we lay in our beds on that rocking ship. Her advice remains the same, to forget Sean. But when she speaks of that other man, her voice takes on a softness in remembrance that speaks volumes. She understands what I'm feeling.

And when she talks about him, which she often does now, I doubt Martha has practiced what she preaches to me about Sean. It's clear as crystal that after all these years, she has never forgotten him.

CHAPTER SIXTY-ONE

For days now, I've wanted to ask Martha a question. About that thing that sometimes happens to me in the middle of night. The first time, I was dreaming of Sean when I woke up with my fingers wet in that private place no one speaks of. It's occurring more and more often, and I fear having it happen while I'm sharing quarters with Martha. What if I moan or yell? I don't want to alarm her.

This is nothing I have spoken of with anyone, certainly not my mother, though I do wonder if what happens is a sin and I need to confess it to Father Ruzzo. If it is, I'll surely burn in hell. I could never tell a man about it, even a priest. Especially a priest.

We have talked about so many things, Martha and I, her life in Kentucky as a slave, love and loss, pain and disappointment. But I don't know what to call this thing. Sometimes, I worry that I'm a freak. Surely other girls don't wake as I do, perspiration covering their bodies and their hands exploring that private place. If it happens to other girls, there'll be a name for it, won't there? Martha will know.

She had just climbed into bed with a mighty sigh, but she's not asleep. I haven't yet blown out the cabin's candles to settle down for the night. The timing is perfect.

"Martha, I need to ask you about something personal."

"Uh-huh?"

"Well, this is so personal that I'd absolutely die if you told anyone else."

"Then I won't."

I lie down on my bed. "Even if you think it's something my mother needs to know about me? Something medical?"

"Honey, if you don't want me to tell nobody, I won't do it. My word."

I take in a deep breath, realizing my body is trembling. "Well, see, Martha, sometimes in the night, when I'm sound asleep and dreaming, something happens to me."

"What somethin'?"

"Like a convulsion or a seizure."

She doesn't answer right away. I look to see her eyes are open and staring at the ceiling.

"Are you thinking over there?"

"Yessum. Does this seizure feel bad or good?"

"Good, really good."

"And do you do anything to make it happen?"

"Not intentionally, but . . . but . . . well, sometimes when I wake up my fingers are all wet and I'm wet down there, but not from wetting myself or anything. It's a different kind of wet."

"Ah, my lil' girl's growin' up." She gets out of her bed and comes to mine. She sits on its edge and takes my hand in hers. With the other hand, she brushes the hair back from my forehead and smiles at me. "Honey, you just gettin' your marble rolled."

"What's that?" I sit up and she cradles me in her arms as if I'm a baby.

She releases me and looks deep into my eyes. "You dreamin' over a young man when this happens?"

"Sometimes."

"Well, honey, you knows how people love each other when they get married?" Her voice is deep and warm like smooth, sweet honey. "What's happenin' to you at night is gettin' you body ready for that."

"But I'm not married. I don't even have a gentleman friend. I've never even been kissed, except on the cheek."

"No matter," she continues to hold me and soothe me with the honey of her words. "When a marriage is good, real good, that's what happens with a man, too."

"Did that happen to you?"

She stops rocking and lays me back down in my bed. She remains seated there. Her eyes take on a dreamy, faraway look as if she's remembering a time long ago in another place. "Uh-huh, but only with my baby's daddy; never with anyone else."

"But did you ever feel that way alone? Isn't that unnatural?"

"Unnatural? Don't be silly, girl. Sure, it happens sometimes in your sleep. That's just God's way of helpin' you shake out some of your problems. Don't happen to me no more—ever. Wish it did."

"Do you think it's a sin?"

She straightens to attention. "A sin? That's crazy talk, girl. How can a gift from God be a sin? Besides, God made you the way you is, an' God don't make no mistakes, does he? Uh-uh, no way that's a sin."

All the worry and guilt washes away from me. It's like a baptism. I feel clean and light. Martha is right. It's not my fault. None of this happens because I will it. It just happens. God wants me to feel the rapture. I'm healthy and normal. Martha knows.

"But what if I marry someone someday and it doesn't happen?" I ask her.

She shakes her head. "No way, honey. If he loves you back, he'll make sure it happens. That's one way to judge his love before you marry 'im. A man who loves you right takes care a his woman. You be able to tell."

The next morning, I find Rosie reclining in a lounge on the deck. My curiosity is intense. Sitting in a chair beside her, I say, "Rosie, when you and Sean coupled, did it feel, uh, wonderful?"

"What?"

"Heat all over your body, with everything tingling and vibrating?"

She stares at me as if I have grown another head. Her mouth is open and her eyes bulge. "I don't know what you're talking about, Nellie. It only happened a couple of times. The first time, it just hurt like blue blazes. The second time, he finished in a flash and left. I didn't feel anything . . ." her eyes brim, "except regret."

Strangely, I'm not surprised. Martha says the man has to love you back to make it happen. But I do feel ever so sad for Rosie. Here she is going to be a mother without ever having her marble rolled.

CHAPTER SIXTY-TWO

It is the following Saturday after breakfast that Neo runs into the dining room.

"Nellie, come out!" he yells. "We see land!"

I run up the steps to the upper deck, pulling Martha and my mother behind me. When we arrive at the rail, it's crowded with passengers. Uncle Kam motions us over to join him. We're all there except Rosie who remains in bed. We lean out over the rail, covering our eyes with our hands and stare across the waves to what appears to be a speck on the horizon.

"Is that Ireland?" my mother asks, screaming over the noise of the steam engine.

"Yes, ma'am," answers a passing porter. "Sure is."

"Oh!" she cries out, dancing from one foot to the other. "I feared I'd never see her again in this lifetime. Isn't she beautiful?"

I strain my eyes trying to see what she is seeing, but there's nothing but a dot out there. When I glance at her, her eyes are closed in bliss as if she sees some scene etched in memory; a memory from twenty-eight years ago when she left her home.

After an hour, we are close enough to see the green of the hillside. It looks like a patchwork quilt of every shade of green in the world's imagination. Emerald, hunter, moss, and mint are divided by dark green borders, which, on closer look, seem to be hedgerows.

"That's to separate properties," my mother explains when I comment on the borders.

The verdant landscape is breathtaking. As the sun peeks in and out of the clouds, the colors change, sometimes dancing brilliantly, sometimes subdued. This constant visual transformation would feed a soul and imagination forever, I think. Ireland looks to be a magical place. No wonder my parents hated leaving her.

When I turn to my mother, tears now glisten in her eyes. "Oh, Nellie," she hugs me tightly, "welcome home."

I remember back when her words would have annoyed me. I wanted nothing to do with being Irish. I associated it with poverty, lack of education, and ignorance. But now, looking at this shimmering island, I see why my parents' voices turn soft and almost mystical when they speak of her.

"Look, Mother, a lighthouse!"

"Ah, the Poolbeg Lighthouse. That stretch of beach it sits on is the Great South Wall. Long, isn't it?"

"Four miles long, actually," Neo hands me his binoculars, "I read about it."

Through the glasses, I see people on that strand of beach, sunning themselves. I hadn't thought of Ireland as having beaches, but that's a beach, and a busy one, too.

My da took me to Carson Beach in South Boston once, but since neither of us were swimmers, we just walked around and laughed at the funny swimming outfits.

On this beach, the bathing costumes are more elaborate than the ones in Boston. The women are in puffy belted dresses over bloomers, their heads topped with pert straw hats. The men wear something akin to my father's long underwear. The women's costumes are colorful, but the mens' are drab and gray. None of the women are actually swimming, though they wade into the water and mince around daintily as if the water freezes their ankles.

Our ship takes a hefty turn to the right and everyone runs across to the other railing to get a better view.

"May I see the binoculars?" Mother asks.

I hand them to her and she puts them to her eyes. "Oh, I can see the harbor now. About eight ships anchored there, most of them sailing vessels. It's quite different than I remember the harbor at Queenstown; not as bustling."

"Actually, it's a busier harbor than Cork. It's the most active port in Ireland," Uncle Kam says.

"Must have been the famine," my mother answers. "Everyone was frantic and scurrying to get away back then. Now it's different." She lifts the binoculars again. "But I still see British flags on most of the ships." Her voice is deep with disgust. "'Tis enough to make me sick. Will they ever get out of Ireland?"

I put my arm around her waist and hug tight. She turns to me, surprised at my sudden gesture of affection, and then smiles and kisses me on the cheek.

Somehow, seeing Ireland has made me more compassionate toward my mother. She was just a little girl when she left here. She had buried her mother and sister and was venturing across the sea alone to find her father. I glance over at Uncle Kam and see in my mind's eye the boy he was when she first saw him. Young, brash, but certainly terrified. He must have been dreadfully frightened after being ripped away from his family in Africa and thrust into the cruel world of the sea.

They turn to each other and a look passes between them that is much deeper than understanding. It is a bond of compassion and love that saved them both when survival itself seemed impossible.

"I won't see my home again," Uncle Kam says. "The Congo is now ruled by Belgium, and Europeans are raping the entire continent for cotton, rubber, and diamonds. And the slave trade still goes strong. I wouldn't be safe there."

"Do you wish you could go back, Father?" Neo asks.

He shakes his head. "Nah, there's nothing there for me anymore."

"Me, neither," Martha agrees.

Neo and I glance at each other, both, I think, realizing how lucky we are. What have we suffered that compares with what these people have gone through? My days of pouting over losing Sean must end. It's time to grow up.

CHAPTER SIXTY-THREE

When we are one-quarter mile from the harbor, the steam engines are shut down, and the tugboats set out from shore toward us. One latches onto our ship and, with a lurch, we are pulled toward the dock.

Neo grabs the binoculars back from my mother. "Excuse me, Mrs. Kelly. I'm just so anxious to see her."

She hands them over with a smile.

He raises them to his eyes and scans the pier. It is not crowded with people, and very soon he sees Angelique. He gasps. "I see her! My angel!"

His excitement reverberates through our small party. We know how long he has longed to be with this girl.

Uncle Kam asks, "May I look, Neo? I want to see my new daughter."

When he looks through the glasses, he asks, "Is she wearing a green dress?"

"Yes, Father. That's Angelique."

"Exquisite," Uncle Kam murmurs.

We take turns looking through the binoculars. She looks even more beautiful than I remembered. Her brother, Jean, stands beside her. Her blonde curls are swept up and back into a comb of green crystals and then cascade down her back. Her emerald silk dress has a low scooped neckline over an elongated bodice.

The skirt of Angelique's dress is in the new fashion featured in the last issue of *Godey's Lady Book*. The overskirt swoops up and back to a soft bustle over an underskirt of white ruffles. She looks fashionable and elegant and so very grown up, though she's just two years older than I am.

"She has to be wearing a corset," my mother whispers to me. "Her waist looks tinier than yours, and her bosom larger."

A tinge of jealousy makes me pull myself taller and draw my shoulders back. It passes quickly as I see Neo gazing adoringly at his soon-to-be bride. The utter joy wreathing his face makes me happy. I haven't seen that expression since we left the circus.

When she sees Neo waving from the railing of the ship, she stands on tip toe and waves back to him, her smile a burst of pure joy. Yes, she loves him every bit as much as he loves her.

"She's a beauty, Son." Uncle Kam wraps his arm around Neo's shoulders.

"And her spirit is as beautiful as her face, Father."

It seems to take forever, but soon we are at the dock and the tug boat unhooks us with a lot of clamor and cheering from passengers. Anchors are dropped into the water, and we pull to a jolting halt.

"That was a very long four weeks getting here," I comment.

"Kam and I were on that coffin ship three times as long." Mother hugs my shoulders. "Thank your lucky stars for steam engines."

Earlier, all our trunks had been placed in the hallways for the porters to unload them down to the harbor. So when the gangplank lowers, we run toward it. Neo is the first down. He pulls

Angelique into his arms and kisses her. I feel as if I'm intruding on something very personal and look away.

Martha stirs beside me. "Good thing those two's gettin' married soon. Otherwise, stuff gonna happen between them pretty quick."

I laugh. "Martha, how can you say such a thing?"

"Honey, I knows human nature better'n you I knows passion when I see it, and it's right there in front of these eyes. Some marbles gonna roll quick like for those two."

Laughing, I breathe in the scent of Ireland. The sweetness of it is so different than Massachusetts or New York. It feels clean and crisp and a little damp, though it's not raining. I fill my lungs and heart with air from the land of my ancestors.

My mother searches the crowd. "Where's Rosie?"

In the excitement, I'd almost forgotten her. Gazing up towards the ship, I see her coming down the gangplank. Her expression is in stark contrast to the joy I feel. She scowls and holds onto the rope of the gangplank with a death grip. Again, cracker crumbs cover the front of her dress, her bonnet is askew, and she walks as if her feet hurt. I suppose I should pity my old friend, and I nearly do. Mostly, I'm grateful I'm not in her situation. I shake the thought away. No reason to ponder that now. I don't even have a suitor. At that moment, Sean O'Halloran seems a million miles away.

When I hit the dock, my legs are wobbly and I nearly fall down. "Oops!" I say, giggling at myself.

"Sea legs, girlie," a passing sailor says. "Happens to every-one."

Jean and Neo begin to load our belongings into two carriages parked there. Drivers sit up top. Behind them are two open seating areas. The eight of us will fit into them, barely. It's a good thing no one in the group is stout.

Jean tells us in heavily accented English that he has arranged lodging at two houses here in Dublin. Uncle Kam and Neo will stay at the house that he and Angelique occupy, and the rest of us at a house next door.

CHAPTER SIXTY-FOUR

As we unload our trunks in front of our respective houses, Angelique comes to me. "Ah, Nellie, dear Nellie, it is good to see you again. You look beautiful. I didn't ask earlier, but I would like for you to stand with me as my bridesmaid. I would have asked you by mail, but I didn't have your address, and letter writing in English is still a challenge for me."

I am touched by her words. Neo is as close to a brother as I'll ever know, so Angelique is almost like my sister. I hug her around that tiny waist and say, "I would be honored, Angelique. Do I need to wear anything special?"

"No, I'm certain that any dress you have will be appropriate. Or, if you wish, I'll lend you something. The designer I modeled for in Montreal gave me the gift of a wonderful trousseau."

Looking at that impossibly small waist, I laugh. "I don't think I could fit into anything that fits you; not without a very strong corset, and then I wouldn't be able to breathe."

She laughs back. "I know. I'm squeezed so tight now I fear I'll turn blue."

That makes me feel better. Perhaps I'm not that much bigger than she is, and perhaps my bosom would be high and round like hers if I had a corset pushing it up. I haven't worn one since I left Boston, but it is packed, just in case I want it for the wedding.

Neo has finished loading our trunks into the wagon, and Angelique runs to him. "Love, Nellie has agreed to be my bridesmaid. Isn't that perfect?"

He grins and wraps his arm around her and me. "Can't think of anyone better."

Oh, I'm going to miss Neo when I leave Ireland.

"Tonight, we dine at a real Irish pub," Jean announces. "I have registered at Trinity College for a degree in business management, and my student adviser is playing at The Brazen Head. I told him we'd come there. The food is adequate, and the whiskey *tres bon.* The Irish aren't much on wine, but they make it up in spirits."

"A pub?" Mother is excited and shocked at the same time. "A real Irish pub? Oh, Kam, wait'll they get a load of you. There are few blacks in Ireland. You and Neo and Martha will be feted like celebrities."

"Is it all right for women to go to these pubs?" Rosie asks. "In Boston, they have back rooms where the women remain. I went to one with . . . er, um . . . with a friend."

No doubt, she means Sean. Before she left for school, his sister, Molly, told me he loves pubs, but I'll guarantee he didn't take her to O'Halloran's. His father would scream if he set foot in there with an Italian girl. Uncle Tommy calls them Eyetralians and Wops. I'm surprised he doesn't hate Negroes. Mother says he always liked Uncle Kam. He even let him tend his bar one St. Patrick's night. Called him Black Irish.

Jean laughs. "Not in Ireland. The women rule the roost and go where they wish." "Do Irish women work after they marry?" I ask, most interested in their independence.

"Some do, I think. The Irish Times ran a story last week about Irish suffragettes. Women trying to get the right to vote."

"Here, too?" Mother chuckles. "I guess that's happening everywhere, just like in Boston. I wish them well but doubt the vote'll happen in my lifetime."

Our lodging is a quick fifteen-minute ride from the dock. It's a charming two-story wooden home with flowers blooming around a white wooden fence in the yard. At the door, a plump Irish woman greets us warmly, "Ah, look at that face, will ye. It has the map of Ireland on it," she says, touching my cheek.

"Looks just like her da, she does," my mother answers. "He's a looker, too." I notice my mother's brogue is back and stronger than ever.

When our hostess sees Martha, her eyes widen for a second. It's clear she doesn't see many black people at her door. But she recovers quickly and opens her door wider.

"Well, come in, come in. I'm Mrs. Conley, the proprietress of this house. Would ye care for a wee cup of tea?"

"That'd be grand," my mother answers.

My mother, Rosie, Martha, and I sit in her parlor and she bustles off to the kitchen.

"Isn't this lovely?" Mother asks, touching the white lace curtains covering both windows. The room is painted a tranquil blue and family portraits cover the walls. A small piano sits in the corner.

"I have two rooms fer ye upstairs," Mrs. Conley says, setting the teapot and cups on the table. "After tea, I'll show ye up." We all sit down.

The tea is black and delicious, accompanied by small cookies served on thin, luminescent white china plates. My mother lifts one and exclaims, "Mrs. Conley, this china is exquisite."

"It's Belleek from County Tambour in the North. They just started making it. Isn't it lovely, though?"

"Indeed, it is," my mother answers, turning the cup in her

hands. "And might I ask where you got these lace curtains? I have some at home, but they don't compare to these."

"Ah, yes," Mrs. Conley replies, pride lighting her eyes. "They are fine lace from Limerick; the best in Ireland."

"Beautiful," my mother breathes softly as she rises and crosses the room to examine the curtains more closely.

After we finish our tea, Mrs. Conley says, "All right then, I'll show ye to yer rooms now."

Each room holds twin beds and its own closet and chest of drawers. Light filters into them through more lace curtains covering sparkling windows. Martha's and my room's walls are covered with beautiful wallpaper of pink roses. I've never seen wallpaper in Boston. My mother's and Rosie's room has a yellow daffodil pattern on all the walls.

Rosie touches the wall and studies it closely. "Oh my, isn't that lovely?"

"Will these satisfy?" Mrs. Conley asks.

"Indeed, they look very comfortable," Mother answers.

Martha nods vigorously.

When Mrs. Conley goes back downstairs, Mother suggests, "Well, why don't we unpack now and perhaps take a short rest before dinner?" She takes a small pocket watch from her purse. "It's four o'clock, Irish time. Let's meet downstairs when the clock strikes half past five."

I think I'm much too excited to sleep but am surprised when I awaken with a start as the grandfather clock downstairs strikes five chimes.

Rising from the soft bed, I creep across the room and look out the window. A light rain is falling. Martha is still sleeping, her mouth ajar and her eyes shut tight.

I head into the small bathroom and quickly wash my face and hands, then tiptoe to the rack where I have hung my dresses and select a new yellow frock my mother bought me for this trip. I don't bother with a corset, although it whittles my waist down to a tiny size. Comfort is important tonight. I intend to have fun during my first visit to a real Irish pub.

By the time I'm dressed, Martha is sitting up on the side of her bed. "Oh, honey, don't you look pretty. Here, let me do your hair up for you."

She pulls the sides up to the top of my head and ties them with a yellow ribbon that matches my dress and then pulls a few curly strands down around my cheeks.

"Now, you be perfect." She smiles at me with such affection that I turn and hug her.

"Thank you, Martha."

She finishes dressing quickly and looks quite lovely in a lavender dress bordered in crocheted lace. "Miss Imani got me this here dress an' another one for Neo's wedding," she explains. "That woman's so good. I just wish she was here."

"And I wish my da was here," I answer. "But we mustn't spend our time in Ireland missing people, Martha. We're going to a pub."

She shakes her head in wonderment. "Ol' Martha going to a Irish pub in Dublin, Ireland. Now don't that beat all?"

I lock our door with the little key Mrs. Conley gave me and toss it in my drawstring purse, then down the stairs we go.

CHAPTER SIXTY-FIVE

My mother stands in the foyer. When she sees us, she explains, "Rosie says she doesn't feel like going out tonight. I told her to rest up. The voyage was hard on her."

Suddenly, I realize that my mother is stunning. She wears a bright green dress with a high bustle and a cameo brooch at her throat. She loves that brooch. My father gave it to her for their twentieth anniversary last year. She turns and examines her reflection in a hall mirror.

"Mother, you look beautiful."

She turns back to me, surprised. "Thank you, love. My brooch reminds me of your father. How I wish he was here with us."

"So do I, but Martha and I were just discussing that we are not going to spoil our time in Ireland mooning for those we left back in America."

Martha joins us, wrapping her shawl around her shoulders. "That's right, Mrs. Kelly."

Mother loops her arms through Martha's and my arms. "You are absolutely right!" she answers gaily. "Let's celebrate!"

Mr. Conley bustles into the foyer, announcing, "Let's go, ladies. Your carriage awaits." He wears a smart suit and a chauffer's cap.

The carriage sitting out front is quite grand. I'm certain it was arranged by Uncle Kam and Neo.

"Climb aboard, ladies." Mr. Conley bows gallantly. "We're off to The Brazen Head." He takes Martha's arm and helps her up and then my mother's. I'm last, and I jump up with no assistance.

As we drive through the streets of Dublin, the people on the street wave cheery hellos our way. It's still light, and our ride is festive. After fifteen minutes, we pull in front of a two-story stone building. A brass plaque by the front door states *The Oldest Pub in the World, Founded 1198 as a Carriage House.* A large sign hangs in front of it. *The Brazen Head.* Under the sign is a board upon which is written, TONIGHT, DAIRE O'BYRNE.

I climb out, and Mr. Conley helps Martha and my mother down to the street. "Ladies, I'll be just across the way." He points across the street. "Stay as long as you wish. I'll drive you home when you're ready." He pulls the horse across the street and parks, lighting a cigar and opening a newspaper.

I can't imagine that this building has stood here for so long. Nothing in Boston dates back that far. I begin to get a sense of a world that existed centuries before I was born. I can almost imagine people scurrying by on these stones back then.

When we enter the pub, Neo and Jean see us and rush to escort us to their table. It is a shadowy world of smoke, wood, and the strong scent of Guinness. As our eyes adjust to the scene, the smell of the black beer mixes with the tobacco odor in a way that pleases me. I've never liked the odor of cigarettes much, but here, for some reason, it is fitting . . . and exciting.

"Watch your step, Martha," I say. This new world is dim, although candles burn everywhere. All the tables are all filled, as is the bar. I see mostly men, but there are a few women scattered among them; some looking none too respectable. Laughter peals around the place. It seems the gaiety is related to the number of bottles on the tables.

As we take our seats, all eyes turn to a tiny stage in the center of the pub. A young man sits on a stool, his fiddle beside him on a small table. He wears a homespun shirt and pants held up by a rope at his waist. He picks up his fiddle and breaks into a fast-paced tune that sets everyone clapping.

"Nellie!" my mother exclaims. "A jig!" She stands and begins dancing in front of the table. Her feet fly so fast they seem almost blurred. Suddenly, she grabs my hands and pulls me to standing. At first I am embarrassed to try this unfamiliar dance, but quickly my feet mimic hers. It's as if I dance to an ancient memory I never knew I had. We hold hands and twirl around the floor, laughing and dancing faster and faster. When she drops my hands, she puts hers flat down to her sides and dances even faster. From the waist up, she looks rigid, but her legs stomp and tap and spin her body around the tiny floor. Imitating her steps, I plaster my hands to my sides, too, and love the contrast between the upper and lower parts of my body. We dance until I can hardly breathe, but Mother doesn't even seem winded.

When the music stops, she falls back to her chair, laughing and gasping. "I haven't danced like that in years. Nellie, that's how it feels to be Irish. It's all in the dance."

Sitting myself back in my chair, I grab my chest. "I don't know how you do it, Mam. You're not exactly a young colleen anymore."

She starts at my use of the familiar Irish term but grins, then laughs and hugs me. "When a jig plays, I'm thirteen years old. Ah, how wonderful it felt to dance again."

The young man playing the fiddle puts it beside him on a table. The lights dim even more as he lifts his head and opens his mouth. In a soft, deep voice, he begins a song.

The pale moon was rising above the green mountain,
The sun was declining beneath the blue sea,

When I strayed with my love to the pure crystal fountain,
That stands in the beautiful vale of Tralee.

My mother grabs my hand and squeezes. "Nellie, that's the song they played at my wedding party when I married your father," she whispers. "'Tis the story of a beautiful young maid named Mary who loved her employer, William Mulchinock. He loved her as well, but the story ends sadly. Ah, but listen, listen to the lovely words. It's an old Irish tale and a true one." By now, my eyes have adjusted, and I stare at the man-boy singing. His sandy hair is cut short. I think he's used pomade to control his curly tresses, but one unruly shock rebels against control and strays forward. He brushes it back to no avail. As the emotion of the song closes his eyes, he leaves it to do as it wishes.

I glance at my mother and see there are tears in her eyes, so I put my arm around her shoulders and say, "Da's with you in spirit, Mam."

I study the young man once again. He is surely good looking, but not like Sean. He's rougher wrought with skin burnished by wind and sun. There are creases around his blue eyes when he grins, and his smile has the look of a devil in it.

"Isn't he a corker, though?" Mother squeezes me tight.

"That's Daire, though everyone calls him Derry," Jean tells us.

I continue to stare at Daire, or Derry, and he catches my eye. As he sings the last verse of the song, he never takes his eyes from mine, though I look away.

She was lovely and fair, as the rose of the summer, Yet t'was not her beauty alone that won me. Oh no, t'was the truth in her eyes ever dawning, That made me love Mary, the Rose of Tralee!

As the last strains of the song fade, he stands, leaving his fiddle on the table, and walks over to us. His body moves easily through the crowd, and he's greeted by many, slapping him on the back and complimenting him. As he draws near us, Jean rises to greet him but the young man shakes his hand and then stands directly in front of me. "Is you name Mary?" he asks.

Everyone is staring at us, and I feel heat rising from my collarbones up to my hairline. I open my mouth to speak, but nothing comes out. I am speechless.

Mother finds her vocal chords, "No, lad, her name is Nellie, well, Ellen really. I'm her Mam, and my name is Mary. Your song so touched my heart for it was played when I married her da."

His senses seem to return to him then, and he shakes my mother's hand. "Derry O'Byrne, ma'am. Sorry to be so bold, but your young wan knocked me sox off for a bit."

"Then you must meet her," she answers, rising. "Nellie Kelly, shake hands with Mr. Derry O'Byrne himself."

CHAPTER SIXTY-SIX

"So, what'da you do with yourself in Boston, Miss Kelly?" he asks, his violin tucked under his arm. Somehow, he had finagled my mother into letting him walk me home after dinner though I can't believe she agreed. He assured her he'd watch out for me and be a perfect gentleman, and she seemed quite taken with this y0oung Irishman; didn't question the propriety of the situation. Before I can answer, a young man calls out, "Hello, Derry. Were you playin' at the Head tonight?"

We stop for a minute, and he introduces me to the man. "He goes to Trinity with me," Derry explains. As we walk on, others greet him, most of them women, and one looks none too respectable.

"How do you know so many people?" I look at him questioningly.

"Lived here all my life . . . and I'm a friendly sort. My mam says I never met a stranger, and I guess she's right at that."

A light rain begins to fall, and he pulls an umbrella from a satchel slung over his shoulder and covering me quickly, wraps an arm around my waist, and pulls me in to his side. "Excuse my familiarity, Miss Kelly. We need to be close enough for this brolly to cover us both."

I can hardly complain about this intimacy since I don't want to get drenched. Besides, it feels good to have him so near. He's warm and muscular and, most of all, knows his way around Dublin. Without him, I'd be lost on these unfamiliar streets and lanes. Signs are written in an indecipherable language—Ascaill Assam and Bo'thar Brian, and Sra'id Cliara. "What's this language?" I am perplexed.

"'Tis Irish," he answers, pulling me still tighter against him. "Do you not speak it?"

"Of course not, I'm American. But once in a while, my father says such words."

"Where's your da?"

"He couldn't come with us to the wedding. He has a court date."

I feel him stiffen beside me. "A hooligan, is he?"

I giggle. "No-o-o, he's a lawyer. He had to defend a man at his trial in Boston and do some contracts for some Italian business men."

"A lawyer, huh? That's handy to have in a family."

"He's a wonderful lawyer. Lots of our Irish neighbors get sued for crimes they haven't committed, like horse thievery and petty larceny. Bostonians who've lived there forever don't care for the Irish."

"And why not?"

"I think it's because so many came over during the famine and took jobs nobody else would do."

"That seems daft, doesn't it? A man's right to support his family is God given, don't you think?"

"Yes, I do, and so does my da. That's why he studied law."

"Good man, I say."

"The best."

"Will I meet him?"

"I don't know how. We live in Boston."

"Well, you see, Miss Kelly, when I graduate from Trinity next year, I plan to sail to America. I want to see for myself how a Republic like America is put together. That's part of my advanced education. I plan a political career one day."

How funny—another politician.

"Does Boston have a port?" he asks.

"Yes, a big one." For no reason I can fathom, my face flames. Dark as it is under the gaslights, I doubt he can see my blush, but just in case, I turn my face down away from him.

"I already knew that. Just testing your geography skills, Miss Kelly. Sooo . . ."

"So?"

"So, maybe I'll look you up when I land in Boston. It'd please me to meet your da."

Before I can stop myself, I say, "He'd like you."

"That's good. 'Tis good to have friends in a new country, don't you think?"

"I suppose it is, Mr. O'Byrne." I laugh, surprised at how happy his words make me feel.

"Let's stop with the Miss and Mr., shall we? Call me Derry, won't you?" He sticks his hand out. "The rain's stopped." He pulls his arm from around me and puts his umbrella back into his satchel. I feel less safe without that strong arm around my waist, though I'd never say such a thing to him. I could never be so bold as to say that.

"So, will you call me Derry, Nellie?"

I turn to look up into his eyes. "Yes, yes, I will, Derry. It's good to have a friend in a strange country, don't you think?"

He laughs and his eyes crinkle up like they did in the pub. "Indeed."

As we continue toward my lodging house, he tells me to

always prepare for rain in Ireland. "It doesn't last long, usually, but it comes and goes just as the sun rises and falls. That's why it's so green here.

"Now again, what is it you do in Boston, Nellie? You never answered me question."

"I just completed my first year at Wellesley. That's a woman's college near Boston. I'm studying to be a teacher."

"A teacher, is it? That's a fine job for such a smart girl as yourself. Do you like children?"

His question gives me pause, but after a few seconds, I say, "I think so. I haven't had a lot of experience with them as I'm an only child, but I love the children in my neighborhood. I used to watch them while their mothers shopped for groceries." Then I remember little Lizbeth at St. Augustine and smile. "Yes, I do like them. Actually, I love most of them."

"That's good. I love 'em as well. I'm the oldest of three. I believe God made us perfect as little lads and lasses, then grownups messed with our heads and tried to change us. If we can just remember the wonder of ourselves when we were young wans, we'll all be better off."

I smile and chuckle softly.

"What's funny?"

"It's not funny. I agree with you." Seeing Neo, Angelique, and Jean together had reminded me. "When I was thirteen, Neo and I ran off together to join the circus. That's where he met Angelique."

He spins me to face him. "You did? You ran off to the circus?"

I bob my head up and down; the memory of tights and Bianco dancing in my head. "Though it nearly drove my parents daft, I never had so much fun in my life. At thirteen, I hadn't yet learned to be proper, you see. Sometimes, I wish I were still that bold young girl."

"That's smashing, Nellie. A girl with *Gaisgeachd*, that's what you are."

"*Gaisgeachd*?" I stumble over the pronunciation. "What's that?"

"Ah, 'tis the Irish for courage, or guts. You know, gumption."

Gumption, just like my mother.

CHAPTER SIXTY-SEVEN

When we arrive at the Conley house, Derry takes my hand. "Tell me, Nellie Kelly, when ye return to America, will you write me?"

"I'd like that, I think." I lower my eyes lest he see how pleased I am.

"That's good. Then I'll have your address, so that when I arrive in Boston, I can come over some time. I'd like to meet your da." He is staring into my eyes.

"I must go in," I murmur, aware of my mother's eyes which are surely watching for me from behind those lace curtains. I turn to go up the steps.

He calls after me, "Tell me, is Wellesley close to Boston?"

"Yes, very close, indeed."

"Good. Close enough for courting, it is." He stands there grinning at me.

I walk up the stairs to the front door, then turn to wave him off after I open it.

His foot is cocked on the bottom step and his eyes twinkle. "Nellie, save me a dance at the wedding, won't you? Or every dance?"

Flustered and happy, I grin and go inside. *Close enough for courting?*

I was right about my mother. She waits in the parlor. "That was a long walk."

"We ran into some friends of his, Mam. Derry was a perfect gentleman."

"Very well, then. I'm going to bed. We have an early day."

When I open the door to my bedroom, I'm humming the song he sang at the pub, "Rose of Tralee." I remember how his eyes looked at me when he sang, . . . *she was lovely and fair as the rose of the summer.* Then, I remember I'm not alone.

Martha sits up in her bed, her hair tied up in a bandana, her nightshirt buttoned primly up to her chin.

"Where you been?"

"Walking home, that's all."

"Sure took you a long time."

"It's quite a distance."

"Uh-huh." Her eyes are narrow with suspicion.

"Martha, we just walked."

"Now looky here, Miss Nellie, you might be a-foolin' your mama with your innocent blue eyes and dainty manners, but you ain't fooling old Martha."

I go into the bathroom to change into my nightgown and brush my teeth. When I return with my hairbrush in my hand, she's still sitting up, arms crossed over her chest.

I begin to brush my hair its usual hundred strokes; she goes to her dresser to get some chaw.

"You gonna do that stinky stuff now?" My nose is scrunched.

"Yessum. You made me nervous, goin' off with that strange boy in this here strange country."

"Oh, goodie," I say sarcastically, continuing to brush. "Just when my mother is letting up on the reins a tiny bit, you're going to start pulling me in, are you?"

"You ain't no horse, Miss Nellie. You're a young girl far away from home. I don't want you gettin' in no trouble with that smooth-talkin' Irishman."

I stop brushing and turn to face her. "Don't you like him?"

"Don't know. Don't even know him yet, 'cept he sings real sweet an' plays that fiddle like he was born with it in his hands. Never seen nothing like that. I could scarce follow his hands on that thing."

"Why don't you like him?"

"Didn't say I don't like him. Just don't know him an' don't want to see you gettin' your heart broke again. That boy brought you home from that circus was a bad one. Then he gets poor Rosie in the family way. I knowed he was no good from the first time I laid eyes on him."

"Do you think Daire O'Byrne is a bad one, too?"

"Don't know. Just worried about you."

"Well then, Martha, you shall get to know Mr. O'Byrne better over the next several days. He's a groomsman at Neo's wedding on Saturday and will be at all the parties leading up to it. So, you'll have plenty of opportunities to get to know him very well."

"Humph, that's good, I guess. Gonna keep a close eye on you two."

I begin to laugh. "Good. But you're being silly. We only just met tonight."

"Uh-huh, I knows, but I also knows what's percolatin' in men's minds when they see a pretty thing like you standin' in front a them. You gonna be careful, ain't you?"

I hold my hand up as if I'm swearing on a Bible. "I promise."

Still grumbling under her breath, she squirms to lie down and pulls the covers up to her chin. "This here country cold," she murmurs.

I put my brush on the dresser and climb into bed, but my eyes won't close. I keep replaying that pub song in my head over and over again. Tomorrow, all the men are going to get together to plan their clothes for the wedding. It won't be formal, but I find myself musing about how handsome Derry might look in a navy-blue suit. I wonder if he'll ever be able to tame that forelock of hair.

CHAPTER SIXTY-EIGHT

The smell of potatoes and meat wafting up from below awakens me. I didn't eat much last night; distracted by the music and the gaiety of the pub. And, if I'm to tell the truth, by an Irishman named Derry.

I'd had a pint of Guinness, my first ever. At first, it tasted awful, but after three or four tentative sips, it was delicious, sweet and thick. I thought I'd order another but knew my mother would have given me that look, so I ordered sarsaparilla instead.

I creep to her room and tap on the door. She opens it. Rosie is snoring in her bed. "Mother," I say. "Do we get dressed for breakfast or can we wear a robe and slippers?"

"I'm not sure, Nellie. Let's dress today and I'll ask Mrs. Conley what's the custom in her house."

As I enter back into our room, Martha is stirring.

With breakfast smells causing my mouth to water, I dress quickly and tell Martha, "I'm going down to breakfast. Come when you're ready."

"You sure it's all right for a colored woman to sit with all you's down there?"

I turn back, sit on the edge of her bed, and kiss her on the cheek. "Yes, I do. The Irish don't seem to have problems with colored people like in Boston. Maybe it's because they didn't have slaves here."

"No slaves, huh?" She stretches and takes my hand. "Did I ever tell you how scared I was the day my master freed me?"

"I don't think so." Though my stomach is rumbling with hunger, this is important for me to hear and for her to say. "Tell me."

She sits up straight and her eyes rise in her head as if remembering. "I was born on a plantation in Kentucky back in 1818. My mammie was born there, too. She was still a child when she had me. Never did know who my daddy was."

"What happened to your mammie?"

"Died real young. Kept having babies till her little body was plain wore out. They needed more workers in the tobacky fields, and she kept providin' 'em."

"Did you work in those fields?"

"Sure nuf did. Soon as I was weaned, just about. Little ones could get the low leaves. I loved bein' with Mammie out there. It was hot, but she made sure I always got the first drink of water. She loved me half to death." Tears glisten in her eyes, but she brushes them away. "Anyhow, she died real young, an' I thought I might just die with her, but then I had to watch out for all the little ones, so I didn't."

She gets out of bed and goes into the bathroom. When she returns, she's pulled on a dress. "I'm ready. Just let me get my boots on."

"Before we go downstairs, tell me what happened when you were freed?"

"Well, by then I was pretty old, but my master had a kindly streak to 'im. He'd met Mista Okafor when he'd sold him some fool tonic. I guess the tonic worked just fine cause he wrote a letter to Mista Okafor an' told him old Martha was a good cook and a trustworthy nigger." She pulls her boots on. "Biggest problem was my hair. Before they put me on that train, the Missus tried with all kinds a contraptions and smelly stuff to straighten it. Nasty. She fin'ly gave up an' tied an old bandanna over it and sent me on my way." She smiles. "Scariest day of my life."

"So that's how you got to Boston?"

"Uh-huh. Sure is. That train ride took a long time, but my master knew he could trust me to stick it out. I gots to see parts a this country I never even heard of." Her eyes glow with memory. "And Missus Okafor met that train. You shoulda seen herer. Prettiest thing I ever saw. And kind. Gave me a sweet lil' room all to myself. Never beat me once. Even tried to teach me to read, but I never could do it. Too old, I reckon."

"How old was Neo then?"

"Just two. Missus Okafor was plain tuckered out chasin' after him, so I took care a both a 'em till I got her back on her feet. Loved that baby boy like my own." She stands up brushing the front of her skirt. "That's enough talk for me. That food smells mighty good. Let's go."

In the little dining room, my mother and Rosie are already seated. Rosie looks less strained than I've seen her in a long time. I'm glad to see that. Seeing her in so much trouble began to trouble me a lot on the ship. I kept remembering how fun and lively she once was.

"You look good, Rosie," I say.

"I slept like the dead last night," she replies. "Think I was catching up on all the sick nights on that ship."

My mother smiles. "Not easy to spend so much time on a ship when you're expecting, dear. It's enough to wear anyone out."

We join them at the small table set for four. A white table-cloth covers it and coffee cups and cutlery are already placed.

As Martha and I sit down, Mrs. Conley comes into the room. "Top o' the morning, good morning," she chirps cheerily. "Will ye have the full Irish breakfast this morning?"

My mother whispers. "Say yes."

Both Martha and I nod yes. Mrs. Conley claps her hands and hurries back to the kitchen. I pour Martha and myself coffee and begin to look around at this room. It's painted a buttercup yellow; bright and charming, with more of those lovely lace curtains covering two sparkling windows. The clouds are heavy outside.

"I think it's going to rain," I say, staring through the pane.

"That's typical here, Nellie," Mother explains. "It'll burn off later, then cloud up and rain, and then clear again. Trust me on Irish weather. I remember it well. That's why you won't see all the fancy hair styles people wear in America. No point in that. It's just too damp."

"And green," I murmur. "So green."

Today, we will tour Dublin. Uncle Kam and Neo are being fitted for their suits for the wedding, so it'll just be me, Martha, Rosie, and my mother. Angelique has a fitting for her dress.

We start out after breakfast and head for a bustling Dublin thoroughfare called Grafton Street. It's lined with shops and restaurants, and it appears most of the women in Ireland are shopping here today. People do stare at Martha, but then smile. A dark face here is a curious thing but clearly nothing to fear or disdain. How different this is than Boston where it would be scandalous for three white women to share a shopping day with a Negress. People would whisper and point with gloved hands. Some might even call her vulgar names. Not in Ireland. I am so glad Neo has chosen to live here with Angelique.

Martha visibly relaxes in this strange new place. She is

smiling broader than I've ever seen her do at home. In one store, she even touches the fabric of a dress, something she wouldn't dare do at the mercantile in Boston.

In late morning, all four of us visit Trinity College, which Jean will enter in September. I wonder if Derry lives on this campus. It's enormous, covering forty-seven acres. When we pass through the gates into the College Green, I am struck with a sense of peace and serenity quite different from the hubbub of Grafton Street. Trees line the wide pathway, and the only sound comes from the birds fluttering in them.

"Look at that bird," I exclaim, pointing to one sitting on a branch. He is the most glorious shade of turquoise with an orange breast and a long, black beak. Suddenly, he opens his beak. "Che-kee!" he shrieks, sounding like the Colt revolving rifle my father brought home from the War Between the States.

It's an ugly sound, rapid and raspy. I figure God gave him an ugly call to make up for the exquisite colors of his plumage. The beautiful bird flies off in a flutter of turquoise.

Most of the buildings here are stone. "The Book of Kells is kept in the library here," my mother tells us.

"What's that?" I ask.

"A medieval illustrated collection of Bible verses handed down by monks from one century to the next. I've heard it's quite beautiful."

"Is Trinity a Catholic College?"

"No, it's Anglican, though I heard they teach every religion known to man there, even Buddhism."

I wonder if Derry is Catholic. *Nellie, stop it. Why should that matter to you?* But I do wonder.

We stop in the magnificent library with its soaring stone ceilings and stacks of books as high as I can see. The line to see The Book of Kells is quite long, though, so we don't wait to see that.

Tired of walking, we all sit down on a bench and watch students earnestly crisscrossing the campus. All are male.

"Isn't this exciting, Nellie?" Rosie prods. "Won't it be wonderful when you go back to college? Maybe sometime I can visit you there."

I see the faraway yearning in her face. She was as determined to go to Wellesley as I was, maybe even more so. She was smart enough and planning to be the first in her family to go to college, just as I was. What a mess she's gotten herself into. Looking at her swollen belly and anxious eyes, I remember when those same eyes sparkled with fun and expectation. I take her hand. "I hope you will visit, Rosie."

She squeezes my hand and whispers, "And I swear I'll never try to get another boy away from you either."

We leave the campus walking hand in hand. It feels good to forgive.

Most of the architecture on the main thoroughfares in Dublin is stone or brick, but on side streets, there are brownstones and wooden houses, much like you see in Boston. Here many of them have beautiful, ornate doors painted bright dazzling colors. *That* you would never see in Boston. It would be considered scandalous.

And there are pubs and churches on every corner. No one will go thirsty or without spiritual guidance in this city, that's for sure.

At lunchtime, we stop at a tearoom across from the Liffey River, which runs straight through Dublin's center, with two bridges connecting the land masses. While Rosie and Martha order lunch for all of us, my mother and I walk across the O'Connell bridge. The water looks dirty and deep, and I mind my gloves lest I drop them into it.

Later, as we walk back to Mrs. Conley's house, Mother yawns

and says, "I think I need a nap." That's odd. She never naps at home, but I understand completely. I think I could use a rest, too. Martha and Rosie agree.

Since none of us is hungry for supper, we retire to our rooms for the evening. I brush my teeth, put on my nightie, and climb into bed with a magazine I found in the parlor. It's still daylight, but I'm tired enough to sleep. It doesn't grow dark here until nine or ten at night. Tomorrow is Sunday. We'll attend Mass and take Rosie to the convent where she'll stay and have her baby.

Thinking of her, I remember when we first met and she became my best friend. She was so lively and adventurous, and oh so very bright; the first girl I ever met like me with ambitions and the brains to accomplish them. We'd planned on going to Wellesley together, and she planned to study nursing. How things have changed for her in those few years. Her plans are ruined. Instead, she will be alone in a strange country having her first baby. Afterward, she'll leave the infant, never to see it again.

Does she wonder if it's a girl or a boy and if its hair will be dark and curly like hers or golden like Sean's. Will her baby be beautiful? I imagine it will. Will she ever kiss its head and nuzzle its tummy? I wonder if Sean ever thinks of that baby. I wonder if he even cares.

CHAPTER SIXTY-NINE

"Nellie, wake up," an urgent voice startles me awake from a dream of green rolling hills and craggy cliffs towering over a rough sea. I open my eyes to bright sun pouring through the window of my room. When my eyes adjust and I realize that I'm still in Dublin, I know the voice belongs to my mother. I sit up and stretch my arms toward the ceiling.

"Mass is at 11:00, and it's 9:00 now. We must clean up a bit and get a move on. Rosie's already up and dressed. Hurry."

Martha is sound asleep and will stay in bed until she decides to get up. That was decided last night. She's tired from the trip and needs to rest. I sometimes forget that Martha is well into her seventies now. On occasion, she seems like a young woman to me. She's become a close friend and a second mother all rolled into one. Martha is wiser than anyone I know, and I'll be forever grateful for her counsel.

I dress in minutes and go downstairs for a quick bite. Rosie's already sitting in the small dining room, and my mother is arranging with Mrs. Conley for transportation. "We need a buggy to take us to Mass and then on to the Mercy Convent."

"Oh, then ye'll want to go to St. Kevin's," Mrs. Conley suggests. "The convent is just across the street. My husband will take ye.

Make sure he goes to Mass with ye. Don't let him go sneaking off to a pub."

My mother laughs. "Oh, don't worry about that, Mrs. Conley. I've lots of experience in taking Irishmen by the ear and booting them out the front door of a pub. I worked in one for years when I first went to America."

"Well, he's a wily one, he is. Keep yer eye on him. And make sure he receives communion, too."

At ten o'clock, we meet Mr. Conley out front. He is clean-shaven now, but his face seems ruddier than it did when he drove us to the Brazen Head and I smell a distinct scent of alcohol. When he spots us, his eyes dance with naughtiness. Seated in the driver's seat of a four-seater carriage, he greets us loudly. "G' mornin', g' mornin', ladies. 'Tis me pleasure to escort such beautiful women as ye to St. Kevin's this fine day."

"And I'm the one who will make certain you sit with us at Mass and receive The Christ in Holy Communion." Mother climbs up beside him.

He turns to her and grins. "Ah, I see the Missus has been weaving wicked tales about me again."

"And probably with good cause, Mr. Conley," Mother answers with a laugh.

"That woman will be the death of me yet." He shakes his head in mock despair.

"And the one who makes sure your soul goes up, not down," she responds.

As we ride along, he delights us with tales of St. Kevin. "He was the monk who built Glendalough in the 5th Century. Ye must visit there while you're here. 'Tis said it's the most sacred place in Ireland. Ye'll feel it the minute you walk on the grounds. The spirits of saints roam that old monastery. 'Tis said they've never left. A bit spooky for my taste, but the Missus loves it."

St. Kevin's soon rises before us, a beautiful stone cathedral. Recently completed, its marble floors and soaring ceilings take my breath away. I'm used to little St. Augustine's Chapel, modest and dwarfed by this magnificent church. The Mass is in Latin, just like at home, but the homily is in English. The priest's voice rises dramatically to the arched pinnacle, lyrical and dramatic.

Rosie elbows me in the ribs. "Do you know what he's saying?"

I shake my head. His brogue is so thick it could almost be another language. Later we learn from my mother that the priest was interspersing his English with words from the Irish language throughout his long sermon.

After the last peals of the organ fill the massive cathedral, we walk back down the stone steps to the street. Mr. Conley returns to the buggy and climbs up front again.

The Sisters of Mercy Convent is directly across Harrington Street from St. Kevin's. Mr. Conley assures us he will wait for us right where he's sitting. My mother raises an eyebrow to him, and he crosses his heart in response to her skeptical look.

We each take one of Rosie's arms as we cross the street. My heart hurts for her. She looks so young and scared and so very pregnant. I recall the first day we met on the steps of Girls High. That day, her dark eyes sparkled with fun and mischief. Now they are filled with fear.

On this long journey, we have mended some of the tears in the fabric of our friendship. When she says she's sorry about taking Sean away from me, I believe her. And now, here she is, alone in a strange country preparing to give birth to a baby she will not keep. How would I feel in her circumstances?

Our knock is answered by a small nun with a cheery smile. "Welcome, ladies." She turns to Rosie. "And are ye Rosie?"

Rosie lowers her face miserably.

"Now don't be looking so down in the dumps, Rosie. These

things happen sometimes. I know God has forgiven ye, and no one here will judge ye harshly. I'll go tell Sister Mary Helen, our Mother Superior, that ye're here. She'll be down shortly." She runs up the carpeted staircase, her tiny feet gliding so soundlessly you'd think she was flying.

We enter a parlor and sit down to wait. My mother whispers, "I chose the Mercy nuns because they're not strait-laced like some orders. They were founded to help and educate women, and they've done just that for over a hundred years."

Sitting on a flowery tufted divan are three young women in various stages of expectancy. My mother goes to them and kneels on the floor in front of them. "So, how're you feeling, girls?"

The largest girl answers, "Pretty well, ma'am."

"Well, I run a birthing hospital in Boston, in America, and I must say you all look splendid."

They murmur their thanks and she comes back to sit next to Rosie. "These girls look very well cared for, Rosie. Mercy nuns are saints. They saved many in my village during the famine, and here they are now, continuing God's work with His most vulnerable children."

Rosie takes my hand. When I turn to face her, I see absolute terror in her eyes.

"Rosie," I say, "in one year, this problem will be behind you and you'll be back in Boston where you belong. You'll visit me at Wellesley and who knows, maybe you'll even attend there."

Her eyes fill with tears and it breaks my heart. Rosie, the most wonderful friend I ever had. Funny, happy Rosie, looks so scared and trapped. How could Sean abandon her like this?

"Nellie," she asks, tears welling, "do you think he'll take me back when I return?"

And then I know, with a sinking certainty, Rosie will never go to Wellesley.

CHAPTER SEVENTY

As the convent door closes behind us, my mother puts her arm around my shoulders. "She'll be all right, Nellie. She's young and strong, and Sister Mary Helen will watch out for her."

I do not tell her that Rosie's concern is whether Sean O'Halloran will welcome her back. It's crazy and demented and beyond foolish, but Rosie loves Sean. *I understand. I have loved him, too. Perhaps, I still do.* As I acknowledge that thought, I feel as frightened as Rosie looked. *Am I insane? He's an uncaring lout for what he did to Rosie. He might do the same to me, given the chance. He says I'm different, but who knows what he said to Rosie.* I know beyond any doubt Sean is not a good man. But when I think of him, I still feel that rush of excitement that tells me I'll probably have the dream again tonight.

Was what happened with Derry just a one-time thing? After all, I'd just met him, and now I can scarcely remember what he looks like. But Sean's golden hair and laughing blue eyes are imprinted on my memory as if I'd seen him minutes ago. I've had a crush on him since I was twelve and time hasn't dimmed that infatuation in all these years. *What if it's real? What if Sean's my true love, my destiny?*

We climb into the buggy with Mr. Conley who is sitting exactly where we last saw him. "I'll give you a sterling report when I speak with your wife, Mr. Conley." Mother is quite pleased.

He grins and pulls the horse away from the curb, "As well ye should, Mrs."

As we ride along, I notice young men in the streets carrying signs and chanting, "Home Rule for Ireland!"

"What's that about?" I ask Mr. Conley.

"They're a group started up about five years ago by a gent called Isaac Butt. They campaign in the British House of Commons for Irish home rule."

My mother sits straighter and stares at the men with the signs. She stands and yells out. "Good for you, lads. Keep up the good work."

I pull on her sleeve. "Mother, sit down."

She pulls away from my hand. "Not on your life, Nellie. 'Tis the only way Ireland will ever be free of the bastards that drove me and your father out of here."

Mr. Conley turns around and grins at her. "Such language from a fine American lady." After a few moments, he says, "There's a home-rule meeting tonight on Liffey Street. I'm planning to go. Want to come along? You, too, Miss." He gestures toward me.

She sits down and turns to me. "We have no plans for the wedding scheduled tonight. What time is the meeting, Mr. Conley?"

"Half after seven."

With barely a breath of consideration, she utters, "Yes. I'll meet you out front around seven. You, Nellie?"

"Let me think about it, Mother."

When Mrs. Conley hears Mother plans to attend the meeting, she shakes her head. "Mrs. Kelly, 'tis not a good idea ye've got. Those meetings can get rowdy."

"You've been?" my mother asks.

"Just once was enough for me," she answers. "The language drove me out. It's a rough crowd. They started these meetings with a group called The Fenians who've struggled for years to get free of England."

My mother's gasp is audible. "That settles it then. I'm going. My father, Sean Boland, was a Fenian. He spoke at their meetings often. Had he remained in Ireland, I wager he'd be marching with those men . . . and perhaps he'd still be alive." She shakes her head in sadness.

"Well, all right then, if ye're hide-set on going. There will be other women there." Mrs. Conley fluffs a pillow on the sofa. "Suffragettes campaigning for the vote."

"Suffragettes?" I pipe up.

"Indeed," she answers. "Some Quaker women started them up, and now there's quite a lot of them, I hear."

"I didn't know there were Quakers in Ireland."

My mother chimes in. "Ah, yes, Quakers have lived here for decades. Back during the famine, they worked with the nuns, setting up soup kitchens and such."

"That's amazing. I thought Quakers lived mostly in Pennsylvania," I mutter.

"Live and learn, Nellie. Live and learn," my mother answers, smoothing her skirt.

"Mother, I worry about you going off like this. What if something happens to you?"

She laughs. "Now you know what I go through when you're out on the town with a strange young Irishman, Miss."

After a moment's pause, I say, "Mrs. Conley, tell your husband I'm going to the meeting, too."

"Brilliant, Nellie," Mother answers in a flash. "'Tis time you learn about your heritage."

At seven on the dot, the two of us stand in front of the

Conley house. I shift nervously from foot to foot until we see Mr. Conley pull up in his buggy. "Come along then," he says, helping Mother up into the back.

It is dusk as we ride to the meeting place, and the lamplighters are preparing to make their journey through the busy streets of Dublin. As we pass them, they wave a cheery hello. Mr. Conley expertly navigates our buggy around the people and carriages. At a pub on the corner of Thomas and Aungier Streets, a woman screams at a man. "You filthy blackguard. Drinking away your children's milk money."

My mother grimaces. "Ah, memories of my days at O'Halloran's."

Mr. Conley drops us in front of a simple two-story meeting house where women mingle in front of it with the men. They, too, carry signs, but theirs say Voting Rights for Women. These women look tough and weathered, and I recognize one as the rough girl who spoke to Derry when he walked me home. She smokes a cigarette and casts me a glare that freezes my blood. She walks up and stands so close to my face I feel her breath. I smell beer.

"Ye're a friend of Derry's, are ye?"

I feel my mother's arm tighten beside me.

"I guess so," I answer.

"Well, girlie, keep yer mitts to yerself. I've got plans for that one."

In any other situation, she would scare me, but strangely, all I feel is anger. "Look, I'm not looking for trouble with you. But if you want it, you'll find I'm stronger than I look."

"Nellie!" Mother's face is shocked, but I see a tiny hint of pride in her eyes.

The girl who is several inches shorter and several pounds heavier grits her teeth as though she's ready to punch me, but then she glances out at the street as a wagon approaches.

"Derry," she changes completely, "ye're here."

CHAPTER SEVENTY-ONE

He ties his horse and strides straight up to me. "Nellie, what're ye doing here?"

The girl spoiling for a fight with me takes his hand. "Derry, sit with me?"

"Not this time, Clairdey."

She sulks away.

I stammer in surprise as he looks down into my eyes. He's close, ignoring my mother beside me and the girl who fancies him glaring in our direction. "My mother wants to support the home-rule lads."

He angles his head toward her and grins that devilish grin of his. "Well, Mrs. Kelly, I'm one of them, and I'd love your support . . . in many ways."

She laughs out loud. "Oh, you're a bold one, aren't you? I read you like a book, young man, and I expect nothing but gentlemanly behavior from you, or you'll feel my banshee wrath for sure."

He raises his hands in protest. "Ah, no, Mrs. No banshee threats at all, at all. I will remain a gentleman in every way. You have me word on it."

"Good," she answers, taking him by the arm. "Now, will you be so kind as to escort me and my daughter into the meeting?"

Putting himself between the two of us, he extends both arms. She takes his left arm and I his right. His arm is hard under my fingers, muscular and strong. Once again, the firmness of him makes me feel safe. And once again, I feel that stir of excitement I've only experienced before when fantasizing about Sean. *What's wrong with me? If I truly love Sean, how can I feel attracted to this stranger?* It almost feels sinful, but then I remember Martha's words. *'God made you the way you are. How can that be a sin?'*

My prayer is silent, *Dear God, please make it clear to me what to do.*

We sit in the sixth row as the meeting is called to order by a well-dressed man in his sixties.

"See, Nellie," Mother whispers, "that man would be about the same age as my da. I bet he'd be here were he still in Ireland."

The man speaks of the injustices done to Ireland through the centuries of British rule and finishes with a rousing yell. "Bring Irish rule back to the Irish!"

The crowd joins in a chant, repeating his words in a deafening chorus. Before I know it, my mother is on her feet joining the chant. She raises her right hand in the air and pumps her fist in time to the words. I've never seen her acting like this. The blood has rushed to her face, and she looks almost frightening in her passion.

More speakers take the stage, each one's words blazing with anger and frustration. Their fervor makes me appreciate my country in a way I've never thought of before. America is truly the land of the free. That's all these people want, their freedom. And I want it for them, too.

After the home rule meeting, a suffragette takes the stage. She is not a young woman. Her hair is gray and her back bent.

But her voice is strong as a girl's as she speaks to the injustice of women having no say in their government. "Women are the backbone of Ireland. Women hold this country together while the men fight for their own justice. We deserve the vote every bit as much as the men do."

All the women in the room cheer her on, and some of the men as well. Derry is one of them.

"Do you think women are equal to men?" I whisper to him.

"How could ye ask that? My mother and sisters are every bit as good as I am." He laughs then. "Probably a hell of a lot better." He turns to my mother. "Excuse my language, ma'am. Just a slip."

She laughs. "I've heard such language before, young man."

At the end of the meeting, we file out to the street, Derry taking both our arms once again. "So, what'd ye think, Nellie?"

"It was magnificent; all those people speaking for their rights."

"Aye, an argument that's gone on much too long and cost too much Irish blood."

"Let alone all of us who were driven off during the famine," Mother adds. "Had the Brits left us any sustenance, I'd have never left my country. I'll never forgive them for what they did to my family."

For the first time, I realize what she and my father spoke of so often, and the longing in their voices when they spoke of Ireland. It is a beautiful nation, and its people, brave and filled with passion.

As we stand there with Derry, Mr. Conley rushes up to us. "Mrs. Kelly. We must get home right away. There's a problem."

CHAPTER SEVENTY-TWO

"Mr. Conley, tell me what's going on," Mother pleads as the horse races back to his home. "What's happened?"

He continues, silent, his face intent on navigating around the people crowding the streets. But then he glances at Derry who had insisted on coming with us and shakes his head. People stare as if our horse is a runaway and scatter quickly out of our way.

A man yells, "Are ye daft, man? Slow down. Yer rig will slip its wheels."

Mr. Conley ignores the shout and brings the whip down again on the horse's back. I wince for the poor animal but am too busy calming my mother to question its mistreatment.

When at last we arrive at our lodging, he jumps from the buggy and ties the horse to a post out front, then begins wiping it down. "Go on in there, Missus and Miss. You, too, Derry. Me wife is wanting to speak with ya."

We walk into the house and are shocked to find Uncle Kam and Neo sitting in the parlor with Mrs. Conley and Martha. Martha's eyes lower when she sees me.

Without removing her shawl, Mother runs into the room. I follow her, with Derry on my heels. "What's happened?" Panic takes her voice up to nearly a scream.

"Mary, sit down." Uncle Kam rises from the sofa, gesturing to the place beside him. "You, too, Nellie."

Blindly, we obey him. He takes my mother's hands into his own. Martha sits across the room in a big, overstuffed chair, wringing her hands. She never takes her eyes from me.

Neo and Derry, sit close to me on a loveseat like bookends. Neo puts his arm around my shoulders. He is trembling. That frightens me. Neo is always so self-contained. My first thought is that Angelique has canceled their wedding. I turn to console him. "Are you all right, Neo?" I ask, looking deep into his eyes. He nods but doesn't answer.

"Mary, we have bad news." Uncle Kam is holding my mother's hands and Neo takes mine.

In that moment, the world moves into slow motion. I am aware of Mrs. Conley hovering over us, arms crossed over her chest, tears in her eyes. Mr. Conley runs in the front door and, seeing all of us, heads into the kitchen. The clock in the corner chimes nine times, and each note sounds more and more foreboding.

"What is it?" *Is that my panicky voice I just heard?* Derry's hand tightens on my shoulder. I hadn't noticed him putting it there.

Uncle Kam takes a piece of paper from his waistcoat. "This wire was sent to me. It arrived an hour ago. There's been a tragic accident back in Boston."

"Is it Imani?" my mother asks, immediately reaching to touch Uncle Kam's face and searching his troubled eyes.

He lowers his head. "No, Mary. It's Daniel."

Time freezes.

My mother stares at me, her face stricken. Unable to speak, she shakes her head from side to side.

But this must be heard, and so I force out my words. "Uncle Kam, what's happened to my father?"

"We're not certain, Nellie. All this says," he waves the wire in the air, "is that Daniel Kelly suffered a gunshot wound." He pauses.

"Where? To his arm or leg? Was it an accident? Was he loading a gun for someone and it went off?" Mother is frantic, her voice rising.

He turns to her. "The wound was to his head, Mary."

She turns to me, gasping for air. "That's impossible. He has no enemies."

Uncle Kam sighs and crumples the piece of paper. "The wire states the police think it was suicide."

"That can't be! He doesn't own a gun anymore."

"I told them that by reverse wire, Mary. And I told them Daniel would not kill himself."

"He's gone then?" she whispers, barely able to get the words out.

He takes her in his arms. "Yes, Mary, he's gone."

She moans, then breaks free of him. "It's not suicide. Daniel would never commit suicide. Never." She turns to me, "Nellie?" Her eyes beseech me to speak.

I jump to her side, wrapping my arm around her waist. "She's right. My da would not kill himself. I know that. He was happy. He loved us dearly. He'd not do that to himself or to us."

Uncle Kam shakes his head, eyes clearly about to overflow. "That's what I told them."

I feel my mother collapse into a trembling mass of dry grief. Her eyes brim but do not spill. She seems like a child, needy and terrified.

I urge her back to the couch and sit beside her, pulling her into my arms, holding tight. The tears come now in a keening wail. I grip tighter. "Mam, dear mam, we'll get through this. I promise we will. We'll find out who did this to Da. It wasn't by his own hand. We both know that."

She collapses into my arms; women joined by love and pain and desperation. We stay there, the two of us, for a long time. I rock her like a baby. Her moans break my heart. I keep telling her we'll get through this, but how? How can I bear my own heartbreak and help her? How will I go back to school? What will happen to us?

Uncle Kam's voice breaks our embrace as he pulls Mother to her feet. I stand, too. "Mary, Martha will take you upstairs now so you can rest. She's prepared a potion to help you sleep. I've found a ship that leaves tomorrow for Boston and booked you and Nellie passage. I wish I could come with you."

"So do I," Neo says, wrapping his arm around my waist.

Uncle Kam continues. "But we can't. Neo will marry Angelique this Saturday, and I'll sail back to Boston to help you immediately after the ceremony. It's all arranged."

My mother looks at him with blank eyes. I don't think she comprehends what he's saying, but Martha takes her hand.

"Come now, Miss Mary. Don't you think about tomorrow. Let's just get though right now. That's enough."

Her words penetrate my awful unreality. She's right. I mustn't think about what will come. I must stay present to this moment and let the future take care of itself. It's the only way I'll survive this.

"We need to get you in bed," Martha coos as she leads Mother to the staircase. "You sail out early in the morning. You'll get through this, Miss Mary. Old Martha gonna take care of you tonight."

CHAPTER SEVENTY-THREE

Uncle Kam turns to me. "Nellie, we're going back to our lodging now. Can we do anything to help you before we turn in? You sail at nine in the morning, so you'd better pack up."

I shake my head, numb and wordless.

Neo squeezes my shoulder. "Will you be all right?"

I stare at nothing and ask myself, *Will I?*

They walk to the front door and open it. Neo casts a final, worried look at me as they leave.

I have never felt so alone in my life.

Derry asks, "May I stay a wee bit with you, Nellie?"

I cannot speak, but my eyes, about to spill over, plead with him not to leave. I am so grateful to have his sturdy shoulder beside me. He leads me to the small sofa before the fireplace. I collapse onto it.

Mr. Conley stokes the fireplace until the flames leap strong and tall. "Take care of her, lad." He pats Derry on the back.

"Aye."

Mrs. Conley sets out tea makings for us and scones leftover from breakfast. "I hope these are still fresh enough." With that, she takes her husband's arm and they go upstairs.

When we're alone, Derry wraps his arm around me, but doesn't speak. I can't say a word. I just can't. I'm unable to believe my beloved da is dead. I see his face as we waved to him from that ship. He was big and strong and vital and his smile wrapped from one ear to the other, delighted we were to have this adventure in Ireland.

How can this have happened to him? Not him. As the reality begins to set in, my shoulders convulse under Derry's hand. He holds me tight as I begin to cry. He doesn't let go. I cry and cry until no tears are left in me, and then I remember Da's smile and cry more. Derry hands me his handkerchief, but never leaves me.

After a long time, I turn my sodden face to his. "Derry, my father is gone."

He squeezes my shoulders and rocks me gently in his arms.

"You'll not meet him."

"I know, and that saddens me greatly."

"But he would have liked you." I can barely get the words out.

My eyes are so blurred, I hardly notice him moving closer. Then, his lips meet mine. It's a soft kiss. It feels good and natural and reassuring. When our lips part, I relax and lay my head on his shoulder."

"That was my first kiss," I whisper.

"Not mine," he answers, "but perhaps my favorite." He lifts my chin and looks into my eyes. "I wish I could come with you to Boston, Nellie Kelly. I wish I could help you with what's ahead. But I know you're strong enough to handle whatever comes your way, and help your mam with it, too."

"Am I?"

"Without a doubt. And, you're smart and funny. Plus, the prettiest girl I've ever seen in my whole life. When I first laid eyes on you in that pub, I knew we had something ahead for us. Something good."

"How can you know that?"

"I don't know yet. All I know is I'll finish off my year at Trinity and you'll graduate and become a teacher. Then we'll figure out what comes next. Whether it's in Boston or here in Ireland, we'll figure it out. Good teachers are always welcome here. Education is so important to us Irish."

For a second, I feel guilty that his words make me happy. *How can I feel this way with my father dead at home?* Guilt washes over me, but he's so close and so warm and so strong I soon forget. He tips my chin up and kisses me again. He starts softly, but then his lips become more urgent, pressing hard into mine. His arms tighten around me pulling me closer on the loveseat. *I should stop this now*, I think, but don't.

After a time, he pulls me to standing. He turns off the lamp; the only light now comes from the fireplace. He takes my hand and leads me to a corner of the room, out of sight of the stairway. I follow ever so willingly. He lifts my arms up around his neck and moves tight up against me. He feels good, so very good. I don't stop him. My body melts against his. A good Catholic girl should stop this now, but I don't want to.

He reaches inside the bodice of my dress and squeezes my breast gently. A jolt of pleasure shoots down to that place I only knew existed in dreams. But this is stronger. As he caresses my breasts, I feel his body press closer, rubbing himself into me. He is hard, persistent, and constant. I cannot stop this. It feels too good.

Suddenly, the rapture begins, lifting me higher and higher. I am gone. I must let it take me to its fullness. There's no stopping it. And I don't try. My body begins to vibrate into bliss, a rapture like nothing I've ever experienced. At its peak, my knees buckle and I find myself hanging onto him, my breath coming in quick gasps.

When I am able to stand up on my own legs and look into his eyes, he is smiling. "Good," he smiles. "A passionate filly I see."

I stammer foolishly. "I'm sorry. I'm so embarrassed. I don't know what happened." But that's a lie. I know exactly what happened. Martha had told me.

"I'd like to take this further, Nellie, but this isn't the time or the place. Someday I will, lass, and it'll be in a soft bed with clean sheets." He starts to kiss me again and then stops. "Go home, Derry," he says to himself, willing his emotions under control. "You promised her mother you'd be a gentleman."

CHAPTER SEVENTY-FOUR

The next morning when Kam and Neo drop us off at the dock, Derry's standing there. They must leave for a wedding rehearsal, so Mother and I kiss them goodbye.

Derry presses a piece of paper into my hand. "My address, lass. Write me."

My face flames with embarrassment over the wanton way I'd behaved last evening. Does he think me a harlot? No nice girl would have allowed that. I know that and he must know it, too. But last night, I felt nothing but the passion of my own body, wild and free. At first sight of Derry, the tightening began again, low in my belly. I think he knew it. *Not now.* I take the paper from his hands and look away. "I will write."

He turns me toward him again, looking down into my face. "Miss Kelly, please don't regret what we felt last night. It was normal and natural."

As I begin to walk away, he captures my hand. "We'll see each other again, Nellie. Mark my words." He squeezes my fingers as if in promise, then goes to my mother. "Mrs. Kelly, I know your heart is breaking. I'm sorry your return home has been marred by such tragedy."

She brings a handkerchief to her red-rimmed eyes. She looks desperately tired now, as though she could fall. He grips her by her elbows, then puts his arms up around her shoulders, pulls her to him. "Easy now, Missus, easy. Come back home to us when you're able."

She lifts her tear-filled eyes to his face. "Thank you, young man. I will."

The voyage back to Boston is turbulent; the fury of the waves somehow matches the anger growing in my heart. *Who could have shot Da? Why? He had no enemies and did nothing cruel to any living creature. Why would anyone do this to him?*

My mother becomes a wraith-like creature, hardly eating or sleeping. I hear her sobbing in the night when she thinks me aslelep. Once, she screams out, "Daniel, love, where are you?" Her moans, coming from some barely conscious place in her soul, are the most piteous sounds I've ever heard. She frightens me. She, always so strong, so capable in helping others, so able to navigate every one of the many storms in her life, is now power-less in her grief over losing the man she has loved so deeply.

Will she ever recover?

Finally, on a day too filled with sunshine to hide away, we hear a crew member shout, "Boston at Starboard."

We climb to the deck and peer out. There it is, the familiar pier from which we had disembarked only one month past, gleaming in the brilliance of the afternoon.

"We're home, Mam," I say.

"Not my home. Not anymore. Not after what happened. This city took my father and now my husband. It's no home to me." Her bitter words curl from a mouth twisted by hatred in a face I hardly recognize. Who is this woman?

We walk down the gangplank and into the arms of Father Ruzzo and Sister Sarah. The old nun coos and weeps around my mother until Mam pushes her away with a stiff arm. "Stop your keening, Sister. Tell me what happened." She trembles and sways. I grasp her arm lest she fall to the deck, shocked at how fragile she seems.

The nun stutters and answers, "I don't know. There're rumors, but no one knows for sure, Mary."

She turns to Father Ruzzo. "Father?"

"Mary, Sister's right. Rumors abound about Daniel's demise, but we have no answers. We just don't."

"You must have an opinion, Father."

His swarthy skin flames. "An opinion? Yes."

She stands before him, now looking as though her feet are cemented to the wooden pier under them. It is clear she will persist until she gets an answer. "Where's my husband? Where's Daniel?"

He lowers his head. "Buried at St. Augustine's, Mary. We couldn't wait any longer."

Again, she sways until he catches her arms and holds her firm. "He's buried? I should have been here. I'll never see my Daniel again in this life."

Her eyes spill over with tears and she moans incoherently; pitiful and unending, coming from so deep in her soul I fear it will carry her away to the land of insanity.

Sister takes her arm and leads her to a carriage, then helps her up and into it. In spite of the warmth of this early July afternoon, Sister covers her knees with a blanket and holds her in her arms, rocking back and forth and keening a soft chant. "*Beidh biseach ort go luath.*"

I don't know what the words mean, but my mother does and finally calms and quiets, her head resting on the nun's shoulder.

Sister whispers, "Mary, dear, Mrs. Okafor took the liberty of buying mourning dresses for you and Nellie. They're at your house. A neighbor let us in."

Mourning dresses? How considerate of Imani. Neither my mother nor I had considered them. *I wonder how long I must wear black. I'll ask Sister later.*

I turn to the priest standing with me. "Father, what do you think happened? Tell me."

He sputters for a moment and then regains his speech. "At first, they thought suicide. It was a single gunshot to the head. The Monsignor didn't want him buried in the church graveyard. I fought that."

"You know my da would never commit suicide, Father. Never."

"Exactly. That's what I told Monsignor. I wouldn't allow them to refuse him a Catholic burial. Thank God, he listened to reason. And, there's something else."

"What?"

"Did they tell you Mr. Marino was also killed?"

"Rosie's father!?" I am shocked beyond comprehension. *Both of them gone? Poor Rosie, alone and in Ireland. Her father murdered.*

"Yes, on the same day, two hours later. He, too, was shot. Apparently, they were both involved in some negotiations with business acquaintances of Mr. Marino's. It's rumored the talks turned ugly."

"Ugly? In what way? My father was cool headed. What did they ask him to do that would make their talk turn ugly?"

"No one knows. It might just be my own opinion, but you know how your father would react if anyone asked him to do something illegal."

This information stuns me. I knew my father was working with Mr. Marino on some contracts. That was why he couldn't accompany us to Ireland. He said that Mr. Marino had urged him to be here for the meetings and had offered to "make it worth his while" if he stayed. So, he did.

Could it be someone asked him to go against his legal prin-ciples? Father Ruzzo isn't an irrational man. If he mentioned such a possibility, it might exist. My mind whirled.

As soon as possible, my mother and I will visit Rosie's mother. She might know something.

CHAPTER SEVENTY-FIVE

Father Ruzzo takes us to our house; offers to come in, but we decline. I know he understands. When we walk into our home, it's so quiet. I run to my father's bedroom. His clothes are still in the drawers. His white shirt is on the bed, stained with blood. I snatch it up and hide it under my skirt. I don't want my mother seeing that.

She wanders aimlessly around the kitchen, checking the icebox. "Oh look, it's full of food. The neighbors must have done that . . . or people from the church. How kind of them."

A knock at our front door makes us both jump. I open it. It's Mrs. Honeycutt from next door, accompanied by her daughters, Norah and Edith. Mrs. Honeycutt's chin and jowls tremble, and her eyes are red and look threateningly close to spilling over.

Don't cry, I think desperately. *Please don't cry. We can't stand that.*

"Oh, Mary, this is awful what happened to your Daniel," Mrs. Honeycutt chatters on. She points out to the back porch. "Right there in your own backyard."

I hear my mother's deep inhalation. "That's where it happened?" She stares outside, her eyes blank and dazed.

"Oh, yes! Didn't you know? Right out there under the maple." She points to the tree. "Tuesday morning, four weeks past. I was the first to find him. I heard the shot and ran over."

My mother, instantly alert, gestures them to sit down at the kitchen table. "Was he alive then?"

"I think so, but it wasn't long before he was gone," the woman says, plopping her ample backside onto a kitchen chair. Her daughters do the same. "His head was so bloody."

Mother's moan stops the woman's prattling. Mrs. Honeycutt looks toward me, her gaze stricken with guilt, then her eyes dart away. The room is completely silent for several seconds.

When she has again composed herself, Mother asks in a quiet voice, "Who was with Daniel that day, Mrs. Honeycutt? Did you see anyone?"

"No, no. I was still in my nightie when I heard the shot, and by the time I was decent and got over here, he was on the ground, alone . . . with the gun beside him. The police thought the shot was self-inflicted."

"No! That can't be true!" I shout, then realize how loud my outcry was, "I'm sorry for yelling, Mrs. Honeycutt, but Mother and I know my father did not kill himself. He just wouldn't."

When I turn to comfort her, Mother is already out the back door heading for the maple tree. By the time I get to her, she is on her knees, scouring the ground under it, looking for something, anything that might tell her about my father's last minutes. "Nellie, look!" she exclaims frantically as she comes to standing. "There's a hole here that looks fresh. Perhaps that's where the bullet lodged."

The hole is above our heads, a bit more than six feet off the ground. The height of my father's temple. As her fingers dig at the hole, my stomach lurches. I reach a nearby bush before it empties all over the blooming roses.

When I recover, I join her at the tree, wiping the spittle off my mouth with my sleeve. "Mother, stop digging at that. It's probably a woodpecker." I take her hand and gently lead her back to the house.

The Honeycutt women call from the kitchen door. "We'll be taking our leave now, Mary and Nellie. If you need anything at all, please just knock on our door any time, day or night."

Mother tips her head numbly and waves at them as I take her inside. We walk into their bedroom. She finds his trousers on a chair. She pulls them into her arms, inhaling their scent deeply, then carefully hangs them on a peg at the side of the room. "He must have worn his blue suit for the funeral. It was his favorite."

She lies down on the bed, and I crawl beside her, caressing her hair away from her damp face. Finally, her eyes close. I join her in blessed sleep within minutes . . . until someone pounds on the front door.

"You stay resting, Mother. I'll get it." I pull myself to my feet and head for the door.

Sister Sarah and two women from St. Augustine's Church stand on the front porch. The parishioners' dresses are as black as Sister's habit. In their hands, they hold large black cloths.

"We're here to do the draping, Nellie. Is this a convenient time?" one asks.

My mother, hearing their voices, comes out of the bedroom. "Come in Sister. Come in all of you."

They offer brief condolences to me and my mother, and then like three fussy crows, busy themselves, hanging black drapes over every window and mirror in the house. It takes them less than an hour. When they have finished their task and left our home, we look at each other in the gloom of the living room.

"How long must we leave these up, Mother?"

"I think tradition says a full year. We'll ask Father Ruzzo."

"I don't think I can stand all this darkness for a whole year."

She hangs her head in agreement. "We'll take them down after a month. The crepe hangers will be scandalized, but to hell with them. Let them gossip." She falls onto the couch and removes her boots. "As soon as I'm rested a bit, we must see where your da kept his will. I know he had one."

"Can't that wait, Mother? You're so tired."

"It'll give me something to do."

Two hours later, she discovers the will hidden in an empty coffee can on the top shelf of the pantry. She yells for me to come. Running to her side, I find her sitting in a chair, crying so hard that the ink on the document is blurring. I take it gently from her hands and blot it dry as best I can. "We'll read this later, Mother. We're hungry."

She looks at me as though food is nowhere in her thinking. I take her hand and lead her to the kitchen table and then take a dish out of the ice box. It is chicken salad with celery, grapes, and red peppers. I dish up generous portions onto two plates, wondering who left it for us as I say a silent prayer of gratitude.

She scarcely takes a bite, though I urge her to eat. After I wash the dishes and cover and put away the leftovers, we read the will. She traces each line carefully. "He wrote this . . ." She has a faraway look in her eyes as she runs her finger gently over the text. It is as we expected. He's left everything to her—the house, the wagon, the horse, and a small bank account. "This won't keep us for long," she murmurs. "I'll have to charge more at the Haven."

That day and for the four days that follow it, everything she touches reminds her of him. His clothes in the dresser and his boots inside the front door set her again weeping. When she finds a glass on the floor of the living room with a trace of stout left in it, she holds it to her cheek until I unfold her fingers one by one and take it to the kitchen.

Neighbors bring over more food, and I love them for their kindness, but getting Mother to sample any of it is an almost futile struggle. She eats little, and though she has always been a strong woman, she's never carried much flesh on her bones. Now she's blatantly frail.

On the fifth day, Molly O'Halloran, who has managed the birthing center in Mother's absence, visits. She is alarmed. "Mary, you are very thin; thinner than I've ever seen you." She takes a stethoscope out of her black bag and puts it to her ears. As she examines my mother, her eyes narrow. "You must eat more, dear. You're running on skin and bones. Your body can't sustain itself."

Mother jumps to her feet. "I must finish straightening up this house. A policeman is coming here at four o'clock." She grabs a broom and starts sweeping an already immaculate floor.

CHAPTER SEVENTY-SIX

Sargent O'Malley states matter-of-factly, "Frankly, Mary, we have zero leads on who killed your husband and Mr. Marino. At first, we thought Daniel committed suicide, but when the Southside precinct informed us that Marino was shot two hours later, we changed the investigation to homicide. The attacks were too similar."

"Who do you think did it?" I ask him. "You must have some opinion."

He hesitates for s second then speaks. "We're not supposed to speculate on these things, Nellie, but it seems there's an unsavory group from Sicily that Mr. Marino was associated with." He hesitates, as if he questions sharing more information, but then speaks again, "Frankly, we suspect they asked your father and Marino to do something illegal and that one or both of them refused and threatened the Italians with exposure."

Mother, sitting on the sofa, comes to her feet and begins pacing back and forth in the room. "Yes, that makes sense. Daniel would not tolerate criminal behavior from anyone. He had important meetings with Mr. Marino's associates set up that he couldn't miss. That's why he didn't come with us to Ireland."

The Sargent nods. "Yes, but now the problem is those associates are long gone from Boston. We've checked all the ship records but haven't found a clue."

Three days later, we make our trip to the Marino's home. "I must talk to Maria." Mother is determined. "Perhaps she knows something."

"How?" I ask. "She doesn't speak English."

"We always find a way to make ourselves understood to each other. We will again."

When our wagon pulls up to the tidy house in South Boston, I am surprised to find the grass long and weedy. Their yard was always perfect. I climb down from the wagon and tie up our horse. Mother heads for the front door. She knocks for five minutes but gets no response. We walk in different directions around to the back, checking every window on the way. Everything is locked up tight as a drum.

"This was a wasted trip, Mother."

"No, it can't be. We must find out what happened." She goes to the house next door and raps loudly on the front door. I run to stand with her.

A tiny, dark woman comes to the door, looking confounded. "*Si?*" she says.

My mother points to the Marino house. "Where are they? I must talk to Maria."

A light comes on in the woman's eyes. "Ah, Maria?"

"*Si*, Maria," Mother answers.

"She gone." She holds up two fingers. "Two weeks." She gestures to the Marino house. "House for sale."

"Gone where?" I ask, frustrated at our inability to communicate.

She clearly doesn't understand my question but asks, "You Kelly?"

We both say, "*Si, si*, Kelly."

"Friends of Maria and Rosie," I offer.

She opens the door wide and gestures us inside. I am assailed by the delicious scent of tomatoes and garlic, as the little woman rushes to the wood stove to move a large pot off the fire. She motions for us. "Come, come."

She leads us into an immaculate bedroom with a picture of Jesus on the wall, his heart blazing from his chest. I pass a grotto to the Blessed Mother on an end table. The woman goes to a dresser and pulls an envelope out of the top drawer. Scrawled on the envelope is the name 'Mary Kelly.'

My mother takes it from the woman's hands, saying "*Grazie, grazie, senora.*"

The tiny woman smiles and touches my mother's shoulder.

When we get back to our wagon, I say, "Mother, open it. What does it say?"

"No, not until we get home. We must be home when we read this."

"What if it's written in Italian?"

"Then, we'll go to Father Ruzzo. He still speaks the language."

We arrive home more than an hour later. Mother brews us each a cup of tea and takes the cups into the living room where she sits down and takes off her boots. Tucking her feet up under her, she gestures me down beside her.

It's not written in Italian. Mrs. Marino explains that she dictated it to her son, Matteuso, and he translated into English for us. It is dated the day after my father died.

Dear Mary,

My heart is broken that our friendship has come to this. You, who were so good to me when my Rosalia found herself in trouble, do not deserve this tragic outcome. Neither does your daughter. And neither do I and Matteuso.

I think our husbands were murdered by criminals from my home country. We fled Sicily ten years ago because they wanted Matteo to join them in their evil pursuits and he refused. After that, he no longer felt safe and brought us to Boston.

I fear now for my son. Matteuso and I will board a ship soon for Ireland. That way we can be with Rosalia when her time comes. I don't know if we'll ever go home or come back here because of the danger to us.

Please know, mi cara *Mary, that you are the only friend I had in Boston. No one could have done more for me.*

Grazie,
Maria

CHAPTER SEVENTY-SEVEN

The letter from Mrs. Marino didn't help my mother very much, but at least it enabled us to stop wondering who killed Da. Now it was clear. "We must get on with our lives," she proclaimed in her usual staunch voice.

She went back to the birthing center today, and I have started preparing to return to Wellesley come September.

Letters from Derry begin to arrive at our post office. Sometimes, they're wrapped two or three to a bunch and tied up with twine. I learn what days the mail ship arrives from Ireland and get to the post office to get them that day. They are filled with exciting news about his classes and work to free Ireland. I remember well the fervor of that meeting we attended the night we got the awful news about Da.

Each time a letter from Derry arrives, my mother questions me about him. "Do you care for him, Nellie? Do you think he cares for you?"

I laugh at her questions as if nothing could be further from the truth. "Mother, he lives in Ireland, for heaven's sake. Do you want me to leave you and go there?"

She just smiles that lopsided grin she only has when she's plotting something. "I always said that losing you or Daniel would be the end of me, but here I stand, a bit skinny and grey, but still standing. Who knows? Maybe I'll go with you."

That's a shocker, for sure, but it makes me ponder things a bit more deeply. I guess the world is full of options for both of us.

I know her heart is still breaking, but when she "stiffens up her back," she's able to survive anything. Only I hear her soft cries at night after she has gone to bed. Each morning, she's back up and bustling, though her red eyes speak volumes about what's happening inside her.

And from Derry's letters, he misses me and still plans to see me when he graduates. He even says I can be a teacher in Ireland after I get my diploma; that an education has always been important to the Irish; that the Sisters of Mercy would welcome me at their school in Dublin. Especially since his father is the one who built their new convent. I wonder if that means I could be teaching both boys and girls. Here in Boston, I would never be permitted such a thing.

It seems that life is one big puzzle after another. Just when you think you have one piece fitted into place, something jolts it out of position and you have to start looking for a different solution.

He still plans to visit Boston after his graduation to study our democracy, and that excites me more than I would ever admit to him. When I think of that night in the Donnelly's parlor, the memory still thrills me . . . and confuses me terribly.

For as long as I can remember, I have loved Sean O'Halloran from a distance. So, the passion I experienced with Derry doesn't make sense. Perhaps I will experience the same feelings if Sean takes me in his arms? I intend to find out this Saturday.

In the afternoon, we will gather with friends in the cemetery for a communion service Father Ruzzo has organized. After that, Uncle Tommy is having a remembrance party at his pub for my father. At first, it seemed disrespectful to have a party soon after his death, but Uncle Tommy was adamant, "Daniel Kelly, of all men, deserves a proper Irish wake. He got cheated on it before, so now we'll make it up to him."

Friday night in bed, I finalize my plan. I will get Sean to kiss me. He never has, and I want to know how his lips feel. Perhaps it's wrong to think of finagling Sean into an embrace, but how else can I sort out my feelings about him. Mother tells me that the front porch of O'Halloran's was the first place my father ever kissed her. When it's late enough to be dark and everyone has had a good amount of stout or spirits, I'll get Sean on that porch.

One thing is certain, I need to figure out my feelings for both Derry and Sean. Hopefully, things will become clearer after Saturday.

Uncle Kam and Martha arrive back from Ireland on Friday and will come to the party, too. I am anxious to see both of them. I want to know all about Neo's wedding. It broke my heart not to be there, but not the way losing Da did. That's a heartbreak I'll never get over. Neither will my mother. People say it takes time, and we have plenty of that ahead of us, but Da was such an immense presence in our lives. When he was here, nothing could harm me. He was a giant and if anyone hurt me, he'd take care of them in a heartbeat. Who will protect me now? Who will protect my mother?

I guess we'll just have to learn to protect ourselves from now on.

CHAPTER SEVENTY-EIGHT

As Saturday dawns, the police are no closer to solving the mystery of who shot my father and Mr. Marino. They've checked the manifests for every ship that sailed in and out of Boston during the weeks before and after the crimes but haven't located anyone suspicious. I'm not usually a vindictive person, but honestly, I'd enjoy watching someone hang for what they did to Da. I miss him more with each day that passes.

In yesterday's letter, Derry says he's decided to study law in hopes for election into the English Parliament. He believes he can best effect change from the inside. He will visit Harvard Law School when he comes here after graduating from Trinity. Apparently, Harvard has developed a new curriculum that is being copied by every major law school in the nation. He's so on fire about the home rule movement in Ireland. I am thrilled he's so passionate about it. I let Mother read the letter, too. She says "You could do worse, girl."

"Mother, he lives in Ireland. Do you want me to leave you to be with him?"

"As I said before, maybe I'll go with you."

She's so brave. I would have sworn that if something bad happened to Da, she'd fall apart, but some strength sustains her.

I hope I have that kind of fortitude if I ever need it. She says I will, and I love her for saying that, but I still wonder.

Today, we'll walk to St. Augustine Cemetery at four o'clock for a prayer service at my father's grave.

We went there yesterday to ready ourselves. We don't want to cry in front of his friends. The dirt over his coffin was so fresh, but small shafts of grass began to cover over the small mound in the earth. I still can't believe that under that dirt, my father's body is rotting away. Looking at that grave is one of the hardest things I've ever done, but I need to stay strong for my mother.

We stood there, the two of us, weeping and praying, and then she took my hand. "Let's go home now, Nellie, and have a cup of tea. We need to keep our strength up."

And that's exactly what we did.

At two o'clock on Saturday, she's ironing our black dresses. Father Ruzzo has invited several of my da's friends and legal associates to say a few words at the grave. It'll be hard to hear them talk about Da in past tense, but I must focus on the joy of seeing Martha again.

She finishes my dress and holds it up for me to see. "It's perfect, Mam," I say. "Thank you."

"Oh, my, you're calling me mam!" she exclaims. "I've wanted that for so long."

I think back to all the times I called her mother with an edge of coldness in my voice. Back then, I was embarrassed by her hair, by her brogue, even by her love for my father. What a little snot I was. So, when I take the dress from her hands today, I pull her close and kiss her on the cheek. "I love you, Mam."

For just a moment, tears well in her eyes, but then she smacks me on the bustle. "It's time to get dressed, girl. Let's get moving."

When I turn to go to my room, I hear her soft words, "I love you, too, dearest."

Pulling the dress over my head depresses me, though it fits perfectly. Of course, it fits. Aunt Imani chose it. When my mother sees me in the dress, she laughs. "You look so morbidly black."

It is humid with a miserable drizzling rain as we walk to the cemetery. Opening my umbrella, I remember being under the bumbershoot in Dublin with Derry. I was so happy then, so carefree. Nothing bad could happen to me or those I loved. Why should it? We all followed the rules, lived moral lives, and prayed to God for redemption. But bad had happened. I take my mother's arm as we huddle together under the cover of the umbrella.

At the grave, Tom Courtenay speaks of my father's skill in the courtroom. "No judge could resist his arguments." He chuckles. "I should know. He kept me out of jail when that lying Jack Maloney accused me of stealing his horse. I told the judge that if I wanted to steal a horse, I could do better than Jack's godforsaken old pile of bones."

Others reveal stories of small kindnesses: how my father never charged them during hard times; how he chose to stay here with his people rather than putting on airs and moving to a posh area of Boston.

"Dan Kelly was a real Irishman." John Hughes's tears spill from his eyes. "No airs, no four-flushing, no scabbing on another man's misfortune. A real Irishman. A real man."

Afterward, I say to my mother, "What's four-flushing mean?"

"Being fake. Pretending you have a full flush when you're one card short."

We arrive at O'Halloran's at five thirty, and the place is decorated in green ribbons inside and out. Inside, a fiddle plays a brisk Irish jig. Compared to Derry's music, this fiddler falls far short, or maybe I'm prejudiced.

Uncle Kam comes to us as soon as we walk in the door. He takes my mother's hands in his. "How're you faring, Mary?"

She shakes her head. She can't pretend with him. He knows her too well. He wraps her shoulder up in his arms and hugs her close. Looking around, I see some faces registering shock at the sight of this tall, distinguished black man embracing my red-haired mother, but I'm not surprised at the sight. These two have been soul brother and sister since they were children. Nothing will ever change that.

I run to Martha who is sitting at a table alone. She stands and embraces me. "Miss Nellie. Oh, girl, it's so good to see you again."

"Tell me about the wedding," I answer. "I want to know every detail."

"Oh, Lordy, that Angelique was just about the prettiest bride I ever did see. She had on a white lace dress that some fancy designer made for her and a veil so long and soft it just floated behind her all the way down the aisle. The train on that dress was a good four feet long and she kicked it around like she was born wearing it. She had on lip rouge and some coal dust 'round her eyes. But not too much, uh-uh, not too much at all. Beautiful, she was. Just beautiful."

I close my eyes and can almost see the image of Angelique walking down the aisle of the church, staring into Neo's eyes. How happy he must have been at the vision of her.

"And Neo? Tell me about Neo."

Martha clasps her hands to her chest. "That boy! Ah, beamin' ear to ear, that boy. And handsome. He was so handsome in his navy suit. Mister Okafor tells me his coat was a frock coat and his waist coat was pure silk. Fit him like it was made for him, and it prob'ly was. I know Mister Okafor visited some mighty fine tailors in Dublin."

"I'm sure he did. Who stood up with Angelique?"

"Oh, some girl from a shop she used to work in. She told me, though, how much she missed having you there with her. Said you like a sister to her. That made me feel real good. After all, you and Mister Neo just like brother and sister, so it's good she thinks a you as a sister, too."

It is then I ask the question that's been deviling my tongue since I first saw her. "And his groomsmen?"

Martha cocks her eyebrow; knows who I'm asking about. "Well, there's just two a them. One was another friend of Angelique's brother, and the other . . ."

"The other was Daire O'Donnell," I say.

"Oh, yes, the fiddler from that pub we went to." She grins in an impish way, and I want to push her for stalling.

"Martha?"

She giggles. "Yes, Lordy, he looked mighty fine, too. Had on a plain blue suit; not so fancy as Neo's, but a matchin' waist coat and a pretty ascot over his shirt. He sat with me at dinner and was pumpin' me with questions 'bout you. What boys you fancy back here, if you been keepin' company with anybody; that kind of questions."

"And?"

"I told him you the prettiest girl in Boston and all the young men here be after you like geese after bread crumbs. That's what I told him."

Her words make me happy, but I try not to grin. "So, Martha, what did you think of him? I mean, if you sat with him, you must have an opinion. You were pretty skeptical in the beginning."

"Still am, but he be nice enough, and for sure he be hankerin' for you like a stallion for a mare, Miss Nellie."

Now I giggle and blush a bit as well, because her words fill me with more joy than I would ever admit. *He's still thinking of me, too. He says so in his letters, but he must be really interested in me if Martha picked up on it.*

At that moment, a strong hand lands on my shoulder.

"Nellie, hello. You look beautiful."

Chapter Seventy-Nine

I recognize his voice as soon as I hear it. Actually, even before he speaks, I feel him close behind me. His presence excites me as it always has. I turn slowly and gaze up into his eyes. "Hello, Sean."

He is even more handsome than memory reminded me. He's so tall, and his blonde hair seems lit from within. It is a golden halo encircling the head of a perfect male, an Adonis dropped down from Mount Olympus to share his beauty with us mere mortals. And, I think he knows it. His posture seems expectant of a startled reaction of reverence.

His blue eyes grow earnest as he leans down to me. "I'm so very sorry about your father, Nellie. Boston lost a great man."

"Thank you, Sean."

He takes my hand and points toward a table in the back of the room. "Let's sit down and talk privately, shall we?"

I turn to Martha and say, "Excuse me, I'll be back later."

She shakes her head, disappointed, and turns away.

I catch a glimpse of my mother's worried expression as I follow him to the table. She's not fond of Sean, even though it was her own hands that brought him into this world. Maybe she resents him for the loss of Kathleen, but it wasn't his fault. Everyone knew Kathleen was too old to safely deliver another baby. I glance at

Uncle Tommy behind the bar pulling pints of Guinness. He's in his element now, giving free beer to my da's friends and acquaintances, grinning like a Cheshire cat. For some reason, I'm angry.

Once I heard Da tell my mother, "He knew she was too old, but he wanted what he wanted with no thought of what it might do to his wife."

Uncle Tommy has always been good to me, but now, looking at him with his skinny wife gazing at him with her adoring eyes, a twinge of resentment wells up. *How is it right that a woman dies because of the two men she loves most in the world? That's plain foolish and unfair. A woman must learn to take care of herself.*

As we seat ourselves, Sean takes my hand. "How's school, Nellie?"

"Wonderful, I can't wait to go back and to actually start teaching children, which I'll do next term."

"Why do you want to teach anyway? I've never understood that desire."

His words stun me. How could anything be more exciting than training a young mind to think, to read, to understand the world in a new way? "I don't know, Sean. It's what I've always wanted to do," I laugh nervously, "ever since I decided I didn't want to be a trapeze artist."

He shakes his head. "Oh, yes, the circus. Well, that was a crazy summer, wasn't it?"

"I suppose so, but I wouldn't trade that time for the world. I learned so much about people, about kindness, about acceptance."

"You mean with the freaks? I saw that bearded lady who took you under her wing. She was disgusting."

His words sting, and I can't ignore them. "No, no, she wasn't, Sean. She was kind and absolutely lovely once you got used to the hair; one of the dearest people I've ever met."

He shakes his head. "All right, Nellie. I meant no offense to your friend. She was just . . ." He shudders and then continues, "Speaking of friends, I heard Neo married his Frenchie in Ireland."

"Yes, he did, and I wish you wouldn't call her that. Angelique loves him very much, and he her. I was supposed to stand up with her at the wedding, until—"

"That must have been awful, I mean to get such bad news about your father when you and your mother were so far away."

My eyes fill with tears. I'll never forget the horror of learning about Da, and I'll never forgive whoever murdered him.

He crosses his long legs nonchalantly. "So, hear anything from Rosie?"

"Not since we got home." I wonder what he wants me to say. "She lost her father, too, you know."

His expression is blank.

"She's with the nuns in Dublin. They'll take care of her and get the baby adopted. *Your* baby, Sean." I stare at him.

He puts up his hands in front of him in mock defense. "Oh, no, now! I'm not so sure I'm the father. I've talked to a number of fellows who say it might be them."

"Then they're lying. You're the only one she was with." My words surprise me, but they're true. He flinches but then recovers and his chest puffs out.

"Who do you believe, Nellie, me or her? It's my word against hers after all."

"You sound like a lawyer."

"Well, that's what I am. I passed the Massachusetts Bar last week."

"Congratulations." My voice is flat, but he doesn't notice.

"Thanks. I plan to practice law for a year and then get into politics. I'm right on track to be the first Irish Catholic Mayor of Boston."

"That's what my da wanted, once; to be the Mayor." Remembering hurts.

"Timing is everything. The Irish population has grown enough to make it possible now; even probable from what people tell me." His speech is brisk, excited.

Doesn't he realize how my mother and I might be feeling about Da? I shake my head and tell myself to be less sensitive. *But how can he be so callous as to not realize how his words might hurt me?*

"Good for you," I say, feeling dispirited and distant from him.

"So, Nellie, people tell me that to succeed in politics, I'll need a proper partner, a Boston wife who is Irish Catholic. Beautiful won't hurt either. You are all those things. Interested?"

Why does this feel like a business deal? Why is my heart cold to his words as he sits there, his smile smug and assured? He's everything I ever thought I wanted. I dreamed of this day since I was twelve years old, but I'm not excited. Perhaps it's just the sadness of losing Da. Or does it have something to do with Derry? Oh, I don't know!

"I have to finish school. I start my student teaching next year and will graduate in two years."

His smile crumples a bit. "Really? Once you get married and start having babies, you won't be able to teach. Why bother to get a degree?"

"Because it's important to me. I've worked hard to get into Wellesley. I don't want to throw all that away. I'll be an excellent teacher. The entire staff says so."

"You can certainly teach our children. I want at least five."

I am dumbfounded. *Five children? Why so many? Because it would look good in the Boston Globe? A handsome young mayor and his perfect Irish family? Is that what matters to Sean? My mother has advised some women to limit the number of children they have to what they can handle. Five?* I can hardly breathe.

"Slow down, Sean. I'm not sure I want children." I turn away from him.

His eyes fill with disbelief. "Not want them? But you're Catholic. How would you prevent them?"

I smile to myself. I am well versed in ways to avoid pregnancy. I've heard my mother teach many an overburdened Catholic woman how to keep another baby from catching hold in her body. "There are ways."

CHAPTER EIGHTY

"We need to talk about all this, Nellie. I hope to change your mind. May I walk you home?"

"My mother will expect me to walk with her." I say this more as an excuse than a reality. Mother can have plenty of company walking with her when she's ready to leave. My resistance, though, seems to embolden Sean.

"Then can I come to your house this evening and talk further?"

Suddenly, I'm so very weary. The service at Da's grave tired me more than I realized. With little energy to resist, I say, "Oh, very well. Come over at eight."

"Will do." He stands up and walks away.

I leave the table and search for Martha. As soon as I'm beside her, I hug her close. "I'm sorry I left you before. I have missed our talks so much."

"Yeah, well I seen who you was just talkin' to."

I laugh and poke her softly in the side. "Martha, you have to let me grow up. Most of my friends are already married; some even have babies."

"They ain't my Nellie. You be special, girl. Gonna be a teacher."

"Yes, I am."

"Good."

Mother appears next to Martha. "Are you about ready to go home?"

"What time is it?"

"Nearly six. I have some leftover beef in the icebox. We'll have sandwiches."

I hug goodbyes to Martha and Uncles Kam and Tommy and then to Molly and Shannon who is large now with another baby. She looks worn out. I can scarcely believe she is the same girl Mother says was the prettiest girl she'd ever seen. Three little ones tug at her skirt, wanting dinner.

The drizzle has stopped and the streets have that just-washed feeling that follows a summer rain. Things smell sparkling clean and I take in a deep breath. Before long, that clean smell will be fouled with the scents of horse dung and cigarette smoke. But for now, everything smells like fresh grass.

"Mam, Sean is coming over tonight at eight."

"Oh, he is, is he?"

"Yes, we'll just sit on the porch and talk."

"Fine with me, as long as he doesn't expect me to join you. I plan to crawl into bed with a book as soon as we've eaten."

We pass Mae Cavanaugh on the street, a fellow St. Augustine parishioner. "Mary, Nellie, I'm so sorry I haven't paid my respects. When I heard what happened to your Daniel, I couldn't believe it. I'm so sorry."

Mae is what my mother calls *a nervous talker*. "That woman can't abide a moment of silence," she has said. "Has to fill it with mindless chatter."

Knowing we're both too tired to remain polite for long, I take Mother's arm and say, "Thank you, Mrs. Cavanaugh. We'd love to see you another time. Right now, we're both fairly ready to drop. Excuse us, please."

Her expression tells me she'll be complaining to everyone at church that I acted highfaluting to her, but I don't care. I need to get a cup of strong black tea down my throat.

I make sandwiches while Mother rests. We eat them with tea on the front porch. She barely takes the last bite before saying, "Well, girl, that book is calling my name. Make my excuses to Sean; not that I care what he thinks, but we must be polite."

I check the clock in the living room. It is seven. I go to the pump and draw up a small bucketful of water, which I splash on my face, then brush my teeth and hair and start to go through the catalogues and class information newly arrived from Wellesley. By the time I'm finished, it's seven-fifty. *Sean will be here soon.*

When the clock strikes eight, a knock sounds. *My, he's punctual.*

When I open the door, he asks. "Where's your mother?"

"Sleeping. She's exhausted."

He smiles and takes my hand. "Let's sit out here a bit, Nellie. It's a beautiful night."

"Would you care for something to drink?"

"Whiskey?"

From the smell of him, he's already had a bit of that, so I lie, knowing there's a bottle of Tullamore Dew stashed on the back porch. "I meant lemonade."

He looks disappointed. "Very well."

I pour us each a glass and join him on the swing outside.

"So, when do you go back to school?"

"In September."

"Let's talk about an alternative."

Chapter Eighty-One

"An alternative?"

"That's right. I've been thinking about this ever since you came to see me about Rosie's baby." He pauses.

I wait for him to continue, wondering what I said then that has caused so much pondering on his part. It was a simple discussion during which he refused to accept responsibility for Rosie being pregnant. Actually, he said some pretty nasty things about her, and I left confounded and confused.

Ready to explain his alternative, he puts his lemonade on the porch railing and sits beside me on the swing. He takes my hands in his and swivels me around to face him. "Nellie, I want you to marry me."

"What?" Stars explode behind my eyes. This is what I've dreamed of. Sean O'Halloran has asked me to marry him. It's what I've always wanted, or at least what I used to want. Right now, I'm so confused I can hardly remember that desire. I mustn't let what happened with Derry cloud my judgment. That was a one-time happening in a foreign land, at a time when I was emotionally shattered about Da's death. I wasn't in my right mind that night. It mustn't influence what I say to Sean now. Because nothing is certain about Derry. This is serious. Sean O'Halloran has asked me to marry him.

"Sean, what's brought this on so suddenly. You've never courted me. Never even kissed me. We hardly know each other."

He laughs. "We've known each other all our lives. Practically grown up together. Our parents were friends. We go to the same church; know a lot of the same people. We have everything in common."

"Yes, I know, but when you get married, you're supposed to be in love. Do you love me?"

"In my way, I do love you, Nellie."

"In your way?"

"Yes, you're beautiful and smart and clever. Who wouldn't love you?"

"That isn't exactly what I mean about being in love. I mean, I've watched my parents my whole life. They couldn't keep their hands off each other. They rushed into the other's arms at the end of a working day. When my mother walked into a room, my father's eyes lighted with a gleam that never happened with any other woman. They were truly in love with each other."

He chuckles. "Guess I've never seen a marriage quite like that. My da is partial to his wife, but certainly doesn't love her in that way."

"Too bad. According to my mother, he did feel that way about your mother before she died."

"I wouldn't know." For the first time since I've known him, Sean's eyes flicker with doubt.

His head slumps a bit, and a wave of sadness for this big handsome man washes over me. I put my hand on his shoulder and rub it. Perhaps I could teach him to love me the way he should. Perhaps it's not too late. But the moment of hope is fleeting.

"The thing is, Nellie," he says, lifting his head. "I wanted to get this straight between us. You can complete this year if you wish, but there's really no reason for you to finish your education.

When we get married, which I hope is in one year, you wouldn't be able to teach anyway. I'll be running for Democratic precinct leader then, and I'd want you beside me all the time. That's the first step in my political career and an important one."

Exciting? Of course. But what of my career? I have wanted to be a teacher ever since I decided the circus was not for me. I'm excelling at Wellesley. This coming year, I will begin shadowing teachers in elementary grades so I can decide where to focus my studies. I love the idea of informing young minds.

Is my destiny to be a decorative political wife and mother? Do I want that? Most girls would be thrilled with such a future, but would I? After all, I've lived all these years with a mother who made a difference in people's lives. Can I make a difference?

"So, what do you think, Nellie?" His voice interrupts my musing, intruding on what may be the most important decision I'll ever make.

I look into his eyes. "Stand up," I say.

"What?"

"Stand up," I repeat.

He chuckles for a moment, looking at me as if I'm crazy. "All right." He stands.

By now, it's very dark outside. I remember my mother's story of the first time my da kissed her on the porch of O'Halloran's. That's when she knew he was part of her destiny. I must find out if Sean could be part of mine.

"Sean, move over to the far end of the porch."

He laughs but obeys me, moving into the deep shadows. I follow him and stand directly in front of him. I lift my arms around his neck and stand on tip toe, never looking away from his eyes. I bring my face closer to his. Though he doesn't move immediately, I stay in this position. Surely, he'll know what to do now.

He brings his lips to mine and wraps his arms around me. My dream is coming true. Sean O'Halloran is kissing me. I wait for the stirring of passion that has given me such delicious night raptures over the past five years. They don't come. Perhaps I need to be closer to his body.

I press against him and part my lips. I feel him harden. I rub myself against him. It begins to feel good, very good. Maybe I do love Sean.

Suddenly, his hands grip my shoulders and push. My eyes fly open to see the shock on his face. "Sean, what's wrong?"

"What's wrong? I want to marry you because you're a nice Catholic girl. Nice girls don't behave that way. If I'd wanted a trollop, I'd have married Rosie."

I am so shocked I nearly fall over. He takes my hand and leads me to the swing.

"Let's sit down again, Nellie. I want to discuss what we were talking about, getting married. I think you should finish one more year of college and we'll marry after that. I'll give you the ring my father gave my mother as soon as you say yes. I just want to be certain we agree on some very important matters."

"Such as." I wait for his response.

"Well, the fact that you'll take care of our home on Beacon Hill and our children, and forget the foolishness of wanting to be a teacher."

"I see." *Foolishness?*

Taking my words as agreement, he continues. "And there's one more thing I must insist on."

"What's that, Sean?"

"I can't have my wife consorting with certain people. When I heard that you shared quarters with that woman, Martha, I almost decided against asking you to marry me. What were you and your mother thinking?"

"I grew up with Martha. She's a second mother to me. I love her."

"But how would it look if the wife of the Mayor was out sashaying around Boston with a nigger?"

What did he call Martha? Nigger? Red heat starts in my toes. It flares up my legs and into my body. And then, it hits my brain. A fury so deep and primal it will not be denied. It is as if I am possessed by another creature, ancient and angry. Slowly, I turn to face Sean. My fist clenches as my right arm rises. He doesn't notice my movements.

I swing. My fist connects with his nose bringing a rush of blood. He screams. "Nellie! What the hell?" He feels the blood and burrows in his pockets for a handkerchief. He raises it to his nose, looks at it in disbelief, and jumps to his feet. "You might have broken my nose," he whines; tears gather in his eyes as he turns, wanting to get away from me quickly before I hurt him again.

"Goodbye, Sean."

He runs down the street dabbing at his nose with his handkerchief. I sit down, my relief as welcome as a long-lost friend.

CHAPTER EIGHTY-TWO

I don't hear the front door open and am surprised when my mother sits beside me on the swing.

"You were listening?"

"Of course."

"For how long?"

"The very beginning." She pulls up her knees and turns to face me. "You didn't really think I'd let you be out here in the dark with that one, did you?"

I smile. "I should have known."

She puts her hand on my shoulder and squeezes.

"Did you see what I did?"

"Oh, yes."

"Are you scandalized? Mother, I may have broken his nose."

"Maybe. I've wondered when the Banshee would show up for you. I guess tonight was the first time."

"Banshee?"

"Yes. Don't forget, you have O'Brien blood in you, just as I do. The O'Briens provided Ireland with more Banshees than any other family."

"Is that what happened to me?"

"No doubt. You acted the same as I did on the ship with the sailors, without control or reason."

"That scares me, Mam. What if it happens again, with someone who doesn't deserve it?"

"Oh, it won't, Nellie. What you experienced was your fiery Irish temper. I have one, too. That happens with me when I've been confronted with someone evil or pompous. Someone so full of himself he's intolerable to others. Like those sailors. Like Sean."

"Are you certain?"

"Sure as I am that a shamrock brings luck. That's how certain I am. And frankly, I'm relieved to see you have her in you."

"You are?"

"Of course. Every woman needs a bit of the Banshee in her to thrive in these days so dominated by men. It wasn't always that way, you know. Back in the days of the Druids and Faeries, women ruled the world. Hopefully, they will again."

Embarrassed, I say, "Did you see me kiss him?"

"Indeed, I did. That's when I knew you'd never marry him. A man afraid of a woman with passion isn't fit for any daughter of mine."

I open my mouth in astonishment. "You don't think it's a sin for a woman to want a man in that way?"

She throws her head back, opens her mouth and lets out a belly laugh. "Of course not, girl. Why should the man have all the fun? That's something I'll miss most about your da. He loved being wed to a passionate woman. You'll meet a man like him one day."

Perhaps, I already have.

"Now let's go to bed. I must go to work tomorrow after church and you'll start school soon. Time's a wasting."

We stand and I put my arm around her waist. "I love you, Mam."

"And I you, Nellie Kelly."

ABOUT THE AUTHOR

Jeanne Charters is a veteran of the broadcast television industry. She was vice president of marketing for Viacom TV and opened her own broadcast ad agency, Charters Marketing.

Charters grew up believing she'd be a stay-at-home mom and live in her hometown in Ohio for the rest of her life. However, after four children and a divorce, Charters ended up in Albany, New York, where she met and married Matt Restivo, her husband of thirty-five years and counting. Charters and Restivo moved to Asheville, North Carolina, after retirement. Beyond her novels, she has also written for magazines and newspapers.

DAUGHTERS OF IRELAND

FROM OPEN ROAD MEDIA

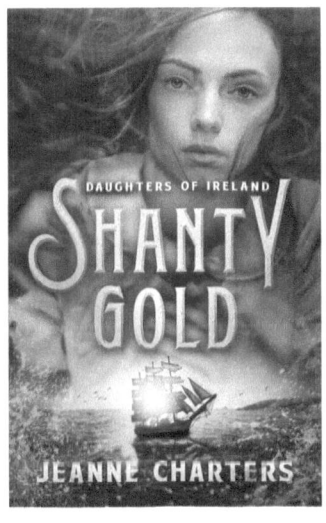

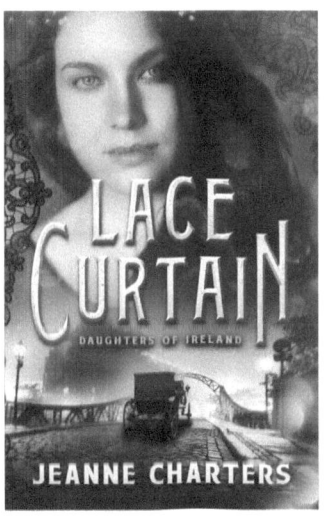

OPEN ROAD
INTEGRATED MEDIA

Find a full list of our authors and titles at www.openroadmedia.com

FOLLOW US
@OpenRoadMedia